ALIEN BOUNTY

A fragile peace between the Il Ronnian Empire and humankind is about to crumble—because space pirates have made off with one of the aliens' holiest relics. Only one man can hunt down the sacred object. A man with a score to settle with the pirates: bounty hunter supreme Sam McCade.

McCADE'S BOUNTY

Six years ago, McCade and his men destroyed the deep-space empire of pirate Mustapha Pong. Now Pong's back—with a vengeance. He's kidnapped McCade's daughter. This time, there's no reward. The bounty belongs to McCade—and it's personal.

McCADE ON THE RUN

WILLIAM C. DIETZ

ACE BOOKS, NEW YORK

THE BERKLEY PUBLISHING GROUP
Published by the Penguin Group
Penguin Group (USA) Inc.
375 Hudson Street, New York, New York 10014, USA
Penguin Group (Canada), 10 Alcorn Avenue, Toronto, Ontario M4V 3B2, Canada (a division of Pearson
Penguin Canada Inc.)
Penguin Books Ltd., 80 Strand, London WC2R 0RL, England
Penguin Group Ireland, 25 St. Stephen's Green, Dublin 2, Ireland (a division of Penguin Books Ltd.)
Penguin Group (Australia), 250 Camberwell Road, Camberwell, Victoria 3124, Australia (a division of
Pearson Australia Group Pty. Ltd.)
Penguin Books India Pvt. Ltd., 11 Community Centre, Panchsheel Park, New Delhi—110 017, India
Penguin Group (NZ), Cnr. Airborne and Rosedale Roads, Albany, Auckland 1310, New Zealand (a di-
vision of Pearson New Zealand Ltd.)
Penguin Books (South Africa) (Pty.) Ltd., 24 Sturdee Avenue, Rosebank, Johannesburg 2196, South
Africa

Penguin Books Ltd., Registered Offices: 80 Strand, London WC2R 0RL, England

This a work of fiction. Names, characters, places, and incidents either are the product of the author's
imagination or are used fictitiously, and any resemblance to actual persons, living or dead, business es-
tablishments, events or locales is entirely coincidental.

McCADE ON THE RUN

PRINTING HISTORY
Ace trade paperback edition / February 2005
Alien Bounty: Ace mass market edition / May 1990
McCade's Bounty: Ace mass market edition / December 1990

ACE trade paperback ISBN: 0-441-01242-6

This book has been registered with the Library of Congress.

PRINTED IN THE UNITED STATES OF AMERICA

10 9 8 7 6 5 4 3 2 1

CONTENTS

ALIEN BOUNTY

This one is for the guys:
Ron Crawford, Steve Bachelder,
Mike Davison, Rion Dudley,
Ron Hand, Nick Kirchoff,
Jim Potter, George Rigg, Craig Riss,
Marvin Straus, and Joe Walsh.

ONE

"Prisoner McCade!" The guard's voice cut through the soft murmur like a knife. What light there was glazed the surface of things and left the rest dark.

The other prisoners drifted away leaving McCade to stand alone. They had enough trouble without borrowing any of his.

McCade was dirty, his leathers were ripped, and his black hair fell down around his shoulders in thick, greasy coils. But there was no fear in his cool gray eyes or in the set of his long, lean body.

The guard shifted his considerable weight from one foot to the other and gripped the nerve lash more tightly. "Are you McCade?"

McCade smiled. "No . . . I'm Grand Admiral Keaton. Is my fleet ready?"

A wide variety of rude noises issued forth from the surrounding darkness. Behind his face shield the guard flushed. "Very funny, pit slime. Now move."

McCade obeyed. Something heavy fell into his stomach as he stepped aboard the lift disk. Bad though Pit 47 was, there'd been reason to hope. Maybe Rico would come back. Maybe he'd escape slavery in the mines. But that was gone now. Each day the guards took one or two prisoners away and now it was his turn.

"Hands."

McCade held out both hands, wrists touching. The guard gave a grunt of satisfaction as he locked the nerve shackles in place. Any attempt to remove them would result in unbelievable agony.

The guard was a big man with thick eyebrows, meaty lips, and an enormous jaw. "This is Duncan in Pit 47. I've got prisoner McCade on disk two."

The voice in his ear was bored. "Code."

Duncan subvocalized so McCade couldn't hear. "Mary four Mary."

"Roger."

The disk hummed softly as it floated them upward. It, and another just like it, were the only way in or out of Pit 47. Each disk would lift two, and only two, people. Even if the prisoners killed the pit guards and took both disks, only four of them could lift. And without the proper code they'd be killed long before they reached the reception station up above.

The anti-grav disks were expensive, but what the hell, the Molarians had credits to burn. Molaria, was the single known source of Nerlinium Crystals, and as everyone knows, Nerlinium Crystals are a very important component in hyperdrives.

Molaria was an artifact world, one of the mysterious planets once home to a long-vanished race, now part of the human empire. Having learned the secrets of hyperdrive from artifacts the aliens had left behind, humans had also discovered the value of the ancient mines that dotted the surface of Molaria. From those mines came Nerlinium Crystals, and from the crystals came untold wealth, some of which had gone into lift disks for Pit 47.

All of which did very little to comfort Sam McCade as the disk carried him upward. More than a hundred feet of smooth featureless wall went by before the disk stopped and the guard motioned for him to get off.

A muscle in his left check began to twitch as McCade stepped off the disk. He'd been in a lot of tight spots during his years as a bounty hunter, but this was one of the tightest. What had started out as a routine trip to buy some spare drive crystals had turned into a nightmare.

After a routine landing he and Rico had approached a crystal dealer with a perfectly reasonable offer. She'd countered with an attempt to rob them, and even though they managed to escape, both men were soon running for their lives.

Running out of her store, they spotted three of the local riding animals. Having climbed aboard two of the creatures, they shot the third in a futile attempt to delay pursuit and headed for the spaceport at top speed. Once aboard McCade's ship they stood a good chance of getting off-planet alive. *Pegasus* was well armed and damned fast.

But they'd have to get there first and that wouldn't be easy. Like most dealers this one had her own security guards and they gave chase. Minutes later the guards were joined by a squad of Molarian mounted police and a posse of bloodthirsty citizens, all of whom were experts at riding their three legged bouncers.

Each of the sauroids has two powerful hind legs and a single foreleg located at the center of its chest. As the rear legs push off the foreleg functions as a pivot bearing the animal's weight until the hind legs hit the ground again. As a result the animals bounce up and down, which explains both their name and why it takes some practice to ride them.

McCade was thrown off time after time. The falls hurt and burned precious seconds at the same time. Seconds they desperately needed to reach the spaceport in time.

Maybe it was his childhood on a farm, or the many years spent living on primitive worlds, but whatever the reason Rico took to the bouncers naturally. He seemed glued to the plastic saddle as he shouted for people to get out of the way and led McCade through a maze of side streets.

But their pursuers were catching up and as McCade went down for the sixth time he yelled for Rico to leave him.

Rico was a big man, a friend who had fought at McCade's side many times and who rarely ran from anything. But as he spun his animal around, Rico saw the situation was hopeless. The posse was closer now, only a thousand yards away, and if it came to a fight, the two of them wouldn't stand a chance.

Rico tossed McCade an informal salute and shouted, "Keep an eye peeled, ol' sport, I'll be back." Then he wheeled his bouncer and took off.

The mob was closer now with only the narrowness of the street to slow them down. It was a thundering mass that rippled up and down as it moved.

McCade drew his weapon and fired over their heads. Suddenly the mob came apart as groups of riders spurted into side streets and alleys.

But they were back moments later brandishing a wild variety of hardware and screaming at the top of their lungs. But Rico had a good head start by this time and McCade was lying facedown spread-eagled on the pavement. He hoped they'd take him alive.

And they had, though not without a beating, and a quick trip to Pit 47. All for nothing though, since Rico hadn't come back, and they were taking him to God knows where.

"Strip."

McCade did as he was told, stripping off his leathers and submitting to a body search. There were four guards now and they were visibly disappointed when they failed to turn up a homemade blaster or nuclear warhead. Something like that would justify a beating and beatings were their main source of entertainment.

They shoved him into a cubicle with a lot more force than was necessary and slammed the door. It was small and dark like the inside of a coffin. McCade was about to attack the door when a red light came on and a hard spray hit him from every direction. The dirt seemed to slide off his skin and the spray reeked of disinfectant.

McCade gave a sigh of relief. It was some sort of decontamination booth. They didn't want him spreading any nasty diseases to the good citizens of Molaria.

When the chemical bath was over the booth beeped and the door popped open. McCade felt very naked as he stepped outside.

"Come on, pit slime." It was the guard with the enormous jaw.

"How 'bout my clothes?"

"Clothes?" the guard asked with a big grin. "You don't need clothes. You're beautiful just the way you are. Isn't that right, guys?"

There was a loud chorus of guffaws and rude suggestions as the other guards assured McCade that he didn't need any clothes.

"Move." The word was accompanied by a shove between the shoulder blades.

McCade moved. The guard with the enormous jaw walked in front with a second guard following along behind. The second guard enjoyed prodding McCade with the handle of his nerve lash.

At first there wasn't much to see, just the perfect smoothness of ancient walls and the guard posts located by each pit.

The pits were vertical shafts that the long-lost aliens had drilled searching for crystals. Being a practical people, the citizens of Molaria had put the shafts to use. All it took was a small investment of time and energy to make them into excellent holding pens. A lighted sign marked each pit head, and McCade noticed that the numbers were getting smaller, twenty-one, twenty, nineteen, and so on.

The numbers eventually dwindled away, four, three, two, one, and a bank of lift tubes. One was designated "Prisoners Only," and that was the one they stepped into.

The platform carried them smoothly upward and stopped at a busy corridor. McCade recognized one of the main subsurface tunnels that crisscrossed Molaria Prime.

The city had three distinct levels. The surface where McCade was captured, the subsurface level where he was now, and the deeps where he would go next.

That's where the slaves worked, lungs gasping for breath, eyes bulging as they searched for the glitter of a Nerlinium Crystal in the dark matrix of ancient rock. A crystal meant a double ration of food, a day off, and sex for those who still cared.

But all that was invisible up here where well-dressed citizens strolled the brightly lit tunnels talking business or just killing time.

McCade felt completely and terribly exposed as the guards led him out into the tunnel. He thought all eyes were on him at first, seeing his nakedness, his complete vulnerability. But then he noticed how their eyes slid past him to look at something else. They didn't *want* to see him. He might remind them of the slaves, of the crystals they scratched from the rock, and the tainted money that flowed into their hungry pockets. No, it was better not to see, not to know where the naked man was going or what would happen to him.

McCade wondered if he'd done the same thing. He too had walked these halls and for the life of him couldn't remember any naked prisoners. Had he tuned them out? Too busy with his own affairs to really see? He couldn't be sure.

McCade forced his head up, straightened his back, and put a spring into his step. He made it a point to meet their eyes and smile. Maybe one of them would see and remember.

The guards led him through a maze of tunnels and corridors until they arrived in front of a steel gate. A pair of guards lounged to either side, their blast rifles hung on slings, their visors tilted up and back. The smaller of the two spoke. "What's this, Dunc? More pit slime?"

Duncan nodded as the other guards opened the gate and shoved McCade inside. "That's about the size of it, Mac. You'll like him. He's got a sense of humor."

"Oh, goody," Mac said approvingly. "Maybe he'll tell the judge some jokes. The judge likes jokes."

Duncan laughed and slapped Mac on the back. "Take care, Mac . . . I'll see you at shift end."

"Sounds good," Mac replied. "You can buy me a beer."

Duncan waved as he walked away, secretly glad to be rid of the man with the gray eyes, and ashamed of feeling that way. The man scared him, and since *he* was the one with the nerve lash, that didn't seem right.

The gate crashed closed and McCade found himself in a tiled room. A stiff spray lanced down to sting his skin and wash the slime off his feet.

Sixty seconds later the water stopped, a beeper beeped, and a door hissed open. "Prisoner McCade, step forward and be judged." The voice came from nowhere and everywhere at once.

There was little point in doing otherwise. McCade stepped through the door and found himself in a large, noisy room.

To the left, row after row of shabby theater-style seats slanted up to a dingy ceiling. The aisles were filled with garbage, and for that matter so were the seats, for McCade had never seen a sleazier crowd.

There were spacers waiting for an outbound berth, prospectors building a new stake, and even a sprinkling of aliens doing God knows what. All were talking, gesturing, and loudly vying for one another's attention. McCade felt like the main attraction at a Roman circus.

A raised platform stood off to the right. On it there was a formal-looking desk, and behind the desk there was a vast fat man, busily eating a large meal. At the moment his greasy fingers were busily dismembering a small carcass. The scattering of bones around his chair suggested that the meal had been under way for some time.

A quick check of the audience revealed that many of them were similarly engaged, although at least one pair of Zords seemed to be making love, though it's hard to tell with Zords. To the untrained eye Zordian sex acts look very similar to the ritual wrestling patterns they use to mark the summer solstice.

McCade looked for somewhere to go, something to do, but a burly guard shook his head. So he stood there instead, shivering under a cold air vent, and hoping the fat man would choke on a bone. He didn't.

He ate until the food was gone, belched his approval, and tossed his plate aside. Then he wiped his fingers on the front of his robe, blew his nose, and cleared his throat.

This was such an obvious signal that McCade expected the crowd to quiet down. But they didn't and the noise continued unabated.

The fat man frowned. Reaching inside his robes, he brought out a huge slug gun. Pointing it toward the audience, he pulled the trigger. The gun roared and a pimp sitting in the last row lost his hat.

The room fell silent. The fat man grinned his satisfaction and made the gun disappear. "That's better. We'll have order in this court or I'll know the reason why."

The fat man picked up a printout, blew the crumbs off it, and turned toward McCade. "My name's Benjamin Borga, a duly qualified judge in the courts of Molaria and a helluva nice guy."

Borga turned his attention back to the printout without waiting for McCade's response. "Let the record show that one Sam McCade stands before the court accused of serious crimes and subject to Molarian law."

Here Borga paused and smiled at the crowd. They cheered in anticipation of what he'd say next. "Also present is a jury of McCade's peers, duly sworn in and ready to earn the princely sum of fifty credits for a hard day's work."

The crowd cheered even louder.

Now McCade understood. The crowd was a paid jury. That's why it was heavily loaded with indigents, drifters, and petty criminals.

"The law clerk will now read a list of McCade's crimes."

The stentorian voice was back, and this time McCade realized it was a computer, and a somewhat pompous computer at that.

"Citizen Sam McCade stands accused of attempted fraud, animal theft, destruction of private property, reckless riding, felonious flight from the law, attempted murder, resisting arrest, and disrespect for an officer of the law."

Borga slumped back in his chair and stared at the ceiling. "So, McCade, how do you plead?"

McCade looked around. Some of the so-called jurors were still eating, others were asleep, and the rest were talking among themselves. The whole thing was a joke. He was about to say so when the courtroom doors burst open, a section leader yelled, "Freeze!" and twenty Imperial Marines trotted into the room.

They wore full armor and carried their blast rifles at port arms. Within seconds they had established interlocking lines of fire that covered the entire audience.

An uneasy murmur swept through the crowd. Some of the jurors got up to leave but took their seats again when the section leader used his energy rifle to punch holes in the durocrete wall over their heads.

A tall, slim man strode into the courtroom a few seconds later. He wore armor with the stars of a full admiral welded to both shoulder plates and carried a helmet tucked under his right arm. He was good-looking in a carefully groomed way, and as he approached the bench, he surveyed the room with obvious distaste.

Borga was on his feet. His face was beet red and his piggy little eyes glared with malevolence. "Who the hell are you? How dare you invade my courtroom? I demand to know the meaning of this!"

The admiral stopped, looked at Borga, and frowned. "It *means* that you are in deep trouble. My name is Swanson-Pierce. Now shut up and sit down."

Swanson-Pierce turned toward McCade. "Hello, Sam." He looked the bounty hunter up and down. "You've never been an example of sartorial elegance . . . but this is absurd."

TWO

Swanson-Pierce gave McCade a VIP cabin and a robo steward called "Slider." Thus equipped he ate and slept his way through two planetary rotations. The weeks in Pit 47 had taken their toll. He was tired and unendingly hungry.

It became a routine. He'd wake up, eat the food Slider brought, and go back to sleep. But the periods of sleep became shorter and shorter as time passed until he finally rolled out of bed early in the third rotation.

He took a shower, put on a set of new leathers, and lit his first cigar in months. He took a drag and decided the cigar was a bit on the sweet side. But sweet or not the cigar was free so what the hell. McCade settled into a comfortable chair and blew a long, thin steamer of smoke toward the overhead.

Slider extruded an olfactory sensor, detected airborne impurities, and sprayed the air with deodorant. As with most military robots, form had been allowed to follow function and Slider looked like a box on wheels. "I'm sorry about the smell, sir. I'll notify the ship's atmospheric control center if it's bothering you."

McCade smiled. "Thanks, Slider, but that won't be necessary. I like the smell. That's why I set these things on fire."

"Oh," the robot replied, "I understand," although it was quite clear that he didn't.

The intercom chimed and faded up from black. Swanson-Pierce was at his impeccable best. His space-black uniform was completely unadorned except for the gold stars that marked his rank. "So you're up and around. I must say you look better with some clothes on."

"And I'm warmer too," McCade replied. "Thanks for the timely court appearance. You made one helluva character witness."

"It was my pleasure," Swanson-Pierce replied solemnly, and McCade knew he was telling the truth. The two of them went way back and the relationship was anything but friendly. Finding McCade naked in the middle of a courtroom was a dream come true, an incident Swanson-Pierce would hold over his head for years to come.

A new belt and holster hung from the arm of his chair. McCade pulled the Molg-Sader recoilless from its oiled leather and aimed at the screen. "And there's all the goodies you've been handing out. I guess I should thank you for those as well."

The naval officer lifted a single eyebrow and smiled.

As McCade lowered the gun he knew the bastard was up to something. The VIP cabin, the cigars, the new handgun, it was all part of an effort to soften him up. Make him willing to do something. The question was what.

McCade forced a smile. "How's Rico? I assume he's the one who told you where I was."

The naval officer nodded. "Rico's just fine. As usual he's down in the officer's mess eating. Just a moment. I have a surprise for you."

Swanson-Pierce stepped out and Sara stepped in. She held Molly in her arms. Both were smiling.

Sara was beautiful. A softly rounded face, large hazel eyes, and full red lips. He no longer saw the scar that slashed down across her face. Like the battle that had caused it, the scar was part of the past.

Both were satisfied to simply take each other in for a moment. Then Molly waved her chubby arms, kicked her legs, and said, "Gaaa!"

Sara laughed, McCade grinned, and Molly gurgled.

Swanson-Pierce stepped into the picture and smiled. "We sent a destroyer to get Sara, and a good thing too. She was getting ready to come after you. Why don't you join us? Your robo steward will show you the way."

McCade stared at the screen for a full minute after it had faded to black. It was wonderful to see his family again, but why all the hospitality?

Yes, he had some friends in high places, including the Emperor himself. After the second Emperor's death Princess Claudia had tried to usurp her brother's place, and would have, if McCade hadn't tracked Alexander down and helped him to assume the throne.

Knowing that, Rico had used his friend's relationship with the Emperor to summon help. Allright fine, but why the VIP treatment? And why bring his family from Alice?

Well, there was no point in putting off the inevitable, and besides, Sara was waiting. With Slider out front to lead the way, McCade took to the ship's busy corridors.

McCade's leathers were those of an officer, and even though he wore no badges of rank, he was on the receiving end of more than a few salutes. It brought back memories of a younger time when he'd worn lieutenant's bars and the wings of an interceptor pilot. Of a time when he'd blasted out to fight the pirates off the planet Hell.

They'd called themselves rebels back then, the stubborn remnants of a larger force that had been all but wiped out during a protracted civil war. Refusing the first Emperor's rule, they had forced one last battle and McCade had been there.

He could see the pirate ship locked in the electronic cross hairs of his sight, feel the firing stud under his thumb, and hear the pirate's desperate voice. "Please, in the name of whatever gods you worship, I implore you, don't fire! My ship is unarmed. I have only women, children, and old men aboard . . . Please listen to me!"

McCade could hear the second voice as well, Captain Ian Bridger's voice as he screamed: "Fire, Lieutenant! That's an order! She's lying. Fire, damn you!"

But McCade had refused. And in doing so he ended his naval career and wound up as a bounty hunter.

An interstellar police force would cost a great deal of money, so inter-planetary law enforcement was carried out by bounty hunters, men and women who pursued fugitives for a price. They were a strange breed hated by those they sought and feared by those they served. The perfect profession for a cashiered naval officer in need of funds.

So when Ian Bridger uncovered the existence of an artifact planet called the "War World," and decided to give its secrets to the alien Il Ronn, Admiral Keaton had asked McCade to track him down. McCade met Bridger's daughter Sara in the process, fell in love, and settled on Alice.

Slider arrived at a busy intersection, tried to stop, and slid into a burly chief petty officer. The CPO lost his balance, his omnipresent coffee cup, and a considerable amount of his dignity as he hit the deck.

The chief scrambled to his feet, kicked Slider in the rear power port, and stalked off down the corridor.

McCade helped the robot back onto its rollers. "Don't tell me, let me guess. This is why they call you Slider."

Slider nodded his torso miserably. "I'm afraid so. It's very disconcerting. RoboTech Hu can't find the problem."

"Well, it could be worse," McCade said. "At least they think you're worth fixing."

Slider was silent for a moment and then seemed to brighten up. "That *is* good, isn't it?"

McCade nodded. "It sure beats a future in the spare parts business."

From there it was a short walk to Swanson-Pierce's day cabin. A pair of marines stood guarding the door. They snapped to attention as McCade approached, and waved him inside. He was surrounded by people the moment he stepped through the hatch.

Rico was there, slapping him on the back and saying, "Good ta see ya, ol' sport."

Sara was in his arms seconds later, her eyes large with concern, the clean smell of her filling his nostrils. "Are you all right? You look so skinny."

As their lips met McCade felt two little arms wrap themselves around his right leg. Looking down, he saw two bright eyes, a mop of brown hair, and a big grin. "Da?"

McCade scooped Molly up into a three-way hug, kissed her, and laughed as she grabbed his nose.

Glancing toward Swanson-Pierce, he saw something completely unexpected. A look of envy. It reminded him that there was a man under that uniform, a man who'd never been married, and had only his career to keep him warm at night.

He shook the feeling off. When Swanson-Pierce wanted something he'd use anything to get it, including McCade's sympathy if he knew it existed.

Swanson-Pierce smiled and gestured toward some comfortable-looking furniture. "Have a seat, Sam . . . I rarely get a visit from friends . . . so this was too good to pass up."

"It's hard to visit with something you don't have," McCade mumbled under his breath.

Swanson-Pierce ignored it, Rico grinned, and Sara gave him a sharp look as they took their seats.

There was a wall-sized viewscreen behind the naval officer. Molaria was a brown ball marbled with white clouds and streaked with blue. It hung in the middle of the viewscreen like a painting in a frame.

The naval officer saw McCade's look and pointed a thumb over his right shoulder. "Things have changed since you left. A marine division went dirtside two rotations ago. They've taken control of the government, the armed forces, and the judicial system."

Swanson-Pierce smiled. "Judge Borga is looking for Nerlinium Crystals in the deeps, his so-called jury has been dismissed, and we're sorting out the people in the pits. We've known about Molaria for some time. Your situation gave us a good excuse to move in and clean things up."

McCade felt a strange sense of pride. Since taking the throne, Alexander had launched a concerted effort to clean up some of the worst planetary governments. The effort was long overdue, and while McCade couldn't take credit for that, he'd certainly helped make it possible.

"How is Alex anyway?"

The naval officer winced. No one else would dare refer to the prince as "Alex," but it wouldn't do any good to complain, since McCade had permission from the Emperor himself.

"Just fine. As you know he and Lady Linnea are married now, and she's expecting. They both send their best."

McCade nodded. "They're good people. Maybe there's hope for us yet."

Swanson-Pierce was strangely quiet as he reached inside his jacket and brought out a sealed envelope. Wordlessly he handed the envelope to McCade.

The envelope bore the Imperial crest, Alexander's seal, and McCade's name. He opened the envelope and, with Sara looking over his shoulder, read the contents.

Dear Sam,

> *I was sorry to hear about your problems on Molaria, but Walter will sort it out and probably rub you the wrong way in the process. Please forgive him. He acts in my behalf, and pompous though he may be, Walter is doing a great deal to hold the Empire together. And God knows the Empire is all that stands between us and final darkness.*
>
> *We need time, Sam, time to make it stronger, and time to make it better. I know you have no love for empires, ours or theirs, but consider the alternatives. Entire worlds burned down to bare rock, billions of lives lost, and a future filled with tyranny. So if Walter asks for a favor, listen, and if you won't do it for him, then please do it for me.*
>
> *Regardless of what you decide, anything within my power is yours, and that includes my friendship.*

Alex

A host of thoughts swirled through McCade's mind as he tucked the note into its envelope. So there *was* more to his rescue than an Imperial favor.

Alexander had a problem, a problem he hoped McCade could solve, a problem that threatened the Empire.

McCade felt mixed emotions. Resentment toward another intrusion into his life, fear of what the task might entail, and yes, like it or not, a rising sense of excitement.

Swanson-Pierce tried to hide his curiosity as McCade lit the envelope and turned a cigar over the resulting flame.

When the cigar was drawing to his satisfaction, McCade dropped the remains of the envelope into an ashtray and allowed the flame to burn itself out. Molly made a dash for the ashtray and McCade picked her up. "Alex says you have a problem."

The naval officer nodded and flicked an invisible piece of lint off his sleeve. "I suppose you could call it 'a problem' though that might understate things a bit. You'll recall our policy regarding the pirates?"

Sara spoke for him. Her voice was grim. "You bet we do. We think of it every time they attack, every time they steal our supplies, and every time they kill more of our friends."

As head of Alice's planetary council Sara had strong feelings about the pirates. Although the rebel forces had been defeated in the Battle of Hell, some had escaped and taken to piracy along the rim. Alice and the rest of the rim worlds were the constant victims of their raids.

However, the pirates had one redeeming virtue, and that was their antipathy toward the Il Ronn, something the Imperial Government used to its advantage.

Mankind had encountered many alien races among the stars but only the Il Ronn had an empire to rival their own. The Il Ronn were an ancient race, much older than mankind, and were already traveling between the stars when humans had lived in caves. Had they shared mankind's impetuous nature, they might have rolled over Terra and kept right on going.

But theirs was a slow and methodical culture based on consensus and dedicated to predictable outcomes. So while their empire grew, it did so in a slow and conservative manner.

Humans by contrast moved ahead in great spurts, leaping from caves into space in a geological twinkling of an eye, before spreading outward to settle hundreds of star systems. Unfortunately, however, huge gains were often lost through internal dissension and laziness.

The net result was two empires of roughly equal size, each eager to better itself, and to do so at the other's expense.

So both sides staged occasional raids but stopped short of all-out war. A war which neither side was sure it could win.

And that's where the pirates came in. Living as they did out along the rim, the pirates helped keep the Il Ronnians in check. That meant a smaller navy, lower taxes, and happy citizens. It also meant eternal victimization for the rim worlds.

Year after year the colonists struggled to make a living, and then, just when it seemed they'd made some headway, the pirates would come to take it all away.

It made them angry and that's why Sara's eyes burned with hatred, her hands gripped the armrest of her chair, and Molly looked up with concern. The pirate raids were something every rim worlder agreed on.

Swanson-Pierce held up a hand in protest. "I agree, believe me. If I had my way, we'd clean out the pirates and live with the higher taxes. But things aren't that simple. If Alexander raises taxes his sister Claudia will use them to build political support for herself, and that could lead to civil war."

"So we're damned if we do, and damned if we don't," Rico added philosophically, lighting a cigar of his own.

The naval officer shrugged. "I'm afraid so. But our present problem is even worse. The pirates staged a major raid into Il Ronnian territory not long ago. Apparently they caught the Il Ronnians napping because they managed to loot a small city and escaped with minimal losses."

Swanson-Pierce paused for a moment, looking at each of them in turn, adding weight to his next words. "And among their loot was an Il Ronnian religious relic. A relic so precious that our pointy-tailed friends are preparing a holy war to get it back."

The cabin was silent for a moment until Molly saw her mother's expression and started to cry.

McCade awoke in a cold sweat. He was surprised to be alive. The dream had been so real, so intense, that reality paled by comparison. *Pegasus* hummed around him, her systems running smoothly, somewhere toward the end of her long hyperspace jump.

McCade swung his feet over the side of his bunk and held his head in both hands. It hurt. This was the fourth bracelet-induced dream. God help him if there was a fifth.

In the first dream he'd been an Ilwid, an uninitiated male, living with his sept in a series of underground caverns. As such he'd learned many things, including a respect for his elders, the importance of hard work, and the value of water.

In the second dream he was an Ilwig, a warrior candidate undergoing the rites of malehood, spending twenty day cycles in the desert alone. During his wanderings he'd killed an Ikk, watered himself with its blood, and stumbled across a sacred chamber.

Everyone knew about the sacred chambers the old ones had left behind, but few were lucky enough to see one, much less bear the eternal honor of finding one. Once, the chamber had been filled with wonders, but all had crumbled to dust by the time he found it, all that is except the bracelet.

It was still intact, its single blue-green stone glowing with internal light, its smooth metal warm to the touch.

He knew the bracelet was something special from the moment he slipped it on. A tremendous peace rose to fill his spirit, strange new ideas filled his mind, and his body trembled with excitement.

Through the bracelet he learned that he was the chosen one, that he must lead a life of flawless purity, and that one day his teachings would spread to the stars above.

In the third dream he was an Ilwik, a revered teacher, sought out and honored for his wisdom.

McCade also learned that while almost all Il Ronnian males advance to Ilwig, perhaps one in a thousand goes on to become an Ilwik, or warrior-priest, and of these only a handful are called "great."

He learned that the Ilwik were the leaders of Il Ronnian society. The most senior Ilwik sit on the Council of One Thousand that governs the Il Ronnian homeworld and the empire as well.

The lesser Ilwik run local governments, perform scientific research, teach at universities, lead the armed forces, and perform a hundred other important tasks.

But that was later. McCade would eventually learn that many others had worn the bracelet after the great Ilwik's death, giving it knowledge of recent times, knowledge it had passed along to him.

In the great Ilwik's day the Il Ronnian people had only recently graduated from a hunting-gathering society organized along tribal lines to a slightly more sophisticated social structure, incorporating some rudimentary specialization, but still dependent on subsistence farming.

Among the areas of emerging specialization were farming, metal working, and the priesthood. So it was that the great Ilwik shunned worldly ways and chose to live in a cave that the holy fluid had carved from solid rock eons before.

By late afternoon each day the sun would disappear beyond the rim of the canyon, throwing dark shadows into the valley below. As the heat gradually died away, he'd come forth to meditate, and as their first work came to an end, his brethren would join him. They would arrive by ones and twos, find seats, and wait to receive what he had to give.

Sometimes he spoke, telling them what he knew, and sometimes he remained silent, losing himself in the cosmic flow, inviting them to feel that which can't be said.

And then as the sun began to set, and second work began, they would seek his blessing. Sometimes a blessing was his to give, and he would heal the sick, and sometimes his touch brought only comfort. Either way his brethren gave thanks, paid him honor, and left the gifts of life.

In the fourth dream they killed him. Jealous of his powers his fellow Il-wiks denounced him and presided over his death. They stripped the flesh from his body inch by bloody inch, chanting their empty prayers and capturing his tears in a vial of beautiful crystal. Over and over they ordered him to recant his teachings, and over and over he refused.

So when death finally came it was a release, a gift from God that he gladly accepted. It was from that death that McCade had come, his body drenched with sweat, nerves still tingling from the pain.

Were the dreams true? Was he reliving the actual experiences of an Il Ronnian messiah? It seemed hard to believe, but the dreams were too real, too vivid, to be easily dismissed.

And what about the bracelet? Was it the same one the Il Ronnian teacher had worn? Perhaps so, because the Il Ronn had sent the bracelet and instructed that it be worn.

They'd neglected to mention that once he put the bracelet on, it wouldn't come off. He tried everything short of a cutting torch, and no matter what he did, the bracelet wouldn't budge.

Logic told him the bracelet was an artifact, an ancient device left behind by the same race who had extracted crystals from the mines of Molaria and left enigmatic ruins on a dozen other planets. If so, it might be some sort of recording device, capable of storing memories and transferring them to someone else. Perhaps the messiah had picked the bracelet up, worn it, and in so doing unknowingly recorded his life for others to share.

That would explain the dreams, but it wouldn't explain their content. Why *those* particular dreams in *that* particular order? Surely an ancient machine would transfer memories serially, or even randomly, but this one did neither. There were huge chunks of time missing between the dreams, yet each dream did an excellent job of summarizing a period in the Ilwik's life, and taken together they told his entire life story. Surely that was no accident.

McCade had even wondered if the bracelet was alive, a sentient being of some kind, with its own hidden motives. While he'd never heard of such a life form, it could still exist. After all, he'd encountered a Treel once and seen it take the shape of a woman. But Naval Intelligence had run the bracelet through every test known to man and pronounced it inert.

Of course, what did *they* know? They were safe and sound on Terra, while he ran around Il Ronnian space with a bracelet that wouldn't come off, and someone else's memories doing a tap dance in his head. Assholes.

McCade stood, took two pain tabs, and stepped into the fresher. The hot shower felt good. He blew himself dry and headed for the tiny lounge. He didn't bother to dress since there was no one else on board.

As McCade plopped into a chair he felt something poke him in the right buttock. Reaching down between the cushions, he pulled out one of Molly's toys. A model of *Pegasus* that Phil had made for her.

The toy had a slim, fast look like the ship herself. A onetime navy scout converted to a yacht. He placed it on a shelf and felt a magnet lock it into place.

He wondered where Sara and Molly were, and what they were doing. Swanson-Pierce had promised to take them home, so maybe they were on Alice by now, preparing for another hard winter. He didn't love Alice the way Sara did, but she lived there and that made it home.

And that's why he'd find the Vial of Tears and return it to the Il Ronn. Not for the Empire, not for Swanson-Pierce, but for Sara. For his family. Because if he didn't, the Il Ronnians would come looking for it, and the first battles would be fought out along the rim, over and around planets like his.

And according to Swanson-Pierce, the Il Ronn stood a good chance of winning. Years of budget cutbacks had weakened the Empire's navy, and it would take time to gather what ships there were and shape them into a cohesive force.

So it was his job to find the vial and get it back. And barring that, he'd use up as much time as possible, time the Empire would use to prepare.

Getting the vial back from the pirates would be hard enough, but the Il Ronnians had imposed some conditions as well.

Only one human would be allowed to search for the vial, and first that human must pass the initiations of the Ilwig, or warrior-priest. None other could be allowed to find and touch the sacred relic. It was a frustrating waste of time, but, like it or not, one he'd have to accept.

That was the bad news. The good news was his bounty, the price the Imperial Government had agreed to pay for his services.

The truth was that he'd have done it for free, but they didn't know that, and he felt honor bound to gouge them if he could. It was his form of revenge, his way of getting back at them for the court martial and the years of hardship that followed.

That's why he'd specified five million credits, more money than he could spend, but the exact price of the new hospital Sara wanted. For years the citizens of Alice had been in need of a good medical facility and now they'd have it.

He lit a cigar and activated a viewscreen. What he saw was a computer simulation of what the stars would look like if he and *Pegasus* were travelling in normal space. Real or not they were pretty, glittering like diamonds thrown on black velvet, each one an unfathomable mystery.

FOUR

Hundreds of red, yellow, and green eyes stared out at McCade from their electronic lairs. He blew smoke at them and waited for something to happen. *Pegasus* was about to make a hyperspace jump, and as usual, there was little for him to do but wait. *Pegasus* would leave hyperspace in a few moments at the precise point specified by the Il Ronnians.

While routine in toward the center of the human empire, hyperspace jumps were a little more exciting when you were deep inside Il Ronnian space and dependent on *their* coordinates. What if they'd given him the coordinates for a sun? Or a planet? He'd be dead, that's what.

But why bother? There're lots of easier ways to kill a single human.

Nonetheless there was a rock in his gut as the ship's computer made the shift to normal space. The viewscreens shimmered as they switched from simulated to actual input. He felt slightly nauseated but the sensation quickly passed.

Suddenly a host of proximity alarms went off. Someone was waiting for him. A lot of someones. It looked like half the Il Ronnian fleet had turned out to greet him. Battleships, cruisers, destroyers, and hundreds of interceptors all swarmed around his tiny ship.

The Il Ronn had been afraid that the treacherous humans might send an entire fleet instead of a single ship. And McCade couldn't blame them. After all, why trust the same folks who ripped you off in the first place?

The dulcet tones of the ship's computer suddenly flooded the control room. It had analyzed the situation and given itself permission to speak. "Due to this ship's current tactical situation, the chances of a successful engagement are zero. Under these conditions any decision to engage will nullify the hull warranty and the manufacturer's responsibility to honor it. If you prefer suicide to surrender, I will dump the ship's atmosphere."

"Gee thanks," McCade replied dryly. "But in this case I think I'll surrender. Now shut up."

Clearly disappointed, the computer snapped, "Have it your way," and returned to its regular duties.

The com set chimed and McCade flicked it on. "Sam McCade."

As the com set came to life McCade found himself face to face with an Il Ronnian naval officer. Although he'd dealt with Il Ronnians before, including a rather unpleasant naval commander named Reez, it was still a shock.

Like all Il Ronnians this one looked like the traditional human image of the "Devil." The alien's eyes were almost invisible under a craggy brow, long pointy ears lay flat against his head, and his leathery skin had a slightly reddish hue. He even had a long tail with a triangular appendage on the end. And McCade knew that down below the range of the vid pickup, there would be two cloven hooves. Everything in fact except horns.

The similarity between Il Ronnian physiology and the traditional Judeo-Christian image of evil had long been a matter for academic debate. Some scholars thought the Il Ronnians' devillike appearance could account for the instant enmity that had sprung up between the two races at first contact. They suggested that after a thousand years of negative conditioning humans weren't capable of liking a race that resembled the devil.

This argument was very popular with those who opposed war with the Il Ronn.

Meanwhile, other scholars disagreed. They maintained that ancient depictions of the devil were based on early visits to Earth by Il Ronnian explorers. Explorers so brutal that their very appearance had come to symbolize evil.

They pointed out that the Il Ronnians had a stardrive long before man, were known to use brutal tactics on less advanced races, and *were* evil.

As a result this second group of scholars felt war was inevitable, and felt the human race might as well get it over with.

Whatever the truth of the matter this Il Ronnian seemed no friendlier than the others McCade had met. His tail twitched back and forth behind his head and he wore a thin-lipped scowl. He spoke flawless Standard like most Il Ronnians of his rank. "I am Star Sept Sector Commander Ceel. You will kill your drives and allow us to take you aboard."

McCade tried for a nonchalant smile. "Valet parking, how thoughtful."

Ceel's scowl deepened and the com set dumped to black.

McCade smiled as he killed his drives. Tractor beams lashed out shortly thereafter to lock *Pegasus* in a powerful embrace and pull her toward a huge battleship.

The ship was miles long and roughly triangular in shape. Designed for travel in deep space, it had none of the aerodynamic smoothness common to smaller ships. An endless array of weapons blisters, solar collectors, cooling fins, and communications antennas covered almost every square inch of the ship's hull. *Pegasus* seemed like a toy as she was pulled into an enormous launching bay and gently lowered into an empty berth.

The outer hatch closed and a thin atmosphere was pumped into the launching bay. This was a sign of his importance, although McCade didn't realize it.

The bay was kept unpressurized most of the time for the convenience of the shuttles and interceptors that constantly came and went. But when important visitors came aboard it was customary to pressurize the bay, saving them the discomfort of wearing space armor.

Of course, outside of his space armor McCade would be more vulnerable, and that too could have played a part in their decision.

A soft chime told him someone was at the main lock. Punching up a surveillance camera, he saw that an entire squad of Il Ronnian Sand Sept troopers stood waiting outside. They were heavily armed.

He activated the intercom. "Hi, guys. Are twelve enough? Maybe you'd better send for reinforcements . . . I'm real grumpy today."

Either the troopers didn't understand him or chose to ignore him, because their stony expressions remained unchanged.

Knowing what to expect, McCade changed into summer-weight trousers and a short-sleeved mesh shirt. Just for the fun of it he strapped on his sidearm as well. It didn't mean much since he was outnumbered a thousand to one, but he was used to wearing one, and the weight of it made him feel better.

He took one last look around to make sure all the ship's systems were powered down, grabbed a fistful of cigars, and headed for the lock.

He cycled through, stepped out onto a set of rollaway stairs, and grinned. Twelve pairs of eyes went to his handgun and back to his face. To his surprise they made no attempt to take it away.

An Eighth Sept Commander stepped forward, cleared his throat nervously, and said, "Star Sept Sector Commander Ceel bids you welcome. Please follow me."

McCade did as he was told. His honor guard, with the emphasis on *guard*, followed along behind. As they marched their steel-capped hooves crashed to the deck in perfect cadence.

They cycled through one of the many locks providing access to the interior of the ship. After the pleasant coolness of the launching bay, it was like stepping into the center of a blast furnace.

Having been on an Il Ronnian ship once before, McCade had prepared himself for the heat but was still surprised by the intensity of it. The Il Ronnians liked to keep their ships warm like the desert planet they came from, and that's why McCade had worn the lightweight clothing, and was soon soaked with his own sweat in spite of it.

The ship was so huge that it took a full fifteen minutes to reach their destination. They marched down sandy brown corridors, rode up lift tubes large enough to accommodate a quarter sept, and rode the rest of the way in a pneumatic tube system.

Wherever McCade went members of the ship's crew stopped to stare. Many had never seen a human before, and those who had were still surprised to see one inside an Il Ronnian warship.

And while McCade had dealt with many alien cultures over the years, he couldn't remember a time when he'd been so completely immersed in one without so much as a single human face to keep him company. It made him feel like a freak, a curiosity led about on a leash, and he didn't like it.

Unlike humans who constantly sought ways to create open spaces in their ships, the Il Ronn preferred the coziness of their traditional underground dwellings, and built their spacecraft accordingly.

So the approach to Sector Commander Ceel's quarters was small and narrow, suddenly opening up into a circular space similar to an underground cave.

As McCade followed the Il Ronnian officer through the passageway, he realized it would force intruders to attack one at a time, giving the defenders one hell of an advantage. A sensible precaution that had found its way from caves to spaceships. As he stepped inside the air crackled around him.

A sensurround gave McCade the impression that he was standing in the middle of a desert. It stretched away in every direction, reddish streaks hinting at a time when the Il Ronnians' skin color had served as protective coloration, finally blending into a purplish sky on the far horizon. Some very real sand crunched under McCade's boots and added to the overall reality of the scene.

He wondered what happened to the sand during zero G maneuvers. Did they vacuum it up or something? There was no way to tell.

Ten Il Ronnians sat in a semicircle before him. They seemed to be sitting on a bench of native stone but appearances were probably deceiving.

In their view the Il Ronnians outranked him, so in keeping with custom, they remained seated. Sector Commander Ceel was the first to speak.

"Welcome, Sam McCade. I see you come before us armed."

McCade tilted his head backward, exposing the major veins in his neck. "A warrior is always armed in defense of his people. My life is yours."

It was a calculated move, a traditional saying straight from the messiah's memories, and it got the desired effect. Ceel was caught entirely off guard, as were most of the other Il Ronnians. They looked at one another in amazement. A polite human? Unheard of!

But one Il Ronnian wore the red cloak of the warrior-priest rather than the purple of the Star Sept. And he was not impressed. "Yes, your life *is* ours, human, and to keep it you need more than a passing knowledge of Il Ronnian custom."

The warrior-priest gestured toward the single rock facing the semicircle of Il Ronnians. "Take a seat."

McCade did as he was told. Real or not, the rock was damned hard and slightly pointy. He was in no danger of falling asleep.

The priest spoke again. "I am Teeb the interrogator. Understand from the start that I oppose your admittance to the honored ranks of the Ilwik. But I must bend before the wishes of my peace-loving brethren and will give you every chance. Every chance that time allows. Unfortunately we must accelerate your testing due to the urgent need for action. Under normal circumstances testing takes place over a period of ten year cycles."

Teeb paused as though giving McCade time to absorb what he'd said. "There are two levels of testing, an initial phase in which we will determine your worthiness, and if you qualify, a second phase in which you will undergo the three trials of the Ilwik, or warrior-priest. The first phase will start in a moment. You noticed our battle fleet as you came out of hyperspace?"

McCade nodded. "Yes, holy one. It was hard to miss."

Teeb's tail appeared over his head, the pointy appendage shading him from the sun. "Good. The fleet is here for two reasons. The first is to defend against treachery, something we expect from your kind, and the second is to launch a surprise attack against the human empire should you fail the first tests. Shall we begin?"

FIVE

McCade tried to remain calm. It wasn't easy. A test? So soon? What if he failed? He imagined a thousand Il Ronnian vessels flashing out of hyperspace, blasting their way through a scattering of navy ships to destroy planet after planet. Thousands, maybe millions, would die, all because he'd failed some stupid test.

Teeb smiled as though reading his thoughts. "Yes, it is a large responsibility, is it not? I hope your superiors chose well, for their sake, as well as yours."

McCade replied with a crooked smile. "We'll soon know, won't we? Let's get on with it."

"My sentiments exactly," Teeb replied. "You are wearing the holy bracelet of Nik. Millions of candidates have worn it before you, including myself many year cycles in the past."

McCade looked at the bracelet in surprise. "This same bracelet?"

Teeb frowned in annoyance. "That is what I said. Those who the bracelet finds worthy are given certain knowledge, knowledge that I am about to test. Do you understand?"

Sweat poured off McCade's body. He should have taken some salt tablets but hadn't thought to do so. If the test took very long, he'd pass out from heat prostration. If so, he'd kill as many of them as he could before he went under. Teeb and Sector Commander Ceel would be the first to go.

McCade wiped the sweat off his forehead and swallowed to lubricate his dry throat. "Yeah, I understand. Like I said before, let's get on with it."

Teeb looked at the other Il Ronnians as if checking to make sure that they'd heard McCade's response. "Good. Here is the first question. When the great teacher was still an Ilwid, or uninitiated male, his egg mother taught him a lesson about the holy fluid. What was that lesson?"

McCade's mind was a complete blank. All he could see was hell bombs falling and entire planets erupting into flame.

A slow smile started across Teeb's thin lips at McCade's silence. It was just as he'd predicted. The human could not answer the question and the farce was almost over. He was just about to call the whole thing off when McCade croaked, cleared his throat, and spoke.

One moment there was nothing but death and destruction, and next Mc-Cade had been transported back in time, to a planet he'd never seen. And as the words poured out he knew they were right, because he'd been there, and lived the entire incident along with the young messiah.

He'd been playing hide and seek with a young female named Lees. He was small for his age and often excluded from the rough and tumble male games. As a result he was left to play by himself or with females.

He didn't like being left out, but Lees was more fun than the males, most of whom had little or no imagination. They delighted in seeing who could throw rocks the farthest, run the fastest, or lift the most weight.

Lees, meanwhile, created armies for him to lead, wars for him to fight, and entire kingdoms for him to conquer. She also invented games, his favorite being hide and seek, played in the labyrinth of tunnels shared by their sept.

They would play for hours alternating between excruciating suspense and gleeful discovery. Such was the case the day he violated one of the sept's most important taboos.

It happened because he was having such a good time. The feeling had been there for some time, the unmistakable urge to urinate, but that would mean a long trip through the tunnels to the recycling vats, followed by an equally long trip back. By that time Lees might have lost interest in the game, or gone off to do something else. Besides, he'd found a wonderful hiding place and hated to give it up.

He listened carefully. Nothing. Lees was still a long ways off, probing small airshafts and searching the many storage rooms. This particular storage room was fairly spacious, having its own series of mirrors to bring light down from the surface, and the usual dirt floor.

Stepping in between some huge earthenware pots, he opened his shorts and extruded his penis. It felt good to relax his muscles and let the urine flow out. It made a small puddle before disappearing into the greedy soil.

He had just withdrawn his penis when someone grabbed him from behind. It was Weea, his egg mother. She'd come looking for an empty pot and found her son using the holy fluid to water the sterile soil of a storage room.

Without a word she dragged him through tunnels, up a ramp, and out into the hot sun. The fields were small. Each had been wrested from the grasp of the desert by constant toil and the careful application of holy fluid.

One belonged to his father, a stern male of unyielding discipline, and as Weea jerked him along fear grew in his belly. What would his father do? He'd knowingly violated one of the sept's most closely held taboos. Whatever the punishment it would be swift and terrible.

His father looked up at Weea's approach, his eyes lost in the shadow of his supraorbital ridge. His tail came up to shade the back of his head as thick fingers wrapped and unwrapped themselves around the handle of his hoe. "Greetings, Weea. What brings my mate and youngest son out into this heat?"

Weea bowed her respect. "Greetings, Deeg. Your son asks many questions about male work . . . and wishes to observe your labors."

Deeg frowned. "His interest is fitting. But the sun is hot, too hot for one as young as my son, perhaps another time."

"Your concern for your son's health does you honor, Deeg, but I ask an exception this day, for I believe the experience will teach him much."

Deeg was puzzled. Weea was rarely this assertive, but when she was, he'd learned to listen, so his tail signaled assent. "It shall be as you request. Come over here, son, and sit down on that boundary rock. Watch, and you will learn of male work."

For the next four hours he watched his father work. Watched as his father broke the ground with an iron bar, watched as he placed each seed into the thin soil by hand, and watched as he watered each seed with the holy fluid.

The merciless sun beat down all the while, leeching every bit of moisture from his skin, heating the rock until he could no longer bear to sit on it.

Finally, after what seemed like an eternity, first work was over and his father led him from the fields.

Nothing more was ever said to him regarding the importance of the holy fluid. There was no need. He'd seen his father work, felt the searing heat of the sun, and understood what Weea wanted him to learn. To waste water was to waste life itself.

As the memory faded away McCade found himself looking at Teeb. The alien's eyes glowed and his voice was tight with anger.

"This proves nothing. The story is a famous one often told to Il Ronnian children. Who knows how the humans learned of it, but it makes little difference since he will fail the next test."

McCade thought the others looked doubtful, but being no expert on Il Ronnian facial expressions, he couldn't be sure.

"The candidate has passed the first test," Teeb said grudgingly. "Two more await him prior to acceptance. Is the candidate ready?"

McCade tried to concentrate, but he was dizzy, and Teeb's words seemed to come from far, far away. It was hot, so very hot. He heard himself croak something in reply, and did his best to listen as Teeb asked the next question.

"It is known that the great one went forth as an Ilwig to test himself in the desert. While there he found the bracelet you now wear, but he found something else as well, something he later claimed was even more important. What was it?"

Teeb's voice seemed to echo off into the distance and McCade spoke without knowing that he did so. He felt the bracelet on his wrist, a warm and glowing presence, anticipating the excitement it would generate when he came home. But that would have to wait since three day-cycles remained before he could return.

Always hungry, he decided to test his skill as a hunter, and approached a lonely water hole. Like most water holes this one was a sometimes thing, here briefly during the spring, quickly sinking out of sight as the hot hand of summer gripped the land.

A thousand tracks crisscrossed the sands leading up to the water hole. And when the muddy little depression came into sight, he knew he'd see the vicious Ikk drinking side by side with the gentle Vidd. Such was the power of the holy fluid. All creatures needed its essence and must trust their enemies in order to get it.

The sun beat down on his shoulders as he climbed the sandy slope, his broad platelike hooves floating on top of the sand rather than sinking into it, his tail hovering behind his head. Just short of the rim he dropped to hands and knees and crawled the rest of the way.

Peeking over the edge, he saw the usual assemblage of animals, all lapping at the muddy water, all keeping a wary eye on one another. Many of them were good game animals and if he could get closer would fall easily to his spear.

He knew from experience however that the moment he appeared they would run in the opposite direction, never allowing him close enough for a kill. Still, they were packed so close together that a spear thrown far enough was almost certain to bring one down.

He slid backward down the slope until he could stand without being seen. He withdrew the short spear-thrower from its sheath, fitted the butt of his spear into its socket, and assumed the correct position. It was hard to run uphill and launch the spear at the same time, but he did so, the extra leverage provided by the thrower hurling the spear high into the air. For a moment it was a short black line against the lavender sky. Then it fell straight downward and disappeared beyond the rim of sand.

He ran to the top of the slope and looked. All sorts of animals hopped, scurried, and ran in the opposite direction, leaving one of their number pinned to the sand. He was jubilant at first. His idea had worked!

As he bounded down the slope he screamed his victory for the heavens to hear and waved his spear-launcher over his head. And then he stopped, for he had seen his spear, and the life it had taken.

The Fueek was the most beautiful of all the desert birds, a pink vision against the violet sky, its wings beating with the same rhythm as the Ilwig's heart. And now it was dying, its head jerking pathetically, its beautiful wings beating feebly against the sand.

Unable to give life, he took it, and threw himself down beside the Fueek's body, begging for its forgiveness, as his tears mingled with the bird's blood.

And in that moment he learned many lessons. He learned that each life has its own special value, that random violence is not a tool of the sane, and that the price of sentience is responsibility for one's actions.

This time total silence filled the room as McCade's story came to an end. Slowly, one by one, all heads turned toward Teeb. His head was bent, his eyes on his lap. For a long moment he was perfectly still. When he looked up, McCade saw tears running down his cheeks, and when he spoke, there was wonder in his voice.

"It is true just as the human told it. I am awed and humbled at the power of the great Ilwik. His teachings are so powerful that even a human can understand them. The candidate has passed the second test. One more awaits him prior to acceptance. Is the candidate ready?"

McCade was burning up. He knew he should pull the handgun and kill them, but feared he didn't have the strength to do it. He wavered and almost fell off the rock. He felt his lips crack as he spoke. "I'm ready."

Teeb seemed almost sympathetic as he asked the last question. "I can see that our heat troubles you. I am sorry tradition does not allow a rest period, but your ordeal is almost over.

"Toward the end of the Ilwik's life a great drought came upon the land. The water holes soon dried up, and before long, even the deepest wells began to fail. The crops withered, the animals of the desert disappeared, and soon his people began to die. Saying that 'to understand a problem you must journey to its heart,' the great Ilwik went into the desert alone. What happened then?"

McCade found himself transported into the past once again, placing one weary hoof in front of the other, a lonely figure in the middle of endless desert. For five day cycles he marched out into the desert, and for five day cycles he prayed, until so exhausted he could go no farther. Falling to his knees, he cried out in his agony, "Please, God, we need the boon of your holy fluid to live. Surely you did not make us for the purpose of dying. Where *is* the water we need so badly?"

And suddenly he was someone else, a tall, thin being with long, thin legs that kicked strongly and propelled him forward. It was a strange sensation like flying might be if air were liquid and terribly cold.

Liquid! He was suspended in liquid, not just any liquid, but the holy fluid! This was no vision sent by God, but a horrible profanity, sent up from some dark corner of his soul. What greater waste could there be than to immerse one's body in holy fluid?

But wait, what was that on his long, spindly arm? A bracelet. The same bracelet he'd found in the sacred chamber? It certainly looked the same. If so, this might be part of the bracelet's magic, a memory from its previous owner, a memory called forth by his desperate need for water. Maybe there was meaning here, something he could learn to help his people.

Looking around, he saw there were others like himself in the water, splashing and calling out to one another. No wonder they treated the holy fluid with such casual disregard. They were swimming toward the edge of a huge vat of it, more holy fluid than he'd ever seen, and more than his people could use in years. But where was this liquid treasure?

His host turned to float on his back, allowing him to see a rock ceiling far overhead. So wherever the water was, it was far underground and safe from the sun's hot breath.

It was also cold, colder than anything he'd ever known, so he was joyful when his host turned and headed for shore.

His feet soon found bottom and walked up onto a sandy beach. Picking up a long white cloth he wrapped it around himself and fastened it in place with a large brooch.

A large blue-green stone was set into the very center of the brooch, and the Ilwik noticed it was a perfect match for the one in his bracelet. What had happened, he wondered, that the bracelet was there for him to find and the brooch wasn't? Did the brooch have magic powers as well?

But he never learned the answer because the ancient slipped on some sandals, stepped onto some sort of platform, and floated upward. The ancient stepped off as soon as the platform came to a stop, touched a panel of light, and waited while a heavy door slid open.

As the ancient stepped outside he somehow knew that his host hated the heat and regretted the need to pass through it. And because of that the ancient hurried, not giving the Ilwik a chance to look around or see where the holy fluid might be.

Up ahead he saw a construction of shining metal, enough metal to make a million spearheads, and it was toward this metal that the ancient carried him. A hole opened in the metal as if by magic and the ancient stepped into the coolness within.

Taking a seat on something shamefully soft, the ancient picked up a large bowl and put it on his head. Much to the Ilwik's surprise he found he could still see as the ancient reached out to touch one of the many lights that glowed before him. It was then that solid metal came to life and vibrated with hidden vitality.

The ancient touched another light and suddenly the Ilwik could see for miles around. There were the three mountain peaks called the "Fingers of Zeek," the long narrow valley called "the place where sun shines not," and stretched out before him the desert called "the land of bones."

He felt the metal lift under him and his spirits soared with it. He knew exactly where he was! Where the holy fluid was! Where his people would come to survive!

And survive they did. Most anyway, though many died on the long trek through the desert and in the mountains beyond. But eventually they found the great reservoirs of the ancients, and the mighty subsurface rivers that fed them, prospering and growing until their eggs hatched in the sands of other planets.

McCade opened his eyes as he croaked out the final words, saw Teeb start to say something, and fell face downward into the hot sand.

SIX

"Drink this."

McCade opened his eyes and found himself looking up at the ugliest Il Ronnian he'd ever seen. He'd never seen a really good-looking Il Ronnian, of course, but even by their standards, this one put the ug in ugly. He had a bulging forehead and one eye that was slightly higher than the other.

But the Il Ronnian held a cup of water in one taloned hand and McCade was extremely thirsty. Thirsty enough to accept water from the devil himself.

McCade propped himself up on one elbow and drank greedily.

The Il Ronnian shook his head in mock dismay. "Teeb would have a heart attack if he saw you sucking H_2O like an Ikk at a water hole. You must drink the holy fluid reverently like this."

The Il Ronnian used both hands to pick up a cup of water. Then he bowed his head over it, closed his eyes, and said, "Let life flow through me." Opening his eyes, he drank the water in a series of small sips.

McCade put his cup down and swung his feet over the side of his bunk. Cool air flowed around him. He was back aboard *Pegasus*.

"Take it easy," the Il Ronnian advised. "You're still suffering from the after-effects of heat prostration. Since we're a bit short of human doctors, we asked your computer for a course of treatment."

McCade rubbed the back of his neck. "And?"

The alien grinned. "Your computer suggested we put a bullet between your eyes. Do all your computers joke around like that?"

"What makes you think it was joking?" McCade asked.

He got up, groped his way to the medicine cabinet, and fumbled two pain tabs into the palm of his hand. It seemed as if pain tabs were becoming a regular part of his diet. He dumped them into his mouth, squirted some water into a glass, and lifted it to his lips.

Finding the Il Ronnian's eyes on him, he dropped his head, mumbled "Let life flow through me," and gulped the water down.

The Il Ronnian shook his head sadly as he cranked up the gain on his heat cape. "Better . . . but still something short of civilized."

McCade padded down the corridor into the lounge and collapsed into a seat. The Il Ronnian did likewise, his red cape swirling around him.

McCade opened a humidor, took out a cigar, and puffed it into life. His throat felt raw, but he sucked the smoke into his lungs anyway, and blew it out in a long gray stream. He eyed his companion through the smoke. "I don't want to seem ungrateful, but what the hell's going on, and who the hell are you?"

The Il Ronnian smiled. "I'll take your questions in reverse order if you don't mind. My name is Neem, I'm your nif, or tutor. You are an Ilwig, the first human to ever achieve that honor, and you're getting ready for phase two of your testing."

"I passed phase one then?"

Neem nodded. "With flying colors. You really shook 'em up. Up till now everyone had assumed that the bracelet spoke only to Il Ronnians. A bit ethnocentric . . . but understandable nonetheless."

McCade looked at his wrist. The bracelet was missing.

"It came off when you fell," Neem said in reply to his unasked question.

"That's strange," McCade said, rubbing his wrist. "The damned thing wouldn't budge when I *tried* to take it off."

"I had the same problem," Neem agreed. "But it came off quite easily once my testing was over. Our more rational theologians think the bracelet is some sort of artificial intelligence device that knows that it's become part of our religion and goes along with the gag."

Neem shrugged. "Nonetheless, we continue to take it quite seriously. In fact, if someone else heard you call the bracelet a 'damned thing,' they'd shove a stake up your anus and leave you in the desert to die."

"Sorry," McCade said humbly. "I didn't mean it that way. It's an amazing artifact. I wish my race had one."

Neem gave a very human shrug. "Why? In spite of the bracelet we killed our greatest teachers, including the great Ilwik, and continue to ignore most of his teachings. Wonderful though it is, the bracelet cannot bestow wisdom on those who haven't earned it."

McCade tapped some ash into an ashtray and regarded the Il Ronnian anew. There was something different about him. Where most Il Ronnians were rigidly formal, he was informal. Where most Il Ronnians were distant, he was friendly. And where most Il Ronnians were secretive, he was open. In fact, now that he thought about it, Neem seemed more human than Il Ronnian. Even his manner of speech was more human than Il Ronnian.

McCade pointed his cigar in Neem's direction. "No offense, but you strike me as different somehow, more like a member of my race than yours."

Neem smiled and revealed some razor sharp dentition in the process. "True. I wondered when you'd notice. As it happens, I'm an expert on human culture; in fact, I have the equivalent of a Doctorate in exoanthropology. Added to that is the fact that I'm not exactly normal."

"Not exactly normal?" McCade asked. "In what way?"

"Well," Neem replied, looking down at his lap. "I'm insane."

McCade choked on some cigar smoke. "Insane? They gave me an insane tutor?"

Neem held up both hands in protest. "It's not as bad as it sounds, Sam. I'm not psychotic or anything. It's just that I'm excessively individualistic. That coupled with an unhealthy interest in humans renders me clinically insane. That's why they made me your nif, because a computer search found that I'm one of the few Il Ronnians who like humans enough to tutor one. Have you noticed how ugly I am?"

McCade tried to look surprised. "Ugly? You look fine to me."

Neem shook his head. "Nice try, Sam, but among other things, I'm an expert at human facial expressions. The point is that I look like this because of a birth defect. Like the deformed members of most cultures, I was excluded by my peer group throughout childhood and left to my own devices. As a result I was poorly socialized, developed a rather rich fantasy life, and eventually went off the deep end. Or so my shrink says."

McCade raised an eyebrow. "And what do you say?"

Neem grinned. "I say exactly what any insane person would say. I'm fine . . . and everyone else is crazy." Then Neem leaned forward as if sharing a secret.

"Actually this could be my big break. Hanging out with a human is pretty weird, but it sure beats hell out of a rubber room, and if I do well, maybe they'll let me teach again."

McCade took a deep drag on his cigar and did his best to look sympathetic. Just his luck. An impossible mission, a bizarre initiation into an alien religion, and an insane tutor. What next?

SEVEN

The Il Ronnian homeworld was called Imantha, or "home of the people," and was quite beautiful according to Neem. McCade had to take his word for it because the shuttle put them down on the planet's dark side where he was whisked underground.

While this struck McCade as an unusual time to arrive, Neem assured him it wasn't, pointing out that his people had always been partially nocturnal, and when technology freed them from tending crops during the day, they had become even more so. Now hardly anyone ventured out onto the planet's surface during midday unless forced to do so.

Technology had also allowed the Il Ronn to greatly extend their ancient system of caves and tunnels into a huge network of cities that underlay the surface of Imantha.

One thing hadn't changed though, and that was the Il Ronnian love of warmth. Even though Neem had provided him with a cool suit, McCade's head was still exposed and it was damned hot.

Neem provided a running commentary as a series of anti-grav platform carried them downward. It seemed the levels nearest the surface were taken up with tightly packed technology. Mines, processing plants, factories, hydroponic farms, defense installations, communications equipment, and more.

Next came the governmental levels where the Council of One Thousand met, and the great septs held their annual conclaves. And below those came the shopping plazas, vast open spaces where the septs hawked their wares, and the residential levels where most of the population lived. An arrangement that also placed the bulk of population deep underground and safe from attack.

It was there that the platform stopped and they got off. Eight Sand Sept troopers went with them.

Neem pulled him into a side passageway after a short walk down a gleaming tunnel. As McCade stepped out onto a small balcony the troopers took up positions outside. A series of lights popped on and a flock of globular vid cams swooped in to hover around him as his eyes fought the sudden glare.

As his eyes adjusted to the light McCade found himself looking down at a hundred thousand Il Ronnians. Even though Neem had warned him what to expect, it was still a disconcerting experience.

The hall was huge and roughly rectangular. McCade saw an endless sea of Il Ronnian faces as he looked down its length. As he bowed the traditional greeting four huge McCades did likewise on wall-sized vid screens. The crowd hissed its approval.

Even though Neem had assured him that Il Ronnian hissing was equivalent to human applause, it still sounded like an army of snakes preparing to strike and made his hair stand on end.

A male voice began to speak in Il Ronnian, and McCade knew that millions, maybe even billions, of Il Ronnians were looking at him on vid screens and holo tanks all over the planet. Much as he detested the whole thing, Neem insisted it was a matter of political and religious necessity.

McCade was coming to understand that Il Ronnian politics were a good deal more complicated than they appeared at first glance.

It seemed that the Council of One Thousand was split into two groups. The conservatives, who tended to be younger and more aggressive, favored a surprise attack on the Empire. The liberals meanwhile were generally older and more experienced, and wanted to give the humans a chance to recover the vial themselves.

The liberals had sponsored this public appearance in an effort to sway public opinion, an important factor in a society governed by mutual consensus.

While the Il Ronnian public was understandably upset about the loss of the holy relic, they were also curious about the human who had promised to find it and were eager to learn more about him. So the liberals hoped McCade would make a good impression and buy them some time.

He knew the Il Ronnian voice was introducing him, telling the public that he'd already passed the first phase of testing, and inviting them to witness phase two. It seemed there were plans to televise his activities from this point on. Neem said this would serve to build liberal support and provide the population with some free entertainment to boot.

"But what if I fail?" McCade had asked.

"Then the conservatives will get their way and attack," Neem had replied with a characteristic shrug. "And since I'm certifiably insane, they'll make me a full Sector Commander."

McCade saw very little humor in the Il Ronnian's joke considering the implications for the human empire.

McCade felt Neem jab him in the back as the Il Ronnian voice stopped. It was his turn to speak. His words had been carefully rehearsed during the trip to Imantha, and computer-checked to make sure the translation from human Standard to Il Ronnian wouldn't introduce any inaccuracies. As he spoke an Il Ronnian translator would echo his words a fraction of a second later.

"I bring greetings from my people to yours. It is a privilege to visit your home planet, to undergo the trials of the Ilwik, and to speak to you this night."

The crowd swirled slightly and a great hissing filled the air. McCade waited for it to die down. "Thank you. There has long been tension between our two races as is natural when two great empires come together and almost touch. And where we come together sparks sometimes fly, lives are tragically lost, and neither race profits. Such was the case when some humans raided the planet you call Fema and took the holy Vial of Tears."

At the mention of the holy relic a deep growling filled the air, and sweat popped out on McCade's forehead as he found himself looking down at one hundred thousand devils, each one voicing his or her hatred. He swallowed dryly as the noise died away.

"Yes, I understand your anger, and ask you to understand that those who took the vial acted on their own without the knowledge and consent of the human Emperor. And, God willing, that's why I will hunt them down and kill them, taking the vial and returning it to the Il Ronnian people."

Now the hissing became a sibilant roar, as thousands of tails lashed their approval, and the crowd surged forward in its excitement.

McCade had questioned his last statement, pointing out that he couldn't promise to find the vial, much less kill the people who'd taken it.

But Neem had waved his objections away. He said the statement was simply a sop to the conservative party that shouldn't be taken too seriously. Looking out at the roaring crowd McCade wasn't too sure. They seemed to believe he could do it. How would they react if he failed?

For the hundredth time he cursed the various forces that had conspired to put him where he was, lifted an arm to wave to the crowd, and watched as the four gigantic McCades did likewise.

He waved one last time as he felt Neem tug on the back of his cool suit, glad to have the whole thing over.

As he left the balcony the Sand Sept troopers closed in around him once more. Together they marched through a series of passageways and down a wide escalator. Additional Sand Sept troopers had been positioned to keep a lane clear for their use.

As he stepped off the bottom of the escalator McCade found himself on a broad platform. Fifty or sixty Il Ronnians were scattered across the platform. Beyond it was a huge tube of some transparent material. He couldn't tell if they'd witnessed his recent performance or not, but they turned to watch him with curious eyes as he arrived.

Moments later there was a soft whooshing sound as an enormous train arrived inside the transparent tube and a series of doors hissed open. It was clearly some sort of underground transcar system, but on a scale McCade had never seen before.

"The second car back is ours," Neem said, "or so I was told. It would seem that you're getting the VIP treatment."

McCade glanced at the Sand Sept troopers and back to Neem. "VIP? What does that stand for, very important prisoner?"

Neem smiled but refused to meet his eyes. "You're not looking at this the right way. The troopers are here to protect you. I'm not the only crazy Il Ronnian on the planet. There're others, some of whom are diehard conservatives and quite violent."

"Thanks," McCade replied dryly. "I feel a lot better now."

Once inside McCade discovered the train was as large as it appeared. While no other passengers had been allowed to board their car, he could tell that it normally held hundreds of riders.

He noticed that the bottom of each seat had a three-inch slot that ran front to back. At first he couldn't figure out what it was for, until he saw Neem take a seat and saw how neatly the Il Ronnian's tail slid back through the slot. Then the tail arched up and over the back of the chair to appear over Neem's shoulder. Now it could become part of the alien's nonverbal communication once again. Later McCade would notice that almost all Il Ronnian chairs featured this same design.

Like everything else the Il Ronnians used, the inside of the train was warm, way too warm. McCade opened the two nozzles located on the chest of the suit and directed the cool air up toward his face. He knew this would put an increased demand on the power pak, but what the heck, he'd just ask Neem for another.

Feeling somewhat better, McCade turned his attention to the large windows that lined both sides of the car. There was nothing much to see. Just solid rock flashing by at incredible speed. Neem volunteered an explanation.

"If you build most of your cities underground, it only makes sense to put your major transportation systems there as well. This particular train runs on the surface for short periods of time, but since it's night up there, you still won't see much."

McCade nodded, kicked his feet up onto the opposite bench, and watched the rock walls flash by until he drifted off to sleep.

"Well, this is it," Neem, said cheerfully. "After this morning, phase one of the testing will be out of the way."

"Or I'll be dead," McCade answered as he fastened the last seal on his cool suit. The long train ride had left him tired and grumpy. After the train trip he'd been transferred here, to the Wa'na, or sacred testing grounds.

He was in a rather Spartan dressing room at the moment. The only furnishings consisted of an Il Ronnian water shrine and a table heaped high with weapons. The shrine was a scaled biosphere that depicted a natural spring bubbling up between lichen-covered rocks.

The walls were made of bare durocrete and were completely featureless except for an ominous-looking metal door. When he stepped through it the testing would begin.

Neem had already explained that like the first phase of testing, the second involved three separate tests, each corresponding to one aspect of life. The first, and the one he would tackle today, was the physical. It included athletic ability, the martial arts, and an appreciation of physical beauty.

The second level was mental. It included the ability to reason, academic as well as experiential learning, and the ability to manipulate the environment through use of tools.

The third level was the spiritual, and it involved a mastery of both the first and second levels, but a mastery that incorporated certain concepts. Primary among them was love and compassion.

But love and compassion were far from McCade's mind as he approached the table and eyed the weapons laid out on its surface. He'd been told to expect physical combat, but that's all he knew, and it made the choice a difficult one. After all, depending on who your enemy is, some weapons are more effective than others.

But he'd always found that slug guns serve a variety of needs, so he left the Molg-Sader belted around his waist and checked to make sure that he had two extra magazines.

Of course, energy weapons have advantages too, so McCade hedged his bet and picked up a brand-new blast rifle. He noticed it was marine issue and wondered how it had fallen into Il Ronnian hands. Whatever the answer, he knew he wouldn't like it.

Then he passed a bandolier of energy paks over his head and decided to call it a day. There were lots of other weapons he could have chosen, everything from frag grenades to rocket launchers, but each additional weapon would add weight and slow him down. So if the Il Ronnians had a main battle tank waiting for him out there, he was just plain out of luck.

McCade recognized Teeb's voice as it flooded in over some hidden speaker. "It is time for the candidate to enter the Wa'na. Please enter through the metal door. Good luck, Ilwig McCade.

Much to McCade's surprise, Teeb sounded as if he meant it.

McCade had his hand on the door when he remembered something. Acting on impulse he returned to the water shrine and intoned the traditional prayer. "As you flow through heaven and earth, flow also through me, watering my spirit and making it grow."

As he opened the door and went through he missed Neem's smile and the words that went with it. "Assuming you survive you'll make one hell of an Il Ronnian someday. Good luck!"

EIGHT

McCade squinted into bright sunlight. Sheer canyon walls rose on every side exposing layers of sediment stained here and there with streaks of red.

An island of solid rock stood in front of him. It had once forced a mighty river to divide itself in half forming two channels, one right and one left.

The river was gone now, but rocks both large and small remained as silent witnesses to a time when Imantha had been very different. A time when the holy fluid had leaped and splashed its way through the canyon on its journey to a distant sea.

Gravel crunched under McCade's boots as he turned a full circle. He held the blast rifle up and ready. Would his opponent attack without warning? Or would he hear some sort of official statement first?

McCade knew as all bounty hunters did that real violence comes without warning. But when violence has been institutionalized and turned into entertainment, it must be justified and explained for the comfort of those who view it. The violence might otherwise seem primitive and uncivilized, and that would never do.

Knowing this, McCade smiled as a flight of vid cams appeared overhead and Teeb's voice echoed between the canyon walls. "In a moment the first phase of your testing will begin. As you know the test will measure your ability to deal with the physical world. Violence is a part of the physical world and to recover the Vial of Tears you will be forced to fight many battles. So we will confront you with five armed opponents.

"All are humans captured during a raid on one of our planets. You may deal with them in whatever fashion you think appropriate. All are experienced warriors, all are well armed, and all will go free if they kill you. Do you understand?"

"I don't want to seem ungrateful or anything," McCade said dryly, "but there's no need to be so generous with opponents. Wouldn't one be enough?"

"For most candidates it would be," Teeb replied evenly. "But you are a professional killer. So to ensure a fair contest we gave you five opponents. Do you have any other comments or questions?"

Although he didn't agree with Teeb's description of him as a "professional killer," McCade decided to let it go.

"Nope, I think that about covers it. It's good to know that you're keeping everything fair."

"Very well then. Your opponents have been released about two of your miles down canyon. The rest is up to you."

With that the vid cams darted in every direction and took up new positions that would allow them to cover the action.

McCade began to run. He chose the right channel, dodged between boulders as he searched for a hiding place. Given the odds he'd prefer to hole up somewhere and let them come to him. All he needed was some cover and a rear exit. Unfortunately he didn't see anything that even came close.

He rounded the other end of the island and came to a sudden stop. There was an open stretch up ahead where the two channels came back together, and while some large boulders dotted its surface, they didn't offer much cover.

Beyond that some upthrust rock formations had forced the river to divide once again and form a number of smaller channels. The river was gone but the channels weren't and they formed a natural maze. Not the sort of place where McCade wanted to play hide and seek with five killers.

He turned and ran full speed at the island. As he ran McCade picked a path through the jumble of rocks and headed for the top in a series of long jumps.

From up there he'd be able to see them coming and establish a good angle of fire as well. They'd have him trapped of course, but there's no such thing as a perfect plan.

It wasn't long before the easy jumps gave way to a serious climb. The ancient river had worn the boulders smooth and footholds were hard to come by. For every two feet of progress made, it seemed as if one was lost.

Meanwhile there were five killers headed his way. He wouldn't know they were there until a slug took him between the shoulder blades. He wanted to look but couldn't. Looking would waste precious time.

He told himself that they'd come slowly. They'd be on the lookout for an ambush and their progress would be slowed by the same maze of channels that he'd decided to avoid.

His arguments made sense, but there was still a hard itchy feeling between his shoulder blades as McCade pulled himself over the top and rolled out of sight.

Moving on hands and knees, McCade hid behind a jumble of rocks, unslung the blast rifle, and flipped the sight to high mag. He swept the weapon from left to right and checked for signs of movement.

Except for shimmering heat waves and the occasional bird, everything was still. A Fueek bird flapped its way upward to soar against the violet sky. McCade remembered the great Ilwik's love for Fueek birds and decided that this one was a good omen.

It was suddenly warmer inside his cool suit and McCade turned over to check for damage. Sure enough, there was a four-inch tear just above the right knee. He could feel cool air spilling out when he held his hand over the hole. Damn!

If he tried to repair the tear, his opponents might break into the open when he wasn't looking. And if he didn't repair the tear, he'd run the very real risk of heat prostration.

McCade swore under his breath as he opened a pocket on his left sleeve and withdrew a small patch kit. He tore it open with fumbling fingers and spilled precut patches all over the ground.

Picking up a rectangular patch with one hand he used the other to squeeze bonding material onto its inside surface. The moment the entire thing was covered McCade slapped the patch into place and felt the temperature begin to drop. It worked!

Then he caught movement from the corner of his eye. Two of the hovering vid cams suddenly jumped upward and spun toward the rocky maze. Someone knew something he didn't.

Grabbing his blast rifle, McCade rolled over to peer through the sight. One, two, three, wait a minute, yes, there they were, four and five. The suited figures had just emerged from the maze and were working their way up channel toward the open space. They were out of range, but it gave McCade a chance to check out the opposition.

Number one was a woman. Her shoulder-length black hair swayed around her face as she moved and her weapon was pointed at the ground. She had the point, which suggested a leader, either elected or self-appointed.

But wait a minute. Look at number two. Was he wrong, or was number two's weapon aimed at number one's back? Number two was a hefty man with a large bald spot and a hard face. What was this? Mutiny? Or something else?

McCade swept his sight across the other three. There were two men and a woman. As they advanced they were close enough to communicate but too far apart to nail with a single burst. Very cool, very professional. These people knew what they were doing.

McCade felt the muscle in his left cheek begin to twitch. Okay, three, four, and five were hard bodies who knew one end of a blaster from the other. But what about numbers one and two?

Maybe two was just a wee bit careless about the way he held his weapon, or maybe there had been a falling out among thieves, or maybe number one was being *forced* to take the point. She'd draw the first fire and give the others a chance to find cover. If so, then number two was the leader, and a prime target.

Number one paused at the edge of the open area clearly hesitant to cross it. But number two gave her a shove and she stumbled forward, almost falling before regaining her balance. And number two was right behind her as she ran from one scrap of cover to the next, his weapon centered on her back.

McCade found himself wishing for a cigar and forced the thought away. It was time to reduce the odds a little. He seated the rifle butt against his right shoulder, flicked the safety off, and centered the sight on a patch of open ground.

This particular patch was directly in front of number four's position. In order to reach the next rock four would have to pass through it, and when he did, McCade would nail him.

It would be a simple shot. Energy weapons aren't subject to the effects of wind or gravity as are slug throwers. Of course they don't pack much kinetic energy either, so if you're trying to drop a charging Envo Beast, you might choose something with a little more wallop. But an energy beam does go where you aim it and for this situation the blast rifle was ideal.

Number four took off like a jackrabbit and ran right into the energy beam. It sliced down through his left shoulder and cut diagonally across his chest. The two halves of his body separated in a bright shower of blood.

A vid cam swooped down for a better shot as McCade turned his attention to number five. Something winked to the right and fire splashed the rock by his head. Number five was shooting back!

McCade rolled left as another energy beam screamed through the space he'd just vacated. Number five was a good shot.

McCade eased the barrel of his weapon through a gap in the rocks, caught a flash of movement, and fired. His energy beam punched a hole through number five's right leg, causing her to stumble and fall.

Using her hands and one good leg, number five managed to drag herself behind a ledge.

McCade let her go. Two down and three to go.

Swinging his weapon left, McCade searched for numbers one and two. He just caught a glimpse of them as they made it to the base of the island. He'd have to stand against the skyline in order to see them and that would provide number three with an opportunity to blow his head off. Where *was* number three anyway?

Conscious that numbers one and two were busily climbing his way, McCade moved to the right. If possible he wanted to find three and deal with him before one and two arrived.

He could feel the seconds ticking away as he quartered the ground below. Each second brought numbers one and two closer and increased the odds against him.

He was just about to give up when he saw a flash of white toward the top of his scope.

McCade tilted the rifle down and found his cross hairs centered on number three's back. The bastard was running away! His finger touched the firing stud and stopped. Later he might regret the decision, but McCade couldn't bring himself to shoot a man in the back.

He turned and was just starting to get up when numbers one and two popped up from behind a jumble of rocks. They were fast!

Something snatched the blast rifle from his hands and McCade dived sideways hoping to ruin their aim.

He hit hard and felt rather than saw the bullets that followed along behind. They spanged off the surrounding rocks as he rolled onto his back and felt the slug gun fill his hand. It came up and he saw a white suit fill his sight.

It was number one! Number two had an arm around one's throat and was using her as a shield! One struggled and two's bullets went wide.

McCade screamed at her. "Drop, damn you, drop!"

Number one dropped. McCade felt the slug gun buck in his hand as she did and saw three red flowers blossom down the front of number two's cool suit. Number two staggered, the slug gun flew from his hand, and he fell over backward into a pool of his own blood.

McCade kept the slug gun centered on number one as he struggled to his feet. He hoped it was over but couldn't be sure. For the first time he noticed that she was very, very pretty, with wide-set brown eyes, a long, straight nose, and a generous mouth.

Her voice trembled when she spoke. "He took the power pak out of my weapon. Are you going to kill me?"

McCade bolstered the slug gun and patted his pockets for a cigar. "Not unless you think I should."

She looked at number two and shuddered. "All of them outranked me so they made me take the point." She paused. "They call me Reba. I'm surprised to be alive."

McCade found a broken cigar, stuck it between his teeth, and puffed it into life. "I know what you mean, Reba. So am I."

NINE

McCade was allowed to rest for one rotation before the next test began. He spent some of his time eating and sleeping and the rest being tutored by Neem.

Among other things McCade learned that the Il Ronn had fifteen different words for heat. Each one conveyed a slightly different quality of heat, and was associated with a time of day or a type of activity.

While this kind of complexity made the Il Ronnian language difficult to learn, it also made it extremely precise and a joy to scientists and poets alike.

Though not sure what to do with this sort of information, McCade found it interesting and the time passed quickly. Before he knew it the rest period was over and Teeb was leading the way to the next test site.

The warrior-priest was no longer hostile. If anything, he'd assumed a proprietary air as if McCade were his invention and a rather clever one at that.

Neem trailed along behind, his tail swishing back and forth in amusement. At this rate they'd have to make room for Teeb at the Institute for Mental Rehabilitation. After all, anyone who liked humans *must* be crazy.

Meanwhile, Teeb had continued his conversation with McCade. Although his tone was friendly, the Il Ronnian's eyes glowed like red coals. "Well, human, what did you think of the first test?"

McCade considered his answer carefully before speaking. "As the great Il-wik once said, 'All things are connected.' In retrospect the test was not entirely physical."

"Yes!" Teeb responded eagerly. "*None* of the tests are entirely what they seem. Tell me, *how* did you pass the test?"

McCade had already given the matter some thought so his answer was ready. "I passed because of things I *didn't* do."

Teeb gave McCade a friendly pat on the back. The impact drove him forward a step and a half. "You amaze me, human! You are correct. You passed because you *did not* panic, you *did not* make stupid assumptions, and you *did not* kill unnecessarily. All virtues of the warrior-priest. But best of all you knew *why* you did as you did."

Actually McCade hadn't figured it out until *after* the test, but since Teeb was so pleased, he saw no reason to straighten the alien out.

The corridor was long, tubular, and increasingly busy. Many Il Ronnians stopped to stare as McCade and his entourage passed by.

McCade did his best to ignore them, but found that somewhat difficult when juveniles ran up to pinch him. Most were intercepted by the Sand Sept troopers, but some got through, and it hurt when they pinched him. Fortunately his cool suit absorbed most of the punishment.

Teeb's long red robe made a soft swishing noise as it dragged along the floor. "During your second test you will play a game called 'Encirclement.' It requires a good memory, an agile mind, and other qualities as well."

They paused as the Sand Sept troopers intercepted a flying squad of young Il Ronnians before continuing on their way.

"I want you to know that we have gone to extreme lengths to make the game fair," Teeb said seriously. "Encirclement is something of a passion with many Il Ronnians, and since you have never played before, it took some effort to locate a suitable opponent. I think that is our door just ahead."

The door was one of many that lined the corridor. Each bore a number and some serpentine Il Ronnian script. McCade tried to open it but was brushed aside by a rather large Sand Sept trooper.

Moments later the trooper was back, signaling the all-clear with his tail and holding the door open so they could enter.

McCade followed Teeb into a large circular room. The walls and ceiling radiated a soft violet light, and like every other Il Ronnian room he'd been in, it was hotter than hell.

A beautiful mosaic covered the floor. Thousands, maybe millions, of stone chips had been used to fashion pictures, each beautiful in itself but part of a much larger whole. Darker stones framed the pictures and went together to form a large grid. And when viewed as a whole the grid formed a desert landscape. And the landscape was filled with Il Ronnian birds, animals, and legendary beasts.

McCade noticed that a large number of red rocks had been stacked on one side of the room, while an equal number of green rocks had been piled on the other. The rocks were highly polished and of uniform size and shape.

"Here is your opponent now. Eena, this is the human called McCade."

McCade turned to find himself looking down into the serious face of a young Il Ronnian female. As far as he could tell the only difference between male Il Ronnians and female Il Ronnians were the colorful sashes the females wore over their loose robes. Apparently the Il Ronnians could tell the difference however, since there were plenty of them.

"I hope you will not be offended by the fact that Eena is not an adult, but given Encirclement's popularity, it was difficult to locate a suitable opponent. However, Eena is the best player in her hatching and I think she will offer you a sufficient challenge."

Although Eena was no more than ten cycles old, and came no higher than his waist, McCade saw her eyes glitter with anticipation. She planned to clean his clock.

McCade bowed his respect. "Greetings, Eena. May you grow and hatch many eggs."

Eena bowed in return. She spoke Il Ronnian, but the translator pinned to her robe turned it into flawless Standard. "Greetings, human. May you eat feces and die an agonizing death."

McCade looked at Teeb with a raised eyebrow. "What's the problem? Have I got bad breath or something?"

The warrior-priest grinned his amusement. "Eena means no disrespect. She is using psychological warfare. She hopes to unnerve you. Such ploys are an accepted part of Encirclement."

McCade nodded his understanding. "Fair enough. If you'll explain the rules, Shorty and I will get this game off the ground."

Eena winced at the term "shorty," and McCade grinned. This could be fun.

Teeb cleared his throat importantly. "Here is how the game of Encirclement is played. You will notice that the floor has been divided into a grid. There are nineteen vertical and nineteen horizontal lines. As a result there are three hundred sixty-one intersections or positions where you can place the stones that are either red or green. Please choose a color."

McCade looked at the piles of red and green stones and then at Eena. He noticed that her face was carefully neutral. She wanted one color over the other. He took a guess. "I'll take the red stones."

Eena's mouth turned down into a scowl. Her red sash had given her away.

"Good," Teeb acknowledged, his tail signaling approval. "The two of you will take turns placing stones, also called warriors, on the intersections where the vertical and horizontal lines meet. Each of you will attempt to encircle as many vacant intersections as possible. When both of you are satisfied that all the potential territory has been taken, you will count the vacant points encircled by your warriors, and subtract the number lost through capture. The individual with the most points wins."

"Capture?" McCade asked. "How does that work?"

"A good question," Teeb answered approvingly. "When two or more of your opponent's warriors occupy adjacent positions on a vertical or horizontal line, they are considered a sept and can be captured when encircled by your stones. As long as one of its members adjoins a vacant intersection the sept is free, but when the sept is completely surrounded, it is taken hostage and removed from the board. Understood?"

"Understood," McCade answered.

"Excellent," Teeb said approvingly. "In that case I'll leave you to it. Have a good match." Teeb's tail waved good-bye as he headed for the door.

Neem sidled up to McCade as Eena went over to inspect her stones. Speaking softly he said, "Don't forget to cheat."

"What?"

Neem looked around nervously and said it again. "I said, don't forget to cheat. I'm an expert on human culture remember?"

"Yeah, so?"

"So many humans disapprove of cheating. We don't. We don't talk about it, but everyone cheats if they can get away with it. So unless you keep an eye on Eena, she'll steal the match out from under you."

McCade nodded thoughtfully. "Thanks, Neem. I'll keep it in mind."

Neem left as a swarm of vid cameras entered and took up positions in various parts of the room.

As one came to hover over his head McCade wondered how many Il Ronnians were watching and whether they were for or against him. According to Neem, McCade had quite a following, liberals mostly, but a scattering of independents as well. Of course, none of them were really rooting for *him,* they were opposed to war and wanted him to succeed for that reason.

"Make your move, human scum."

McCade turned to find Eena scowling up at him. Her attempts to intimidate him were kind of cute. And even though she'd eventually grow up to look like the devil himself, there was something appealing about her pinched little face and big determined eyes.

He patted her shoulder. "Thank you, Eena. You're pretty cute for a short person. I'll grab a rock and be right back."

He headed across the room without waiting for a response and picked up a red rock. For some reason he'd imagined the stones were artificial and therefore lighter than they looked. Nothing could have been further from the truth.

The stones were real and weighed about twenty-five pounds apiece. Later he'd learn that this particular court had been designed for male grand masters. Most courts were a good deal less fancy, and many Il Ronnians preferred to play on miniature boards or computer terminals. But this was a full-blown traditional court complete with real rocks.

McCade carried his stone to the middle of the grid, picked an intersection, and plopped it down.

He saw a look of enormous satisfaction come over Eena's face. The human had placed his first warrior in the middle of the desert! At this rate the ugly alien would beat himself!

Eena selected one of her own stones, struggled to pick it up, and staggered over to the far corner of the grid where she carefully lowered it into place.

The stones were way too heavy for her and McCade was tempted to help. But should he give up an advantage? Perhaps the weight of the stones had been factored into the match as part of her handicap. And what if he *had* to win in order to pass this test? By helping her he might call down a nightmare of destruction on his own kind.

With those thoughts in mind McCade decided to let Eena fend for herself. Meanwhile he'd do his best to win the match.

Having analyzed Eena's last move, McCade realized that the corners of the grid were easier to defend than the middle. Like her he would start in the corners and work his way out.

He selected another stone, placed it in close proximity to Eena's, and stepped back to watch her reaction.

What he got was a look of resignation, as though she'd realized that his stupidity couldn't last forever, and been forced to accept it.

Well, he *thought* it was a look of resignation, but how could he be sure? He'd picked up on some Il Ronnian facial expressions from Neem, but still couldn't tell if Eena was resigned, or just suffering from indigestion. He decided to assume the former and placed another stone near hers.

And so it went stone after stone, intersection after intersection, until McCade was almost completely surrounded. Eena had also captured small contingents of his warriors so now he was outnumbered as well as poorly positioned. He was going to lose, that much was certain.

Nonetheless, McCade was determined to make the best showing he could. So there was only one thing left to do. Follow Neem's advice and cheat.

By now the weight of the stones had started to take their toll on Eena. McCade estimated that each of them had around two hundred stones at their disposal, and at twenty-five pounds apiece, that came to more than two tons of rock.

So each time Eena went for another stone her movements were a little slower, her steps a little more uncertain, and her eyes a little more out of focus.

McCade's heart went out to her, but he steeled himself with visions of what might happen to Molly if he failed the test and set about using Eena's predicament to his advantage.

Usually it was a simple matter of sliding her warriors off one intersection and onto another less important position. And sometimes he moved his own stones, subtly improving their positions and worsening Eena's.

The vid cams swooped and hovered throughout all this, picking up his activities and transmitting them to thousands of Il Ronnians all over the planet. What did they think of his cheating? There was no way to tell.

Eena came close to catching him more than once, returning from the pile of stones to find the board slightly altered, frowning as she tried to remember where all the pieces had been. Had he been a peer, or had she been less exhausted, maybe she would've said something. But she didn't and the game went on.

Time after time she returned to the ever dwindling supply of green stones, and time after time she hauled one back, until it was obvious that she was on the edge of physical collapse. But the little Il Ronnian had guts and refused to give up.

By this time McCade had begun to feel sorry for her. He kept looking up at the hovering vid cams, waiting for Teeb to declare that the game was over, that Eena could stop. But nothing came.

Damn it! Why continue this farce? Eena had won all but a final victory and could hardly keep on her feet.

McCade set about reversing the effects of his cheating. Making almost no effort to conceal his movements, he rearranged Eena's warriors so they surrounded twice the intersections they had before and captured half his remaining warriors in the bargain. Maybe he'd lost the match, maybe he'd failed the test, but he couldn't bear to watch Eena carry more rocks.

Eena finally staggered up with her last stone, dropped it onto an intersection with a heavy thud, and surveyed the grid. Then she realized that her warriors dominated the entire grid and her features lit up with delight. She gave a whoop of joy and her tail stood at attention as she jumped up and down. "I won! I won!"

The vid cameras spun and dipped as they picked up final shots, and McCade wiped the sweat off his forehead with the back of his hand. He looked down at Eena and grinned. "You sure did, Shorty. You won fair and square."

TEN

It seemed like a long time before Teeb came. McCade spent it smoking cigar after cigar until his room was thick with dark blue smoke. Finally coughing and hacking, Neem left McCade alone with his own dark thoughts.

Had he passed their stupid test or not? The least the pointy-eared bastards could do was tell him. The whole thing was silly. Yes, he understood how much the sacred vial meant to the Il Ronnian people; yes, he understood that according to tradition only a full Ilwik could undertake a holy quest; yes, he knew what was at stake.

But it wasn't fair. The tests had no clear rules, the odds were stacked against him, and the penalty for failure was way too high.

If he failed, would the Il Ronnian ships really blast out of hyperspace and lay waste to the rim worlds? Was a vial full of liquid really worth an interstellar war? Unfortunately the answer came back "yes," and the knowledge plunged him even deeper into despair.

In typical Il Ronnian fashion Teeb didn't knock when he entered McCade's room. Instead he barged right in waving some sort of printout over his head.

"You know what *this* is, human?"

McCade did his best to look bored. "I haven't got the slightest idea."

"It is an audience consensus . . . that is what it is!"

"A consensus?"

"Yes, our society operates on consensus, as you know, and the only way to test consensus is to sample the population on a regular basis. And according to the people you passed the second test by an even larger margin than the first one!"

McCade was suddenly on his feet. "What? You mean *the audience* decides whether I pass or fail?"

Teeb looked momentarily mystified. "Yes, of course. Who else would decide?"

McCade's jaw dropped. "I don't know. I assumed there was a committee or something."

Teeb dismissed the idea with a wave of his tail. "Only humans would let others make such an important decision for them. On Imantha everyone has a say."

A feeling of tremendous relief swept over McCade as he fell back into his chair. He'd passed! Never mind that the whole thing was completely insane, he'd passed!

Teeb paced back and forth, his tail twitching, his eyes glowing with enthusiasm. "What a match! You are without a doubt the worst player in this sector of space! Eena out positioned you from the start, and cheat, my goodness that youngster could cheat!"

"Cheat?" Even though Neem had warned him of the possibility, and even though he'd done it himself, it hadn't occurred to McCade that Eena had cheated too.

Teeb laughed. "Of course. Eena moved your warriors around more than you did!"

McCade felt suddenly defensive. "Well, if I performed so poorly, how come I passed the test?"

Teeb was suddenly serious. "Because you did the best you could in a situation where all the odds were stacked against you, because you managed to adapt to changing circumstances, because you chose to risk all to help the weak."

McCade was silent for a moment and then he spoke. "The audience said all that?"

Teeb's tail signaled agreement. "That is correct, human. The audience said all that."

McCade nodded soberly. "I see. So what's next?"

"That," Teeb replied with a toothy grin, "is for me to know, and for you to find out."

ELEVEN

The trumpets made a long mournful sound as McCade walked down the broad aisle toward the Rock of Truth. To his right and left ten thousand Il Ronnians stood and bowed their respect. He noticed that most wore the uniform of the Star Sept.

Gravel crunched under his boots and he heard the sound of his own breathing as he walked up a curving path to emerge on top of a flat rock.

It was from this spot that the great Ilwik had ministered to his followers so long ago. As the sun dropped behind the canyon walls they had come forth to hear him speak, and in his latter days trumpets had announced his arrival.

And even though the canyon had been roofed over five hundred cycles before, and its floor made smooth for the comfort of the people, it was the same place. A holy place imbued by time and use with a sense of profound peace and quiet.

A shiver went down McCade's spine as he looked out over the assembled multitude. The usual vid cameras danced here and there as filtered sunlight streamed down from huge skylights and twenty thousand devils waited for him to speak. It couldn't, shouldn't, be happening, yet here he was about to judge and be judged in return. He held up both hands as an audio pickup moved in to hover near his mouth.

"In the name of the great Ilwik I bid you welcome. Please be seated." Thanks to translating devices his voice spoke perfect Il Ronnian as it boomed the length of the canyon.

As the twenty thousand Il Ronnians took their seats they made a loud rustling sound like the wind passing through dry vegetation.

McCade sat on the same rock the Ilwik had favored and pulled out a cigar. The Il Ronn didn't smoke so they had no prohibitions against it. McCade puffed the cigar alight and blew out a column of smoke with his first words.

"My name is Sam McCade. Although I am not an Il Ronnian, I have worn the bracelet and seen through the great Ilwik's eyes. I come before you to judge a crime, and to be judged in return, for if I fail there will be a terrible war. Let us all pray that justice will prevail. The prosecution may begin."

Neem and he had rehearsed everything up to this point, but he'd have to wing it from here on out, and that wouldn't be easy. Ilwiks had dispensed justice at the tribal or sept level of Il Ronnian society in ancient times. But as the need for specialization grew, they had gradually transferred that function to occupational groupings.

So, if a clerk in the Department of Census beat his mate, the matter would be heard by an Ilwik from that same department, and the judgment would be confirmed or modified by a jury of his peers. Il Ronnian theory held that they alone were truly his peers and best able to confirm or deny his punishment.

And according to Neem it wasn't unusual for some cases to be assigned to individuals in the final stages of testing. For in the Il Ronnian view, justice and religion were part and parcel of the same thing. And what better way to test a candidate's spiritual readiness than to cast him in the role of judge? And since his decision would be subject to ratification by a group of the defendant's peers, what could go wrong?

Everything, McCade thought to himself as a group of Il Ronnians approached the rock. Just about everything could go wrong. Especially considering the fact that he didn't even know *what* crime had been committed. In order to assure their impartiality judges weren't given any information about the crime prior to the trial.

A short Il Ronnian dressed in the uniform of the Star Sept was the first to speak. "I am Sub Sector Commander Deex, and I speak for those who seek redress."

McCade noticed the latticework of scars that crisscrossed Deex's leathery face and the gleam of metal where his left arm should have been.

"Thank you, Commander Deex. Who speaks for the accused?"

Now another Il Ronnian stepped forward, this one attired in the robes of the merchant marine, the nonmilitary ships that conducted commerce between Il Ronnian worlds. "I am Captain Oeem. I speak for the accused."

McCade saw that Oeem was older, his skin hanging in loose folds around his neck and wrists, a slight stoop hinting at years spent within the close confines of merchant ships.

"Thank you, Captain Oeem," McCade replied. He waved his cigar. "Let the accused step forward."

At this point a youngish Il Ronnian took a single step forward. He wore the uniform of a Star Sept Sixteenth Commander, the lowest commissioned rank there was, roughly equivalent to an ensign in the Imperial Navy. He was obviously scared but held his back rigidly erect and ramrod straight. "Sir, I am Sixteenth Commander Reep, sir."

"Thank you, Commander Reep." McCade turned to Deex. "Please read the charges."

Commander Deex stepped forward. "Sixteenth Commander Reep is accused of refusing a direct order from his commanding officer. His offense is made worse by the fact that his group of interceptors were engaged in combat at the time, and by the fact that he is completely unrepentant. His actions set a dangerous precedent and if allowed to go unpunished would endanger all members of the Star Sept."

McCade stirred uneasily in his seat. There was something funny going on here, at least it seemed like there was, but it was still too early to know for sure. He tapped some ash off the end of his cigar and turned to Oeem.

"Thank you. Captain Oeem? Do you wish to make an opening statement?"

Oeem's tail indicated his assent. "Yes, I would. I do not contest the fact that Commander Reep disobeyed a direct order from his superior, but maintain that he was correct in doing so, given the situation he found himself in."

McCade nodded. "I see. Thank you. Commander Deex, please state the case against Commander Reep."

Deex stepped forward once again and assumed a position similar to parade rest. If he thought it strange that a human was judging the case, he gave no sign of it.

"Yes, sir. A tenth cycle ago my squadron was assigned to patrol part of the Necta Sector. The Necta Sector forms part of our frontier with the human empire, and because of the unusually large number of star systems in that sector, human pirates use it as a way to enter Il Ronnian space. Over time they have become extremely adept at jumping from one system to the next using planets to shield their activities from our sensors."

McCade dropped the cigar onto the rock and crushed it out. "Was your squadron at full strength? And if not, how many ships did you have?"

McCade saw the Il Ronnian's tail twitch in surprise. These were military questions coming from a civilian. And if there was any form of life lower than a human civilian, Deex couldn't think what it was.

Nonetheless this human held a position of power, and power was something Deex understood quite well. He chose his words carefully. The Star Sept was woefully thin along the frontier and in constant need of more funding. On the other hand his superiors wouldn't want him to suggest the frontier was undefended either, especially to a human.

"We had a carrier, two destroyers, and a light cruiser. So while the squadron was slightly under strength, it was more than sufficient for our mission." There. Deex hoped he'd hedged all his bets.

"Thank you," McCade said. "Please continue.

Deex cleared his throat. "Yes, sir. We had been on station for six standard cycles when one of our scouts spotted a formation of five human ships attempting to slip across the frontier. We positioned our vessels along their path and laid in wait. The moment they came into range we issued a warning and called on them to surrender."

This last part wasn't exactly true since it was SOP to fire on human pirates without warning, but Deex couldn't say so, because it wouldn't square with standing orders.

"And then?"

"They tried to run and we opened fire," Deex answered. "The carrier launched a flight of interceptors, and they were engaged by human craft of similar design. It was then that Captain Oeem blundered onto the scene."

"Blundered onto the scene?" Oeem demanded, his eyes glowing under a prominent brow. "How dare you! Since when does a merchant ship on its legal and authorized rounds blunder onto anything? My ship had a perfect right to drop out of hyperspace in that sector. A sector I might add that would be safe for merchant vessels like mine if the Star Sept spent more time on patrol and less time sitting on their rear ends!"

McCade cleared his throat. "Gentlemen, Please. You will have your chance in a few minutes, Captain Oeem. Until then Commander Deex has the floor. Go ahead, Commander."

"As I was saying," Deex continued self-righteously, "we had just engaged the enemy when Captain Oeem's ship *arrived* on the scene. As luck would have it, he came out of hyperspace in close proximity to the human ships. Immediately identifying Captain Oeem's ship as Il Ronnian, the humans locked some heavy-duty tractor beams on it and started to retreat while using the merchant vessel as a shield."

McCade could imagine the pirates' surprise as the Il Ronnian merchant ship dropped out of hyperspace and into their laps. A quick mind had seen the vessel's potential and reached out to capture it. By keeping the merchant vessel between themselves and the Il Ronnian warships the pirates could reduce the volume of incoming fire and escape with their loot. Though careful to conceal it, McCade couldn't help but admire the pirates' audacity.

"And then?"

Deex scowled. "Fearing that we might kill innocent civilians, our commanding officer ordered us to cease fire and withdraw. The pirates would escape but Captain Oeem, his crew, and his passengers would survive."

"And did you follow that order?"

"Yes, sir, all except for Sixteenth Commander Reep." Deex turned to skewer Reep with an accusing look. A look the younger officer managed to ignore by keeping his eyes focused on a spot somewhere over McCade's head.

"And what did Commander Reep do?"

Deex turned back to McCade, and when he spoke his voice was grim. "Ignoring repeated orders to withdraw, Sixteenth Commander Reep dove his interceptor in toward the enemy formation and fired two torpedoes. Both torpedoes found their mark, destroying the largest of the enemy ships and releasing Captain Oeem's vessel. Seeing this, our commanding officer ordered the rest of the squadron to attack and all the enemy ships were destroyed. By disobeying orders Sixteenth Commander Reep endangered civilian lives and those of his comrades as well. Star Sept Command requests that Reep be sentenced to five annual cycles in a military prison and be stripped of his rank."

McCade watched the older officer's words hit Reep one at a time, and knew he'd been had. Although the circumstances were slightly different, the whole thing was too similar to his own court martial to be pure coincidence. Reep and he had both disobeyed a direct order involving civilian lives. And each had been court-martialed as a direct result.

How much information had Swanson-Pierce given them anyway? Enough to give them an edge, to force him into judging himself along with Reep, and to bring it all back. The anger, the fear, and the shame.

McCade forced those thoughts down and back. "Thank you, Commander Deex. Captain Oeem, would you present your side of the case please?"

Oeem's tail twitched in agreement. "I would be happy to. Commander Deex has done an admirable job of explaining how the battle came about, but has chosen to leave out certain facts that have a bearing on Commander Reep's actions. It is well known that the pirates kill Il Ronnian prisoners. There is no market for Il Ronnian slaves within the human empire, and the pirates refuse to feed and clothe us. No, a beam through the head is much quicker and simpler, something that Commander Deex and every other Star Sept officer knows quite well. So when our ships obeyed the order not to fire, they did so for *their* sakes not for *ours,* preferring inaction to the possible criticism that might result from the destruction of my ship."

At this point Oeem held out his right arm to point a quivering talon at Reep. "Only this young warrior had the courage to lay his life and career on the line for us . . . and now, when he should be receiving our highest award for valor . . . he stands before us accused of crimes. Each and every one of us should be ashamed of this day!"

McCade was impressed with Oeem's oratorical skill and decided that in spite of whatever bad luck had befallen Reep up till now, winding up with Oeem as his representative had been fortunate indeed.

"Thank you, Captain Oeem. Sixteenth Commander Reep, is there anything that you'd like to add?"

Reep seemed to grow another inch as he snapped to attention. "Sir, no, sir. Captain Oeem has done an excellent job of stating my case."

McCade nodded. "All right then. I will withdraw to consider the evidence. When I return I will render my verdict. You may return to your seats."

As McCade stood and made his way across the rock ledge and into the cave he heard a growing murmur behind him. Twenty thousand Il Ronnians were discussing the case. What would the human decide? A good question, and one he'd like an answer to as well.

It felt strange to enter the great Ilwik's cave. He'd been there countless times in his dreams and knew every nook and cranny of the place. Over there, where a thousand cook fires had blackened the wall, the great Ilwik had prepared his simple meals. And there, where a replica of the teacher's thin mattress lay, was where he'd slept. Slept peacefully until they came in the night to take him away.

And even as they tortured the life from his frail body and milked the tears from his dying eyes, he had forgiven and blessed them saying "I shall return."

And through the bracelet he *had* returned, a thousand times and more, as an unending chain of minds relived his life. And through his teachings the great Ilwik still lived on as an example of what sentient beings could be if they so chose.

A sudden flood of anger and determination rose to fill McCade's mind and emotions. On one level the Vial of Tears was stupid. A religious artifact that the great Ilwik would laugh at if he were alive. Yet on another it had value as a connection between the past and the present, as a symbol of one being's sacrifice, and of the things he'd stood for.

Suddenly McCade was determined to find the Vial of Tears, not just for Sara and Molly, but for the Il Ronnians as well. First however he had to become a full-fledged Ilwik and that meant reaching a judgment about Reep and himself.

Dropping onto the concave surface of a ledge where the Ilwik had loved to meditate, McCade stuck a cigar between his teeth and turned the case over in his mind. Like his own court martial the case revolved around a conflict between military discipline and compassion for others. Like McCade, Reep had been forced to choose between the two, and opted for compassion.

Unlike McCade however, Reep had a judge who was both sane and sympathetic. That suggested a verdict of not guilty.

Yet McCade had been an officer himself. He understood the need for discipline and he knew that disobedience had cost far more lives than it had ever saved. What to do?

He rolled the unlit cigar between his fingers, and as he did, an answer came.

From his subconscious? From walls that had absorbed the great Ilwik's wisdom? He didn't know or care, but the words certainly came from the great teacher.

"True justice lays outside the jurisdiction of the sept and is not ours to give. All else is symbolic and therefore less than perfect."

McCade stood, stuck the cigar in a pocket, and walked out of the cave with his mind made up.

As he came into sight the murmur of conversation gradually died away until perfect silence filled the room.

Stepping onto the Rock of Truth, McCade looked out at twenty thousand Il Ronnian faces, then down at the three who more than all the rest waited for him to speak.

Deex wore an expression of rock-hard determination, while Oeem looked concerned, and Reep tried to keep his features blank.

McCade cleared his throat, but the cigar butt he'd dropped earlier caught his eye and he bent over to pick it up. He slipped it into a pocket of his cool suit and lifted his eyes to the audience.

Two vid cams moved in for a closer look. "I've reached a verdict that I now submit for your consideration."

Forty thousand red eyes stared back at him in stony silence.

"It is my judgment that both sides of the case have considerable merit. Commander Deex is correct. Discipline is absolutely essential to any military organization, and as Commander Reep admits, he refused a direct order from his commanding officer. In light of that fact a prison sentence and loss of rank seem quite appropriate."

McCade saw Deex smile and Reep sag momentarily before forcing himself back to attention.

"On the other hand, we must also look at the effect of Commander Reep's actions. Through his valor a loss became a victory, innocent lives were saved, and the pirates were vanquished. Under normal circumstances his name would be submitted for a Medal of Eternal Valor."

Now Reep brightened and Oeem looked hopeful.

"So as punishment for his crimes I sentence Sixteenth Commander Reep to five annual cycles in prison, suspended, and reduction in rank to noncommissioned officer status. And in recognition of his bravery, I award Commander Reep a Medal of Eternal Valor and congratulate him on behalf of the Il Ronnian people."

As McCade's words echoed away the silence grew long and thin. And then, just when McCade's heart had begun to sink, a tiny hissing was heard. It grew louder and louder until finally it filled the canyon with its force.

As Deex glowered, Oeem hissed, and Reep grinned, twenty thousand tails lashed their approval. Justice had been served.

TWELVE

The transcar was still moving when the Sand Sept troopers jumped out and checked the platform. After a quick look around they gave the all-clear and McCade stepped out with Teeb at his side.

A long red cape swirled around McCade as he moved, causing bystanders to turn and stare transfixed by the sight of a human Ilwik.

McCade's relationship with Teeb had entered a new phase. The Il Ronnian was genuinely pleased with McCade's success and considered himself to be the human's mentor. In fact, Neem had disappeared, apparently relegated to lesser duties somewhere else.

So Teeb and McCade followed along behind as the Sand Sept troopers cleared a way through the crowd.

"So, Sam, one ordeal ends and another begins."

"True," McCade agreed. "I wish the second ordeal had a better chance of success. Finding the Vial of Tears will be like searching for a grain of sand in the middle of a desert."

Teeb waved the saying away with the tip of his tail. "Do not be so quick to doubt, egg brother. I once said you would never pass the tests, but now you wear the red, and the people honor you as one of their own. Where one miracle comes another can follow."

"I hope so," McCade replied doubtfully. "I sure hope so."

And there was reason for concern. McCade had one standard month in which to find the holy relic, and if he didn't, the conservatives would reach consensus and declare war on the human empire. He hoped the human empire was using the time to get ready.

A sharp right carried them into a heavily used corridor. It was full to overflowing with Star Sept troopers, administrative personnel, and spidery maintenance bots. All but the most senior officers hurried to get out of the way, and even they bowed their respect, entranced by the sight of an alien Ilwik.

A host of familiar odors filled McCade's nostrils as they neared the underground hangar. There was the smell of hot metal, the stench of high octane fuel, and the ever-present stink of ozone.

A set of heavy blastproof doors cycled open at their approach and revealed a waiting aircar. It was oval in shape with rows of bench seats. As they took their seats Sand Sept troopers jumped on the running boards and the car began to lift. Seconds later it was scooting full speed toward the far end of the hangar.

The hangar was huge. A deep rumbling came from up above as massive doors slid back to reveal a violet sky. A black wedge slid into sight, its navigation lights strobing on and off as it dropped toward the hangar below. Its shadow quickly shrunk until the rumble of the hangar doors was lost in the scream of the ship's repellors. Dust flared as it touched down and robo tenders rolled out to refuel it.

Farther down five interceptors took off on a training exercise. They seemed to float upward, riding their repellors until clear of the hangar and free to engage their main drives. Then they were gone, mere specks at the far end of long white contrails, arrows headed for the blackness of space.

Meanwhile the aircar passed rank after rank of ships. Some were military, some were civilian, all were in various stages of maintenance or repair. Technicians and robots swarmed around them like acolytes around a series of altars.

And everywhere smaller craft swooped, darted, and dived as they went about their various chores. It made such a spectacle that McCade was taken by surprise when the aircar came in for a landing next to a smallish ship.

Not just any ship, but his ship! McCade ran a critical eye over her hull as he got out of the aircar. *Pegasus* looked just the way he'd left her; in fact, she looked even better. Light reflected off the new coat of heat reflectant paint that covered the hull and a number of small dents had disappeared.

"We took the liberty of doing some maintenance on your ship," Teeb said. "There is no cause for alarm. While we are not really set up for maintenance on human ships, we do capture them from time to time, and our technicians have become quite adept at working on them."

"Well, it certainly *looks* good," McCade said cautiously. "Send the bill to Prince Alexander."

"I would not think of it," Teeb answered with a straight face. "As an Ilwik you have a generous expense account plus a salary of one hundred thousand rang a year."

"Really?" McCade asked, brightening at the thought of additional income. "Well, here's hoping I live long enough to spend it."

Teeb stuck his hand out human style and McCade took it. The Il Ronnian's grip was strong and leathery. "Good luck, Sam."

"Same to you, egg brother," and to McCade's surprise, he found he meant it.

McCade had climbed the rollaway stairs, and was just about to enter the ship's lock when Teeb called after him. "Sam!"

"Yeah?"

"I left some presents for you. I hope you'll find them useful."

McCade waved. "I'm sure I will. Tell Neem I said goodbye." And with that he entered the lock.

It felt good to be inside his own ship again. For one thing it meant he could shed the cool suit and enjoy some honest to goodness air-conditioning.

Stripping to the skin, McCade stepped into the fresher, took a shower, and blew himself dry. Much refreshed, he made for the control room clad in nothing more than a good cigar.

He was humming to himself and emitting small puffs of smoke when he stepped into the control room and came to a sudden stop.

Neem and Reba looked up from their pre-flight check lists and smiled. Reba was the first to speak. "Welcome aboard, Captain. Is that the uniform of the day?"

As *Pegasus* headed for the human empire McCade relaxed in the ship's small lounge and thought about Teeb's "presents." Reba and Neem. Beauty and the beast.

On many rim worlds Neem would be shot on sight. People don't like Il Ronnians out along the rim, especially on planets like Arno that had been settled by a fundamentalist religious sect. They would see Neem as the devil incarnate and would either shoot him or run screaming for their temples. Either way it was a problem, so Neem would have to stay aboard the ship.

Of course, Neem *could* command the cooperation of any Il Ronnian warships that happened along, and *if* they actually found the vial, he could take it home, a trip McCade could do without.

Even so, McCade wondered if Teeb secretly hoped Neem wouldn't come back at all, and was using the situation to unload a nutcase.

Reba on the other hand was a definite asset. Or so it seemed anyway. She was a qualified pilot, a fairly good medic, and fun to look at besides. All skills that could come in handy.

She also swore that her pirate days were over, that she owed McCade a debt of gratitude, and that nothing would give her greater pleasure than to help recover the Vial of Tears. Well, time would tell.

McCade really didn't care as long as she stuck around long enough to give him what he needed most, access to the planet called "The Rock."

McCade requested a Terran whiskey from the autobar and lit a cigar.

Neem entered the lounge, nodded politely, and plopped down in front of the holo player. He put on a set of earphones and stared intently into the holo tank. Another whodunit most likely. The Il Ronnian loved them.

McCade forced his thoughts back to the problem at hand: "The Rock." Once, back during Confederation times, the planet had teemed with life. Thick jungle had wrapped the planet in green, mountains had soared to the sky, and rivers had cut their way down to seas rich with life.

But that was gone now, erased by the hell bombs used to sanitize the planet's surface.

Even then the Il Ronnian empire was expanding, and forts were needed to stop the inexorable advance, forts powerful enough to stand off an invading fleet. So a planet was chosen and prepared. And by the time the engineers finished there was nothing left. Not a tree, not a mountain, not a single body of water. All of it gone right down to the bedrock.

A fortress was constructed. It covered more than a hundred square miles and drew its power from the planet's core. Powerful weapons were placed around the circumference of the planet and aimed toward space. More weapons were placed on orbiting weapons platforms and these too were aimed outward.

Years passed and an Il Ronnian attack never came. The Confederacy destroyed itself instead and gave rise to the Empire. But some continued to resist the Emperor and in so doing gave the fortress a new purpose.

Thousands of prisoners vanished into the sprawling complex and rechristened the planet "the Rock" after a famous prison on old Earth. And like its namesake the Rock offered no chance of escape. No one could survive on the planet's sterile surface, and even if they did, there was no way off.

Sure, they could take over the complex itself, but why bother? The weapons on the orbiting platforms, like those on the planet's four moons, were now turned inward and manned by marines. Nothing could move without their approval.

As things turned out that was a serious mistake.

The attack seemed like a joke at first. A pathetic attempt by the remains of a rebel fleet to rescue their comrades, strike one last blow for a defeated cause, and go out with a bang.

Though defeated by Admiral Keaton at the Battle of Hell, what was left of the rebel fleet had split up and come back together at prearranged times and places. They knew the war was over, but sympathy for their imprisoned comrades drove them to one last desperate act: an attack on the Rock.

Knowing the planet was heavily defended, the rebels expected to lose, to die fighting, but much to their own surprise they won.

The Imperial Marines fought bravely, but their weapons were aimed in the wrong direction, and they were badly outnumbered. Thousands died.

So the planet's defenses were turned outward once again, and the rebels went about making their prison a home, and in the process transformed themselves as well.

They knew they couldn't rest. The existing supplies of food wouldn't last forever, and given the planet's barren surface, there was no possibility of growing more. Even the thin atmosphere required artificial maintenance.

So the rebels used fighting skills honed during years of war to raid other planets for supplies. They saw themselves as liberators, taking what they needed to continue a glorious cause.

But their victims saw them as pirates, taking what they weren't willing to make themselves, spreading pain and misery wherever they went.

Time passed and once-bright ideals became increasingly tarnished. Loot became the purpose of their existence, and not as a means of mere survival, but as a means of wealth and privilege.

Disliking the term "pirates," they called themselves "the Brotherhood," and styled themselves as an occupational democracy.

But McCade had been to the Rock and seen the way the pirates lived, and there wasn't anything democratic about it. A council made up of a few powerful individuals ran everything and vied with each other for ever larger slices of a rather fat pie.

And they didn't take kindly to unauthorized visitors. McCade knew that from personal experience. On his last visit to the Rock he'd managed to rip them off, blow up half a spaceport, and destroy a number of their ships. As a result he wouldn't be able to sneak in the same way he had before, and once there, he would be in even greater danger.

"A penny for your thoughts."

McCade looked up into Reba's brown eyes. Damn, the woman was pretty. If it weren't for Sara . . . He shoved the thought down and back.

"Only a penny? Surely you're worth more than that. I was thinking of you."

Reba smiled as she dropped into the seat next to Neem. He didn't even look up from the holo tank.

"I'd be complimented if I hadn't seen the holopix of Sara all over the ship. But I have, so I'm worried instead. What's on your mind?"

"I was thinking that you're the key to getting on the Rock. And unless I miss my guess, that's where we need to go."

Reba frowned. "Why?"

McCade examined the ash on his cigar before tapping it into an ashtray. "The vial was taken during a raid, right? And while the pirates who took it didn't realize its true value, I understand the vial is quite pretty, and therefore valuable in its own right. And since all loot goes to the Rock for auction, that's where it went."

"That's true," Reba agreed. "But things sold at auction usually go off-planet with whoever buys them. By now the vial could be anywhere."

McCade nodded his agreement. "Exactly. But once we find out *who* bought the vial, we can track them down. Make sense?"

Reba's eyes dipped toward the deck and back up again. She had reservations but wasn't willing to share them.

"It makes sense," she agreed reluctantly. "But how will I get you onto the Rock? And more importantly, how will you get off? I was on patrol when you trashed port twelve. But I heard about it, and I know the executive council would love to get their hands on you. They might allow you to get dirtside, but they'll never let you go."

McCade blew smoke toward the overhead and smiled. "Then we won't tell 'em I'm there."

FOURTEEN

Spin was a desolate place, so unremarkable that its name stemmed from its one redeeming virtue, earth normal gravity. Gravity that served to hold a small collection of dilapidated domes in place in spite of the fact that it wasn't worthwhile.

The planet had little to recommend it. The vast majority of its surface was dedicated to rocky wasteland, and if Spin hadn't marked the nexus of two minor trade routes, it would've stayed uninhabited.

McCade had been there once before. A fugitive called Crazy Mary had led him there after a long and weary chase. He'd ordered her to surrender, but she'd just laughed and gone for her blaster as she had so many times before.

But this time it was her turn to fall, it was her body they dumped outside for the scavengers to pick clean, and it was someone else who walked away.

McCade felt his cheek twitch as Reba lowered *Pegasus* onto the scarred surface of Spin's single spaceport.

Three other ships had landed there before them. There was a beat-up Confederation-era freighter, a sturdy-looking tug, and a sleek little DE that had "pirate" written all over it.

Good, McCade thought to himself. The first part of the plan had fallen into place. With a little luck the rest would follow. He eyed the DE's scarred flanks.

Destroyer Escorts were just right for small one-ship raids. They were fast, heavily armed, and large enough to carry some loot. Small stuff like isotopes and rare gems.

The com screen swirled to life as Reba cut power to the ship's repellors. On it was a man who just barely qualified for the name.

Hair crawled over his bullet-shaped head, sprouted from his ears, and covered his face. His eyes blinked constantly as he spoke.

"It's gonna cost you a thousand credits to park that play pretty on my pad."

Reba scowled. "A thousand credits my ass. A hundred, and not a penny more."

The man grinned evily. "Your ass ain't worth a thousand credits. Not even here. Nine hundred."

Reba made a rude gesture. "Two hundred."

The man displayed yellow teeth as he laughed. "Seven hundred."

"Three hundred."

"Six hundred."

"Four hundred."

"All right, all right. Five hundred credits. But don't expect any free drinks."

The screen went suddenly black.

"You humans crack me up," Neem said from the hatch. As usual he wore a red heat cape wrapped around his skinny torso. "All that bargaining for a simple landing fee. Whatever for?"

"Entertainment mostly," McCade replied as he released his harness. "The less formal entertainment there is, the more bargaining we do. Now, does everyone understand the plan?"

Reba nodded and Neem's tail twitched in agreement.

"Good, let's get ready."

An hour later Neem stood by the lock to see them off. "Good luck, Sam, I hope everything goes smoothly."

"Same to you, Neem. And remember, keep a close eye on the sensors. If someone tries to board, dust 'em off."

"Dust 'em off," Neem said experimentally. "I like that. Another alternative to waste 'em, grease 'em, and ice 'em. You humans certainly have a grisly language."

"You've been watching too many holo dramas," McCade said patiently. "Just do it, okay?"

"Okay," Neem replied happily. "If anyone tries to board, I'll dust 'em off."

"Good. I'll see you in a week or so."

Pulling the rebreather down over his head, McCade checked the neck seals and looked at Reba. Hers was already in place and she gave him a thumbs-up.

McCade palmed the lock control and waited while the inner hatch cycled open. When Reba stepped through he followed.

Both waved at Neem until the hatch had cycled closed. There was a wait while Spin's noxious atmosphere was pumped in, and a slight pop as the hatch cycled open and pressures were equalized.

Needless to say there were no robo stairs to meet them, so Reba was forced to deploy a ladder and wait while McCade clanked his way down it. The leg shackles were noisy and slowed him down.

As Alice's one and only peace officer, McCade had other more modern restraints aboard the ship. But the leg shackles were the most dramatic by far and therefore appropriate to the situation.

As Reba made her way down the ladder McCade took a look around. The DE looked larger now, looming above him like some sort of metal monster, partially hidden by wisps of poisonous fog. Was that gun turret pointed his way on purpose? Or had it been positioned like that all along?

His thoughts were interrupted as Reba gave him a shove and growled, "Get a move on, stupid. This ain't no sightseeing trip."

McCade tied to catch himself, but his leg shackles tripped him and he fell.

Reba jerked him to his feet with a growl of frustration and gave him another shove.

Head hung low, shackles clanking, McCade shuffled toward the nearest dome. Someone could be watching or monitoring their radio traffic, so Reba was right to establish their relationship.

But did she have to shove so hard? Should he put this much trust in her? What if she betrayed him the moment they got inside?

Then Neem would come to his rescue. He'd try anyway. While Reba was asleep the two of them had cooked up a plan. Neem would lift *Pegasus* on her repellors, cripple the DE, and cut a hole through the skin of the main dome.

Assuming Neem managed to carry out the first part of the plan, McCade would don his rebreather, release his leg shackles using the electronic key taped to the inside of his left forearm, and escape via the newly created exit.

The plan was complicated and vulnerable to a sorts of unforeseen problems, so McCade hoped they wouldn't be forced to use it.

Reba gave him another shove and he stumbled forward.

Piles of debris were heaped left and right. It was SOP to throw garbage outside the lock until it threatened to engulf the dome itself. At that point someone would climb aboard an ancient crawler and shove the garbage into a nearby ravine.

Reba palmed the lock. The hatch made a grinding sound as it cycled open. It too was overused and undermaintained.

Long before it was fully open the hatch began to iris closed. They hurried to get inside and just barely made it. Seconds later a noisy pump went to work evacuating Spin's noxious atmosphere.

A slush of water and mud covered the bottom of the lock. Plastic sacks full of garbage lined both sides of the chamber and the walls were covered with a variety of graffiti. None was especially original.

The place was still the same. Fortunately he wasn't. In the unlikely event that someone remembered him, McCade figured that his five-day growth of beard, filthy rags, and beaten demeanor should be a sufficient disguise.

A tired buzzer announced a breathable atmosphere and the green indicator light in McCade's rebreather confirmed it. As he shuffled toward the inner hatch McCade pulled the rebreather down off his face and let it hang by its straps.

Continually urged on by a series of shoves and insults, McCade followed a muddy path down a poorly lit corridor and into a circular room.

The air was thick with blue smoke. It hung in layers of blue-gray with the heaviest smoke on the bottom and the lightest on top.

A few things *had* changed since he and Bloody Mary had faced each other in the center of the room. The bar was kitty corner from where it had been, a new holo tank took up a large part of one wall, and the layer of grease that covered everything was even thicker.

Conversation stopped and every head turned as they entered. Not too surprising since they were the most exciting thing to happen all day.

McCade was careful to maintain his submissive posture as Reba pushed him toward the center of the room and swaggered along behind. Watching from the corners of his eyes he saw the bar was about half full. It wasn't difficult to sort them into groups.

The pirates sat by themselves toward one corner. There were eight of them, nine if you counted the woman passed out on the floor. Their table was loaded with empties. They seemed dazed as if the two strangers were apparitions only half seen and partially understood.

Unless they were short on personnel McCade figured there were two or three additional crew members still aboard the DE.

The male pirates watched Reba with a certain amount of interest, but no one jumped to their feet and called her name, so none of them knew her. Good. They had a story prepared just in case, but McCade didn't want to use it.

The freighter's crew sat on the far side of the room. They were as far away from the pirates as they could get and still be in the same bar. McCade didn't blame them. It's a wise sheep who stays as far away from the wolves as possible.

There were four of them. The captain was a solid-looking black woman in her forties. To her right sat a youngish-looking woman with the flashes of a power engineer on her nonreg cap. Next to her sat a brutish-looking Cellite and a beat-up android. The latter was sucking an electronic cocktail via a wall outlet. Like the pirates they'd left one or two people aboard their ship.

There was a scattering of other people in the room as well, an older man and a boy who might have been a match with the tug, plus the usual assortment of drifters.

One of these was a man of indeterminate age with flat dead eyes, expensive clothes, and a blaster with custom grips. Just as the pirates looked like what *they* were, the gambler looked like what *he* was. His eyes drifted across McCade and came to rest on Reba. A smile touched his lips.

"Greetings. At the risk of sounding trite, what brings someone like you to a place like this?"

Reba smiled. "Gravity, the need for a number four power board, and a powerful thirst."

The gambler nodded understandingly. "Would you care to join me? I don't bite."

Reba looked around as if considering her other options.

It's perfect, McCade said to himself, don't overact.

McCade heaved an internal sigh of relief as she grabbed a chair and shoved him toward another. "Sure, as long as you don't mind gark breath here. He gets into trouble if I leave him aboard ship alone. Isn't that right, gark breath?"

Reba kicked McCade just as he tried to sit down. He fell and the pirates laughed.

McCade swore under his breath as he picked himself up and claimed a chair.

"What was that, gark breath?"

"Nothing," McCade mumbled.

"Good," Reba said, turning toward the gambler. "Now where were we?"

"Just getting acquainted," the gambler replied smoothly. "Can I buy you a drink?"

"Does a Zerk monkey like fava fruit? You bet your ass you can."

The gambler summoned one of the saloon's two staff members, a slovenly woman who doubled as Spin's only prostitute, and ordered drinks. After accepting two glasses of black brew, the gambler paid and offered Reba a toast.

"To quick money and just enough time to spend it."

"Amen."

Both upended their glasses. Reba choked, coughed, and came up grinning. "I don't know what that was, but I'll bet you could run my ship on it."

"They call it a Tail Spin," the gambler answered as a deck of cards appeared in his hands.

Reba eyed the cards and licked her lips. A nice touch, McCade thought admiringly. Not only was Reba keeping her word, she was doing it with a certain amount of class.

The gambler saw her hungry look and smiled. The cards jumped from one hand to the other and back again. "Do you play?"

"Sometimes," Reba answered with just the right amount of hesitation. "Not very well though. Would you be interested in a friendly game of Flash?"

The cards made a graceful arc as they rippled through the air to patter down in front of her. The gambler smiled. "Deal."

Reba was good. Maybe *too* good since she was winning instead of losing.

It was the gambler's deal. He'd just lost a long series of small pots, and although he kept his face professionally blank, McCade could see the sheen of perspiration that glossed his forehead. The gambler had upped the ante in hopes of recouping his losses. But would it work? If not, he'd lose his entire stake. A stake he'd need to buy his way off Spin. It was just a theory, but a theory that fit the situation like a glove, and would explain the gambler's anxiety. An extended stay on Spin would be less than pleasant.

The cards made a gentle slapping sound as they hit the surface of the table. Before long there were ten cards facedown in front of each player. Reba looked up. "Dealer flashes first."

The gambler inclined his head slightly. Long white fingers lifted the cards one at a time and showed or "flashed" them at Reba. She had approximately one second to see and memorize each card before the gambler flipped it over and tucked it into his hand.

Then it was Reba's turn. She held each card up for a full three or four seconds before hiding it away. But the gambler was *still* losing in spite of that advantage. Maybe Reba had a better memory than he did, or maybe she just outclassed him, but whatever the reason things were *not* going according to plan.

McCade shifted his weight from one side to the other. He wanted to yell, "Lose damn it, lose!" but bit his lip instead.

Now both players were taking turns replacing up to five of their ten cards in an effort to build a full system. A full system included twin stars, six planets, a comet, and one moon. But a full system was pretty rare, so lesser hands usually won.

So when Reba said, "Read 'em and weep, a full system takes the pot," McCade groaned in disgust.

The gambler managed to smile as Reba raked in the pot, but McCade could see the perspiration running down his neck. Chances were the gambler was close to tapped out. If so, he'd pull out pretty soon.

And the gambler was just about to say something when the pirate saved the day.

The pirate was young, no more than twenty-five, and walked across the room with a drunken swagger. He wore a slug gun low on his right hip, like someone who fancies himself a quick-draw artist and worries about what other people think.

From McCade's point of view the pirate was a godsend, just what he'd hoped for in the first place and failed to get.

"Any chance of dealing myself in?"

The gambler spoke quickly. "It's all right with me if the lady has no objection." Maybe another player would change his luck and reduce the magnitude of his losses.

Reba made a show of thinking the proposition over as she tossed off her latest Tail Spin.

Finally, when McCade thought she'd pushed it too far and the pirate would leave in disgust, she gestured toward an empty chair. "Sure, why not. Let's see the color of your money."

The pirate fumbled around in a pocket for a moment before dragging out a wad big enough to choke an Envo Beast. He slapped it down on the table, called for a drink, and shuffled the cards.

Reba's luck took a turn for the worse a few minutes later. The pirate won, and continued to win, until the gambler's eyes narrowed in suspicion. Was she throwing the game? But that wouldn't make any sense. Why cheat to lose? Besides, he was winning, and so long as that continued he'd keep his mouth shut.

An hour passed, and as it did Reba became increasingly careless, forgetting which cards her opponents had and making a series of stupid mistakes.

The others put it down to her heavy drinking, and McCade would have too, except he'd seen her surreptitiously pour them into the semiliquid slush that covered the floor.

Finally it was over and Reba's money was nearly gone. A large pot occupied the center of the greasy table and Reba burped as she threw down her remaining credits. "Well, thaz it, gentlemen. Outside of gark breath over there, and juz enough to cover a number four power board, I'm broke."

The pirate looked down at his hand and up to Reba. His bloodshot eyes gleamed with anticipation. "Fine. Throw in gark breath and I'll show you what I've got."

A frown creased Reba's forehead as though she was trying to understand the pirate's proposal and, finding that hard to do, was pretending to think it over.

The gambler had decided something was fishy. He didn't know what and didn't care. He was slightly ahead and wanted to stay that way. He spread the fingers on both hands. "It's getting too rich for me. I fold."

Reba tried to focus bleary eyes on his face. She nodded heavily. "Zur, just when things get interestin' you bail out. Well, not me. I hereby add gark breath to the pot. Read 'em and weep."

Though not overly thrilled about the name "gark breath," McCade was happy that things were finally moving in the right direction. He watched Reba and the pirate spread their cards out on the table.

There was a long silence.

Reba was the first to frown, followed by the pirate, followed by McCade himself. He couldn't see the cards from where he sat, but something was wrong.

While Reba *should* be frowning, the pirate *should* be jubilant, and he wasn't. Suddenly McCade understood. Reba had won! The miserable so and so had won the pot! All that work, all that hobbling around in shackles, all of it a waste of time!

And that's when Reba did the only thing she could. She swayed in her chair, held a dramatic hand up to her forehead, and fell over backward. Her chair hit the floor with a tremendous crash.

Conversation stopped, heads turned, but things were back to normal a few seconds later. No big deal, just another drunk hitting the floor. A somewhat routine occurrence in that or any other rim world bar.

The gambler looked at the pirate. The pirate looked at the gambler. They grinned. "Fifty-fifty?" the gambler asked.

"Done," the pirate agreed. And the two men wasted little time splitting the pot. With that accomplished they turned to McCade.

"You have a ship and I don't," the gambler said thoughtfully. "Give me a hundred credits and gark breath is yours."

McCade knew that fifty percent of a prime slave was worth more than a hundred credits and so did the pirate. "Agreed. One hundred credits it is."

The pirate counted out a hundred credits, stepped over Reba's prostrate body, and jerked McCade to his feet. McCade cringed, thanked the pirate for hitting him, and shuffled toward the lock.

Meanwhile the rest of the pirates were headed for the lock as well. Two were busy trying to out belch each other, while the rest bumped into furniture and cracked crude jokes.

McCade felt his new owner give him a push, and heard him say, "Hurry up, gark breath, we're headed home."

McCade did his best to snivel. "And where would that be, master?"

"Why the Rock, gark breath, the Rock. Where else would members of the Brotherhood go?"

SIXTEEN

McCade spent the first part of the trip locked up in a small storage compartment with a broken-down maintenance bot. McCade ignored the robot at first, but eventually the loneliness wore him down, and he tried to make conversation.

"Hi there. What's a nice robot like you doing in a place like this?"

There was a whir of servos as the robot turned its bulbous head. "I have a defective logic board. I am awaiting repair."

McCade nodded sympathetically. "That's a tough break. Say, you're a maintenance bot, aren't you?"

"That is correct."

"Well, if you're a maintenance bot, and you need maintenance, why not fix yourself?"

Time passed during which the robot made no reply. Finally, just as McCade was about to drift off to sleep, the robot spoke.

"I apologize for my delayed response. At first I couldn't understand why you would ask me such a question. Then I realized that you were stored in here for the same reason I was. When did your logic board burn out?"

McCade smiled in spite of himself. "I think it was the moment when I allowed Swanson-Pierce to rescue me from Molaria."

"Oh," the robot replied, and lapsed into silence.

Time passed and eventually, after much boot-licking, McCade was allowed to perform menial chores under the watchful eye of his owner.

His owner was an up-and-coming young pirate who went by the name of Ace, but was actually named Harold, and who lived in fear that his friends might discover his terrible secret.

But it wasn't Ace's friends who discovered the secret, it was McCade. There he was, cleaning up the pirate's filthy cabin, when he came across a stash of letters. They all started out with "Dear Harold," and were signed, "Love, Mommy."

Thus armed McCade blackmailed his owner into some extra food and the occasional cigar. When you're a slave the small comforts mean a lot.

Meanwhile, Ace took very little interest in McCade's past, accepting his lies with bored indifference, eager to sell him and drink up the profits.

This attitude suited McCade to a T, so he made himself the model slave, always cooperative and eager to please.

This strategy worked so well that after a while the crew began to take him for granted and allowed him a certain amount of freedom.

As a result he was in the control room as the ship approached the first weapons platform. The weapons platforms were located approximately one light out from the Rock and constituted its first line of defense. They were heavily armed, completely automated, and capable of identifying friendly ships via a code printed into each vessel's atomic structure. If you had the code, you could pass; if not, boom!

McCade knew that much from past experience. What he didn't know, and wanted to find out, was whether the pirates had added anything new since then.

So McCade was swabbing the deck when the DE came into range of the nearest weapons platform. Never mind the fact that robots normally swabbed the deck. The pirates never asked any questions as long as he did something menial.

"Platform alpha sixteen coming up, Skipper." The pilot sounded bored. And why not? The DE had the proper codes and he knew it.

"That's a roger," the skipper replied, looking up from a skin mag. "Hey, gark breath, how 'bout a cup of coffee?"

"Right away, sir," McCade sniveled, and shuffled his way toward the small alcove at the rear of the bridge.

The pilot ran his hand through a shaggy head of brown hair, picked his cavernous nose, and tapped out a short rhythm on his keyboard.

Peeking out from the small pantry, McCade saw the words "Brotherhood vessel 6456 Delta cleared for planetfall" appear on the pilot's com screen and vanish again as the pilot cleared his board.

"We're cleared for planetfall, Skipper."

"That's real good, Murph. Hey, gark breath! Where the hell's my coffee?"

McCade had an idiotic grin on his face as he shuffled his way over and spilled scalding hot coffee on the captain's leg.

"You idiot!" The skipper jumped to his feet, hit the coffee pot with his arm, and sloshed more hot liquid onto his right foot.

There was quite a commotion for a while as the captain swore and hopped around the control room on his one good foot with McCade in sniveling pursuit.

Finally the officer stopped in one place long enough for McCade to dab ineffectually at his leg and analyze what he'd seen.

The system hadn't changed, and later on that would play an important part in his escape, assuming there *was* an escape. First of course he'd have to get on the Rock, avoid detection, and find the vial. Just take it one step at a time, he told himself, that way you won't realize how completely stupid the whole thing really is.

The skipper was still glowering a few hours later when the pilot put the ship down on the planet's light side on the inner ring of Port Seven.

Being devoted to both military and commercial enterprises the Rock had some sixty spaceports, number seven being entirely dedicated to the repair and maintenance of raiders.

McCade had never seen someone clean out their ears and land a spaceship at the same time before, but the pilot not only pulled it off, he did it rather neatly as well. The landing jacks made only the slightest bump as they touched down.

A small army of robo tenders scuttled out to refuel and perform maintenance on the ship as the whine of the ship's repellors died away.

Eager to see their families, or to tie one on, the crew wasted no time gathering their personal belongings together and heading for the main hatch. And, as one of Ace's belongings, McCade found himself wearing shackles and struggling to keep up with his owner.

As he clanked his way down the robo stairs to the durocrete pad below, McCade took a look around. This was a military spaceport, but with the exception of the ships themselves, it looked a lot like the commercial version he'd seen during his previous visit. Long orderly rows of ships, and beyond them the endless vista of black rock that stretched to the far horizon.

And interspersed among the ships were the black towers. Each one was a hundred feet high and topped off with a bulbous turret that bristled with weapons and sensors. Up there, behind armored glass, members of the Brotherhood's planetary police stood watch, and the knowledge sent a chill down McCade's spine.

Wouldn't they just love to catch him! On his last visit he'd almost leveled a spaceport, destroyed dozens of ships, and caused the destruction of an orbital weapons platform. Now he was back, and if the police found out, slavery would look good by comparison.

His heart leaped into his throat. There were four members of the planetary police waiting at the edge of the pad! Their black uniforms and military appearance were supposed to strike fear into the hearts of miscreants everywhere and it worked. The muscle in McCade's cheek started to twitch and his emotions clamored for attention.

"Run for it!" they screamed. "Kill! Run! Hide! Do something!"

"Now wait a minute," his mind replied. "This doesn't make sense. They couldn't know about me. They're here for some other reason."

"Oh, yeah?" his emotions asked. "And what the hell do you know? We'd have been dead years ago if we listened to you. Hide! Run! Kill!"

McCade was looking for a place to hide when the line jerked to a halt and the pilot dumped his flight bag in front of the police. It was mostly dirty laundry and as the police pawed through it they made a number of crude jokes about his purple underwear. Of course! A customs check!

"See," McCade told his emotions, "there was nothing to worry about."

"Maybe," they grudgingly admitted, "but let's delay the celebration until *after* the customs check."

Having finished with his flight bag, the police were running sensors over the pilot's body. It made sense. Without a search the crew would start to skim loot off the top of their haul and the Brotherhood would lose out.

The pilot was cleared and the line jerked ahead. As Ace stepped up to the table he gestured for McCade to follow.

The police flicked a retinal scanner across Ace's eyes while they pressed his right hand onto an electro pad. Somewhere a computer compared the incoming prints with the ones on file, achieved a match, and signaled its approval.

Three of the police had their visors down, all the more to intimidate you with, but the fourth wore hers tilted up. And surprise, surprise, she had a sense of humor.

"Name?"

"Ace Javers."

The woman consulted her hand-held comp. "Gee, Ace, looks like we've got a mix-up here. The computer thinks you're some guy named Harold."

Ace mumbled something.

The policewoman pretended not to hear. "What was that? Harold? Well, why didn't you say so in the first place? Glad we settled that. Now, who's the guy in chains? Prince Alexander?"

"We call him gark breath," Ace responded, eager to regain some of his lost composure. "I won him playing Flash."

"Witnesses?"

"The skipper was there."

"Good enough. We'll take him from here. Usual deal, ninety percent for you, ten for the Brotherhood."

"Sounds good."

"Okay, give me your seal."

Ace pressed his right hand on the electro pad for a second time and was waved through the checkpoint. He took off without so much as a backward glance at McCade.

The policewoman gestured for McCade to step forward. "Okay, gark breath, let's check you in."

McCade was scanned, printed, and cleared all within a couple of minutes. Even so the seconds dragged by like hours, each one bringing the very real possibility that the central computer would cough up his real identity and finish his mission right there.

But his real identity had never been properly recorded during his previous visit to the Rock, so nothing happened.

The policewoman looked up from her comp and smiled. "Hey, buddy, you're now WM 89546. It ain't much, but it sure beats the hell out of gark breath. Next!"

Two hours and a series of rides later McCade found himself in an all-male holding pen. For someone who'd done time in Molaria's Pit 47, it was all too familiar: the hopeless eyes of his fellow prisoners, the subjugation of the weak by the strong, and the desperate scramble for food. McCade faded into the dog-eat-dog structure of it without conscious thought.

But all things considered, the holding pen was nicer than Pit 47. It was well lit, fairly spacious, and furnished with durasteel furniture. You couldn't move it, you couldn't burn it, but you could sit on it and McCade did.

There were other differences as well. Where Pit 47 had housed the same men for months at a time, there was constant turnover in the holding pen, and that slowed the emergence of a strong pecking order. And that was fine with McCade because beating the hell out of people was not his idea of a good time.

"Aha," said a voice from behind him. "A fellow anomaly I trust?"

McCade turned to find himself face-to-face with a little man with bright inquisitive eyes, a long, thin nose, and ears that stuck out like handles on a cup. Like McCade he was dressed in little more than rags.

"An anomaly?" McCade asked.

"Why yes," the man replied. "You know, a deviation from the norm."

McCade smiled patiently. "Yes, I know the meaning of the word, I just don't understand how it applies."

The little man looked surprised. "You don't? How strange. It's quite obvious to me." The bright little eyes looked McCade up and down. "You're in good shape, you're well fed, and you're wearing nice rags."

"Nice rags?"

"Um-hmm," the little man said. "Nice leathers that were ripped and torn to look like rags. And there's your body language. While most of us are scared, wondering what'll happen next, you're relaxed. So, you're an anomaly. And where there's an anomaly there's a reason."

"And you have a big mouth," McCade said thoughtfully. "Which doesn't qualify you as an anomaly, but could get you in deep trouble."

The little man looked around to make sure that no one else was listening. "Don't worry. Your secret's safe with me." He stuck out his hand. "They call me Chips."

As McCade shook the other man's hand he found it was dry and surprisingly hard. "Chips?"

"Yeah, Chips, like in computers. That's what makes me different than the rest of this herd. I'm smarter than they are."

McCade nodded thoughtfully. "That's just great, Chips, except for one little thing. If you're so smart, how come you're a slave?"

Chips dismissed McCade's comment with a wave of one hand. "This is a temporary inconvenience, nothing more. I work—or should I say 'worked'?—for a large conglomerate. Maybe you've heard of it. Mega Mining and Metals. No? Well, it's *big*, take my word for it, and I am, or *was*, their top programmer.

"I was on my way to restore a major systems failure on some godforsaken asteroid when the company speedster came out of hyperspace right on top of a pirate raider. We tried to run, but they put a tractor beam on us and reeled us in like a dead carp. So, here I am, but," Chips added brightly, "not for long."

Chips looked around and lowered his voice into a conspiratorial whisper. "How would you like to get off this rock?"

McCade had run into his share of deluded prisoners before, Pit 47 had housed some real lulus, but he decided to play along. Although Chips seemed like a flake, he'd seen through McCade's disguise with disconcerting ease and that suggested hidden depths.

"I'd love to get off this rock," McCade replied, "assuming I can pick the time."

Chip's smile revealed some expensive dental work. "Good, because all I need to get us off-planet are these"—he waggled his fingers—"and a willing endomorph." Chips looked McCade up and down like a chef selecting a side of beef.

McCade sighed. From gark breath to endomorph in a single day. Sometimes you just can't win.

SEVENTEEN

As slave markets go it wasn't too bad. It was fairly clean for one thing and they didn't beat you for another. Not much anyway. This didn't stem from latent humanism but from a reluctance to damage the merchandise. And being part of the merchandise, McCade approved.

At the moment he and Chips were standing in a line that led out and onto a small stage. An underground transcar ride had brought them here from the central holding pens.

Like everyone else they were naked, stripped of even their rags, and exposed to the world. McCade was reminded of his journey through the corridors of Molaria, and decided to handle it the same way, forcing himself to stand tall and look people in the eye.

Everything was painted an eye-searing white. White walls, white ceiling, and a white floor.

It seemed strange at first, until McCade realized that the white background made them easier to see. Especially for eyes used to a level of illumination higher than earth normal, and presumably there were some such in the audience.

But no amount of white paint could cover up the feel of the place, the stink of their sweat, or the fear that oozed out through their pores to fill the air. It was a bad place, a place where sentients were bought and sold like hunks of meat, a place from which all compassion had long since fled.

Beyond the stage there was row after row of theater-style seating. The seats were already half fall and the would-be slave buyers were still flooding in. A more variegated lot McCade had never seen.

There were plenty of humans, the usual scattering of Zords, and even a Lakorian or two. Not too surprising since all three races were regular participants in the slave trade.

There were some exotic species scattered throughout the hall as well, but it was hard to tell what they looked like due to their bulky atmosphere suits.

What McCade wanted to see but didn't was Reba. She was supposed to land, buy McCade, then set him free. A workable plan given the fact that she was a pirate in good standing. But the seats were filling up now and Reba was nowhere in sight.

It was as if Chips could read his mind. "So where's your friend?"

McCade frowned. "How the hell would I know? I imagine she'll show up any minute now."

Chips shook his head sadly. His voice was sorrowful, as though McCade had somehow led him astray. "Face it, Sam, she ran out on you. She wasted your friend, took your ship, and sold it. I should never have listened to you. Now it's too late to use my plan."

McCade had provided Chips with a somewhat sanitized version of his current situation. While he'd mentioned two friends, he'd left out the fact that Neem was alien, and Reba a somewhat secretive pirate.

Instead, he'd left the impression that he was trying to recover something the pirates had stolen from him, and that Chips could help. In return McCade had promised to get Chips safely off-planet.

By agreeing to McCade's plan, Chips had given up one of his own. Which was just as well since it called for an endomorph like McCade to incapacitate several guards while Chips accessed the Brotherhood's computer system.

Chips swore that once he obtained access to the Brotherhood's computer system he could fiddle the records and set them free. The only problem was that he hadn't figured out how to get them off-planet afterward.

McCade thought the little man's plan was less than perfect, and would probably generate more than a few unexplained corpses, possibly including his own.

But he did see a certain value in having his own computer expert, assuming of course that he managed to escape from his present situation. What better way to get a lead on the Vial of Tears than to take an unauthorized peek at the Brotherhood's records?

But everything hinged on Reba setting him free so he could set Chips free. Why had she deserted him? Maybe she was scared, or maybe she'd lied to him from the start, but it would be easy for her to kill an unsuspecting Neem and go her merry way. And there wasn't a damn thing McCade could do about it either. Especially if he was busy harvesting yirl deep in the jungles of some godforsaken jungle planet

His thoughts were interrupted by the auctioneer's deep baritone. "If you'll finish taking your seats, the auction will begin in a few moments."

There was a rustling as latecomers found seats, the hum of servos as their chairs adjusted to a variety of physiological differences, and the low murmur of conversation as the buyers gossiped among themselves.

McCade knew that others would follow the action as well, watching the auction on closed-circuit holo and bidding via computer terminal. The thought cheered him. Maybe that was the answer. Maybe Reba would bid by computer.

He remembered what it was like. The vast dome filled with thousands of sentients, the tower that dominated its center, and the countless terminals used to buy and sell stolen merchandise. Merchandise so cheap that victim sometimes chose to buy their goods back from the pirates rather than replace them from other sources.

Yes, Reba could be in that dome somewhere preparing to buy his freedom, but deep down he knew it wasn't true. If she came, she'd come here and do it directly.

McCade scanned the audience one last time, hoping, praying that he'd spot Reba's pretty face among them. No such luck. All he saw were hard faces and calculating eyes.

"Greetings on behalf of the Brotherhood," the auctioneer said portentously.

He was a tall, slender man with slicked-back hair and a pencil-thin mustache. He enjoyed being the center of attention and performed his duties with a theatrical flourish.

"We have some prime humanoids for you today," he said cheerfully, "and I'm sure you'll find something to meet your particular needs. And now time's money so let's get started."

A couple of bored-looking police types shoved a man forward. He was middle-aged, somewhat overweight, and on the verge of tears.

"An excellent specimen," the auctioneer said approvingly. "A little exercise will turn WM 7896-A into a prime field hand."

The auctioneer glanced at a handheld comp. "Skills include operation of simple machinery, some ability at advanced math, and—you'll love this—he plays the violin! Is anyone out there assembling a symphony orchestra? If so, this is the one for you!"

There was general laughter from the humans in the audience and a variety of other noises from the aliens as well.

Bidding started rather low and, in spite of the auctioneer's best attempts to drive it upward, ended with a high bid of three hundred and forty-six credits.

The middle-aged man looked even more dejected as he was herded to one side where a female Zord used her single eye to inspect her newest possession.

He was the first of many. Some made a fuss, crying or calling out for help, but most were outwardly calm, hiding their thoughts and feelings behind blank faces. Then as their new owners led them away, the line would jerk forward and the police would shove someone else toward the middle of the stage.

Finally it was McCade's turn and he scanned the audience one last time. Maybe Reba had slipped in unobserved, maybe he'd missed her the first time around, maybe everything was all right. But no such luck. Reba was nowhere to be seen and his time was up.

The police shoved him forward and the auctioneer tapped his shoulder with a silver pointer. "Now here's a decent-looking field hand. He's in good shape as you can see, young enough to survive in a hostile environment, and healthy as a horse. He has no special skills to speak of, but how much skill does it take to lift a shovel?"

The audience laughed appreciatively and the auctioneer gave a small bow. "Do I hear an opening bid?"

A tough-looking man in black leathers made the first bid. "Three hundred."

"Three fifty." The second voice emanated from a creature in a four-armed atmosphere suit. McCade tried to remember a race with four arms but couldn't.

"Four hundred," said the man in leather. He looked annoyed.

"Four hundred and fifty." The voice had a hollow metallic quality as it came over the suit's external speakers.

McCade felt a heavy object drop into the pit of his stomach and hoped the man in leather would win. There was something ominous about the four-armed creature. Its suit was black and kind of bulky through the middle as if it had a midsection similar to a spider's, and worst of all was the fact that you couldn't see its head. Where a human's eyes would be there was a band of polarized plastic that circled all the way around the thing's helmet. Did it have eyes in the back of its head? There was no way to tell.

McCade was not given to xenophobia but the thing made his hair stand on end. Looking around he saw that others felt the same way too. No one wanted to look directly at the thing, as if afraid of what they might see. Even the auctioneer looked over rather than directly at it.

That was bad enough. What was worse was the thing's motives. It didn't breathe oxygen so what would it want with a human slave? A number of possibilities popped into McCade's mind and none of them were very pleasant.

"Five hundred." The man was beginning to sound bored, and based on the bidding that had gone before, McCade knew they were reaching the upper limits of his worth.

"Six hundred," the creature said levelly, "and five hundred apiece for the next three in line."

Chips snapped to attention, viewing the creature with alarm. "What the hell . . ."

"I'll pass," the man in leather said, "they're all yours." He took his seat with an expression of disgust.

McCade looked on with alarm as the auctioneer nodded his understanding and said, "Going once, going twice, gone. Congratulations, my friend, you've got a fine group of humanoids there. Pay the cashier and collect your merchandise. *Bon appétit.*"

There was nervous laughter as the creature lumbered over to the cashier's window, paid for its slaves, and watched the police shackle them to a length of durasteel chain.

Chips was behind McCade with the two newcomers behind him. One was a big black man and the other was white. Both did their best to avoid looking at the four-armed alien.

Once the four humans were secure the alien used one of its four arms to gesture toward the door. "Move."

"Thanks a lot," Chips whispered as they stumbled forward. "I'm not only a slave, I'm a slave to some alien geek. God knows what it will do with us."

"I hope it gets you to shut up," McCade growled.

Obviously offended Chips pursed his lips and pretended McCade wasn't there.

Once they were outside the slave market they followed the alien into a steady stream of traffic. Slaves were a common sight on the Rock and attracted little attention, but four-armed aliens were something else; even the police hurried to get out of the way.

They hadn't gone far when the alien turned in at one of the planet's less reputable hotels. There was a low rumble of conversation between the alien and the hotel keeper followed by the flash of credits changing hands.

Then they were herded into a small room. The alien pointed at McCade. "You. Come with me. The rest of you wait here. Food will come soon."

McCade's stomach growled at the thought. Why couldn't he stay? But a nerve lash had appeared in one of the alien's gloved hands and it left him little choice.

The thing unshackled the others, ushered McCade into the hall, and locked the room behind him. The fact that this was possible suggested that the room had served a similar function before.

"Come." So saying, the alien lumbered down the hall as if sure that McCade would follow.

McCade thought about running, but knew he wouldn't get far wearing shackles, and decided to obey. Maybe later on he'd find a way to overpower the alien and gain the upper hand.

The alien stopped in front of another door. It swung open at its touch. "In there."

McCade entered rather cautiously since he was unsure of what he might find inside. He needn't have bothered. This room was a shabby duplicate of the first one. He heard the door close behind him and turned just in time to see an incredible sight.

The alien was using two arms to unscrew its helmet. What the hell was going on? Was the alien planning to commit suicide right there in front of him?

The helmet squeaked as it turned and McCade backed away waiting for some kind of noxious atmosphere to spill out.

It didn't. Instead the arms lifted the helmet up and away to reveal Neem's smiling countenance. "Don't just stand there, Sam, find some blankets. It's colder than the tip of an asteroid miner's tail in here."

The computer console was first-class just like everything else in their suite. Chips cracked his knuckles experimentally as he sat down in front of it. He wore a big grin as he brought the first screen up and entered the system. To him this was an electronic jungle in which he was the skilled explorer avoiding all manner of dangers and steadily closing in on the hidden treasure.

McCade checked the door to make sure it was locked and sat down across from Neem. The power lounger sighed softly as it adjusted to his body and radiated a gentle warmth. McCade plucked a cigar from a nearby humidor and puffed it into life. When he spoke it was through a cloud of smoke. "How much does this suite cost per rotation anyway?"

Neem, shrugged as he turned up the heat on his power lounger. "As you humans would say, it beats me. Since I don't plan to pay, I never asked."

Nonpayment of bills. One more offense added to our growing list of crimes, McCade thought to himself. Well, why not? What's another crime more or less when you've already broken every law short of murder?

"So," McCade said, waving his cigar to include the entire room. "Perhaps you'd be kind enough to explain how we came to be here?"

The tip of Neem's tail had slipped up and out of his coat collar. It signaled his agreement. "As things turned out, your departure from Spin triggered an unfortunate series of events. As you'll recall, I was supposed to monitor the ship's sensors in case of trouble. So there I was, monitoring my life away as you were taken aboard the pirate ship. 'So far so good,' I said to myself as your vessel lifted, 'Sam is on his way.'

"Reba came out of the dome shortly thereafter and I opened the main lock to let her in." The Il Ronnian shook his head sadly. "It was a mistake to trust her, Sam. You should have left her on Imantha."

"Oh, really?" McCade inquired dryly. "Wasn't it Teeb who sent her along? And you too for that matter?"

"Let's not quibble over details," Neem replied loftily. "The point is that your treacherous female pulled a blaster on me and forced me off the ship."

McCade raised an eyebrow. "You're in surprisingly good shape for a corpse."

"The female did allow me a breathing unit," Neem conceded, "but that was her only kindness. The moment I was clear of the ship she lifted."

McCade felt a moment of grief. He'd grown attached to the little ship and hated to lose her. Still, a ship is a ship, and not very important when compared to the big picture. Or so he told himself. It didn't seem to help much.

"So what then?"

"So there I was," Neem said dramatically, "cast adrift on the uncharted sea of an alien culture, unable to enter what little shelter there was, and vulnerable to whatever predators might happen along."

"Please," McCade responded, "spare me the sob story. You found a way off Spin or you wouldn't be here."

"Yes," Neem agreed shamelessly, "utilizing my tremendous resourcefulness I found a way to escape the terrible predicament you left me in. Do you remember the small tug?"

McCade thought back to their landing on Spin. He remembered the DE, a freighter, and, yes, a small tug. "Yeah?"

"I stole it," Neem said proudly. "I waited in the shadows near the tug's lock for the crew to approach. Time passed, and with each second that ticked by, my precious supply of oxygen became smaller and smaller."

McCade groaned. "Please, spare me the melodrama."

Neem ignored the interruption. "Then, just when my breathing device was almost empty of life-giving oxygen I saw them. Two humans approaching the tug. Even though I was gasping my last breath I waited for the first one to palm the lock before I hit the second one over the head. It took two blows because the first one hit the forward edge of his breathing device and bounced off.

"Having heard the disturbance, the first human turned and came to the second one's assistance. Such was my speed and skill that I was able to disable him as well, dragging both clear of the tug's repellors prior to entering the ship and taking off."

McCade had conflicting emotions. Having your ship stolen out from under you was about the worst thing that could happen short of death itself, and to have it happen on a planet as desolate as Spin, well that made the situation even worse.

On the other hand he couldn't help but admire Neem's resourcefulness, especially since the Il Ronnian was the human equivalent of a college professor. "I'm amazed, Neem . . . it was a nice piece of work."

"Thanks, Sam, I'm kind of proud of it myself. I'm not much of a pilot as you know, but the tug was equipped with automatics, and having had some experience with *Pegasus*, I had little difficulty getting into space."

"And then?"

Neem's tail assumed a posture of doubt. "Then I didn't know *what* to do. I checked the tug's computer and found coordinates for the Rock, but based on what you'd told me, I knew I wouldn't get past the weapons platforms.

"I'm ashamed to say that I was just about to run home with my tail between my legs, a rather strange saying for you humans to have by the way, when I stumbled across the answer.

"As I entered the new course into the tug's computer it asked me if I *really* wanted to enter a new set of coordinates or use the last ones instead. Just out of curiosity I asked what the last ones were. Well, I couldn't believe my eyes when the coordinates flashed on the screen."

"Your next destination was the Rock," McCade guessed.

"Don't be silly," Neem replied tartly. "I was lucky, but not *that* lucky. No, the next destination was the Asod Cluster." Neem paused dramatically. "To tow a disabled ore barge to guess where?"

"The Rock," McCade said, exhaling a long, thin stream of smoke.

Neem's tail drooped. "You guessed."

"Sorry," McCade said unsympathetically. "So you went to the Asod Cluster. Then what?"

"It was fairly simple after that," the Il Ronnian admitted somewhat reluctantly. "Thanks to the ship's automatics I was able to assist two other tugs in pulling the barge out of orbit. We locked all four vessels together via tractor beams and made a synchronized hyperspace jump."

McCade winced at the thought. It was a common practice but it was damned dangerous. One miscalculation, one hyperdrive slightly out of phase with the others, and all four ships would be lost. Blown up? Forever adrift in hyperspace? No one knew for sure, and McCade had no desire to find out.

"So," Neem added matter-of-factly, "once we cleared hyperspace it was simple. The pirates were expecting us so we sailed right past the weapons platforms. Then we placed the barge in orbit, landed for refueling, and went our separate ways.

"By then I was determined to take Reba's place and obtain your freedom. A disguise seemed in order and it was a simple matter to cut up three of the tug's spacesuits and construct a somewhat exotic-looking alien. I thought the extra arms were especially effective, didn't you?"

"A nice touch," McCade agreed dryly as he stubbed out his cigar. "I owe you one, Neem. A big one."

"Yes, slave, you certainly do," Neem replied through a big grin. "And the next time I purchase slaves, remind me to go for quality rather than quantity."

"How *did* you pay for us anyway?" McCade asked. "And why buy four instead of one?"

Neem gave a good imitation of a human shrug. "I had some time to kill during the hyperspace shift from the Asod Cluster to the Rock. I used it to crack the tug's safe. When I got the safe open I found a thick wad of credits inside. It was as simple as that.

"Once on the Rock I donned my disguise, took a taxi to the hotel where my other two slaves are still under lock and key, and waited for the auction.

One rotation later it started, and not wanting to seem too interested in any one human, I bought four. The rest is, as you humans would say, history."

"Paydirt!" The voice belonged to Chips. "They've got one helluva good system, I'll give them that, but not good enough to foil old Chips! I went around their blocks, defeated their traps, and fooled their tracers. In a few moments you'll have a printout of all the loot taken from Il Ronnian space within one standard week of the date you gave me. Complete with description, estimated value, and final disposition. Then all we gotta do is grab the vial and haul ass.

"That's great!" McCade said, jumping to his feet. "Chips, you're a genius."

The small charge went off with a loud cracking sound and the triple locked door flew open. A small army of armored police rushed in and took up positions around the room.

They didn't say anything. They didn't have to. Their drawn weapons said it all. McCade, Chips, and Neem all froze without being told.

Smoke billowed, eddied, and was sucked toward the nearest vent. That's when Reba stepped into the room and smiled. "Hello, Sam. Greetings, Neem. I couldn't help but overhear that last comment via the bug in the ventilator. Chips is many things . . . but a genius isn't one of them."

McCade treated Chips to a withering look.

The little man spread his hands apologetically and said, "Ooops."

NINETEEN

"Sam McCade, I'd like you to meet Sister Urillo. Sister Urillo, this is Sam Mc-Cade."

Sister Urillo was a cyborg, a beautiful cyborg, but a cyborg nonetheless. It hadn't always been so. During a raid on Carson's World a surface-to-air missile had ignored the electronic countermeasures built into her aerospace fighter and hit one of her stubby wings. Her ship crashed a few seconds later.

Her copilot pulled her from the burning wreck, but she had massive injuries, and even with an unusually fast air evac, she just barely survived.

Doctor after doctor said she'd be lucky to live out her life in a nutrient tank, little more than sentient tissue, stored away in some dark corner of a hospital.

But Urillo refused to give up. She said "yes" to the countless operations, she said "yes" to the experimental bionics, and she said "yes" to the pain.

And finally, when all the parts of her body were meshed into a unified whole, she went a step further. She made a decision to love and accept her new body. So while others might have hidden their bionic parts, Sister Urillo flaunted hers, treating them as ornaments and using them to her advantage.

She had rich brown eyes and a beautiful face. It was almost untouched by the crash, the single exception being her left temple and cheek where smooth brown flesh gave way to golden metal. The metal had been sculpted to match the other side of her face. Fanciful patterns had been engraved into the metal, moving and flowing to surround and enhance the single ruby set into her cheek. It glowed with internal fire and flickered with each movement she made.

Her shoulders were of gleaming chrome giving way to golden arms and fingers. Her red dress was cut low to reveal most of her remaining breast and all of its metal twin. The metal breast was perfectly shaped and tipped with a ruby nipple.

Lower down her dress fell into sculptured lines around beautiful legs, one brown and one chrome. They took turns appearing and disappearing through slits designed for that purpose.

And Sister Urillo's appearance didn't end there. Her combination office-living quarters were a carefully designed extension of her body. A high-tech, glass-topped desk served to complement and echo her metal parts while the rest of the furniture was soft and brown like her remaining flesh.

McCade noticed that her voice had a lilting quality and was only slightly distorted by a hidden speech synthesizer. "Greetings, Sam McCade. Although we haven't met, I was present the last time you left the Rock. It was an expensive and rather spectacular sight."

Even though her hand was metal covered by a thin layer of golden plasti-flesh, McCade found it warm to the touch. Some sort of heating element woven into the plastic?

He smiled wryly. "My apologies, Sister Urillo. Had I known that such a beautiful woman was present I would have stopped to introduce myself."

"It's better that you didn't," Urillo replied with a laugh. "I would've been forced to blow your head off."

She turned to Reba. "He's annoying but gallant as well. You didn't tell me that."

Reba looked from Sister Urillo to McCade and shrugged. "Sam is full of surprises. Like his transformation from slave to computer thief for example. It was a mistake to underestimate him."

"I'm glad you admit it," Sister Urillo said as she went behind her desk. "A little humility is a useful thing. Both of you, please, take a seat. McCade . . . you may light one of those god-awful cigars if you wish . . . though Reba may object."

"Go ahead," Reba said as she selected a seat. "My cancer shots are up-to-date."

The invitation bothered him. He wasn't sure why. Maybe it was their complete control of the situation, or maybe they'd taken the fun out of it, but whatever the reason he refused.

"Thank you, ladies," McCade said, dropping into the deep comfort of an over-stuffed armchair, "but I think I'll pass."

"All right then," Sister Urillo said, her eyes suddenly hard. "Let's get down to brass tacks. By now you realize Reba's something more than a damsel in distress. Most of the time, when she isn't allowing herself to get captured during Il Ronnian raids, she's one of my security agents. I sit on the Brotherhood's governing council and have responsibility for planetary security. So when Reba left Spin, she came straight to me."

McCade nodded. Well, it was his own fault. He'd been suspicious, just not suspicious enough. "I suppose Chips works for you as well?"

Urillo nodded approvingly. "Yes, Chips works for us on a part-time basis."

"Then why the charade?" McCade asked. "Why not grab me off the top?"

Reba shrugged. "We wanted to see if you would contact any Imperial agents. There are some but we don't know who they are."

"And," Sister Urillo added wryly, "you did contact an agent. A crazy Il Ronnian who found a way to escape from Spin, bypassed our security systems, and bought you on the open market. We actually lost track of you for a while, and if it hadn't been for Chips, you might have escaped."

Reba nodded soberly. "Another mistake on my part. I should've killed Neem, but I couldn't bring myself to do it.

"That *was* a mistake," Sister Urillo agreed, "but in retrospect it was a good mistake."

"Speaking of which how *is* Neem?" McCade asked. He hadn't seen the Il Ronnian since the police had broken in.

"Your friend is fine," Urillo replied calmly, "which brings us to you." She leaned forward in her chair. Her eyes narrowed and the light sparkled off the ruby in her cheek. "I should kill you and use your body to help rebuild our damaged soil. And if it weren't for this absurd religious relic, that's exactly what I'd do. But Reba tells me the Il Ronn are ready to come after this thing, and if they do, the Rock's the first place they'll stop. And while we might stand 'em off for a while, there wouldn't be much left when they got done, and some stupid vial isn't worth dying over. So this is your lucky day, McCade. Instead of winding up dead, you're going to find the relic and give it back to them."

McCade felt a big emptiness in the pit of his stomach. "Find it? You've already got it. The Vial of Tears was taken during a raid on an Il Ronnian planet and brought here."

Sister Urillo leaned back in her chair and steepled her golden fingers. Light winked off her forearms and danced across the ceiling. "Unfortunately that's not the case. Oh, it was taken during a raid all right, but it wasn't brought here, and we aren't sure where it is."

"You see," Reba added, "the raid was unsanctioned."

"Meaning that while the raid was carried out in our name and using our ships, we didn't authorize it," Urillo added. "That particular raid was led by Mustapha Pong, an ex-colleague of mine and a complete rogue."

"I was looking for leads to Pong's whereabouts when I was captured," Reba explained. "We want him just as much as the Il Ronn do."

"Exactly," Sister Urillo agreed, chrome flashing as she crossed her long legs. "So I want the two of you to stop screwing around and go find him."

Tin Town. Though not a town in the normal sense of the word the name fit. First because Tin Town was made of metal, and second because it qualified as a collection of inhabited dwellings, and that's what a town is.

So what if this particular town was in orbit around a planet, was equipped with hyperdrive, and had once been an ore barge? To the ten thousand five hundred and sixty-five sentients who lived there, Tin Town was home.

As *Pegasus* drew closer McCade dimmed the main viewscreen. Tin Town shimmered with light. Much of it came from the signs that covered its hull. They rippled, flashed, and pulsated, advertising everything from ***HOT SEX*** to Clyde's Cyborg Clinic. "Check in and check us out."

Some of the light came from Tin Town herself. As the hull turned on its axis an endless array of solar collectors flashed in the sun and generated a belt of light. In addition, there were the winking navigation beacons, the glow of welding torches, and the occasional blue-white flare of steering jets when ships jockeyed for position.

McCade had never been to Tin Town before, but like everyone else, he'd heard of it. The habitat had been founded some seventy years before by a group of people who disliked government of any kind. They believed everyone should accept responsibility for every aspect of their lives, and having done so, they owed nothing to others. As a result they were commonly referred to as "Loners."

The group first tried to live out their philosophy on a succession of rim worlds. Things would be fine for a while, but after a while new settlers would come along and conflict would soon follow.

The new settlers would want to establish a fire department, or a police force, or some other public service, and they'd propose a government to organize and provide it.

The Loners would object, suggesting a privately owned enterprise instead. They felt each person should be free to support the service in question or go without.

"But what about the destitute?" the settlers would ask. "Don't we have a moral duty to help them?"

"Not at all," the Loners would reply. "With the exception of a very few who should borrow money and start again, the destitute failed to provide for themselves. Now they want *us* to take responsibility for *their* lives and protect them from the consequences of their own folly. That's not fair. Why should we support a government we don't want or need?"

Needless to say the rest of the settlers went right ahead and formed governments without them, provided services, and imposed taxes. At this point the Loners were forced to pay or leave, and time after time they left, eventually settling on some other planet where they were forced to start all over again.

Eventually some of the Loners grew tired of the unending struggle and decided on another course of action. If they couldn't have their own planet, they'd create an alternative. A habitat large enough to hold them but small enough to control. Their habitat would be mobile too, so they could leave unfriendly environs whenever they wished, including human space if that became necessary.

Research showed that a conventional ship wouldn't be big enough and a custom-designed habitat would be way too expensive. The solution strangely enough was an ore barge. Unlike most ore barges, this one was equipped with drives of its own and was fairly new to boot. The barge had come onto the market when the company that owned it went out of business. Due to its unusual size and design, other companies had declined the opportunity to buy it.

But the barge was perfect for what the Loners had in mind so they formed a corporation and bought themselves a dream. True to their philosophy each person bought as much of the barge as they could afford, paid for those services they wished to receive, and were in all other respects free to do as they wished.

To protect their newfound freedom the Loners instituted a policy of strict neutrality toward all governments, planetary and galactic alike, and in doing so made themselves accidentally rich.

Throughout the history of human civilization there's been a need for neutral ground. A place where enemies can meet, where money can be stored, and secrets can be kept.

Given their fanatical desire for independence, their utter pragmatism, and their ability to run from trouble, the Loners were perfect candidates to fill this need. And fill it they did, opening banks, storage vaults, and a broad range of related services.

Due to their prosperity, others were eager to join them. And pragmatists though they were, the Loners didn't care whether the newcomers understood or approved of the undeflying philosophy, only that they lived in accordance with it.

Time passed, and before long there were more people than space to put them in, so additions were approved. There was no reason to limit mass since Tin Town was too large to negotiate a planetary atmosphere, and doing so would have compromised its security.

As a result the barge began to change shape. Her once-smooth hull grew bumps and bulges as sections were enlarged. Two globular liners were connected to the barge's bow and stern, making her the bar between two huge dumbbells. Then a forest of sensors, weapons platforms, and cooling fins appeared along with the now-famous name "Tin Town."

A soft chime interrupted McCade's thoughts as the com screen lit up. Where he expected to see a face, there was a request for a damage deposit instead. A rather *large* damage deposit.

Although the Loners placed no political restrictions on their visitors, they did insist on insuring themselves against financial loss. After all, a town without laws tends to attract some nasty visitors and without some sort of controls would soon cease to exist. Therefore each visitor was required to produce a rather substantial damage deposit before they were allowed to land.

The Loners were willing to accept a variety of assets including cash, ships, family members, specialized equipment, bodily organs, and anything else of recognized value.

McCade typed *Pegasus*'s name and legal description onto the com screen, palm printed the agreement, and swore as it faded from sight. If he or any member of his crew caused damage to Tin Town, or any of its permanent residents, *Pegasus* would be forfeit.

He didn't like it, but according to Sister Urillo, there wasn't much choice. Her sources said that Mustapha Pong had been sighted three times in recent months, all of them in Tin Town, and all of them in the company of a local businessman named Morris Sappo. The habitat was in orbit around a planet called Lexor at the moment, but there was no way to tell if that was a significant part of the Sappo-Pong relationship, or just happenstance. But it could be important, and since no one knew when the Loners might decide to move Tin Town somewhere else, time was short. If McCade wished to find Pong or, failing that, Sappo, he'd have to visit Tin Town, damage deposit and all.

Threading his way through a maze of orbiting ships and free-floating junk, McCade guided *Pegasus* into the lighted maw of Tin Town's main hatch.

The hangar was huge, taking up all of what had once been the barge's number three hold. All sorts of ships formed orderly rows to the right and the left. There were scarred freighters, sleek little one-man scouts, richly appointed space yachts, sturdy-looking tugs, and a scattering of pirate raiders. The latter were not too surprising since Tin Town was one of the few places pirates could openly visit.

Lowering *Pegasus* into her allotted berth, McCade killed the repellors and turned to his companions. "Welcome to Tin Town, a monument to money, and an eyesore in the sky. All ashore who's goin' ashore."

Though Neem and Reba didn't seem excited by the prospect, they disappeared into their cabins and showed up a few minutes later ready to go.

Reba was dressed in faded coveralls. She wore a blaster in a cross-draw holster and had a throwing knife sticking out of her right boot top.

McCade had debated the merits of taking Neem versus leaving him on the ship and, based on the Il Ronnian's previous success, had decided to take him along.

Neem was a vision in black. Black helmet, black visor, and a long black cloak that concealed his tail. He had blasters concealed in his copious sleeves, a wicked looking sword strapped across his back, and variety of knives scattered about his person.

McCade wasn't sure how Neem would react to actual combat, but he certainly *looked* like death incarnate, and maybe that would help.

A shuttle bus arrived a few minutes later, sealed its lock against the ship's and welcomed them aboard. There was something wrong with the vehicle's voice simulator that caused it to drop every fourth word.

"Welcome to Tin . . . We hope you . . . enjoy your stay . . . You may pay . . . cash or we . . . be glad to . . . you a line . . . credit secured by . . . damage deposit. Please . . . the payment plate . . . you wish to . . . credit."

McCade palmed the plate and gave thanks that Swanson-Pierce had provided a thick wad of expense money. If a shuttle ride cost fifty credits a piece, how much would a hotel room be?

The shuttle stopped twice to pick up other passengers before heading for the main terminal. Except for a birdlike Finthian and a wealthy-looking Cellite, it was a largely humanoid crowd.

The Cellite wore richly detailed pajamas. They swished softly with each movement of his stocky body and gave off a spicy scent. He wore a matching skullcap on his rounded head and, lacking a nose, breathed through his thin-lipped mouth.

As he boarded the shuttle the Cellite's eyestalks darted this way and that, examining his fellow passengers with the friendly curiosity of a small child. Then the alien caught sight of Neem and developed a sudden interest in a viewport.

McCade grinned. Neem's new disguise was having the desired effect.

The shuttle made lock-to-lock contact with the main terminal, disgorged its passengers, and issued a broken invitation for others to come aboard. Most were more drunk than sober and barely able to stagger aboard with the help of handholds and crewmates.

Reba grinned. "This place makes Spin look like a nursery school." She had to yell it over the noise of the crowd.

McCade nodded and motioned toward a broad corridor that led away from the lock and toward glittering lights. "Make a hole, Neem. We'll be right behind you."

"Having a couple of humans behind me is not my idea of a dream come true," Neem replied good-naturedly, "but everyone should live dangerously once in a while. Follow me."

And they did. Both sides of the corridor were lined with wall-to-wall shops: restaurants, bars, whorehouses, clothing stores, equipment dealers, banks, medical clinics, and weapons dealers.

And these were not passive enterprises but centers of frantic activity packed with merchandise and staffed by sentients ready and eager to unload their present stock and bring in more.

Signs blinked, hawkers yelled, and robots scurried through the crowd bleating out their prerecorded messages. "Dark dreams! Dark dreams! A place where dark dreams come true! Corridor five, cross tunnel fourteen. Dark dreams! Dark dreams!"

The air was filled with a heady mix of smells. Smoke, perfume, food, sweat, and other odors too faint to identify all fought for dominance.

McCade noticed that the crowd seemed to bunch up around the more popular haunts and thin out again to pass others by. And although the crowd was made up of all sorts of sentients, all had one thing in common. It was a look, a look that said they needed to acquire something, or satisfy some hidden need before time and money ran out, and they were forced to leave.

And here and there along the edges of the crowd the predators waited, their restless eyes skimming the crowd in search of profit or pleasure. There were all sorts: whores, pimps, thieves, pirates, mercenaries, bounty hunters, and more, all waiting, all living off the weakness of others.

But the tall black thing didn't look weak, and neither did the man and woman who strode along behind it, so the predators watched but made no move. Strength is difficult to gain and easy to lose so eventually the black thing might still be theirs.

"The House of Yarl." That was the name Sister Urillo had provided and it was right where she'd said it would be, just off the main corridor along cross tunnel twenty-three.

The name was deeply etched into a brass plate that graced an otherwise nondescript metal door. It hissed open at McCade's touch. As the bounty hunter stepped inside he found himself in a small but richly appointed lobby.

A middle-aged woman with a kindly face and two wings of dark hair looked up from a comp screen. "Welcome to the House of Yarl. My name is Portia. How may I help you?"

"We're friends of Sister Urillo's," McCade replied. "She recommended that we stay here."

"How nice," the woman replied evenly. "How *is* Sister Urillo these days?"

"The kinesthetic feedback unit you sent her is much better than the old one. She can dance now."

When Portia smiled her entire face lit up. "Excellent! It is as I hoped. There was a time when she loved dancing as much as flying. One, two, or three rooms?"

"Three," Reba said firmly.

"I don't know about you, but I feel insulted," McCade said to Neem.

"Maybe it's those cigars," Neem replied. "They're enough to drop an Ikk at thirty yards."

The woman tapped away at her keyboard and looked up at the comp screen. "Your rooms are ready. Palm the counter, then palm the doors."

McCade pressed his palm down on the counter, followed by Reba, then Neem.

Portia frowned at the alien's gloved hand but decided to let it go. Anyone wearing gloves could open the thing's door, but whatever lurked behind that visor could take care of itself and wouldn't need any advice from her.

They were just turning to go when Portia turned on her professional smile. "Thank you for choosing the House of Yarl and have a nice stay."

McCade smiled, nodded in her direction, and decided that he'd be satisfied if he got off the habitat alive.

TWENTY-ONE

They'd been walking for about twenty minutes and the bright lights were far behind them. Every third or fourth light was burned out or shot out, McCade couldn't tell which.

The walls were covered with graffiti, and garbage lined both sides of the corridor. The air was humid and carried the strong scent of urine. Every society has an underside and this was Tin Town's.

The people who passed them were the dregs of a society focused on self. They padded the length of Tin Town's less traveled corridors like human vultures, hoping to find the leavings of some predator, or to encounter a victim so weak that they could make the kill themselves.

But the threesome were well armed and moved with the confidence of those who know where they're going and why. And since the vultures were ever fearful of becoming victims themselves, they gave the strangers a wide berth and went in search of weaker prey.

Nonetheless, there was the very real possibility of an ambush. The corridor practically screamed, "Danger! Run for your lives!"

So while Reba managed to *look* calm, her right hand hovered over her blaster, and there was a tightness in the way she moved. Her eyes jerked toward McCade when he spoke and then darted away.

"Where did you say we were going again?"

Reba frowned. "We're looking for a good restaurant. Pay attention, Sam. We're looking for a man called Scavenger Jack. Sister Urillo has him on a retainer. If Pong's here, Jack will know."

McCade was about to say something along the lines of "Well, excuse me," when Neem snarled at the both of them.

"Cut the chatter, you two. Unless you'd like to come up and trade places with me."

Il Ronnians are partially nocturnal and have better night sight than humans so Neem was leading the way. But he didn't relish the assignment and wanted them to know it. Each side tunnel was a potential threat, and if someone started a firefight, he'd be the first to die.

"Tunnel eighty-seven. We're getting close," Reba said, pausing to read faded numbers. "Scavenger Jack lives in ninety-one right."

They passed three more tunnels without incident and found themselves in front of one marked "91." Unlike most this one was partially lit.

McCade stepped into the tunnel. "Watch our backs, Neem. We'd be like rats in a trap if this tunnel dead ends."

"Rats in a trap," Neem said experimentally. "I like that. Is it similar to being up feces creek without a paddle? And why travel on a creek filled with feces anyway?"

"Not now, Neem," Reba replied impatiently. "Just watch our backs." And so saying she followed McCade into the tunnel.

Neem started to make a rude gesture with his tail but remembered that she couldn't see it and wouldn't understand even if she could. He settled for a rude noise instead.

Turning, he backed his way up the tunnel, watching the main corridor for signs of trouble.

They were about a hundred feet into the tunnel when they heard the scream. It was long, drawn out, and undeniably human.

McCade drew his blaster and broke into a run. Another scream followed the first, this one going even higher, before dying into a low gurgle and disappearing altogether.

Up ahead a door slammed open and a shaft of light hit the far side of the tunnel. A shadow hit the wall as a man stepped out and turned their way. He took one look and drew his slug gun. "Come on, guys! We've got company!"

The man used a high velocity slug to punctuate his sentence. The slug blew air into McCade's ear as it passed, hit the overhead, and screamed down the corridor. The chances were slim that it would go through the habitat's hull, but it could happen. Stupid asshole.

McCade squeezed his trigger and punched an energy beam through the man's chest. As he fell over backward more men came through the door and leaped his body. They had better sense and opened up with energy weapons.

Now Neem and Reba had joined the fray. Bolts of blue energy screamed up and down the tunnel. The two groups came together with a collective grunt just as another man fell. Knives flashed in the dim light and it was each person for himself.

McCade found himself paired off with a man in a blue uniform. He was short, ugly, and smelled of cheap cologne.

McCade tried to use his blaster but found his wrist locked in a grip of steel. Light flashed off the other man's blade and McCade blocked it with a grip of his own. Now the two men tried to best each other through strength alone.

Though a full head shorter than McCade, the other man was as strong as an ox, and it was soon apparent that he'd win. He held his knife edge up, and in spite of McCade's best efforts, each second brought the shining steel closer and closer. Any moment now and McCade would feel the first pinprick as the knife point broke his skin. Next would come the excruciating agony as the cold steel slid into his guts. His belly jerked back at the thought.

Neem's voice came from behind. "Turn him around!"

McCade found that if he pulled with one arm and pushed with the other he could turn his opponent to the right.

"Get ready to die," the man rasped through yellowing teeth. "I'm going to split you open like a ripe fava fruit."

McCade didn't waste precious energy on a reply. Instead, he used all of his remaining strength to push and pull at the same time.

It was then that he heard the whicker of cold steel and Neem's Il Ronnian war cry. As the alien swung into sight his sword was already in motion and McCade did his best to duck.

The razor-sharp steel made a sucking sound as it passed through the man's neck and came out the other side. There was a gout of bright red blood as the man's head went one way and his body went another. They hit the metal deck with a double thump.

McCade swayed slightly as he looked around. His arms still hurt where the other man had gripped them. A glance informed him that Reba was okay and that the rest of the assailants had fled. Neem was using a corpse to wipe the blood off his blade.

Seeing McCade's look, Neem grinned behind his visor. "While in college I took a course in the fabrication and use of ancient weapons. Standard stuff for anthropologists and, as it turns out, quite useful as well."

McCade shook his head in amazement. "You never cease to amaze me, Neem. You *are* a crazy bastard."

"You can say that again," Reba agreed. "And a good thing too. Come on. Let's see what's inside."

McCade went through the door fast and low, his blaster searching for a target. There was none.

The inside came as a complete surprise. He'd expected some sort of hovel, a metal cave complete with piles of junk, and a grizzled old man who called himself "Scavenger Jack."

Nothing could've been further from the truth. Far from being a metal cave, Scavenger Jack's foyer was larger than McCade's hotel room and better decorated as well. The floors were marble, the walls were covered with rich red fabric, and the light fixtures dripped crystal. For some reason the man chose to live in a remote and almost deserted part of the habitat.

"Over here." Neem had pushed a door open with the point of his sword.

McCade followed the Il Ronnian through the door and found himself in a formal sitting room. It was filled to overflowing with richly upholstered furniture, fine paintings, and small pieces of Finthian sculpture. Something caught his eye and he moved over to investigate.

"This is amazing," Reba said quietly. "Who'd believe you could find something like this just off tunnel ninety-one? Scavenger Jack sure knows how to live."

"And how to die," McCade added. "Look at this."

Scavenger Jack was lying behind a couch. In life he'd been a handsome man with curly brown hair and a thick mustache. He wore a surprised expression as if he'd known how things were supposed to turn out and this wasn't it.

McCade couldn't blame him. Scavenger Jack was not a pretty sight. Neither was the knife that protruded from his chest. First they'd worked him over, which explained the screams and the condition of his fingernails. They'd pried them off one at a time. McCade wondered why. Did it have something to do with Pong? Or was it totally unconnected? There was no way to tell.

"Damn." Reba made it a comment and an expression of sorrow all in one.

"Yeah," McCade agreed. "Not a very nice way to go."

"There's no such thing as a 'nice way to go,' Neem observed. "And I suggest we leave lest we suffer a similar fate. They might come back."

Neem's suggestion made a lot of sense so they wasted little time slipping out the door and into the tunnel.

There was no way to tell if Scavenger Jack had a next of kin, or if the habitat's founders believed in concepts like legal inheritance, but they closed the door just in case.

It closed with the solid thump common to bank vaults everywhere, and now that McCade looked more closely, he realized the door and frame were made of hull metal. Though a bit eccentric, Scavenger Jack was no fool.

All of which made McCade curious. Given the fact that an energy cannon wouldn't even scratch the door, how had the killers managed to get inside?

The obvious answer was that Scavenger Jack knew his killers and decided to let them in. That, plus his surprised expression, suggested friends. Or people he *thought* were friends.

The bodies were right where they'd left them and Reba's knife flashed as she cut something off the headless corpse, stuck it in a pocket, and moved down tunnel.

The walk back was long but uneventful. As they approached the hotel McCade saw a number of police and, what with his bloodstained clothing and heavily armed companions, felt more than a little conspicuous.

But this was Tin Town, and unless the police had some reason to suspect that someone had attacked one of *their* clients, then there was nothing to fear.

McCade decided to visit his room prior to joining the others. So when he entered Neem's room a half hour later he was showered, shaved, and feeling much better.

McCade noticed that the Il Ronnian had the room temp up to max and was about to complain when he remembered the sound that Neem's sword had made as it passed through the short man's neck. The heat suddenly seemed like a minor inconvenience and he said "hello" instead.

Besides turning the room into an oven, Neem had taken the opportunity to shed his disguise. Freed from all constraints his tail danced this way and that as he spoke.

"Welcome, Sam. Reba has come up with some rather interesting information."

"Good," McCade said as he dropped into a chair. "We could use some interesting information right about now."

Reba had her boots up on a coffee table and was using a piece of the hotel's promotional material to fan herself. She looked unhappy. "Well, it's interesting . . . but not very helpful. You remember the short guy Neem made even shorter?"

McCade nodded grimly. "Who could forget?"

"Well, I cut the insignia off his uniform on the way out. I showed it to Portia and she says it belongs to Morris Sappo's household troops."

McCade lit a cigar and used the time to think. Pong had been seen with Sappo on each of his recent trips to Tin Town. They knew that from the reports Scavenger Jack had filed with Sister Urillo. So it seemed that Pong and Sappo were financially linked and maybe even friends. It wasn't difficult to imagine ways in which one of Tin Town's foremost businessmen could assist a renegade pirate and turn a profit in the process. Having broken off his relationship with the Brotherhood, Pong would have to sell his loot somewhere, and Tin Town was the perfect choice.

Given that, and given the fact that McCade was on Pong's trail, it seemed likely that Sappo's troops had murdered Scavenger Jack in an effort to protect Pong's privacy. But how had they known?

"It appears that there's a leak in Sister Urillo's organization," McCade said, expelling the words along with a column of smoke. "Someone informed Pong and/or Sappo that we were on the way."

Reba nodded her agreement. "I agree. I've sent word to Sister Urillo via Portia. In the meantime we've got a problem. Sappo isn't going to tell us where Pong is, and Scavenger Jack is dead, so what do we do now?"

There was a long silence during which they watched McCade's smoke drift on the heavy air. It was Neem who finally spoke.

"In spite of your best efforts you humans have dropped the globe. So it's time for an Il Ronnian to step in and save the day."

"Oh, really?" Reba asked. "And how will you accomplish that, O wizened one?"

Neem smiled a superior smile. "It just so happens that Tin Town boasts a Class III Il Ronnian intelligence operation. I think it likely that our operatives will know where Pong is . . . or where to start looking. I suggest we drop in and ask them."

TWENTY-TWO

McCade was surprised. It seemed hard to believe that the Il Ronn had spies on Tin Town. Subjugated races spying for the Il Ronn yes, human traitors yes, but the Il Ronn themselves? No.

For one thing there was the obvious physical differences. How could an Il Ronnian possibly pass for human? Or vice versa? Sure, there was Neem's disguise, but he couldn't get away with that forever. No, Il Ronnian spies didn't seem possible. Nonetheless that's exactly what Neem wanted them to believe.

McCade came to a stop as a pink robot trundled out to block Neem's path. A woman appeared next to it. She wore a skin suit and a rather tired expression.

"Step through my door, tall, dark, and handsome," she said. "I've got what you're looking for."

"I doubt that very much," Neem replied dryly as he sidestepped the robo pimp. "You're not my type."

McCade smiled as the woman made a rude gesture. Wouldn't she be surprised to see Neem in the nude!

Lights strobed, people swirled, and mind-numbing noise assailed their ears as they threaded their way through the crowd.

Neem was his usual self, but Reba was a bit grumpy, as if Scavenger Jack's death was a personal affront to her honor. Having been unable to cheer her up, McCade decided to let her sulk.

Level six of Alpha Section was located at the opposite end of the habitat from the House of Yarl and that's where Neem was taking them. A high-speed monorail whisked them the length of the original barge and deposited them in a somewhat gaudy station.

Like the rest of Tin Town, Alpha Section was a sort of capitalistic free-for-all, governed by nothing more elaborate than the law of supply and demand.

Though McCade wondered how Il Ronnians could survive undetected, it was clear that spies would thrive on Tin Town's laissez-faire system of government and profit from the information that changed hands here. Maybe, just maybe, Neem was right.

Neem claimed that he'd been specially briefed by the chief of Il Ronnian intelligence during McCade's last days on Imantha. Though Neem was not normally privy to classified information, the Council of One Thousand had anticipated the possibility that he might need some help and granted him a special dispensation.

Not eager to reveal the extent of the Il Ronnian intelligence network to a human, Teeb had ordered Neem to keep the information secret unless forced to do otherwise. Or so Neem claimed.

McCade wasn't so sure. In retrospect, Neem had been a lot more competent than any college professor had a right to be. First he'd extricated himself from a bad situation on Spin, then he'd shown up to rescue McCade from the pirates, and now he was beheading people right and left. Yes, McCade decided, Neem will bear watching.

They rounded a corner and found themselves on the edge of a circular plaza. Shops and restaurants faced the plaza, which wasn't flat, but fell in levels toward a circular stage. At the moment four jugglers were busy tossing daggers at one another, catching them and pretending not to, thrilling the audience with a series of close calls.

Neem glanced at his wrist term. "Come on. We've got some time to kill." The Il Ronnian made his way down the steps and McCade followed with a disgruntled Reba tagging along behind.

Neem slid sideways down a half-filled aisle. The Il Ronnian seemed to step on every third foot, leaving McCade and Reba to make his apologies.

The jugglers had finished with the knives and were moving on to Rath snakes by the time all three of them were seated. Rath snakes are somewhat irritable to start with, and the process of being thrown around did nothing to improve their tempers.

As they flew through the air the reptiles twisted every which way, hoping to sink their poisonous fangs into an arm or hand. But the jugglers were a blur, anticipating every move, whipping the snakes back and forth like pieces of green rope.

Then something went wrong. One of the jugglers missed a catch. A squirming Rath snake soared out over the audience and started to fall.

The crowd let out a collective gasp and people scrambled to get out of the way. All except for a man in baggy coveralls. He seemed frozen in place as the snake fell toward him, his mouth hanging open in stupefied amazement, his hands opening and closing as if unsure of what to do.

McCade's hand went toward his blaster, but he knew it was hopeless. By the time he drew and fired, the Rath snake would already have its fangs in the man's flesh.

Then just as the reptile was about to land in his lap, the man stood, snatched the snake out of midair, and threw it back.

A juggler caught it, tossed it into the air, and the crowd realized they'd been had. There was loud applause as the fifth juggler took a bow, stripped off his coveralls to reveal a colorful costume, and hurried down to join his friends onstage.

"Now would be the time to pass the hat," Reba remarked thoughtfully. "They should do pretty well."

"Chances are they've done pretty well already," McCade replied. "Look at the crowd they drew. I'll bet the stores fronting on the plaza pay them to perform."

McCade turned to Neem. "By the way, which store belongs to your friends?"

Neem chuckled. "None of them. My 'friends' as you call them are right in front of you."

McCade looked toward the stage. The jugglers had just activated thirty laser torches and were preparing to toss them around.

"You'd better have your eyes checked, Neem, the jugglers are human."

"They *look* human," Neem agreed, "but they aren't. They're cyborgs."

Il Ronnian cyborgs designed to look like humans? It couldn't be. But as McCade watched the jugglers he began to wonder. By now the laser torches were flashing through the air at incredible speed. Speed that defied human reflexes. And why not? If Neem was correct, the reflexes weren't human and never had been. They were wired, servo-controlled, and computer-assisted.

No wonder the jugglers were willing to throw Rath snakes around like so much rubber hose. A bite wouldn't even pierce their plastiflesh skin much less poison them. Much as he hated to admit it, the whole thing made sense. By posing as human jugglers, the Il Ronnian spies had a perfect excuse to travel around and poke their noses into all sorts of places. And given their skill people probably begged them to come!

All of a sudden the enormity of it struck home. There could be hundreds, even thousands, of Il Ronnian spies roaming the Empire sucking up secrets like so many vacuum cleaners. Swanson-Pierce would go crazy!

But wait a minute, what would stop humans from doing the same thing? Among the millions who'd seen him on Imantha had some been human? Fellow Terrans locked inside electro-mechanical bodies deep inside an enemy empire? If so, each and every one of them deserved a medal.

McCade's thoughts were swept away by the sound of loud applause. The jugglers took a series of quick bows, and when the audience started to leave, the cyborgs started to pack.

Neem motioned for McCade and Reba to stay put and pushed his way down toward the stage.

"Where's Neem headed?"

"You're going to find this hard to believe," McCade replied, "but according to Neem the jugglers are Il Ronnian spies."

As McCade explained Reba's eyes got larger. When he was finished she shook her head and laughed out loud.

"Well, I'll be damned. It makes a lot of sense now that I think about it. I'll bet both sides have been at it for years. Sister Urillo will have a fit! She'll see Il Ronnian spies under every bed."

McCade nodded and felt through his pockets for a cigar. The best he could find was broken in two. He stuck the longer half between his teeth and puffed it into life.

Down on the stage Neem had just sealed some sort of agreement with a very human handshake. McCade blew smoke toward the deck and watched Neem climb the stairs. Strange though it seemed, things were looking up.

TWENTY-THREE

Morris Sappo had spent a lot of money to make himself both comfortable and safe. Not satisfied with what Tin Town had to offer, he'd commissioned a sort of annex, a blister on the habitat's hull built to his own specifications.

According to rumor, Sappo's quarters were luxurious beyond compare. A farm boy once, Sappo hated Tin Town's small spaces and hungered for the vast skies of Regor II. In order to satisfy his craving for openness he covered his home with transparent duraplast. If he couldn't have the blue sky of his boyhood, he'd have the heavens beyond.

Having started with the stars themselves as decorations, Sappo was challenged to do them justice. Fantastic holograms, each one a work of art, rippled across his walls in harmony with Sappo's moods. Expensive furniture, much of it specially crafted for his small frame, dotted his combination office and living room. And water swirled this way and that beneath his feet, trapped there between two layers of duraplast, tinted with multicolored dyes and programmed to match the walls.

That's what rumor said anyway, but if their plan worked, McCade would soon know for himself. Two standard days had passed since the Il Ronnian cyborgs had performed in the plaza. Now they were about to take part in a performance of a different kind—an assault on Sappo's private quarters.

Neem had anticipated a certain amount of resentment, even resistance, from the cyborgs, and was surprised by their cheerful cooperation.

Unknown to Neem, or so he claimed, Teeb had provided him with an authorization code so powerful that the cyborgs regarded him as the direct embodiment of the governing council.

In addition, they were astounded to discover that Neem was running around the human empire protected by nothing more than a flimsy disguise. So they not only jumped to do his bidding but hung on his every word as well.

While McCade and Reba found this quite amusing, poor Neem was quite taken aback and spent a lot of time ordering the cyborgs to treat him just like anyone else.

Unfortunately the cyborgs took his entreaties as a form of divine humility and reacted by elevating him to new heights. From Neem's point of view the whole thing was quite disconcerting.

But regardless of their attitude toward Neem, the cyborgs were quite competent. This became clear during the two days spent planning and preparing the raid. Each was a specialist recruited from the various branches of the Il Ronnian armed forces. With but one exception, all had been severely injured during combat prior to recruitment into the Cyborg Corps.

As Leeb, the explosives expert, put it, "The decision becomes relatively simple once your body is almost completely destroyed."

The single exception was their leader Ceex. Ceex was a professional intelligence officer so devoted to his job that he'd voluntarily given up a perfectly healthy body to become a cyborg.

In Neem's opinion Ceex was a few planets short of a full system, but since the anthropologist was a head case himself, this seemed like a case of the pot calling the kettle black. Still, it did seem as if Ceex had taken patriotism a step too far.

But looney or not, once Ceex understood the situation, he wasted little time in coming up with a plan. He didn't know where Pong was but felt sure that Morris Sappo did. The two men were often seen together and it was common knowledge that Sappo routinely purchased large quantities of Pong's stolen goods.

Given that, and given the limited amount of time to work with, Ceex suggested the direct approach. Bypass Sappo's security, break into his quarters, and force him to tell whatever he knew.

It wasn't very subtle, but given the stakes involved, and the need to get moving, McCade was in no mood for subtlety.

A scouting mission by Leeb and weapons expert Keeg confirmed what everyone already knew. Sappo's quarters would be a tough nut to crack. He had guards everywhere. In addition there were elaborate alarm systems, robotic sensors, and automatic defense systems.

"What you're saying is that the front door's locked," McCade had responded thoughtfully.

"Correct," Keeg agreed. He had the appearance of a pleasant young man with blond hair. "The back door, however, looks a good deal more promising."

"The back door?"

Keeg grinned an extremely human grin. "Yes. From what Leeb and I saw, Sappo's security system assumes that intruders will come from *inside* Tin Town. And a quick scouting trip on the surface of the hull confirmed it. Oh, there's plenty of nasty stuff out there as well, but compared with the inside approach, the outside is wide open."

And so it was agreed that they'd attack Sappo's quarters from the surface of Tin Town's hull. Now they were in place and about to venture out onto the habitat's surface. The cyborgs waited patiently while McCade, Neem, and Reba checked their space armor.

When all three had given Ceex the thumbs-up, he palmed the lock and waited for the atmosphere to hiss away. This particular lock was just outside the edge of Sappo's security systems.

Like the rest of the cyborgs, Ceex wore no body armor. He didn't need any. Outside of his brain and spinal cord he didn't have any biological parts. His internal life-support system would keep both organs well oxygenated and protect them from physical trauma. Still, it seemed strange to see a man step outside without a suit.

Tin Town's surface was a labyrinth of harsh shadows. A cooling fin towered off to McCade's right. It was back lit by a large sign that read MAMA SALDO'S SHIPYARD and threw triangles of black across the habitat's gleaming hull as it flashed on and off.

An automatic weapons turret swiveled around and around to McCade's left, its sensors probing the heavens for some sign of hostility, its twin-energy projectors waiting patiently for the order to fire.

And up ahead a maze of ducts, sensor housings, and clustered pipe waited to slow them down. And beyond that McCade could see the Beta end of the spindle, blazing with light and hanging against the stars like a big silver ball.

Movement caught McCade's eye and he looked up to see a sleek freighter fire her steering jets, pause, and slide out of sight beyond the hull's horizon.

The cyborgs drifted between the obstacles like so many ghosts. Their infrared beams probed the darkest corners, their transceivers sampled all the radio traffic in the immediate vicinity, and their optical scanners watched for signs of movement.

But even cyborgs are fallible, a lesson all would learn a few minutes later.

Although Tin Town didn't have any government as such, it did offer a number of police companies, one of which offered robo surveillance service. The service was designed to discourage unauthorized excursions over portions of privately owned hull. And the key to the service were the small globular devices called robo sentries. They didn't have much brain, but they bristled with weapons and flew preprogrammed patterns over the hull's surface.

The robo sentries were launched and retrieved via large pipes that passed through Tin Town's hull at various points. Although McCade didn't see the silver ball sail out of a pipe behind him, he did see it burn a hole through the rearmost cyborg's back and splash blue fire against the hull beyond.

The cyborg, an individual named Seeo, staggered but managed to stay upright. A mist of white fluid rose to envelope him.

McCade's energy rifle spat blue light as the robo sentry spun right and tried to line up on Neem. Though heavily armed, the robots didn't carry much armor and the silver ball exploded in an orange flash.

For a moment Neem was showered with pieces of hot metal and plastic. Then they lost their inertia and slowly drifted away, each one reflecting tiny shards of light.

"Sorry about that." It was Ceex's voice in McCade's helmet. "It looks like the cyborg's out of the bag."

A part of McCade's mind registered the joke. The rest was busy staying alive. The robo sentry had sent out a distress signal before it died and now silver balls were flocking to the spot like sharks to a feeding frenzy.

McCade took cover behind some sort of metal housing and began to pick them off one at a time. First he'd compute a robot's trajectory, next he'd pick a spot just ahead of it, and then he'd squeeze the trigger. Nine times out of ten the robot disappeared in a flash of orange flame. The others joined in and pretty soon robo sentries were popping like so many party balloons.

The battle was not entirely one-sided however. While McCade and the others fought off most of the swarming globes, five or six managed to surround Seeo and soon finished him off. Like the professional he was, Seeo died without uttering a sound.

Seconds later his life-support system confirmed his death, triggered his built-in demo charge, and blew up. Two of the silver balls disappeared along with Seeo's body.

"Damn." Reba's voice sounded hollow in McCade's helmet.

"Yeah," he replied. "Damn."

"Let's move," Ceex said, sounding like every noncom McCade had ever heard. "Sappo's quarters are just ahead."

They were running now, a sort of fast shuffle that ate up the distance but maintained their contact with Tin Town's hull. They knew that each passing second would bring more and more opposition and give Sappo's household security troops that much more time to get ready.

McCade welcomed the movement. After all the deception and delay, it felt good to *do* something for a change. Even if the something was dangerous as hell. His muscles strained, his pulse pounded, and the ragged sound of his own breathing filled his helmet.

Every now and then another robo sentry would appear, loose off a bolt of energy, and disappear in a flash of light as someone blew it away. Once you knew about them they weren't that hard to handle.

"We've got security troops up here," Ceex said grimly. "Get ready to take some heat."

McCade climbed over a low pipe and saw a strange sight waiting up ahead. Four members of Sappo's household troops had exited through his private lock and come face-to-face with the Il Ronnian cyborgs. But Sappo's troops didn't *know* that the men who faced them were cyborgs. And not knowing they stood frozen in place wondering how humans could enter a vacuum and stay alive.

None of them lived long enough to find out. One after another they fell as the strange apparitions shot them down. Two died without firing, the third got off a single shot, and the fourth killed Keeg a fraction of a second before Leeb drilled an energy beam through his visor. The cyborg blew up just as the man's visor shattered and the vacuum sucked him out through the hole in his helmet.

It wasn't a pretty sight, but McCade didn't have the time to look. He was too busy helping Leeb place explosives around Sappo's private lock. A few seconds later and the cyborg was pushing McCade toward cover.

They were just barely behind a boxy piece of duct work when the charges went off. McCade peeked around the corner just in time to see the outer hatch fly off its hinges and spin into space.

Neem and Reba were right behind him as he and Leeb dashed for the lock.

"We've got more troops out here," Ceex warned. "Geev and I will hold them off while you secure the lock."

"Roger," McCade replied.

The tunnel had decompressed as they blew the hatch, but there was another lock just fifty feet in. It had been placed there in case the first lock failed.

"Just a sec and I'll blow it," Leeb said, reaching for his demolitions bag.

"Whoa," McCade ordered. "If we aren't careful, we could decompress Sappo's entire area. He won't be much good to us if he's dead."

McCade palmed the door and it slid open. It seemed all the security measures had been lavished on the outer door, leaving this one unprotected.

McCade chinned his radio. "The lock is secured, Ceex. Time to join us."

The cyborg arrived a few seconds later. His energy rifle had disappeared along with his right arm. White hydraulic fluid spurted from the stump and half his face was burned away. "Sorry I'm late. Geev won't be coming."

McCade remembered Geev's dark plastiflesh, his flashing brown eyes, and his ready smile. He hoped that whatever Sappo had to say would be worth the price, and wondered if that was possible.

The outer door closed, air hissed into the lock, and the inner door cycled open a few minutes later. They were all on the dock with weapons ready, but nothing could have prepared them for the hail of lead and coherent energy that reached out to greet them.

It was Reba who saved the day when she stood up and lobbed a grenade down the corridor. She was still standing there waiting for the grenade to go off when Neem reached up and jerked her down.

The grenade turned the other end of the corridor into a slaughter house and Neem threw another just to make sure. Like the first one it went off with a deafening roar. They waited for a few moments, but there were no signs of life, so one by one they all got up.

All that is but Leeb. A piece of shrapnel had lanced down through his chest ripping his life-support system apart and destroying his motor control subprocessor.

McCade bent to help him, but Ceex pulled him away. "He's gone, Sam, and if you stay here, he'll take you with him."

They were forty feet down the corridor when Leeb blew up. The explosion made a dull thumping sound and no one chose to look back.

Their entrance into Sappo's quarters was almost anticlimactic. As the door hissed open they were ready for anything, but rather than armor-clad troops a domestic robot rolled forward to greet them. Its synthesized voice was stern and unyielding.

"Please leave. Your presence is not wanted here. I will summon help if necessary. Please leave . . ."

The robot never got to repeat its warning because Reba put her hand blaster up against its metal forehead and pulled the trigger. The beam of blue energy went right through the thin metal and out the other side.

On the far side of the room a tank filled with Nuerillium air fish shattered into a thousand pieces, freeing its multicolored captives to flutter about the room.

And what a room it was. If anything the rumors had understated its elegance. Overhead the vast sweep of the starscape made the room seem huge. The holos added to that impression, wrapping the room in color and pulsating to the beat of the exotic music that floated through the air. And water eddied and swirled beneath their boots looking like marble brought to life. The overall effect was beautiful but cold like a piece of sculpture that is seen and not touched.

"All right," McCade said grimly. "Sappo's in here somewhere. Spread out and find him."

No one had taken more than a couple of steps before a section of holo rippled and a man stepped out. He was small, carefully dressed, and as far as McCade could tell completely unarmed. He wore an amused, almost arrogant expression, and frowned when he saw the air fish fluttering around the room.

"I don't know who you people are but you're certainly destructive. If this is an attempt to rob me, I'm afraid you'll be sadly disappointed. I keep my cash and other valuables somewhere else."

"No," Neem answered as he walked across the room toward Sappo. "This is not an attempt to steal your stupid possessions. What we want is knowledge. Knowledge stored in your brain. And we'll do whatever's necessary to get it."

Sappo became visibly nervous as Neem drew closer. "My brain? Knowledge? What do you want?"

The black plastic of Neem's visor was only inches away when he spoke. "We want the location of a man. A friend of yours by the name of Mustapha Pong. Give us what we want and you'll live."

Sappo was scared now. He took a step backward. "You don't understand . . . I can't . . . Pong would kill me."

Neem reached up to remove his helmet. As it came away he said, "No, *you* don't understand. If you *don't* tell, I'll kill you. I'll strip your skin off one inch at a time until you pray for death with every breath you take."

Sappo took one look at Neem's distorted features and began to scream.

A week had passed since their assault on Sappo's quarters. Now *Pegasus* was closing in on asteroid FA 6789-X. It was better known as the Dump, and from what McCade could see via his long-range optics, the name fit. FA 6789-X had once served as an Imperial supply dump, a staging area for some long-forgotten mission, an airless lump of rock to be used and then abandoned.

A long list of temporary residents had come and gone since then, including a succession of miners, an eccentric loner or two, and most recently Mustapha Pong. Or so Morris Sappo claimed.

And McCade was inclined to believe him. For one thing Sappo was scared, and for another he was sitting in the ship's lounge where Neem could reach out and touch him, something the human would do anything to avoid.

Sappo had some rather deep-seated religious beliefs stemming from his childhood on Regor II. There his parents had attempted to beat an understanding of good and evil into his scrawny little body, and even though they'd failed, they had managed to warp his mind. So even though Sappo knew that Neem wasn't the devil, the Il Ronnian's demonic appearance still turned him into a babbling idiot. And babbling idiots can be extremely cooperative.

Thanks to a cooperative Sappo, they'd been able to lift from Tin Town without interference, and without payment for the considerable damage they'd caused. So when Sappo said that Pong made regular use of the Dump, McCade believed him.

The only problem was that McCade couldn't tell if the pirate was in residence or not. McCade spoke without taking his eyes off the screen. "Reba, cycle through the sensors one more time."

"Okay," she replied. "But it won't do much good. There's so much junk on the ground that you could hide the Imperial fleet down there."

Reba was right, of course. The original supply dump had centered around a cluster of domes. When the navy pulled out, all sorts of junk was left behind. Broken-down crawlers, gantries, and other less identifiable chunks of equipment lay all over the place. As the years passed, other tenants had added their debris to the pile so that a jungle of wrecked ships, scrap metal, and other junk filled a good-sized crater.

As a result there was enough metal on Dump to put all of McCade's metal detectors onto eternal alert. On top of that were radiation leaks from junked drives, a lot of vague static, and residual heat emanating from God knows what. It could mean nothing or everything. There was no way to tell.

Reba looked up from her sensors. "Sorry, Sam. There's too much input. If Pong's there, I can't pick his ship out of the background clutter."

McCade nodded and stuck an unlit cigar between his teeth. He could land and risk falling into a trap or stay a safe distance away and wait for something to happen. A day? A week? A month? It made little difference because he couldn't afford to use any time at all. Unless he found the Vial of Tears, and found it damn soon, entire planets would begin to burn.

"Strap in, everybody. We're going down."

It was a simple approach. FA 6789-X had a nice predictable orbit with just the right amount of spin to generate light gravity.

The problem was where to land. The crater was so full of junk that there wasn't much open space left. That seemed to suggest a landing outside the crater's perimeter, but if he did that, *Pegasus* would stick out like a Zord at a Finthian tree dance. And if Pong returned, he'd see the little ship and destroy it. That left the crater, junk or no junk. It might be a tight fit, but once down *Pegasus* would fade into the background. In fact, they could lay an ambush for Pong if that seemed advisable.

As the asteroid grew larger in his viewscreens, McCade swung *Pegasus* to the right and used his repellors to skim across the crater. "Keep a sharp lookout, Reba. Let me know if you see anything funny."

But Reba was silent as they passed over the forest of junk. Light dusted the tops of things and sparkled off the billions of dust motes that were stirred up by the ship's repellors. But outside of the ship itself nothing moved or gave McCade reason to run.

McCade put *Pegasus* down in the shadow of a huge ore processor. It was a tight fit between that and a pile of metal scaffolding, but he made it. He used the ship's sensors to take one last look around. Nothing. If Pong were present, surely he'd have reacted by now.

McCade released his harness, stuck the cigar in a pocket, and followed Reba out of the control room.

Neem, Sappo, and Ceex were already in the lounge when they arrived, so the tiny space was full to overflowing. Now that they were down McCade was anxious to look around.

"All right. With the exception of Ceex, I want everyone suited up. Yes, Sappo, that means you. If anything unpleasant happens to us while we're out there, it's gonna happen to you too."

"Ceex, I want you to stay aboard *Pegasus* and man the weapons systems. If anything moves, blast it."

"Maybe he should "Il Ronnian" the weapons systems instead," Neem suggested with a smile.

"Give me a break, Neem. That okay with you, Ceex?"

The cyborg nodded. Half his face was a mass of melted plastic that dripped downward like wax from a candle. The other half wore a twisted smile.

They'd done the best they could for him, but the truth was that his injuries required the attentions of a fully equipped cyberlab, and an Il Ronnian cyberlab at that. But Ceex had insisted that he be allowed to come along, and this way he'd be useful without slowing them down.

"All right then," McCade said. "Let's suit up and take a look around. I want everyone to carry an extra oxygen supply and a blast rifle. There's no telling what we might run into out there and we may want to stay awhile."

Forty-five minutes later McCade scrambled down to the ground and took a look around. Huge pieces of equipment formed a metal maze on every side. There were thousands of hiding places and everyone of them could harbor an ambush. But why bother? McCade thought to himself. If Pong's here, we would have seen him by now.

They had chosen the original domes as their destination. According to Sappo, that's where Pong stored some of his loot between raids, and if they decided to lay an ambush for him, that would be the place to do it.

McCade and Reba took the point with Sappo following along behind and Neem bringing up the rear. Constrained as he was by McCade's leg shackles, Sappo couldn't move very fast but that was fine. The rest of them were loaded down with extra oxygen and weapons so they weren't moving very fast either. But the light gravity helped as did a certain amount of fear.

It was spooky in and among the junk. Their movements carried them from heavy shadow to bright sunlight and back again. It took very little imagination to turn twisted pieces of metal into homicidal aliens.

Once, McCade thought that he saw a weapons turret on a junked shuttle turn to track them, but when he stopped to look again, he saw that it was just the way the light had moved across its surface.

And twice he thought he saw movement, first between two hydroponics tanks, and then through the canopy of an old crane.

On both occasions he used his radio to ask Ceex for confirmation, but the cyborg hadn't seen anything and swore that all of his sensors were clear.

Over the years a number of natural paths had evolved in and between the larger pieces of junk. These were well marked by crawler tracks, but it was impossible to tell how recently they'd been used. Without the effects of weather to wash them away, many were probably twenty or thirty years old.

Finally the domes loomed up ahead. One had been crushed by a badly piloted ore barge years before, one had been stripped for use somewhere else, and three appeared to be in reasonably good shape.

McCade and Reba approached the first of these while Neem and Sappo hung back. Its surface was checkered with solar cells, beat exchangers, and other less-obvious equipment. Crude patches were visible here and there where someone had modified the dome for a particular use and someone else had come along to restore it.

They circled the dome by carefully working their way along the wall until they reached the main door. It was wide open. Stepping inside McCade saw endless rows of empty shelves. There was something about them, something about the used pallets scattered here and there, and the multitude of tracks that ran every which way that suggested recent use. Had Pong emptied the warehouse? And if so, why?

"Sam! Reba! You'd better get out here!" The voice belonged to Neem.

They came at a fast trot and the moment he got outside McCade saw the problem. It was rather hard to miss. Though not huge, a light cruiser is a large ship and this one was hovering about a hundred feet over the crater. It was roughly triangular in shape and was covered with weapons turrets, torpedo launchers, and a host of other installations. Though too large to land on most planets, the absence of an atmosphere and the asteroid's lighter gravity permitted the ship to come in close.

"The damn thing was hiding in the junk on the far side of the crater," Neem said grimly. "One moment it wasn't there and the next moment it was."

McCade chinned his mike. "Don't try it, Ceex, you don't have a . . ." but he could have saved his breath.

Ceex opened up with everything he had, but it was like a zit bug taking on an Envo Beast. *Pegasus* was heavily armed for a ship her size, but the larger ship's defensive screen shrugged off her puny attack as if it hadn't even happened and then responded in kind.

Huge energy projectors burped blue light and *Pegasus* exploded into a million pieces. They seemed to fall forever due to the asteroid's light gravity and hit with exaggerated force.

McCade simply stood there completely helpless while his ship and a trusted comrade died in front of his eyes.

There was a burst of static in McCade's helmet followed by a voice he'd never heard before. "Welcome to the Dump. I'm Mustapha Pong, and unless you do exactly what I say, you will die."

TWENTY-FIVE

McCade had never felt so helpless. The cruiser hung above them like some dark god, untouchable and omnipotent. With no atmosphere to conduct the sound of its repellors, the ship seemed all the more awesome and mysterious. Pong's voice filled McCade's helmet.

"Which one of you is Sam McCade? Raise your right arm."

McCade gulped and raised his right arm. There was little point in doing otherwise. If he chose to, Pong could turn the entire crater into a lake of molten metal.

A spear of white light flashed down to pin McCade against the ground. His heart stopped beating while he checked to make sure that he was still alive. With a sigh of relief he realized that it was nothing more than a spotlight.

"Good. Now tell me why you're here, and I warn you, McCade, do not waste my time. If you tell the truth, I will allow you and your friends to live. If you lie, or attempt to mislead me, I will know and our conversation will end rather abruptly. Do you understand?"

McCade understood. He understood that in spite of Pong's threats he should say as little as possible. The question was how much did Pong know? It couldn't be much or he'd have killed them by now. No, Pong was curious. He knew McCade was trying to find him and wanted to know why. He knew about Sappo's abduction but little else.

Thank God! If Pong knew about the vial and understood its value, he'd try to auction it off to the highest bidder, use it to extort money from the Il Ronn, or God knows what else.

McCade swallowed to lubricate a dry throat. "The answer's quite simple. The Brotherhood is offering five hundred thousand credits for your head, and I'm a little short on cash. Surrender peacefully and they'll go easy on you."

There was a long silence. And then, just as McCade was preparing to die, there was a loud laughter. When Pong spoke again, there was merriment in his voice.

"McCade, you're something else. You said the one thing that could save your life, and you said it with a certain amount of style. I like that. I like it so much that I'll let you live. Providing of course that you return my property."

McCade frowned and looked around helplessly. "What property is that? I wasn't aware that I had anything that belonged to you."

There was a burst of static followed by Pong's chuckle. "Oh, but you do. Unless I'm very much mistaken that's my good friend Morris standing over there, and while he's been a little too talkative of late, I'd like to offer him a ride home."

Another shaft of light lanced down to bathe Sappo in white. He waved enthusiastically to the ship and shuffled in a circle.

"Just follow the light, Morris, and a shuttle will pick you up."

The spotlight moved off toward the area where they'd landed and Sappo followed.

Something landed in McCade's stomach with a heavy thud. He chinned his mike. "Neem, Reba, move toward me and do it *now.*"

Meanwhile Sappo hurried toward the white circle and came to a sudden halt when the light stopped moving. "That's far enough, Morris," Pong said sweetly. "I lied . . . and you know what that means."

Sappo looked around with desperate eyes searching for someplace to hide, someone to help. "Please, Mustapha, don't do this, they made me tell."

"Oh, really?" Pong asked quietly. "Are your eyes hanging down onto your cheeks? Are you walking on broken feet? Has every tooth been pulled from your lying mouth? If you can show me those injuries, I will spare you and tend your wounds with my own hands."

Sappo made no reply but tried to run. Due to his leg shackles he didn't get very far. A single burp of blue energy consumed Sappo, space armor and all, leaving nothing more than some scorched rock and a puddle of molten metal. In less than a second Sappo's shackles had been transformed into a marker for his grave.

"Good-bye, McCade. I hereby cede the Dump and all that it contains to you and your friends. Like Morris, it has ceased to be useful."

McCade chinned his mike. "In ten or twelve hours we'll run out of air."

Pong chuckled. "I said I'd let you live, but I didn't say for how long. Besides, as Morris just found out, I lie a lot. Bye."

And with that the cruiser drifted over the domes. Blue beams flashed down to burn huge holes in each structure. Then the ship engaged its main drives, lifted, and disappeared over the horizon.

"The bastard!" Reba shook her fist at the point where the ship had vanished.

McCade had never felt as depressed as he did at that particular moment. They'd come close, damned close, and now it was over. Not just for them, but for the millions, the billions, who would die in the coming war. But before he could pursue that line of thought a strange voice filled his helmet.

"Testing . . . testing . . . can you hear me? Hello, can anybody hear me?"

"I can hear you," McCade replied. "Who are you? Where are you?"

"I call myself Henry," the voice replied. "Although my manual says I'm a NAVCOMP IN7808/L. But that seemed so impersonal I decided to name myself after a great navigator called Henry."

"It's a nice name," McCade agreed. "Although Henry had a tendency to hang around Portugal while other folks did the actual navigating."

McCade looked around and tried to spot where the voice might be coming from. "So you're a robot?"

"Certainly not!" Henry replied, obviously offended. "A NAVCOMP IN7808/L is a far cry from some piece of animated junk. I'm a top of the line navigational computer, and proud of it. Pong didn't like me, and well, I thought we could be friends."

"Sounds good to me," McCade replied. "Where are you? Let's shake on it."

"Right here," Henry said as a birdlike creature stalked out of the shadows. Something about its jerky walk reminded McCade of the movement he'd spotted earlier.

Henry had a cylindrical body and three skinny legs. Two arms stuck out at odd angles, one of which boasted a three-fingered hand, the other being equipped with some sort of complicated tool. He had a long flexible neck that extended out and up from his cylindrical body to a ball-like head. An antenna stuck straight out in front to suggest a beak and thereby cement Henry's resemblance to a bird.

McCade extended his right hand and found Henry's grip to be surprisingly delicate. "I'm Sam McCade. That's Reba, and the taller one is Neem. It's a pleasure to meet you, Henry."

"Likewise I'm sure," Henry replied politely. "Hello, Reba, hello, Neem. I'm sorry about your ship. Had I known you were good people I would have warned you, but I thought you were part of Pong's security forces. They try to hunt me down every now and then."

"They tried to hunt you down?" Reba asked. "Whatever for?"

Henry's head drooped toward his metal chest. "They want to terminate me. I was the navigational computer aboard Pong's ship until I made a mistake and miscalculated a hyperspace jump. No one was hurt, and everything turned out just fine, but Pong was angry and had me junked. He said I was stupid, but it wasn't my fault. I told the maintenance tech to check a short in my number four logic sequencer, but he said it could wait."

"So Pong threw you on the scrap heap?"

"That's right," Henry replied, "but I didn't stay there. I was wearing my control console body when they threw me outside. It includes my head and one articulated limb that I use for routine maintenance."

"I still don't understand why they'd try and terminate you," Reba said. "Why bother?"

"I don't know," Henry replied simply. "I guess Pong thought I'd die out here and when I didn't he got mad. Anyway I managed to drag myself into this labyrinth of junk where I went to work on building myself a new body. Bodies actually, since I now have three, each being dedicated to a different purpose. They tend to be a bit asymmetrical since I cobbled them together from junk, but appearances aren't everything. This is the body I use for working on the ship. What do you think?" Henry turned himself around like a model on a runway.

"Very nice," McCade said approvingly. "Did you say something about a ship?" He tried to conceal his eagerness but failed.

"Ship? Oh, yes, the ship. Well, a NAVCOMP IN7808/L isn't worth much without a ship, so I've been repairing an old freighter I found. I can't imagine how they got it here. After I revived the ship's NAVCOMP, I learned it was re-tarded. Poor thing, I put it to sleep."

"I see," McCade replied, not quite sure whether he approved or not. "How long before your ship's ready to lift?"

"With some help I could do it in three or four standards, without help a couple of weeks, a month max."

"If we helped, would you give us a lift?"

"I'd give you a lift even if you didn't help," Henry replied cheerfully. "Though partially sentient, I'm also programmed to help humans, especially where matters of navigation are concerned."

"Excellent," McCade said, his spirits rising. "You've got yourself a crew."

Reba cleared her throat. "Aren't you forgetting something, Sam? You know, the stuff we breathe?"

"Oxygen?" Henry asked. "I don't use the stuff myself, but there's lots of it around." He gestured toward the surrounding junk with his three-fingered hand. "I come across it all the time."

"Well, then," Neem put in. "What are we waiting for? Let's repair the ship and haul rectum."

"Neem that's . . . oh, never mind," McCade said. "Let's do it."

It took three standard days of extremely hard work to ready the freighter for space, and even then the word "ready" was more optimism than reality.

McCade had never seen a ship exactly like it, and guessed the freighter was around a hundred years old. The last twenty or so of those years had been spent in the crater, and thanks to the surrounding vacuum, there'd been little or no deterioration to its hull.

She'd been chock full of number nine core drills when Henry found her. Someone had removed her drives, her weapons systems, and her old-fashioned hydroponics lab before converting her into a warehouse. But her hull was sound, her control systems were intact, and her auxiliary systems were still functional, so Henry went to work.

The first step was to unload the number nine core drills. Even with the asteroid's gravity this was quite a task since each drill weighed about eight hundred pounds. To deal with the situation Henry constructed a body small enough to negotiate the ship's narrow hatches but strong enough to pick up core drills four at a time. It looked like a cross between a fork lift and an all-terrain vehicle.

Once the core drills were removed Henry had systematically checked out every inch of the ship's wiring, run diagnostics on its antiquated subprocessors, and effected repairs wherever he could.

The next step was to find a drive, not just any drive, but one which would fit inside the little ship and could be linked to its ancient systems.

It took Henry the better part of a month to find the drive. And when he did it was in a lifeboat for a much larger ship. Like most lifeboats this one echoed the vessel it was built to serve. It was therefore almost as large as the freighter itself, and while it was twenty years newer, its systems were still compatible. Lifeboat design always seemed to lag behind everything else and for once that worked in someone's favor.

Tests proved that the drive was in fairly good shape but there was still a problem. The lifeboat was trapped under the wreckage of a mobile refinery that hadn't been mobile for ten years or more. And that's the problem that faced his new friends. How to move the refinery and get at the lifeboat's drive?

Difficult though the task was it could have been worse. They could move around freely now that Pong was gone and thanks to the accumulated junk there was plenty of stuff to work with.

First they went from wreck to wreck searching for, and finding, enough oxygen to last them a week or more. Once it was safely transferred to some portable storage tanks they were ready for the task at hand.

Both McCade and Neem were handy enough, but it was Reba who shouldered most of the load. She had a natural aptitude for things mechanical and it was she who repaired a large winch, ran more than two miles of durasteel cable through a series of improvised pulleys, and lifted the refinery clear.

And having done so, it was Reba who worked hand-in-hand with Henry to remove the lifeboat's drive and install it in the freighter.

McCade worked hard as well, but his tasks were more routine and left him time to think. And the more he thought, the more he believed that they still had a chance. If so, Henry would be the key.

But there was no point in discussing something like that until the ship was repaired.

Time passed, work went on, and final tests were run. Then as the drive hummed, and the main accumulators built up a charge, he popped the question.

The control room was the only part of the ship that would still hold an atmosphere and the three of them were sitting around with their helmets off. Since none of them had bathed in three days, the stink was terrible, but it felt good to escape the close confinement of their helmets. "Henry . . . I've got a question for you."

Henry had reverted to his smaller control module configuration and popped out of the console like a prairie dog coming out of its hole. He waved his single arm by way of a greeting. "Sure, Sam. What's up?"

"Does Pong have another base?"

"Yes he does," Henry said matter-of-factly. "His main base is in the heart of the Nakasoni Asteroid Belt. As a matter of fact this asteroid is located on the outer fringes of the great Nakasoni, which is why Pong used it. He needed a place where his business associates could come and go without learning the location of his home base."

Both Reba and Neem were suddenly paying attention. Neem was staring at Henry with an intensity that would've made a human somewhat nervous. "And the course to Pong's base . . . do you know it?"

Henry looked from Neem to McCade and back again. "Of course I know it . . . I'm a NAVCOMP IN7808/L, aren't I?"

TWENTY-SIX

There was zero G inside the ship and that made the space sled easy to handle. McCade used small squirts of nitrogen to hold it in place as he waited for the hatch to open.

Outside, the Nakasoni Asteroid Belt stretched off for thousands of miles. And somewhere inside that vast drift of tumbling planetoids was Pong's secret base and, with any luck at all, the Vial of Tears.

McCade fought back the fatigue that threatened to roll over him and tongued another stim tab. This was number five, or was it six? It was hard to tell since the last few days had become one long blur of nonstop effort.

Sleep. He'd give anything to sleep, but sleep takes time, and time was slipping away. If they moved now, and if the plan worked, there was still a chance to recover the vial and prevent war.

Pong had done pretty well for himself since deserting the Brotherhood, but he'd made some mistakes too. The first was his decision to junk Henry, the second was his murder of Ceex, the third was his destruction of *Pegasus*, and the fourth was leaving McCade alive after committing the first three.

The hatch was wide open now. It served to frame the nearer asteroids and the starfield beyond. There were thousands of asteroids out there, ranging in size from small ones a mile or so in diameter, to larger specimens, some of which were five hundred times that size. And, just to keep things interesting, the asteroids were in constant motion relative to the sun and each other. So, if you didn't know the right way in, you could have one helluva time finding your way out, and that wasn't all. There could be man-made hazards as well.

And that's why Henry and he were about to undertake a one NAVCOMP, one man scouting mission.

McCade chinned his mike. "Thinks for the lift. Don't bother to see us out, we know the way."

"That's a roger," Reba replied. "Neem sends his best. You two take care of yourselves. We'll meet you here in two standards, *Methuselah* willing."

Every ship should have a name, and since the freighter was old, more than a little crotchety, and very dependent on the goodwill of a supreme being, *Methuselah* had seemed perfect.

They had a plan although the word "plan" implied more order and logic than seemed apparent now. The heady realization that Henry could lead them to Pong's hidden base had been followed by an equally sobering discovery.

Henry knew how to get there, but he didn't remember what sort of defenses they might encounter, how many ships Pong had under his command, or anything else of military value.

As a partially sentient computer Henry was largely self-programming. That meant that while he had a predetermined "purpose" he was free to decide which areas of knowledge might be useful to the fulfillment of his mission and which wouldn't. And although Henry didn't like to admit it, the size of his memory was limited, and that forced him to make choices about what he'd remember and what he wouldn't. And while he'd stored away the long strings of numbers necessary to find his way through the great Nakasoni to Pong's base, he hadn't seen fit to memorize whatever defenses lay along the path. On a large cruiser those matters were the province of other computers and not his concern.

So the decision was made to equip a modified space sled with extra oxygen that would allow McCade to scout the path into the asteroid belt. Henry would come along to guide him in and out again.

In the meantime Reba and Neem would take a short hyperspace jump to the nearest Imperial outpost and request help. Marshaling whatever forces were available, they would return and rendezvous with McCade and Henry. An assault on Pong's base would follow.

That was the plan anyway, and it might even work. If it didn't, McCade would spend eternity circling Cypra II with a few thousand asteroids for company.

Even though his part of the plan was fairly chancy, McCade wondered if Reba and Neem's was even worse. After all, a hyperspace shift involves a certain amount of risk even in a well-maintained ship, and *Methuselah* was anything but "well maintained."

One malfunction and they'd end up in a place that mathematicians were still arguing about. It wasn't a pleasant prospect.

When Reba spoke it seemed as if she were reading his mind. "If we don't show up, feel free to go ahead without us."

"Gee, thanks," McCade replied dryly.

"How's the Geezer?" The voice belonged to Henry. Having resurrected the freighter's moronic NAVCOMP, he'd named it "the Geezer. " All the Geezer had to do was plot a single jump, but Henry still didn't trust him.

"The Geezer's lookin' good," Reba said. "He just cycled his self-diagnostics and says he's in great shape. Says he'll be plotting jumps long after you've been recycled into a coffee pot."

Henry gave a snort of derision but lapsed into silence as McCade squeezed both handgrips and launched the tiny sled into the vastness of space. After putting some distance between himself and the ship, McCade released the left grip for a second and then both grips together. The sled turned left and drifted forward on inertia alone.

Methuselah was a black shadow against the stars beyond. "I'm clear."

"Roger," Reba replied. "Take care, Sam. We'll see you soon."

McCade watched as Reba fed power to the ship's single drive and *Methuselah* merged with the blackness of space.

A vast loneliness welled up inside McCade as he watched the ship disappear. Without his companions he was smaller somehow, the smallest and least significant microorganism in the vast ocean of space, and almost completely helpless.

It was Henry who snapped him out of it. The NAVCOMP was attired in a modified version of his control console body. He still resembled a round metal ball with a single articulated limb, but he'd added a small solar collector to augment his battery power, and some wiring to access the sled's primitive control system. He was strapped down beneath McCade's seat.

Henry would take the controls from here on out, freeing McCade to observe and watch for trouble. One of five sleds they'd found stored away in a ruined dome, theirs was designed for external ship repairs or ship-to-ship errands. As such it had no hull, no weapons, and no padding for the skeletal seats.

McCade shifted his weight and tried to find a more comfortable position. His skin was raw where the suit had rubbed against it for the last four days, he had a nonstop urge to scratch places he couldn't reach, and even after the stim tab he was still bone-tired.

"Sam, if you'll release the controls, I'll take over."

McCade released the controls. "You've got the con, Henry . . . take it away."

And Henry did. Using the sled's rudimentary sensors to see where he was going, the NAVCOMP brought the sled up to half speed and headed into the asteroid belt.

The ride quickly became one of the most exhilarating and terrifying trips of McCade's life. He'd taken a number of short trips into open space, some on sleds and some in armor alone. But he'd never gone farther than a few miles and help had always been seconds away. Now he was setting off on a journey of hundreds, maybe thousands, of miles, and doing it through a twisting, turning maze of asteroids.

Although miles apart, many of the asteroids were in sight of each other, and that added to the sensation of movement as McCade passed between them. Time lost all its meaning as the hours rolled swiftly by and the readouts for his oxygen tanks steadily unwound.

Distant specks of reflected light grew larger and larger until they blocked the starfield beyond and hurtled by a few hundred feet to one side or the other. Bright sunlight slid across the surface of slowly tumbling asteroids creating an endless dance of light and dark. It was beautiful, so beautiful that McCade became lost in the majesty of it, and almost missed the first sensor station.

All he had was the momentary impression of light glinting off a metal surface and then it was gone. "Slow down, Henry, and make a note that we just passed some sort of sensor emplacement. Chances are there's more up ahead."

And there were. Moving more cautiously now, Henry eased his way between the asteroids, giving McCade a chance to spot the sensors. They came at regular intervals and each installation looked the same. They consisted of a metal box crammed with electronics, a flowerlike solar collector, and a thicket of shiny antennas.

Thanks to the sensors Pong would receive a running progress report on any ships approaching or leaving his base. When the attack came he'd have lots of warning. It couldn't be helped though. There were way too many emplacements for McCade to destroy by himself, and even if he found a way to do it, the act itself would be a warning.

There was also the possibility that the sensors had picked up the sled and were tracking it all the way. But the sled had very little mass, no radio signature, and its nitrogen-gas propulsion system didn't put out any heat.

So, unless he began a series of loops and barrel rolls, the sensors would probably ignore him. Since this was an asteroid belt, pieces of flying junk were a centime a dozen.

Suddenly the asteroid belt began to close in on itself. Now the rocks were only miles apart, and even though Henry had slowed the sled to a virtual crawl, they seemed to flash by at incredible speed.

Then McCade saw them, one, two, three weapons emplacements up ahead, all positioned to place ships in a cross fire as they came through the narrow passage.

Speaking in a quiet monotone, McCade began to feed Henry information. The NAVCOMP would put it together with the relevant navigational coordinates and produce a detailed report on Pong's defenses.

"The outer ring of weapons emplacements appear to be automated," McCade noted, "since there's no sign of associated living quarters. There could be concealed living quarters somewhere underground of course, but I don't think so. There's none of the junk that seems to pile up when sentients are about.

"Now we're passing through the narrowest part of the passageway. I don't see any fortifications here. That makes sense because opposing emplacements would end up firing on each other.

"Now things are loosening up a bit, wait a minute there's something shiny up ahead; uh-oh, I see emplacements on all the surrounding asteroids. Some are controlled by automatics but some appear to be manned.

"The passageway is wider now and opens up a few miles ahead. There's a large sphere-shaped open space with densely packed asteroids forming the outer surface. In toward the center I see a few free-floating asteroids, and there, right in the middle, I see a reflective surface. It's big, not as big as the larger asteroids, but damned big just the same.

"We're getting closer now . . . I'll be damned . . . it's a ship! Not just *any* ship but a liner. And not just any liner but the *Earth Star*! I'd recognize that H-shaped hull anywhere. It seems she wasn't lost in hyperspace like everyone thought. Pong got her instead. God knows what happened to her passengers and crew.

"This is good enough, Henry . . . put us alongside that chunk of rock over there. This close in they'll be watching the smaller stuff too. Good. Now, starting with the *Earth Star* and working my way around to the right, I see all sorts of ships. I see a DE, three heavy cruisers, two light cruisers, another DE, six, make that seven destroyers, two armed freighters, an ore barge, two hulks, and a tug.

"Based on visible running lights and jet flares I'd say there's plenty of small craft running around and some of them are probably armed. There's no way to tell if he's got any interceptors loaded aboard the *Earth Star* or the cruisers but chances are that he does. In addition, I see that one of the nearby island type asteroids has been equipped as a Class C dockyard. I think there's a ship in the yard but I can't tell what kind. Got all that, Henry?"

"I've got it, Sam. What now?"

"Now we turn around and get while the getting's good."

Henry obediently turned the sled away from the free-floating chunk of rock and headed back toward the passageway. They hadn't gone more than half a mile before a bored-sounding voice boomed in through McCade's speakers.

"Hey, buddy, what the hell do you think you're doing?"

McCade felt his heart jump into his throat as he tried to see where the voice was coming from. There it was about a hundred feet away, a sleek, little four-place gig, complete with an ugly-looking energy projector mounted in its bow. Its approach had been hidden by the same rock he and Henry had used. He swallowed hard.

"Doin'? I'm lookin' for a number three laser welder, that's what I'm doin'. You haven't seen it, have you? Big sucker with three tanks and a safety frame. Belongs to the dockyard."

The same voice again. "I know what a number three laser welder looks like, you blockhead. How did it get away?"

McCade added a whine to his voice. "It wasn't my fault, honest. Logan, he's the lead on my shift, he told me to bring him some insulation. When I went to get it, the welder just floated away."

"And he sent you out here looking for it?"

"That's right. Logan said to find it, or to plan on sucking some vacuum."

The voice laughed. "Well, buddy . . . the welder isn't likely to be this far out. And that being the case, I suggest you get your butt back toward the dock. Maybe next time you'll remember to rig a safety line. *Comprendez?*"

"*Comprendez,*" McCade replied humbly as he took the controls from Henry. He put the sled into a long graceful turn and tried to figure out his next move.

A glance to the rear showed that the gig was still there. If they attempted to contact the non-existent Logan, he'd be well and truly screwed.

Turning forward, he saw something part company with the dockyard and move slowly his way. A ship! As it altered course and headed for the passageway, an idea started to form.

Looking back he saw the gig was gone. Good. Putting the sled on an intercepting course he mentally crossed his fingers. *If* the ship maintained its present course and speed, *if* its crew missed him on their scanners, and *if* the gig failed to reappear, his plan would work. It seemed like a lot of ifs.

Neither the ship nor the sled were moving very fast but their combined speed was fairly high. Given that, and given the fact that if he missed a head-on approach, he wouldn't get a second chance, McCade decided to come in from behind. That way it would be easier to match speeds and there would be less chance of being seen. When you're leaving port there's a natural tendency to look at what's up ahead rather than behind.

As he got closer McCade saw the ship was an armed merchantman. Chances were it had been captured and converted for use as a raider. He put the sled into a tight turn and gave chase. As he straightened the sled out, he saw that the raider was already pulling away from him.

McCade squeezed both handgrips and felt the sled surge forward. The forward motion pushed him into his seat and put pressure on some of his worst sore spots. McCade bit his lip and forced his mind back to the task at hand.

Up ahead the pirate ship grew steadily larger. If they maintained their present rate of speed, he'd be okay, but if they piled on some power, he'd be out of luck. The sled was going full out as it was, and if the pirates upped the ante, he'd never catch up. Not only that, but at the rate he was using nitrogen, he might not have enough to make the trip back.

Angling in to stay clear of the ship's drives, McCade held his breath. Now the raider was huge, blotting out the stars beyond, its black hull absorbing almost all the available light.

Dark though it was McCade saw that the hull was fairly smooth, typical of smaller ships that could negotiate planetary atmospheres, and far from ideal. While the smooth hull would help him land, it would also make him easier to see.

Closer . . . closer . . . almost there, now. The sled touched down with a gentle thump. McCade triggered the electro-magnets embedded in its skids as the sled made contact with the ship's hull. The sled would remain locked in place as long as the power lasted.

"Nice job," Henry said in his ear. "Your navigation lacks a certain mathematical elegance, but it gets the job done."

"Thanks," McCade replied. "Now let's see if anyone noticed us getting aboard. Things might become somewhat unpleasant if they did."

Five minutes passed, ten minutes passed, and finally a full half hour passed. During this time the ship continued to accelerate toward the passage, and McCade began to relax. If the pirates hadn't spotted him by now, he figured they never would.

It felt good to relax. McCade felt suddenly tired. The hard work, the tension, and the succession of stim tabs seemed to catch up with him all at once. "Henry, I'm going to take a little nap. Wake me up when we're half an hour from the rendezvous point."

"You've got it, Sam," Henry replied cheerfully. "Sweet dreams . . . whatever dreams are."

McCade awoke with a struggle. It seemed as if he were far, far away, lost in some place where the air was sweet and his body didn't hurt. He wanted to stay there, tried to stay there, but the voice dragged him back.

"Sam, it's time to wake up, Sam . . ."

The first thing he noticed was the lack of vibration. The ship was gone and he was floating in space but where?

"We're at the rendezvous point," Henry said, anticipating his question. "Rather than wake you up I released the magnets and left the ship about ten standard hours ago."

"Ten standard hours . . ." McCade's eyes flew open. Ten standard hours plus, my God, damn near two days in the belt—what about his oxygen? McCade looked at the readout and saw that he was into the emergency reserve.

"What the hell are you doing, Henry? Why didn't you wake me? I'll be sucking vacuum in a few minutes."

"True," Henry said agreeably. "But I thought it would be rather cruel to wake you up just to point that out. Fortunately you don't need to worry. Take a look around."

McCade looked up and out. Ships. He was surrounded by ships. And not just any ships but a strange mix of vessels. Imperial destroyers next to Il Ronnian cruisers, next to—could it be? Yes, it looked as if the Brotherhood was represented as well, their ships being huddled together as if wary of the rest.

Then he heard Swanson-Pierce's familiar voice boom in over his speakers. "Hello, Sam. While the sled suits your personality to a T, you might want something a little more substantial around you when the shooting starts. How about a drink and a good cigar?"

TWENTY-SEVEN

The assault boat was brand-new. It looked new, it felt new, it even smelled new. McCade was doing his best to change that with a freshly lit cigar.

Reba wrinkled her nose from the copilot's seat and Neem coughed loudly from behind.

McCade didn't notice. Together with the fifty marines riding shotgun in the back, they were about to lead an assault on Pong's base, and his attention was focused on staying alive. As the first boat in, that would be difficult enough without any electronic or mechanical failures.

McCade scanned the indicator lights in groups. Hull integrity, locks sealed, no leaks. Drives on and green. Communications on and green. Jammers on and amber. Countermeasures on and amber. Chaff launchers on and amber. Weapons, primary and secondary, on and amber. They all looked good but McCade decided to cycle the boat's diagnostics one more time just to make sure.

"Henry, let's run the diagnostics one more time," McCade instructed. "If anything's belly up, let's find out about it now."

"That's a roger," Henry answered crisply. Henry had taken on a slightly military air ever since he'd been asked to download the assault path to the rest of the fleet's NAVCOMPs. Not satisfied to serve in any other boat, he'd disappeared into the control panel and taken over from the resident computer. What *it* thought of this arrangement nobody knew.

McCade checked the boat's main battle tank. The fleet made an impressive sight. It resembled a snake, shimmering with electronic scales, each one a ship. McCade's boat was located at the tip of the snake's nose, followed by a delta-shaped head full of interceptors and a long, thick body swarming with destroyers and cruisers.

It was a powerful force but a strange one. Behind his A-boat, Il Ronnian and Imperial interceptors jockeyed for position, each eager to lead the way, each determined to outshine the other.

Farther back pirate destroyers vied with Imperial cruisers for the honor of going in first while an Il Ronnian Star Sept Commander tried to pull rank on both.

It was one of the strangest military alliances ever put together and a rather temporary one at that. The Imperial Navy was attempting to avoid a galactic war, the Il Ronnians were trying to recover the Vial of Tears, and the Brotherhood was afraid of getting caught in the middle. And everyone would go their separate ways the moment their objectives were achieved.

In the meantime the partnership made sense.

Methuselah had practically fallen out of hyperspace seconds ahead of a major control systems failure. Fortunately the old ship emerged almost on top of the Imperial naval base that the Geezer had been instructed to find. Hours later *Methuselah* was in the friendly grasp of a naval tug and on its way to the Kodula Naval Base.

Once in orbit Neem and Reba were rushed down to the surface where they were interviewed by the base commander. And much to Reba's amazement Commander Moreno took their story seriously, fired off a message torp to sector headquarters, and began to organize the few forces she had available.

Like every other senior officer within Imperial space, Moreno had orders to provide someone named Sam McCade with anything he wanted. And the *anything* had been underlined.

The orders didn't mention pirates and Il Ronnians, but Moreno lumped them under *anything* and did what they asked. That included provision of two message torpedoes that were launched toward destinations outside of Imperial space.

Doing so required a certain amount of professional courage on Moreno's part, courage that was severely tested when a small fleet of Il Ronnian ships suddenly left hyperspace and dropped into orbit around her planet.

Within a few minutes the alien was busy gabbing with an Il Ronnian big shot named Teeb, her XO was on the verge of having a heart attack, and Moreno was wondering if she'd committed a serious error.

Fortunately the next group of ships to arrive brought Admiral Swanson-Pierce with them. Otherwise the subsequent manifestation of pirate ships would have shaken even Moreno's considerable poise.

But Swanson-Pierce listened to Moreno's report, promoted her to full captain, and proceeded to invite the senior members of all three groups to dinner.

After a report by the Reba woman and the Il Ronnian civilian, everyone agreed to a joint assault on Pong's base and hoisted a few to seal the bargain. It was then that Moreno learned that Il Ronnians can not only handle alcohol, they can do so in prodigious quantities.

Now the mixed fleet was awaiting orders from a cashiered naval officer/ bounty hunter who claimed to know a secret passage through the thickest part of the Nakasoni Asteroid Belt. If it wasn't the craziest thing Moreno had ever heard of, it certainly ran a close second. However there was no sign of these thoughts on her handsome face when she turned to Admiral Swanson-Pierce and gave her report.

"There's still a little squabbling toward the rear of the formation, Admiral, but ninety percent of our units are where they're supposed to be, and all things considered that's pretty good. We stand ready to attack on your command."

For a naval officer who was about to risk his career on what most of his peers would consider an insane mission, Swanson-Pierce looked very relaxed. He leaned back in his command chair and smiled. "Not this time, Captain. This is McCade's show, and he won't raise the curtain without an attempt to irritate me first."

Unlike McCade's cramped assault boat, the bridge of the cruiser *Tenacious* was both spacious and comfortable. Pilots, electronic warfare specialists, and weapons officers tended their various boards with the quiet reverence of priests before an altar. All wore space armor in case of a sudden loss of cabin pressure.

A com tech appeared at Moreno's side. "I've got a com call from A-boat One on channel three, Admiral. Will you take it?"

Swanson-Pierce grinned at Moreno. "See?"

Then he turned back to the tech. "Put McCade through by all means."

"Aye, aye, sir."

Seconds later one of the four com screens mounted in front of Swanson-Pierce lit up and Sam McCade appeared. There was a half-smoked cigar clenched between his teeth and he was in dire need of a shave.

"Hello, Walt. Well, I never thought I'd say it, but for once your people seem to have their shit together. My compliments to Commander Moreno. According to Reba she's real sharp, although I find that hard to believe, since really sharp people avoid your chicken-shit outfit like the plague."

"It's Captain Moreno now," Swanson-Pierce replied dryly. "And I'll give her your message."

"Thanks," McCade replied, removing the cigar from his mouth and rubbing it out on the heretofore spotless control console. "Now, if you naval types are done polishing your posteriors, we can get this show on the road."

"Lead the way, Sam, we'll be right behind you."

"That's just great," McCade replied sourly. "Try not to blow my ass off." And with that the screen faded to black.

"He really *is* obnoxious," Moreno said wonderingly.

"Yup," Swanson-Pierce replied cheerfully. "And as Mustapha Pong's about to learn, you haven't seen anything yet."

McCade turned to look at Neem. Since his tail was enclosed by his space armor, the Il Ronnian gave him a human thumbs-up, as did Sergeant Major Valarie Sibo. Her marines were out of sight in the main compartment but their status lights were solid green.

"All right, Henry, take us in at full military speed."

The boxy-looking assault boat wasn't pretty but it was fast. As Henry goosed the boat's dual drives, McCade flipped all the weapons systems from amber to full green. After that he enabled all the automatic defensive systems, opened his visor, and lit a cigar. Even at high speed they wouldn't hit the first sensor station for another two hours.

He was just leaning back in his seat when every alarm on the board lit up, went off, or printed out. A single glance at the main battle tank told the story. Two of Pong's ships were on their way out!

He'd known it was possible but hadn't really expected it to happen. Damn!

Cigar ash dribbled down across the front of McCade's armor as he slapped the emergency attack bar and felt the boat jerk in response.

The WEAPCOMP had a flat, emotionless voice. "Two torpedoes away and running, two ship-to-ship missiles in flight, chaff left, chaff left, closing, closing. Target one is full evasive, target two is full evasive, jamming, jamming full spectrum all freq's.

"Both targets have launched defensive missiles, closing, closing, torpedo two has been neutralized, missiles one and two neutralized, we have a hit from torpedo one on target two. Target two destroyed. Target one has launched four missiles, tracking, tracking . . ."

McCade was thrown on his side as the boat banked right and then left.

Henry did his best to take evasive action as the WEAPCOMP continued its dispassionate narration. "Chaff left, chaff right, full spectrum electro countermeasures engaged, defensive missiles, launch, launch. Target one is approaching effective range of secondary weapons, fire, fire, target engaged and returning fire . . ."

The boat shuddered as Henry jinked right, left, and right again.

McCade fought the G forces and did his best to follow the action in the battle tank. Suddenly two green deltas appeared on either side of the red circle that marked the A-boat's position.

"We have side by side friendlies," the WEAPCOMP droned on, "launching, launching. Target one has launched full spectrum defensive, closing, closing, hit, hit, hit, miss. Friendly one has a hit on target one. Target one destroyed. Load, load, all systems cycled to full green."

McCade brought his hand up to wipe the sweat off his forehead and found a cigar butt between his gloved fingers. Making a fist he crushed it out. He chinned his mike.

"Is everyone okay?"

"We took some hits from flying debris," Reba observed, "but the armor handled most of it. We did lose our backup antenna array however."

"Could've been a lot worse," McCade replied. "Neem, how are the passengers doing?"

"Pretty well, Sam. The sergeant major's taking a nap, and the rest of her team is taking bets on whether Private Mahowski will throw up in his helmet or shit his pants."

McCade grinned. Marines are resourceful if nothing else.

Two hours later they hit the first sensor station. It had a fraction of a second to see the assault boat, the wave of interceptors behind it, and squirt a message toward Pong's base. Then the WEAPCOMP launched a single missile and the station was gone, leaving nothing more than a pool of cooling metal to mark the place where it had once stood.

But the sensor station had accomplished its mission. And when its message flashed into the *Earth Star*'s com center, the duty officer wasted no time in taking action.

His name was Farb. He was a slender man with close-cropped blond hair and a predatory face. The prospect of some action made him smile. He thumbed a red button.

All over the ship gongs began to clang, lights began to flash, and thousands of people ran for their action stations.

Electronic signals flashed out, were verified, and immediately acted on. Destroyers and cruisers and interceptors took up their various positions and prepared for battle.

As all of this took place Farb calmly made his way down a broad corridor, past row after row of first-class cabins, and paused in front of a massive hatch. It was made of durasteel bonded to gold and had once opened to admit the Emperor himself.

Farb palmed the entry lock and waited for Pong's voice.

"Yes?"

"Detector Station One reports a large force of heavily armed intruders. We have confirmation from stations two, three, and four. ETA . . . twenty minutes."

There was a moment of silence before Pong replied. "Our ships?"

"Dispersed according to plan two," Farb replied. "Orders?"

"Pipe all incoming data to the tank in my quarters. All ships will fight to the death. Remind them that there's no other way out."

"It shall be as you wish," Farb answered.

Just as he was turning to leave, Pong spoke once more. "And, Farb . . ."

"Yes?"

"You'd better have someone prepare the *Arrow*."

Farb grinned. The *Arrow* was Pong's private yacht. Should things go poorly, Pong, Farb, and two other trusted lieutenants would use it to make their escape. Although very few people knew about it, there *was* another way out.

McCade and everyone else aboard the assault boat very nearly died as they passed between Pong's weapons emplacements.

A bright latticework of coherent energy webbed across the passageway threatening to wrap the boat in its lethal embrace. Missiles accelerated from launchers searching for heat and metal. Other missiles leaped from the boat's rotary launchers to meet those missiles as still more missiles came up to meet them.

Walls of flame erupted as waves of missiles intersected and canceled each other out. Torpedoes followed the tons of hot chaff that the invading ships scattered across the passageway, exploding whenever they came near. And everywhere electronic signals raced, probed, and tried to fake each other out.

Inside the boat they were thrown up, down, and back and forth as Henry tried to keep them alive and the WEAPCOMP droned on. It spoke of torpedoes, missiles, and targets as if they were somewhere else, distant things that were part of someone else's world.

One by one the interceptors assigned to guard them blossomed into flowers of flame and disappeared. It was brute strength against brute strength, missile against missile, computer against computer.

McCade grit his teeth and willed the weapons emplacements to die. And one by one they did die, each wave of passing ships pounding them further into submission, until none were left.

McCade chinned his mike as the A-boat flashed into Pong's inner sphere. "Assault Boat One to Assault Leader."

"We copy, Assault Boat One," a voice answered. "Go."

McCade imagined Swanson-Pierce sitting in his command chair listening to the conversation. The bastard was probably sipping a cup of tea or something.

"Phase one is complete, Assault Leader. Confirm phase two."

"Phase two confirmed, Boat One," the voice said. "You have new friendlies port and starboard, with ground pounders bringing up the rear. Assault Leader sends 'well done.'"

"Copy that ," McCade replied sourly. "Tell the Assault Leader to come up and join us."

A glance at the battle tank showed that a swarm of fresh interceptors had formed up around him. They were followed by a gaggle of boxy A-boats. Each boat held fifty marines.

The interceptors would attempt to punch a hole through the pirate defense allowing the A-boats to close with and board the *Earth Star*. Once aboard they'd try to find the Vial of Tears, and failing that, Mustapha Pong.

Meanwhile the combined force of destroyers and cruisers would move in and fight the main battle. McCade grinned at the thought. Wait till Pong's people got a load of those Il Ronnian warships!

McCade chinned his mike. "This is Boat One. Let's kick some butt."

Henry's response threw McCade back and down. He forced his head toward the battle tank. A whole wave of ships and interceptors were coming toward him. He felt an anvil hit the bottom of his stomach. He thought of Sara and Molly, then thought no more as the boat went into a jerky pattern of evasive maneuvers.

What followed happened too quickly for human hands or eyes to follow.

It was a computer war of launch and counterlaunch, jam, and counterjam, move and countermove.

Whether you lived or died depended on the speed and quality of your computers, upon the effectiveness of your weapons, and on that most fickle of all things, luck.

But their plan worked. Even though Pong's warships were *supposed* to defend the *Earth Star,* many of them were actually tying to escape instead. An attack by the Brotherhood was one thing, but an attack by a combined force of pirate, navy, and alien ships was something else again. They wanted out.

The pirate ships were like a long, thin wall of metal, a tough obstacle to get around, but a relatively easy one to punch through. And that's what the interceptors did.

By concentrating all their firepower on a single point, the interceptors managed to overwhelm two destroyers and a light cruiser, making a hole through which the A-boats could pass.

The *Earth Star* had weapons of her own, but like most liners her defenses were more symbolic than real and were soon neutralized by the swarming interceptors.

"Put us alongside that emergency lock," McCade ordered as he sealed his visor. "And somebody wake the sergeant major."

"That won't be necessary, sir," Sergeant Major Sibo replied calmly. "Just put this crate alongside and we'll do the rest."

The sergeant major was as good as her word. McCade had pumped all the atmosphere out of the cabin by the time Henry put the A-boat alongside the larger ship. As a result there was no time wasted matching locks. Armed with a ship cracker it took three marines ten minutes to cut their way through the *Star*'s outer hatch.

McCade knew that other teams were using the same strategy all over the ship. If nothing else that would force Pong's crew to split up into smaller groups and make them easier to handle.

A large piece of hull metal came free and spun off into space. A satchel charge flew into the open lock and exploded with a brilliant flash. Armored bodies followed it in, their blast rifles burping blue light.

Sergeant Major Sibo's voice dominated the command channel for the next few minutes. "Spread out, you idiots! One grenade'll get you all. What's the matter, Mahowski? Afraid to earn your pay? Shoot those bastards before they shoot you. Wu, you idiot, get your head down before they blow it off. Great Sol, have I gotta wipe your ass too?"

Then it was over and she was in the blackened lock urging McCade to board. "The lock's secure, sir, welcome aboard."

"Thank you, Sergeant Major, nicely done. Have you got the schematic?"

"Yes, sir. It's up on my visor right now."

"Good, let's head for the Imperial stateroom. If Pong's aboard, that's where he'll be."

"Aye, aye, sir," Sibo replied. "Follow me."

McCade followed and was forced to step over a number of bodies in the process. At least two of them wore marine armor.

With Reba and Neem close behind him, McCade followed Sibo through a short side passage to the point where it joined a main corridor. Another lock blocked their way. An indicator showed breathable atmosphere beyond. At the sergeant major's direction four marines cycled through and signaled the all-clear.

As she emerged from the lock, Sibo took a moment to consult her schematic and turned left. Two marines brushed past her to take the point as the rest of them formed a column of twos and jogged along behind.

Like all liners the schematics for the *Earth Star* were on file at every navy base. That was SOP in case of collision or capture. So as each team of marines made their way on board they'd use the schematics projected onto the inside surface of their visors to find their particular targets. Strategic targets came first, like the bridge, the com center, and the drive rooms, followed by storerooms or other places where the Vial of Tears might be stored.

At least one Il Ronnian Sand Sept trooper had been assigned to each team of marines. Once the vial was found the Sand Sept trooper would stand guard over it until one of the several Ilwiks present could take possession.

The journey soon became a running firefight as the marines encountered small groups of crew members and quickly overwhelmed them. Pong did have some well-trained troops, but most of them were aboard his destroyers and cruisers, and therefore unavailable to defend the *Star*.

The marines were able to make good progress as a result. Slowly but surely they made their way ever toward the first-class accommodations and the Imperial stateroom.

Then, just as they left a side corridor to enter the main thoroughfare that led to the Imperial stateroom, they hit an ambush.

Farb had placed his people well, hiding them in two opposing staterooms and an overhead access tunnel. Holding his breath he waited for the marines to pass and yelled "Now!" into his open mike.

The Pirates opened up from both sides as more dropped from above to block any possibility of retreat.

Sergeant Major Sibo died in the first five seconds of the ambush, slumping forward as a crew-operated energy beam punched black holes through her armor.

McCade hit the deck in a forward roll. As he came out of it his hand blaster jumped into his hand. Pirates spilled out of a stateroom to the left. He squeezed the trigger four times and saw two holes appear in a visor that quickly misted over with blood.

Something hit his armor from behind but didn't go through. McCade spun around and gut shot a pirate from three feet away.

Tough though it was the pirate's armor couldn't stand up to that kind of punishment and gave way. The energy beam went through Farb's stomach and splashed against the backside of his armor. The ensuing darkness came as a complete surprise.

Suddenly it was over and the marines had won. Bodies lay everywhere in tumbled heaps. A blue haze filled the air and when McCade opened his visor the smell of ozone filled his nostrils.

A marine appeared at his side. "Sergeant O'Hara, sir. We have sixteen dead, seven wounded, and twenty-seven effectives. Orders, sir?"

McCade could see the golden hatch at the far end of the corridor. "See that hatch, Sergeant? I want it open."

"Open. Yes, sir. Rawlings! Newly! Mobutu! Open up that door and make it quick. The rest of you, cover them. We may run into all sorts of shit in there."

Half a minute later the three marines were busy cutting their way through the hatch. The ship cracker spit ruby red and the hatch sucked it up until the locking mechanism gave way and the door began to slide open.

The marines dropped the ship cracker and scrambled to get out of the way. Thirty weapons were lined up on the open hatch but nothing happened.

"Okay," McCade said, "let's take it nice n'easy."

As the marines moved forward, Reba slipped in from the side. Blue light stuttered out to lance through her body in a dozen places. McCade watched in utter amazement as she brought up her blast rifle and fired back. There was a double thump as two pirates hit the floor.

McCade ran forward and was there to catch her when she fell. White fluid spurted from the holes in her armor. He couldn't place it at first and then he could and didn't want to believe it. Holding her in his arms, McCade looked up at Neem, and when the Il Ronnian nodded, he knew it was true. Reba was, and always had been, a cyborg. As such she'd infiltrated the Brotherhood, been accidentally captured, and been reinfiltrated via her association with McCade. Her voice made a horrible rasping sound when she spoke.

"Sam?"

"Yes, Reba?"

"I'm sorry I lied to you."

"It's okay, Reba. I understand."

"Sam . . . are you really an Ilwik?"

McCade looked up at Neem and he nodded.

"Yes, Reba, I guess I am."

"Good," Reba rasped. "Then give me the prayer for the dead."

The words tumbled from McCade's lips as if he'd said them many times before. "You may leave this one, O holy fluid, for your work is done. She has lived fully, seen much, and served with honor. Now she journeys forth into a new land where you await. Our blessings go with her for she was one of ours.

"Was that okay, Reba? Did I say it right?"

But Reba was silent, her beautiful features frozen in a smile.

Neem pulled McCade to his feet. "It was more than okay, Sam. It was perfect. Now come on before Reba blows up and takes you with her."

McCade was leaning against a wall and looking the other way when Reba blew up. He was tired of killing, and tired of watching people die. No matter how hard he willed his body to move, it wouldn't go. He dimly heard Sergeant O'Hara give the all-clear and heard the marines spread out to search the stateroom.

Pong was gone, of course, having escaped along with two others aboard his yacht, but Neem found something of interest on the surface of the pirate's rather ornate desk. Pong had used it as a paperweight and, being of little intrinsic value, had neglected to take it along.

The object was made of purest crystal and shaped like a vial. Inside the vial a clear fluid could be seen. It was moving. With life of its own? Or in sympathy with the ship?

In either case the vial shimmered with light and threw a rainbow of color against the wall beyond as Neem picked it up and said a silent prayer.

With trembling hands Neem carried the vial into the adjoining room and to the place where the tired-looking human stood. Placing the vial in Mc-Cade's hands, Neem said, "The Vial of Tears, O holy one." And together the Ilwiks cried.

McCADE'S BOUNTY

For Allison and Jessica,
with thanks
for their technical
advice and encouragement.

ONE

For the better part of two rotations the battle raged on and around the ice-world called Alice.

The pirates managed to destroy the planet's small navy during the first few minutes of battle.

Then, expecting an easy victory on the ground, they dropped into orbit. The force fields around their ships disappeared, as hundreds of assault craft spilled out and spiraled down toward the bluish white planet below.

It was a mistake, and one for which the invaders would pay dearly. Missiles rose from the planet's surface followed by man-made lightning. Caught with force fields down, two of the attacking ships were destroyed, and others were damaged.

Then, angered by the effrontery of their victims, the pirates unleashed a terrible fury. Mushroom-shaped clouds marched across the frozen landscape turning vast sections of ice and snow into superheated steam and radioactive glass.

But most of the important targets were located deep underground safe from the planet's harsh winters and pirate attacks. They survived and the battle continued.

The combatants had fought many times before and knew each other well.

On the one side there were the settlers, life-long losers most of them, driven, or drifting farther and farther from the center of the human empire until reaching its very edge. For Alice was a rim world, the last stop before the Il Ronnian Empire, and the great unknown.

Now the settlers eked out a precarious existence built more on hard work than the scarce resources of their planet. They were quirky, independent, and tough as hell when backed into a corner.

The pirates were as pirates have always been, the lowest common denominator, the link between animal and man. Once, years before, they'd been something better.

They were soldiers back in those days. Soldiers who fought valiantly for a cause they believed in. A confederation of planets, each represented in a star spanning democracy, each part of a greater whole.

But in spite of their heroic efforts to hold it together, the confederation had collapsed of its own weight, and given rise to the Empire.

The first Emperor was wise in his own way, and knowing he couldn't micro-manage each planet, he provided all of them with a measure of independence and full amnesty for the confederates.

Tired of war, and preferring order to anarchy, most of them agreed.

But some scorned the offer, choosing to fight a guerrilla war instead, waiting for the day when they would seize power and restore the confederacy. The day never came.

Time passed, and with it, the ideals they'd fought for. Raid followed raid, and death followed death, until the difference between "military" and "civilian" targets started to blur.

There were atrocities, each worse than those that went before, until minds grew weary and hearts became numb.

Now, many years later, they sought loot rather than liberty. Gradually, without realizing it, patriots became pirates and a cause disappeared.

The settlers' command center was deep underground. During the past two days it had survived attacks from air-to-ground missiles, smart bombs, and a flight of robotic subsurface torpedoes. They'd burrowed within one mile of the complex before they were detected and destroyed.

The C&C was large, lit mostly by flickering vid screens, and filled with the soft murmur of radio traffic. Smoke streaked the air, empty meal paks crunched underfoot, and a feeling of weary desperation pervaded the room.

Sara Bridger-McCade focused tired eyes on the surface of the tac tank. She hadn't slept for more than twenty-six hours and exhaustion had taken its toll.

Sara was beautiful, or had been once. Now a long white scar slashed down across her face. It was deathly white against her heat-flushed skin. A grim reminder of her first encounter with the pirates many years before.

Sara wore a plain gray jump suit, light body armor, and a blaster in a cross-draw holster.

Ignoring concerned stares from C&C staff she tried to concentrate. The tac tank was a swirl of color and movement. It was similar to a three-dimensional electronic chess board, in which the green deltas belonged to her, and the red squares to someone else.

But this was no game. These markers represented real flesh-and-blood people. Mothers, fathers, sisters, and brothers. Friends of hers. They were dying and Sara couldn't stop it.

Some of the population would survive as slaves but most would die. It was the pirate way. Take what you want, destroy the rest. Sara peered into the tac tank and looked for an answer.

Hills and valleys were outlined with green contour lines and marked with elevations. Surface and subsurface installations showed up as yellow circles. Civilian domes and factories were light blue. All of it looked so neat and orderly without the sprawl of dead bodies, the stench of burned-out homes, and the cold-blue stutter of energy weapons.

Without ships to bring help, without FTL communication, the settlers had a single ally. The weather. Up above, on the planet's surface, a class-two storm raged. Nothing like an eight or, God forbid, a ten, but just enough to slow the pirates down. Sara had hoped for more, hoped the storm would defeat them in a way that she couldn't, but the pirates were well prepared.

They wore heatsuits, rode in armored crawlers, and knew what they were doing. Slowly but surely the red squares were pressing in, pushing the green deltas toward the underground command center, crushing anything that stood in their way.

Over there, about ten klicks short of Donovan's Rift, Riston's Rifles were still holding against a company of mechanized infantry. And there, just short of the main armory, Colonel Larkin was fighting one last battle.

But that was it, after two days of battle the pirates had come close to wiping the planet clean, and would soon be victorious.

Sara's vision blurred and she rubbed her eyes. Was there a way out? Something she'd missed? A weakness?

No, nothing. The knowledge lay heavy in her gut. The pirates would take Alice within hours. She'd failed. The battle was lost.

But why? Why such determination? Why so well equipped? Why Alice?

"Sara?" The voice was calm and gentle. She looked up to see a man and a woman standing on the other side of the tac tank.

There were five members of the planetary council. Sara, Colonel Larkin, presently defending the armory, Rico, off-planet with Sam, Professor Wendel, and Dr. Hannah Lewis.

Three qualifies as a quorum, Sara thought tiredly, though it hardly matters. There's nothing left to decide.

Professor Wendel smiled wearily. He was an elderly man with bright blue eyes and a white ponytail. "We did the best we could, child. Let's save what we can."

Sara looked at Hannah. She had an open face, beautiful brown skin, and a tight cap of kinky black hair. She had a diagnostic scanner strapped to her right arm and a stethoscope hung around her neck. There were bloodstains on her OR greens. The planet's main medical facility was a thousand yards down the main corridor.

"The professor's right, Sara. Release the remaining troops and let them slip into the bush. The pirates won't find them. Not on Alice they won't."

Sara knew Hannah was right. The locals were experts at cold-weather survival. They knew the terrain, and those fortunate enough to be some distance from the C&C would have a chance of escape. "And the children?"

Hannah looked at Wendel. It was he who answered. "They're gathered in the cafeteria. The pirates will take them as slaves."

Sara felt a terrible sadness roll over her. Which was better? To die? Or live as a slave? She knew what Sam would say, knew he'd want his daughter to live, knew there was no other choice.

Sara nodded. "I'll give the necessary orders." She activated her throat mic and began to speak.

And so the word went out. "Disengage . . . pull back . . . fade into the bush. Save who and what you can. Live to fight another day. Thanks for all that you've done . . . and good-bye."

Then it was over, a kiss on the cheek from Professor Wendel, a hug from Hannah, and a wave to her quickly departing staff.

Some, either because of skills or appearance, would have a chance to become slaves, but most, like Sara with her disfiguring scar, would not. They would tend to last-minute chores, say good-bye to loved ones, and meet at the main entry. There they would make one last stand.

Sara's heels made a clicking sound as she walked down the corridor. Normally it was spotless, with shiny floors and clean walls. Now it was dark and gloomy, stained with smoke, and littered with the debris of war. Lights buzzed on the edge of burnout, bloody dressings littered the floor, and odd pieces of clothing lay here and there.

A horn honked behind her and Sara stepped aside. An electric cart rolled by, loaded down with heat-suited people, headed toward the main entry.

Many of the people wore bloodstained bandages. The wounded, determined to make their deaths count, looking forward to taking some pirates with them.

One waved. Sara waved back. She couldn't remember his name.

The cafeteria was dark and somber. There were fifty or sixty children spread around the room, all were subdued, some were crying. Sara saw small huddles here and there, as parents said good-bye to their children. Many would never have that chance, for they were already dead, or dying somewhere in the cold.

Ten or twelve hard-pressed teenagers moved among the crowd, little more than children themselves, doing the best they could to bring help and comfort.

Some elderly men and women were in charge. One, a woman named Edna, bustled over to greet Sara. She had a wrinkled face and plump hands. Edna wore the same cheerful smile she always did, and Sara admired her courage.

"Hello, dear, come to see Molly? She's right over there. Hurry now, we plan to sing some songs until they come to take the children away."

Sara smiled her thanks, and marveled at Edna's words. ". . . Until they come to take the children away." As if "they" were nothing more than counselors taking the children off to summer camp. But Edna was right. It wouldn't do any good to dwell on the horror of it, to think of what Molly would face, to break down and sob as she desperately wanted to do.

Sara felt angry for a moment. Angry at Sam for being off-planet when the pirates came, angry at the Empire for leaving the rim worlds vulnerable to attack, angry at God for letting it happen. It wasn't fair, damn it!

"Mommy!" Suddenly Molly was there, arms thrown around Sara's waist, face pressed against her stomach. Somehow, much to Sara's pleasure and her daughter's chagrin, Molly had a mop of tightly curled, brown, almost black hair. It was soft and thick, strangely comforting to her fingers, a reminder of Sam.

Suddenly the anger was gone, replaced by a terrible sadness. There was so much she wanted to say and so little time to say it. Sara knelt and took Molly in her arms. They hugged and took comfort from each other. Then as they pulled slightly apart Sara looked into her daughter's eyes. They were big and solemn, filled with knowledge beyond her years, and brimming with tears.

"Things didn't go very well, honey, we lost."

Molly nodded sadly. "I know, Mommy. They told us. The pirates are going to take us away."

Sara forced a smile. "I'm afraid so, Molly. Do you remember how the pirates took me, and your grandmother?"

Molly nodded. She'd heard the story many times. How the pirates had stopped the liner, how Mommy fought them at the main lock, how Daddy unknowingly saved her life a few months later. "I remember."

"Good . . . because you must do as I did. Stay alive, help others, and remember the things Mommy and Daddy taught you." Tears began to roll down Molly's cheeks.

"Are you listening to me, Molly?"

"Yes, Mommy, I'm listening."

Sara scanned her daughter's face, determined to remember it, and take the memory with her. "Good. This is the most important part of all. *Never* give up hope. No matter where they take you, no matter how long it takes, Daddy will come. He'll hunt them clear across the universe if that's what it takes. Be ready. There'll be trouble when Daddy comes, and he'll need your help."

Molly sobbed and pressed her face against Sara's shoulder. "I don't want to go! I want to stay with you!"

Sara gently pushed her away. "I know, honey . . . I wish you could. But Mommy has things to do. You take care of yourself, and remember I love you."

And with that Sara stood, kissed Molly on the top of her head, and turned away.

By the time Sara entered the main corridor she could hear the sounds of distant battle. The pirates were forcing their way in and the command center staff was making one last stand. Tears rolled down Sara's cheeks as she pulled her blaster, checked its charge, and headed for the entry. The bastards would pay.

TWO

The room was small and heavily hung with rich fabrics. Perfume misted the air and shadows filled the corners as the two men regarded each other across the surface of the expensive desk.

The merchant straightened his robes, pouted his lips, and rubbed his chin. The likeness of a serpent wound itself around the merchant's bald skull and terminated at the center of his forehead. The merchant waved his hand and light winked off a golden pinky ring. "One hundred and thirty-five thousand imperials, and not a credit less."

Sam McCade took the cigar out of his mouth, examined the soggy end for defects, and shoved it back in. He had gray eyes, strong even features, and a two-day growth of beard. "You're out of your mind. I'm here to buy fertilizer, not diamonds. I'll pay one-twenty, and not a credit more."

The merchant shook his head sadly. "McCade, you are a crude man. I will lower my price just to be rid of you. A hundred and thirty."

McCade blew foul blue smoke toward the other man's face. "A hundred and twenty-five."

The merchant coughed and pushed a terminal across the surface of his inlaid desk. "Done. Collect the tanks from my private loading dock and never darken my door again."

McCade grinned, tapped in the amount of transfer, and added his personal code. His leathers were worn and stained. They creaked as he stood. "Thanks, Corrus. You're a thousand laughs. See you next time around."

Corrus waited till the other man was gone, sprayed the air with perfume, and allowed himself a big grin. He liked McCade. Only Sol knew why.

Rico waited outside. He was a big man, with a head of unruly black hair and a beard to match. His eyes were small and bright. He wore a loose-fitting shirt, a leather vest, and a pair of black trousers. Like McCade he was armed with a low-riding slug gun.

"Well? Did ya purchase the poop?"

McCade frowned. "Yes, and since it cost Alice more than a hundred thousand credits, I'll thank you to refer to it as 'liquid fertilizer.' Come on. Let's find Phil."

Rico grinned and followed McCade up the corridor.

The asteroid had a little spin but not much. The men moved carefully. Without much gravity it would be easy to bounce up and bang your head against solid rock.

Like most of the passageways within Rister's Rock, this one was courtesy of Rister himself.

Rister had lived on the asteroid for more than thirty years, and during that time, he'd bored tunnels in every direction.

Not because he *had* to, or was looking for minerals, but because he *wanted* to.

It seemed that Rister enjoyed the process of boring tunnels, and, more than that, believed the finished product was a work of art.

The fact that no one else agreed with him didn't bother Rister in the least. He went right on boring tunnels till the day he died. In fact, Rister had been dead for years by the time they found him, a dried-out mummy in a beat-up space suit, grinning like he understood the biggest joke of all.

Now Rister stood in the back of Meck's saloon, where he served as a sometimes hat rack and surefire conversation starter.

But regardless of Rister's intentions, the asteroid had been put to good use. Located as it was on the very edge of the asteroid belt, and close to a hyperspace nav beacon, the planetoid made a handy spot to do business.

In fact, Rister's Rock had a pretty good rep, but still attracted all kinds, and McCade watched as they passed by. There were the roid rats, striding the halls in beat-up armor, and spacers, bored-looking men and women, hunting for something they hadn't tried, and merchants, some as colorful as peacocks, others drab and boring, all watching one another with the wary look of potential combatants.

There were aliens too, not many, but a feathery, scaly scattering of Finthians, Lakorians, and Zords, plumage waving, tentacles writhing, feet stumping along.

From long habit McCade sifted the crowd for fugitives. They could be of any shape, size, or species, sentients who'd committed a crime, or been accused of one, and were on the run.

Pragmatic soul that he was, the first Emperor had decided to rely on bounty hunters, rather than ask his hard-pressed citizens to foot the bill for an empire-sized police force. And like many of his ideas, this one worked.

Most worlds had a police force, but its jurisdiction ended in the upper atmosphere, and that was fine with them.

Once someone fled the planet they were assumed to be guilty. A bounty was placed on their head, so many credits dead or alive, and they showed up in public data terms all over the Empire.

All a bounty hunter had to do was access a terminal, scroll through the possibilities, and select those he or she wished to pursue.

Then, for a very small fee, the bounty hunter could buy a hunting license and track them down.

It had been a long time since McCade had stepped up to a terminal and purchased a license, but he felt sure there were some fugitives in the crowd.

Loud ones, hiding behind carefully constructed false identities; quiet ones, doing their best to escape all notice; and the fortunate few, who by dint of biosculpture and organ transplants, had re-created themselves from the ground up. They'd be hard to catch.

McCade smiled. Well, they were safe from him. His bounty-hunting days were over. Now he was a part-time cop, a part-time purchasing agent, and a full-time husband. It would be good to get home.

McCade's thoughts were interrupted by a racket up ahead.

As the two men stepped out of the tunnel and into the circular area where a number of passageways came together, they found themselves in the midst of a crowd. There were numerous shops, but the largest was Meck's saloon, and people were looking in that direction. McCade craned his neck to see what the excitement was about.

There was an inarticulate roar followed by a loud crash as a spacer came flying through the front of the saloon to land in front of the crowd. Thanks to the light gravity, the man was able to roll over and shake his head. Friends picked the man up and dusted him off.

McCade turned to the roid rat on his left. He was a big man with a hooked nose and a walrus-style mustache. "What's going on?"

The man nodded his head toward the bar. "We were in Meck's having a drink when this bear-thing comes in. It orders a beer and sits at the bar. Then a spacer says 'I don't drink with freaks,' and all hell breaks loose."

The roid rat gestured toward the dazed spacer. "That guy tried to jump the bear from behind."

McCade looked at Rico and the other man shook his head. "Phil's gettin' less tolerant all the time. Must be gettin' old."

McCade sighed, pushed his way through the crowd, and entered the bar. Rico was right behind him.

The place was part saloon and part curiosity shop. Besides a mummified Rister, it boasted other wonders as well, including a cage full of alien birds, miniature landscapes made from human hair, a pickled something that no one could identify, a chunk of rock said to have strange healing powers, and much, much more.

The place was completely empty except for Phil, the man he was lifting over his head, and a distraught bartender. Broken furniture and shattered glass littered the floor.

Phil stood about seven feet tall, weighed in at more than three hundred pounds, and looked like a bear. He had brown eyes, a short muzzle, and thick brown fur. He wore a kilt of his own design, carried a machine pistol as a side arm, and wore a twelve-inch knife strapped to his right leg.

Originally human, Phil had been biosculpted for work on ice-worlds and liked Alice for that reason. Phil was not only a qualified biologist, but a one-variant army, with infrared vision, amplified muscle response, and razor-sharp durasteel teeth.

He could also go into full augmentation for short periods of time, a state that burned tremendous amounts of energy and left him completely exhausted.

In this case however the variant hadn't even worked up a sweat. This was partly due to the asteroid's light gravity but mostly because of his enormous strength. Phil was holding a man over his head and lecturing him at the same time. The man looked scared and, as McCade knew, had every reason to be.

Meanwhile the bartender, or perhaps Meck himself, danced around Phil and begged him to stop. It did little good. Phil had something to say and said it.

". . . So, you can understand how I felt. No one likes to be singled out, identified as different, and subjected to verbal abuse. Especially by low-life cretins like you. Though generally a proponent of positive reinforcement, I think punishment has its place as well, which explains why I'm going to throw you through that wall."

Fortunately for the man in question this particular wall was made of lightweight plastic with a fire retardant foam core. He went through it with no problem at all. As luck would have it, however, there was nothing but solid rock on the other side. He hit with an audible thump.

McCade winced. Some of the crowd had filtered back in and lifted the un-conscious man from the debris. He was alive but would spend the next few days in the rock's infirmary.

Phil ran an experienced eye over the damage, reached into his belt pouch, and produced five gold imperials. "This should cover the damage with some-thing left over. Agreed?"

The bartender, a middle-aged man with radiation-burned skin and a siz-able potbelly, nodded. He had no desire to engage Phil in protracted negotia-tions. "Agreed."

Phil smiled and revealed rows of gleaming teeth. "Good. Now, if it's all the same to you, I'll finish my beer."

So saying Phil hoisted his beer, poured it down in one swallow, and slammed the mug onto the surface of the bar. Tiny bits of foam and droplets of beer flew in every direction.

Phil belched and wiped his muzzle with the back of a hairy paw. "Ah! That hits the spot. Hello, Sam, Rico. Ready to go?"

McCade looked around and grinned. "Ready if you are. Sure you want to leave the place standing?"

Phil waved a dismissive paw. "Just a slight misunderstanding. You have the nutrient solution?"

Rico chuckled. "We've got it all right. More'n a hundred thousand credits' worth o' poop."

Phil frowned. "Rico, you're hopeless. It's not 'poop.' It's a specially formu-lated nutrient solution for use in our hydroponics tanks. Now, if you'd spent as much time looking at the planet's population curve as you do on hunting trips . . ."

Phil lectured Rico on hydroponics, demographics, and planetary ecology all the way up to the planetoid's surface. Once there they dodged a small army of vendors, paid an exit tax, and retrieved their space armor from rented lockers.

With space armor on and checked, they stepped into one of four large locks that served Rister's Rock, and waited for it to cycle them through. Five minutes later it did, and they stepped out on the asteroid's rocky surface. A good-sized landing zone was nearly filled with shuttles and smaller ships, while farther out, the sun made a line of jagged light across the top of a low-lying ridge.

All asteroids looked pretty much the same to McCade's eyes. As he bounced toward the shuttle McCade wondered what had made this one so special to Rister. He'd never know.

The shuttle, like the ship it belonged to, was of military design. Both had been gifts from a grateful Empire after McCade's last ship had been lost while searching for the Vial of Tears.

The Vial, a religious artifact sacred to the alien Il Ronn, had been stolen by a renegade pirate named Mustapha Pong.

The Il Ronn had sworn to regain the Vial no matter what the cost, and faced with the very real possibility of interstellar war, the Emperor had requested McCade's help. But that was history and something he'd just as soon forget.

The shuttle was a squat wedge-shaped hunk of metal, built to haul heavy loads and survive atmospheric landings under combat conditions. It had a blunt nose, a boxy fuselage, and short extendable wings. The shuttle crouched on retractable landing jacks and looked more like a primeval bug than a ship.

McCade punched a series of numbers into the key pad located on the shuttle's belly. A line of light appeared and expanded into a rectangle. Stairs slid down, found the ground, and stopped.

The three men made their way up the stairs, waited for the lock to cycle through, and took off their suits. They attached the suits to wall clips and entered the crew quarters.

Farther back, and almost full of goods and equipment, there was a cargo compartment. It could be pressurized to carry additional passengers or left unpressurized as it was now.

Passing between curtained bunks, through the tiny galley-mess area, and into the control room, McCade dropped into the pilot's position. Rico sat on the right, with Phil one seat back, in one of the two passenger slots.

McCade fired the shuttle's repulsors, got a clearance from the rock's computerized traffic-control system, and danced the ship toward the glare of greenish loading lights.

The loading docks were unpressurized and, outside of one or two space-suited figures, completely automated.

Auto loaders wove complicated patterns around one another, tall spindly robots stepped over and around piles of merchandise, and computer-controlled crawlers towed trains of power pallets toward distant ships.

Acting on a string of radio commands McCade skittered the shuttle over to loading dock seven, opened the main cargo hatch, and watched via vid screen as an auto loader positioned two silvery cylinders in the middle of the cargo bay.

The auto loader had four headlights, and as they swung away, a number of smaller robots scampered through the hatch to lock the cylinders in place. As soon as they were finished the robots left as quickly as they'd come.

McCade sealed the hatch, ran an auto check on all systems, and fired his repellors. The shuttle lifted and dust fountained up from the asteroid's surface. Then, with the ship safely aloft, McCade engaged the main drive.

Seconds later they were free of the asteroid's light gravity and headed out toward the area where the *Void Runner* and some of the other large ships drifted miles apart.

The *Void Runner* had originally been a Destroyer Escort and, as such, was twice the size of McCade's previous ship *Pegasus*.

Although still small enough to negotiate planetary atmospheres, and therefore streamlined in appearance, the *Void Runner* was more ship than one person could comfortably run by himself.

The ship had carried a crew of eight back in her military days, but McCade had modified her to operate with a crew of four, and could fly her single-handed in an emergency.

So, Rico and Phil had come along to keep McCade company and crew the ship. They chatted with each other as McCade sent *Void Runner* a recognition code, countersigned the return password, and slid the shuttle toward the lighted berth on DE's port side.

There was another similar berth on the starboard side presently occupied by a four-place speedster. More toy than tool, McCade justified it as a lifeboat and ignored Sara's disparaging remarks.

Easing the little ship into its bay, McCade fired the shuttle's repellors and lowered it onto the durasteel deck. The outer hatch slid closed shortly after that, air rushed in to pressurize the bay, and a pair of snakelike robo tubes slithered out to connect themselves to the shuttle. The tubes pulsed rhythmically as fuel flowed into the shuttle's tanks.

McCade, Rico, and Phil left the shuttle the moment the bay was properly pressurized. The argrav was adjusted to Alice normal and felt good after Rister's Rock.

Bright lights threw hard black shadows down against the durasteel deck. All around the three inner bulkheads, tools, torches, and hand testers were racked and waiting for use.

McCade tapped a code into the lock and waited for it to iris open. The lock was necessary so that a loss of pressure inside the shuttle bay wouldn't affect the rest of the ship.

McCade still felt a sense of pride when he stepped out of the lock into his ship. *Pegasus* had been comfortable and fast, but nothing like *this*. The *Void Runner* was larger, roomier, more heavily armed, and even faster than *Pegasus* had been. She was three years old, but she still smelled new, and McCade took pleasure in walking her corridors.

As McCade made his way toward the ship's bridge he passed the hundreds and hundreds of items that mean little by themselves but taken together make a warship.

There were com screens, remote status displays, zero-G handholds, navy gray bulkheads, damage-control stations, equipment panels, warning labels, first-aid kits, access doors, radiation detectors, patch paks, ventilation ducts, weapons lockers, maintenance ways, crash kits, miles of conduit, and, yes, brass that did little more than look good.

McCade scrambled up a short flight of metal stairs and entered the bridge. The overhead lighting was subdued. Hundreds of indicator lights glowed red, green, and amber.

There was a command chair located toward the center of the room, fronted by three control positions, one for the pilot, the copilot, and the weapons officer.

McCade dropped into the captain's chair and touched a button. "Maggie? You there?"

A screen came to life. It showed a middle-aged woman. She was all torso and no legs. Both had been horribly mangled during a drive-room explosion and scissored off by her self-sealing space armor.

For reasons only Magda Anne Homby could understand, she'd refused stim growth replacements *and* prosthetics, settling for a custom-designed ar-grav box instead.

But legs or no legs, Maggie was still the best damned engineer for a hundred lights in any direction, and knew it.

Maggie blew a stray strand of red hair out of her eyes. "Of course I'm here. Where the hell did you think I'd be?"

McCade grinned. He knew from experience that Maggie was impossible to please. In fact it was Maggie's personality rather than her handicap that kept her from more lucrative employment on a freighter or a big liner. "My mistake. I'll need the drives about five from now."

Maggie nodded curtly and the screen went black. Though welcome on the bridge, she preferred to ride where she worked, in the drive room.

Rico ran a manual preflight check, while McCade tapped instructions into the ship's navcomp, and Phil sharpened a durasteel claw. Although the variant was a lousy pilot, his keen brain and amplified reaction times made him a crackerjack weapons officer.

With all systems green, and a gruff "go ahead" from Maggie, McCade fired the *Void Runner*'s standard drives. The DE would reach the nav beacon in a few minutes, enter hyperspace, and exit about three standard days after that. A short run later and they'd see Alice.

McCade allowed the seat to make him comfortable and delegated control to the navcomp. He couldn't wait to get home.

The ship's screens blurred momentarily as the *Void Runner* slipped out of hyperspace. McCade felt the usual moment of nausea and scanned his readouts for signs of trouble. Nothing. All systems were green.

Phil tapped a series of keys. Sensors reached out to probe the surrounding vacuum for indications of heat, metal, or radiation. Passive receptors listened, scanners watched for signs of pulsed light, and vid cams searched for movement against the stars.

Phil growled in the back of his throat as the skin along the top of his muzzle formed a series of ridges and his fangs appeared.

Something was wrong. Although Alice couldn't afford remote weapons platforms, she did have deep-space robo sensors, and based on their warnings the *Void Runner* should've been challenged by now.

Phil opened a com link, tapped in a frequency, and spoke into his mic. "This is the *Void Runner*, Delta Beta, six-niner-two, requesting a planetary approach vector. What the hell's wrong with you people? Wake up and smell the coffee."

Silence.

Phil's chair whirred as he turned toward McCade. "I'm worried, Sam. No challenge so far, and no response."

McCade frowned. Maybe there was some sort of equipment failure.

"Try 'em again, Phil, and run a diagnostic routine on our gear. There's always the chance that some equipment went belly up."

Phil tried again and got the same result. He ran an auto check on the ship's com gear. Nothing. The variant turned toward McCade and gave a shrug.

McCade lifted a protective cover and pushed a red button. A klaxon went off and called a nonexistent naval crew to battle stations. The ship's defensive screen went to full military power, weapons systems came on-line, and a three-dimensional tac tank appeared in front of McCade's chair.

The tac tank was empty of movement—outside of symbols representing Alice, her sister planets, and the sun itself. There were no warships waiting to pounce, no fighters vectoring in, no torpedoes flashing through space. Nothing.

The intercom bonged. Maggie appeared on-screen. She scowled. "You're starting to piss me off, McCade. What's all this battle stations crap? You hit the wrong button or something?"

McCade fought to keep his temper. "We can't raise Alice and we're not sure why. They should be all over us by now. Strap in and stand by."

Maggie nodded and the screen flashed to black.

McCade took another longer look in the tac tank. Still nothing. A hard lump formed in his throat. Where were the robo sensors? The usual tramp freighters? The planet's five-ship navy?

McCade swallowed hard. "Rico, full power. Phil, keep your eyes peeled. I've got a bad feeling about this."

It took twelve long, frustrating, tension-filled hours to close with Alice. Hours during which there was plenty of time to worry, to think about Sara and Molly, to imagine all sorts of terrible calamities. But nothing, not even McCade's worst imaginings, could compare with what they actually found.

Alice half filled the view screens when Phil spotted the first wreck. "Sam, Rico, take a look at this."

Phil's claws made a clicking sound as they hit the keys. A magnified image appeared on the main view screen. It was a ship, the remains of one anyway, tumbling end over end. Light and dark, light and dark, over and over again. Torpedoes had taken a terrible toll, ripping huge holes in the vessel's durasteel hull, gutting the interior.

Rico's fist made a loud bang as it hit the control panel. "Damn! That's the *Free Star!*"

"It *was* the *Free Star,*" Phil corrected grimly. "Wait . . . there's more . . ."

McCade bit his lip. The *Free Star* had been a reconditioned destroyer, the flagship of the planet's small navy, crushed like a child's plaything. Who had done this? Pirates? The Il Ronn? It was impossible to tell.

By the time the DE swung into orbit around Alice the crew had seen more smashed ships, a ruptured habitat, and four or five burned-out satellites. Taken altogether the destruction meant hundreds of lives lost.

McCade thought about Sara and Molly. A muscle in his left cheek began to twitch. He had to get dirtside, had to find them, had to make sure they were okay. But what if they weren't? What if . . . Phil interrupted McCade's thoughts.

"Hold it! I've got something on VHF!"

Alice shimmered and disappeared as a new image formed on the main view screen. The shot showed a man, a nice-looking man, with a fleshy something on his shoulder. Was it blue? Purple? The thing shimmered like iridescent cloth. The man smiled.

"Hello. This message is intended for Sam McCade. Everyone else can open the nearest lock and suck vacuum.

"As for you, McCade, I sincerely hope you're dead. But if you survived . . . here's something to think about: 'Do unto others as you would have them do unto you.'

"Or, how about, 'What goes around comes around'?

"Or, the ever-popular, 'Screw with me and I will rip your goddamned lungs out'?

"Take your pick. Just remember. You stuck your nose where it didn't belong, and I chopped it off."

The screen snapped to black.

Rico's chair whirred as he turned toward McCade. "Okay, sport . . . who the hell was that?"

McCade's mind raced. Who the hell was that, indeed? Like most bounty hunters he was good at remembering faces. Yet McCade was sure that he'd never seen the man before. But that didn't make sense. The man had a personal grudge, a grudge so big he'd attack Alice, so surely they'd met. Wait a minute . . . the voice . . . there was something about the voice.

"Play the last part again."

Phil tapped some keys and the man reappeared. ". . . And I will rip your goddamned lungs out.

"Take your pick. Just remember. You stuck your nose where it didn't belong, and I chopped it off."

McCade slammed his fist down onto the arm of his chair. "Mustapha Pong!"

Now it made sense. Pong was the renegade pirate who'd unknowingly stolen the Il Ronnian Vial of Tears a few years earlier. In an attempt to avoid an interstellar war and pocket a sizable bounty, McCade had tracked the Vial to Pong's secret base. Shortly thereafter a combined human–Il Ronnian fleet had destroyed the base and almost all of Pong's ships. That explained the grudge.

And although McCade and Pong had spoken with each other by radio on one occasion, they'd never met face-to-face.

Rico nodded his understanding. "So what's the weird-lookin' thing on Pong's shoulder."

"I can answer that," Phil said grimly. "The 'weird-lookin' thing' as you call it is a Melcetian mind slug."

McCade frowned. "A Melcetian what?"

"Mind slug," Phil replied evenly. "I read a paper on them once. They're nonsentient symbiotic creatures who rarely leave their native planet but have the capacity to amplify human brain activity."

"Amplify brain activity?" McCade asked. "As in think better?"

Phil nodded. "Better, faster, and more creatively."

Rico raised an eyebrow. "Oh, yeah? Then how come I never saw one before?"

Phil smiled, and given his durasteel dentition, it was a terrifying sight. "Because everything has a price. In this case the price involves allowing the slug to tap into your spinal cord, filter your blood for nutrients, and feed you addictive chemicals."

McCade shuddered as he hit his harness release. "Sounds horrible. It makes a certain kind of sense though. No wonder Pong's so good at what he does."

A few seconds later all three of them were headed for the shuttle. Although McCade was the only one who was married, both Rico and Phil had significant others, plus a raft of friends. And as a member of the planetary council, Rico felt a special responsibility to the entire population.

They all hoped for the best but feared the worst.

McCade paused outside the shuttle bay access lock and touched a button. Maggie appeared on-screen. He knew without asking that the engineer had kept abreast of developments via the drive-room intercom and view screens. Maggie didn't talk much but she always knew what was going on. "We're heading dirtside."

Maggie nodded. "It didn't take a genius to figure that out."

"Are you coming?"

Maggie gave him a twisted smile. "No, I don't think so. I haven't got any people down there, and besides, who'd watch the ship?"

McCade had expected something of the kind and was secretly grateful. He hated to leave *Void Runner* unattended. "Thanks, Maggie. I'll call you from dirtside."

McCade was just starting to turn away when Maggie cleared her throat. "McCade?"

"Yeah?"

"I'm sorry."

McCade looked in Maggie's eyes and knew she thought Sara and Molly were dead. It was a logical conclusion but one he refused to accept. A lump formed in McCade's throat and he forced it down.

"Thanks, Maggie. Keep a sharp lookout. There's always the chance that they'll come back."

Maggie nodded silently and the screen faded to black.

The trip dirtside was a dark and somber affair. Heavy winds buffeted the shuttle as it entered the atmosphere and snow fell at lower altitudes.

McCade brought the shuttle down through the lowest layer of dark gray clouds and sent it skimming over pristine whiteness. He flew low and slow. Rocky hills swelled here and there, bare where the wind had scoured them clean, their sides covered with low vegetation.

Then the hills were gone and the shuttle entered the mouth of a long, low valley. Days of snow had hidden most of the damage, with only wisps of smoke and a higher-than-usual radiation count to indicate damage had been done.

McCade knew that to the north and east a number of low-yield nuclear devices had exploded, each destroying a surface-to-space missile battery, but leaving the underground population centers untouched. At least *that* strategy had worked.

Now, as the shuttle neared the capital city of New Home, the damage became more apparent. Shattered domes, covered with a dusting of new snow; wrecked crawlers, sitting at the center of fire-blackened circles; half-blasted radars, still searching the skies for targets long disappeared; and here and there, the pitiful huddle of someone's last stand, now little more than bumps under a shroud of white.

McCade bit his lip and glanced at Rico. The other man's feelings were effectively hidden behind his beard, but his eyes were on the view screen, and they were as cold as the land below.

All was not death and destruction however. Here and there signs of life could be seen. Fresh vehicle tracks in the snow, a hint of underground warmth on the infrared detectors, and the vague whisper of low-powered radio traffic. There was life down there, less than before, but life nonetheless.

McCade stuck an unlit cigar between his teeth. "Run the frequencies, Rico. Someone's talking. Let's see who it is."

Rico flipped some switches and ran the freqs, starting with commonly used civilian bands and working his way upward. "Rico here . . . anybody read me?"

The response was almost instantaneous. A surprisingly cheerful male voice said. "Pawley here, Rico . . . nice of you to drop in."

Rico grinned. "Pawley? What the hell are you doing here? I thought you were down south working the G-Tap."

McCade knew, as did all the planet's citizens, that "G-Tap" stood for "geothermal tap," and was a project to harness the energy resident in the planet's core. A lot of effort and a lot of tax money had flowed into that project, and Brian Pawley was the G-Tap team leader.

"We were lucky," Pawley replied soberly, "either they missed us, or thought us unimportant. In any case we survived and came back to help. Everybody's pitching in. Ranchers, miners, you name it, they're all lending a hand."

McCade saw the landing pad up ahead. Two piles of snow-dusted wreckage marked where a ship and a shuttle had been caught on the ground. Energy weapons had cut a confusing hatch work of dark lines into the ground. McCade cut speed and prepared to land.

"We're about to land," Rico said. "Where should we head?"

Pawley was silent for a moment. When he spoke there was a forced cheerfulness to his voice, as if he felt one way, and was saying something else.

"Stay on the pad . . . I'll pick you up."

McCade killed the shuttle's forward motion, fired repellors, and settled gently onto the pad.

A huge cloud of steam billowed up to obscure the view. As the wind blew it away McCade saw a crawler roll out onto the pad, its white and gray camouflage useless against the burnt area behind it, twin rooster tails of snow flying up behind it.

It took McCade and Rico a good ten minutes to pull on their heat suits and enter the lock. Phil was already there, sans suit, with a big grin on his face. Thanks to his thick layer of fur the variant could stroll through winter snowstorms that would kill Rico or McCade in a few short minutes.

The lock cycled open and they left the protection of the ship's hull. McCade had opted to leave his hood and goggles hanging down his back. The cold cut into his face like a thousand tiny knives. He removed the unlit cigar from his mouth and threw it away.

Unlike Sara, Rico, and Phil, McCade hated the cold, and would've preferred a warmer planet. Sara . . . Molly . . . the names were like spears through McCade's heart.

Their boots made a crunching sound as they approached the crawler. A door hissed open and released a blast of warm air. McCade scrambled inside, closely followed by Phil and Rico.

Pawley was at the controls. He turned sideways in his seat. Though normally clean-shaven, Pawley wore a two-day growth of beard. He had short hair, a crooked nose, and thick rather sensuous lips. "Welcome aboard, gentlemen."

Pawley's words were followed by an awkward silence. Rico was the first to break it. "No offense, ol' sport . . . but let's go straight to the bottom line. Who made it and who didn't?"

A cloud came over Pawley's face. "I'm sorry, Rico . . . Vanessa was killed. She died defending the fusion plant."

Rico nodded, and looked out through scratched plastic at the bleakness beyond. Tears ran down his cheeks and into his beard.

Pawley looked at Phil. The variant stared back, trying to read the scientist's eyes, steeling himself against the worst.

Pawley ran his tongue over dry lips. "We just don't know, Phil . . . Deena's unit went off-air more than a day ago . . . she's missing in action."

Phil gave a grunt of acknowledgment. Missing rather than dead. There was hope at least.

Now it was McCade's turn to look Pawley in the eye. "Well?"

The word sounded harsh, and McCade wished he could pull it back, but there was no need. Pawley understood.

"Good news and bad news, Sam. The good news first. Sara was wounded but she's alive. Doc Lewis says she'll be fine in a couple of weeks."

"And Molly?" McCade croaked the words out. If Sara was the good news, then . . .

Pawley swallowed hard. "They took her, Sam . . . along with sixty or seventy other children."

McCade let his breath out in a long, slow exhalation. At least she was alive. Frightened, lonely, but alive.

McCade's fingers curled into hard fists. First Molly, then Mustapha Pong. Not for money, not for empire, but for himself. McCade's Bounty.

FOUR

Molly McCade bit her lip and refused to cry. She'd done a lot of crying during the last few days and it didn't do any good. The pirates didn't care, and the other girls were just as scared as she was. She didn't know where the boys were and hadn't seen any since the attack.

Molly rolled over, careful not to wake anyone who might be asleep. Sleep was a precious commodity for the children. It was a time of much needed rest and escape from the horror of the ship's small hold.

The girls were packed into four-foot-high sections, with cold metal gratings under their backs, and very little room to move around.

They were allowed to leave the hold twice a day. First came the scramble up ladders to the pressurized launch bay, then a bowl of tasteless protein mush, followed by fifteen laps around the hangar. Then they were forced through a bank of over-used chemical toilets, an antiseptic spray, and returned to the gratings.

And since everything was done in alphabetical order, there was no hope of a better position on the gratings.

Poor Susy Zobrist. She was stuck on the bottommost grating and cried all the time.

Some kids threw up a lot, others had to go to the bathroom all the time, and whoever lay just beneath them took the brunt of it.

But some dribbled past, and ended up at the very bottom of the hold where it coated everyone and everything.

From the pirate point of view it was an extremely efficient low-cost way of transporting a lot of people at once. Not only that, but when the gratings were removed, the hold could still be used for more conventional cargoes.

Looking up through the dark crisscross of metal gratings, and the black sprawl of supine bodies, Molly could see the glow of a single greenish light.

It reminded her of the night light in her room on Alice. As long as the light was on nothing could sneak up and hurt her. There had been two greenish lights originally, but one had gone out two cycles earlier, and now Molly feared that the other one would too.

"Oh, please, God," she prayed, "don't let the light go out. And if Mommy's with you, tell her I miss her, and I'm trying to be good. And, God, if Daddy's coming, tell him to hurry."

FIVE

They used hand blasters to cut down through the permafrost. After that the robo shovels moved in, their drive wheels squeaking in the cold, their scoops biting into frozen dirt.

Steam rose from the temporarily warmed earth, eddied around the mourners like strands of errant ectoplasm, and was whipped away by a steady breeze. It came from the south and made the minister's robes swish and pop. His words were feeble and small against the vast backdrop of frozen wilderness and gray sky.

". . . And so it is that we lay these valiant souls to rest, secure in the knowledge that their essence lives on, looking forward to the time when we shall see them again . . ."

McCade felt Sara shift her weight from one leg to the other. Her right leg still hurt where the slug had ripped through her thigh. It was a miracle that she was still alive. Twenty-seven men and women had defended the main entry. Three had survived.

McCade thought Sara should be in the hospital, but between the pressures of office and her own stubbornness, she'd been up and around for a day now.

McCade tightened his arm around Sara's waist and pulled her even closer. He gloried in the feel of her, and had Molly been there beside him, he would've been secretly happy.

But she wasn't, and that, plus the guilt McCade felt for putting his own family first, pulled his emotions down.

At least Phil was alright. Deena had been found and was recovering in the hospital.

The minister paused, turned a page in the tattered book, and intoned the ancient words. ". . . Ashes to ashes . . . dust to dust . . ."

Sara leaned her head against his arm. She was crying.

McCade watched Rico as the coffins were lowered into the grave. They were all that remained of a full section. The rest would never be found. The second belonged to Vanessa. As her coffin disappeared from sight, Rico whispered a prayer and threw something in after her. McCade caught the glint of gold.

When the last coffin had been lowered into the grave, and blasters had rewarmed the earth, a robo shovel filled the trench.

Then, their shoulders covered with a dusting of snow, the mourners crunched their way back to the line of waiting crawlers. One had been set aside for Sara, McCade, Rico, and Phil.

It dipped and rolled through broken ground to waddle out onto the landing pad. The elevator mechanism that normally lowered ships below the frozen surface was still under repair, but both of the burned-out hulks had been pushed aside, and another shuttle sat beside his own. It was old and extremely beat-up.

A tramp freighter had dropped into orbit the day before. After all the death and destruction it seemed hard to believe that life would go on, that the rest of humanity was still going about its business, but the shuttle proved it. Things, outer things that didn't mean much, were returning to normal.

Somewhere, deep in space, a message torp was on its way to Imperial Earth. There wouldn't be much that the Emperor could do but it was worth a try.

Rico and Phil were quick to buss Sara on the cheek, say their good-byes, and head for the shuttle. The door opened and closed with a rush of cold air.

McCade glanced toward the driver but saw that the connecting hatch had been tactfully closed. Not for him, but for Sara. After all, she was head of the planetary council and a person of some importance.

McCade cupped Sara's face with his hands and used his thumb to remove a tear. "Don't cry, honey, I'll find Molly and bring her back."

"And the rest of the kids too."

McCade nodded solemnly. "And the rest of the kids too."

Sara bit her lower lip and nodded. He no longer saw the scar. She looked so pretty it made his heart ache.

"Be careful, Sam. Pong hates you so much he's willing to destroy entire planets. The possibility of losing Molly is bad enough . . . but if I lose you too . . ."

McCade put a finger over her lips. "It won't happen. Molly's got a good head on her shoulders. She'll hang in there and we'll do the rest."

Sara nodded slowly, her eyes searching every aspect of his face, as if committing it to memory. "Keep a close eye on Rico, Sam, he's hurting, and God knows what he might do."

McCade answered with a kiss, a long one that kindled memories and desires as well. When it was over Sara smiled.

"You'd better get out of here, Sam, or the driver will have a racy story to tell her friends, and I'll never live it down."

McCade laughed, kissed her on the tip of her nose, and keyed the door. It opened and he didn't look back. He was afraid to. Afraid he'd break down and start babbling what he felt. Conflicting things that didn't make sense and were all jumbled together.

That he should've been dirtside when Pong attacked. That he shouldn't leave Sara alone on Alice. That he should've started the search yesterday.

McCade was halfway to the shuttle before the cold cut through his thoughts and chilled his skin.

Every search has to begin somewhere and Lakor seemed a likely bet. A somewhat primitive planet, featuring a mishmash of high and low tech, Lakor was best known for its slave markets. Ugly, sprawling places, filled to overflowing with miserable sentients, they provided a much-needed source of foreign exchange.

In fact, Lakorians claimed the dubious distinction of being the biggest slave traders in all of known space, a claim disputed by the Zords, but probably true.

McCade, Rico, and Phil knew Lakor rather well, since they'd spent some rather unpleasant time there and weren't eager to return.

Still, knowing that pirates generally unload slaves as quickly as possible,

Lakor was a logical place to go. After all, maybe they'd get lucky and find the children right off the top.

It could happen . . . especially if Lif came to their assistance.

While searching for the War World some years before, McCade had been dumped on Lakor by a rather unfriendly Il Ronnian naval officer and taken into slavery. McCade was rescued by Rico, but Sara wasn't so lucky. Together with Phil the two men set off to find her. During the journey they encountered the then Baron Lif, entered a conspiracy to overthrow King Zorta, and eventually did so, rescuing Sara in the process.

This had positioned Baron Lif to take the planetary throne, and assuming he had, they might be eligible for some royal assistance. They could hope anyway.

Most of Lakor was obscured by a thick layer of clouds. The same clouds that dumped vast quantities of rain into the planet's swamps, filled its rivers to overflowing, and created two rather large oceans.

Having received clearance to land, and having left *Void Runner* under Maggie's surly care, McCade, Rico, and Phil rode the shuttle down through Lakor's cloudy skies. They couldn't see a thing and were totally reliant on the ship's instruments.

Even though the shuttle jerked and bucked its way down through the atmosphere it still felt comfortable compared to McCade's last trip.

Along with Sara, and a marine named Van Doren, McCade had been forced into an unpadded cargo module and dropped from orbit. The combination of Lakor's gravity and unpredictable winds had beaten all of them unconscious.

The shuttle dropped out of the clouds over a large bay. Beneath them a fleet of wooden fishing boats left tiny white streaks against the blue-green water. Their lateen sails were bright orange and pushed the boats along at a pretty good clip.

There were hovercraft as well, brightly colored rectangles, dashing here and there without regard for the fishing nets or their owner's safety.

Then the boats were gone, left miles behind as the shuttle flew over quickly shallowing water and a large swamp. Beyond the swamp was a river, a twisting, turning ribbon of reflected light, heavy with debris and brownish silt.

Thick jungle grew down to touch the river on both banks, filling the V-shaped valley with verdant life, much of which was dangerous as hell.

Dropping down so that the valley's steep walls reached upward from both sides, McCade took pleasure in the twisting, turning course. He loved the skill required, the feeling of speed, the hint of danger.

The valley started to widen out. McCade killed speed, missed the look of relief on Phil's face, and followed a series of flashing beacons in for a landing.

The shuttle had no more than touched down when four armed crawlers roared out onto the scorched duracrete followed by a company of mounted soldiers.

The crawlers were of standard imperial manufacture but the cavalry were quite extraordinary. First came the Lakorians themselves. Squat-looking humanoids with greenish skin and stumpy legs. They wore orange uniforms with dark brown trim.

Then there were the Lakorian mounts. Huge six-legged reptilian animals, carrying three riders apiece and wearing bright blue trappings. The lead riders carried lances from which long green pennants flew. Seated behind them were two more soldiers, each armed with an energy weapon and a mean expression. The shuttle was completely surrounded within seconds.

McCade could still lift, but in doing so he would kill some of the riders, and call in whatever navy the planet had. That would not only foreclose any possibility of finding the children but might be fatal as well.

Rico shook his head in pretended amazement. "Sam, ya never cease ta amaze me. We haven't even left the ship and someone's pissed! How the hell do ya do it?"

"By flying too damned low," Phil said sourly.

McCade initiated an auto shutdown sequence, released his harness, and stood up.

"Thank you for the vote of confidence. But as you are about to learn, things are not always as they appear. Where *you* see a group of soldiers bent on hanging me from the nearest tree, *I* see a guard of honor, sent by King Lif to escort us to his palace."

Rico looked at Phil, Phil looked at Rico, and both of them shrugged.

Five minutes later the outer hatch cycled open, McCade stepped out, and a horrible sound rent the air.

The source of this terrible noise was a stout-looking Lakorian noncom with a long-dead animal tucked under his right arm. By blowing air in through the poor creature's nostrils and squeezing its inflated body, he was able to produce a sound somewhat akin to a tortured house cat.

Realizing this was Lakorian music, and suspecting that it might be Lif's anthem, McCade popped to attention. Seeing this Rico and Phil did likewise.

The caterwauling went on for some time, rising and falling to the subtle manipulations of the steadfast noncom, finally ending in an earsplitting screech.

It was at this point that a much-bemedaled officer stepped forward, bowed formally, and said, "On behalf of King Lif, defender of the realm, protector of the innocent, and gift from the gods, I greet you. I am Major Rola. Please accompany us that we might take you into the presence of the king himself."

Like most Lakorians Rola spoke excellent standard. The slave markets drew an unending flow of off-world visitors, and that, plus the Lakorian fondness of things human, meant that the upper class spoke standard as fluently as Lakorian. Some even preferred it, much to the dismay of traditionalists.

McCade turned to Rico and Phil, raised an eyebrow as if to say "I told you so," and turned back to Major Rola. He bowed deeply. Lakor had a strong feudal tradition complete with fancy titles and courtly manners.

"Thank you, Major. We are honored. Please lead the way."

"The way," as it turned out, involved a crawler, and the axiom "that the shortest path between two points is always a straight line."

With their crawler leading the way, a convoy was formed and headed toward the northeast, with the cavalry following along behind.

During the brief moments when McCade wasn't being thrown from one side of the vehicle to the other, he took time to look out the viewports and observe their surroundings. Things were much as he remembered.

All Lakorian dwellings were built on pilings. This made them immune to the comings and goings of the water below them. Most were circular and had domed roofs. Sections of the roofs were hinged so they could be opened during rare moments of sunshine.

All-terrain vehicles were very popular. McCade saw them all over the place. Brightly colored creations with huge balloon tires and lots of dents. Half roared this way and that, while the other half were parked, often right next to the rotting boats that they'd replaced.

The streets were haphazard. They followed the path of least resistance most of the time, or ran along beside sections of the old canal system, now choked with garbage and weeds.

This did not intimidate their driver however, who, true to his straight-line philosophy of navigation, splashed through all but the very deepest canals.

In addition their route carried them down busy thoroughfares, through residential backyards, across at least one swamp and out into a large clearing.

At its center stood a log palisade, and within that, the largest log structure McCade had ever seen. It was huge, boasting thousands of square feet, and like everything else was up on pilings. A pair of gates swung open to admit the crawler.

"Well, here's the palace," Major Rola said proudly as the crawler jerked to a sudden halt. "Unbelievable, isn't it?'

McCade looked out at the muddy courtyard, the domesticated animals rooting in one corner of the palisade, and nodded his agreement. "It sure is," he said dryly. "Don't the taxpayers complain?"

"Naw," Rola replied confidently. "Why should they? The money comes from slaves, not them."

The Lakorian's comment served to jerk McCade out of his role as tourist and remind him of his mission. Molly. Molly and the other children.

The door hissed open to amidst some tired, soggy air. McCade stood. "Thanks for the ride, Major. Let's see the king."

After a short walk across the muddy courtyard they passed through a large door and entered a reception area. It was huge and, outside of the muddy floor, quite spotless.

Three guards flanked each side of the hall. They snapped to attention as a rather junior officer stepped forward.

"The humans will surrender their weapons. The hairy thing also."

McCade took a moment to look the Lakorian up and down. He didn't like surrendering his slug gun, especially on a slime ball like Lakor, and especially to some jumped-up clown in a fancy uniform.

But he did want Lif's cooperation, and even the most generous monarch might resent the loss of his bodyguard and find ways to express his displeasure.

Seeing the human's insolent gaze and correctly interpreting the lack of respect it conveyed, the officer went for the nerve lash secured to his belt. Five strokes would put the human in his place and restore the lieutenant's dignity.

Major Rola was just opening his mouth to object when another voice was heard. "As you were, Lieutenant!"

The officer came to rigid attention.

The Lakorian who stepped out into the reception area was splendidly clad, about a foot shorter than McCade, and by the standards of his race quite handsome.

He had a prominent forehead, intelligent eyes, and a wide, thick-lipped mouth. It was turned upward in a rather human smile. "Greetings, Sir Knight. Squire Rico, Squire Phil, welcome to my humble home."

Lif frowned as he turned to the unfortunate lieutenant. "While I appreciate the zeal with which you carry out your duties, I would recommend a good deal more tact, especially when dealing with humans like these. Any one of them could have killed you and all of your troops long before you pulled that silly nerve lash from your belt. These are not serfs for your abuse! Report to your quarters and give it some thought."

McCade thought he saw some looks of enjoyment pass between the enlisted males as the lieutenant left the room.

Moving in closer Lif shook their hands human style and lowered his voice. "Again, welcome. Imagine my surprise and pleasure when orbital control informed me of your wish to land."

Lif saw McCade's questioning look and waved a negligent hand. "Yes, some visitors are brought to my personal attention, and you among them. I owe you much. I apologize for the actions of my nephew Hora, but he is young and will eventually learn. But enough of that. Come! We must eat and drink. Then we shall speak of many things."

Lif led them into a sumptuous dining room, hosted them to an enormous dinner, and did his best to drink them under the table. While appearing the genial host Lif liked to lubricate his guests as quickly as possible. It gave him the advantage.

Knowing that from past experience, all three of the humans had managed to swallow inhibitors during the early stages of the meal, and were only slightly drunk by the time it was over.

"So," Lif ventured, squinting through the haze of blue cigar smoke that circled their heads, "what brings you to Lakor?"

McCade tried to concentrate. The vak was clouding his thoughts. "A personal quest, sire. Pirates raided our planet. They came in such force that we couldn't stop them. When they left the pirates took more than sixty of our children with them. One was my daughter, Molly."

Lif shook his head sadly. "I'm sorry, good knight. The fault is partly ours. As long as we rely on slavery as a source of foreign exchange we will be partners to such horror. I hope to reduce our dependence on slavery but these things take time. In the meantime you came to Lakor wondering if the children had passed through our slave markets."

McCade nodded. The motion made his head swim. "Exactly, sire. We had hoped for your help and assistance."

"And have it you shall." Lif clapped his hands and an elderly Lakorian appeared from behind a large tapestry. McCade wondered how long he'd been there. He was slightly stooped over and clad in a long orange robe.

"Sire?"

"Murd, this is Sir Sam McCade and two of his squires. Sir Sam is searching for his daughter and sixty other children taken from his native planet. It is possible that they were brought here. Search all of the slave markets and report to me."

Murd bowed. "Yes, sire. It shall be as you say."

He turned to McCade. "Tell me, good knight, would you have a holo pix or other means of identification by any chance? Our markets are large, and there are many cubs."

Rico scowled at the thought and reached inside his vest. He removed a data cube and handed it over. "Photos, descriptions, it's all on this."

Murd bowed once more. "Thank you, squire. Work will begin immediately." Then he backed toward the tapestry and disappeared.

Lif hoisted a pitcher and filled their mugs with more vak. "So, my friends, let us drink to Murd's success, after which I will seek your advice and counsel."

McCade lifted his mug and took a small sip. Here it comes, he thought to himself, the price for Lif's cooperation. Chances were Murd wasn't doing a damned thing and wouldn't until Lif made it clear that he should. Lakorians were shrewd bargainers, one reason why they'd been so successful as slavers, and everything had a price. He decided to move the process along.

"Advice, Your Highness? Surely you have advisors more qualified than we?"

Lif chuckled indulgently. "Yes, good knight, on things like taxes, crops, and fertilizer. But when it comes to matters of war, my advisors lack imagination. Surely you remember this from our campaign against the despot Zorta?"

McCade *did* remember. Though brave, the Lakorian officers tended toward all-out frontal attacks, and were something less than innovative.

Nonetheless, McCade was careful to avoid acquiescence, and an indirect insult to the Lakorian general staff. After all, if Murd liked to hang out behind the tapestry, there might be others as well.

"A successful campaign as I recall, Your Highness, and one in which your forces performed admirably."

Lif laughed. "Your tact does you credit, Sir Knight. But enough of this dancing around. Chances are it will take Murd a few days to check all the slave markets. In the meantime I have a small problem and would appreciate your help and advice."

McCade blew smoke toward the distant ceiling. Lif had set the trap. There was little he could do but jump in and hope for the best. "Of course, sire, we would be happy to help. What's the nature of the problem?"

Lif picked up a carving knife and waved it like a wand. "It's my brother, Bulo, the now Baron Lif. He has taken over a town outside of our ancestral lands and refuses to leave."

"I see," McCade replied with a growing sense of dread. "And how can we help?"

Lif brought the knife down hard. Two inches of the durasteel blade penetrated the wood. It wobbled back and forth as he let it go.

"That should be simple, good knight. Go into the town, find my brother, and do what has to be done."

Molly awoke from a fitful sleep as a hatch swung back on its hinges and hit the ship's hull with a dull clang. The woman they called Boots let go of the ladder and dropped the last few feet to the first level. The gratings shook with the impact.

The nickname stemmed from the way the woman looked from below, like a large pair of combat boots, topped by a black blob. Of course the children saw her at meals as well, a beefy woman with her hair in a bun, but the name still seemed to fit.

Acting on impulse Molly made a rude noise. There was a deathly silence for a moment, followed by giggles and laughter. It was the first time anyone had laughed since the attack on Alice.

Boots stamped a gigantic foot. The grating rang in response. "Who did that?"

Silence.

Boots spoke again. "Give me her name, or lose your next meal!"

Molly was afraid now. They received so little food that meals were extremely important. Most of the kids would protect her, but one was all it would take to give her away. She didn't know what Boots would do and didn't want to find out.

But there was only silence.

Boots climbed the ladder and closed the hatch. The children had sacrificed a meal but gained a measure of self-respect.

Those closest to Molly whispered their congratulations and asked what she planned to do next. Accidentally, and without forethought, Molly had become a leader.

Molly knew Mommy was a leader, and a good one too. She chaired the council that ran Alice. And Mommy said Daddy was a leader as well, the kind you want to have when there's trouble, or when people start to give up.

All of Molly's life she'd heard them talk about politics, about people, about how to get things done. What would they say about this situation? What could she do to help herself and those around her?

Molly could almost hear her mother's voice. "Basics come first. Nobody wants to talk about freedom and justice until their stomachs are full."

Molly winced. Rather than give them food she had taken it away. Sure, the incident had granted her some temporary popularity, but that wouldn't last long. Hunger was stronger than loyalty.

First she must find a way to fill their bellies and improve their living conditions. Then it would be time to discuss things like freedom, which in this case meant escape.

Hours passed. Finally it was mealtime once again. The hatch opened and hit the hull with the usual clang. Boots dropped to the grating.

"All right, any wise comments this time?"

Silence.

Boots grunted her approval. "Good. All right, you little hold rats, time for din-din, top grating first. Hurry up, I don't have all watch."

There were the usual rattlings and clankings as the topmost layers of children crawled toward the ladder and climbed upward. Boots administered an occasional lick to the slower ones urging them to "hurry up or forget the whole damned thing."

Forcing herself to ignore the pain caused when her filth-encrusted clothes came in contact with the open sores on her arms and legs, Molly tried to think, tried to imagine a way in which she could use this brief moment of comparative freedom to better their living conditions. Try as she might nothing came to mind.

The children blinked as they left the darkness of the access way and entered the brightly lit hangar. As usual there was a row of shuttles and interceptors along the far side of the bar, attended by a small scattering of maintenance bots, and some ship-suited technicians.

The mess line cut the space in half and the A's, B's, and C's were already going through it. Molly could smell the yeasty slop and her stomach growled in response.

Shuffling forward when the line did, Molly forced herself to look around. She must remember to think. What could she do to better their circumstances? Wait a minute, who was that?

A rather pleasant-looking man with some sort of lump on his shoulder. What was that thing anyway? Molly had never seen anything quite like it. Whatever it was looked kind of pretty, all shiny and shimmery, like the fabric in Mommy's best dress.

In any case, the nice-looking man was talking to someone else, a man who looked anything but nice. He was big, like a weight lifter, and wore a heavy leather harness instead of a shirt.

Without thinking, without considering the consequences, Molly left the chow line and walked toward them. They were in charge, she could tell that from the way they stood, and the other crew members shied away. She had thirty or forty feet to cover. It looked like a mile.

What was it Daddy had told her? If you're doing something you shouldn't, act natural, look relaxed. People see what they're conditioned to see. So Molly walked when every fiber of her body wanted to run.

And it worked. Molly was only five feet away from the two men when she heard a yell of protest and the sound of running feet.

The nice man turned, laser blue eyes locking onto hers like range finders, a smile touching his lips. The slug thing shimmered wildly and seemed to ooze a few inches to the right. The man didn't seem to notice.

"That's close enough, child. You smell like the bottom of a recycling vat."

Molly stopped and drew herself up straight. "Exactly, sir. Are you in command?"

The man gave a slight nod. "Yes, I am."

Loud footsteps came up behind her and a heavy hand fell on Molly's shoulder. She knew who it belonged to without turning around. Boots sounded half angry, half scared. "Come here, you . . . I'll teach you to disobey my orders!"

The man held up a hand. "Hold. I want to hear what she has to say."

"But, sir . . . I . . ."

"Silence. Let the child speak."

Molly's heart beat wildly in her chest. The blue eyes were cold and empty of compassion. What could Molly say that would move a man like this? Her voice quavered slightly.

"Sir, if you are in command, then we children are your property. It seems safe to assume that you plan to sell us. Yet we receive only two meals a day, no medical care, and spend most of our time on bare metal gratings."

Molly held out her arms. They were covered with infected sores. "Look at the condition of your property. Our value falls further with each passing hour. Eventually some of us will die."

"Is that it?" The man's voice was hard and unyielding.

Molly swallowed hard. "Yes, sir."

The man looked up over Molly's head. The meaty hands disappeared from her shoulders. "The child makes sense. Feed them three times a day. I will send the medical officer. Arrange for clean clothes. See to their quarters." He gestured toward the blond man. "Raz will inspect them once per cycle."

Molly felt Boots stiffen behind her. "Yes, sir!"

The man nodded and turned away. A few seconds later he and Raz were in deep conversation.

A hand fell on Molly's shoulder. It guided her away from the chow line to where some cargo modules were secured to tie-downs in the deck. As soon as the modules hid them from view Boots spun Molly around, grabbed the front of her ragged shirt, and pulled her in close.

"Listen, brat . . . and listen good! You think you're real smart, real slick the way you conned Pong, but you forgot one thing. *He* spends most of his time on the bridge . . . and *I* spend most of my time with you."

And with that Boots slapped Molly across the face. Then came more slaps followed by hard fists and huge boots. Darkness came as a welcome relief.

SEVEN

The hovercraft bumped and shuddered through a series of small rapids throwing the tightly packed serfs left and right. Adults swore, children cried, and a variety of domesticated animals growled, hissed, and squealed their objections.

It was bad enough for the passengers in the main cabin, but for McCade, Rico, and Phil, as well as the Lakorians assigned to assist them, it was part of a long, boring hell.

They'd been locked in the forward hold for two days now, unable to see out, and constantly thrown about.

Light came from a couple of high portholes and some tired chemstrips. And like most holds this one came complete with cargo, some unpleasant life forms, and plenty of strange odors. Their table was a cargo module, crates stood in for chairs, and odds and ends took care of everything else.

At the moment Rico and six of the Lakorian troopers sat around the table, playing poker and swearing prodigiously.

One of the Lakorians was named Ven, a crafty type who'd risen a couple of ranks since McCade's first visit years ago, and commanded the rest.

Ven folded with an expression of profound disgust and pushed the small pot in Rico's direction. The human raked it in.

It was good to see Rico having a little fun. He'd been dark and gloomy of late, something he denied, but the others recognized for what it was . . . grief. Vanessa's death had hit him hard.

McCade climbed up on a box and tried to look out through one of the small slitlike portholes. It was a waste of time. Between the spray thrown up by the hovercraft's fans, the rain that never seemed to stop, and the vessel's erratic motion, he could see little more than a gray-green blur.

McCade climbed down and lit another cigar. The air was already thick with smoke and moisture, but what the hell, it was something to do.

Phil opened one eye, didn't like what he saw, and turned over. The variant had built himself a bunk on the top of some packing crates and spent most of his time in it. The warmth and humidity made him miserable so he was sleeping through as much of the trip as he could.

There was a narrow open space along the port bulkhead. McCade used it to pace back and forth, cigar clenched between his teeth, smoke issuing forth in small puffs. At some point during the next hour or so the hovercraft should arrive in the village of Durn. Then he'd know what they were up against.

The whole thing sucked but there wasn't much McCade could do about it. Without saying so directly Lif had made it clear that the situation in Durn was directly linked to Murd's efforts on behalf of the children.

It seemed that Lif's younger brother Bulo had always been something of an embarrassment, spending most of his time chasing after females, and gambling away his share of the family fortune.

When Lif became king, Bulo had expected his brother to elevate him to an appropriately lofty post. Something lucrative but not very demanding.

So, when the post failed to materialize, and Lif refused his requests for favor, Bulo took drastic action.

Picking out a village, apparently at random, Bulo invaded using his entourage of toadies and young toughs to overwhelm the local police force.

Lif had received the predictable protest from Duke Isso, Lord of Durn and a powerful politician, not long thereafter.

Just as Bulo had intended, Lif found himself in a difficult position, forced to choose between a member of his own family and an important ally. If he used force against his brother, it would be the same as finding him guilty of a crime, and by Lakorian tradition, that guilt would extend to Lif's entire family including Lif himself.

And if the king didn't move against Bulo, Duke Isso would use the issue to make serious trouble in the House of Nobles, possibly leading to war.

Of course he could give Bulo what he asked, and forget the whole matter, but Lif knew better than that. Bulo would want more, and more, until the entire planet groveled at his feet.

No, that would never do. So the answer was to have someone else perform his dirty work for him, someone Lif could deny if necessary, someone like a group of itinerant aliens.

McCade dropped the cigar butt on the deck and ground it out under his boot.

Yes, the whole thing was more than a little transparent, but effective nonetheless. Lakor was a big planet, home to many slave markets, and only by securing Lif's cooperation could they be sure of checking them all.

That meant they'd have to find Bulo, snatch him out from under his army of butt kissers, and get him back to so-called civilization.

McCade was thrown forward as someone cut the power too fast. He caught himself on a cargo module and heard feet thump as the crew ran to get bumpers and boat hooks.

Now McCade was thrown in the opposite direction as the captain ordered full speed astern. Thanks more to luck than skill, the hovercraft hit the pier with a gentle thud and came to a stop. Then the power was cut and the vessel settled down onto her inflated skirts.

McCade scrambled up to the porthole, wiped away the condensation, and peered out. Minus the spray, and with only a slight misting of rain, McCade could see most of the dock. It was surprisingly well made and in good repair. A testament to Duke Isso's provident use of tax money.

He saw some ragged-looking serfs drag the gangplank into position, lift it up into the air. He heard, rather than saw it hit the hovercraft's deck.

At this point some passengers started to disembark but the staccato cough of an automatic weapon sent them fleeing back up the gangplank.

A brand-new group of Lakorians was starting to board. Although heavily armed, they acted more like civilians than soldiers, sauntering up the gangway as if boarding a yacht.

McCade turned slightly, pointing toward the doors and overhead hatch. The Lakorians, all members of Lif's personal bodyguard, took up positions opposite the two main entrances. Phil aimed his machine pistol up toward the cargo hatch and Rico waited with a blast rifle cradled in his arms.

McCade looked back just in time to see the Lakorian dandies disappear from sight. He bit his lip and strained to hear what was going on.

There was a good deal of incoherent shouting as Bulo's followers asserted their right to search the hovercraft and the vessel's skipper told them to shove it.

The skipper had received a rather generous subsidy to carry the aliens in his forward hold, and to do so in complete secrecy. He could double-cross them of course, but that would mean double-crossing King Lif as well, a rather unhealthy thing to do.

The problem was finally resolved with a Lakorian-style compromise, in which the dandies were allowed to search the upper decks, while the holds remained sealed.

This saved face all the way around, and inconvenienced no one, except the peasants, who were more worried about getting enough to eat than notions of personal honor.

Satisfied that they'd carried out their duties, the bullies left the ship and headed for the inn that doubled as Bulo's headquarters.

The next hour or so was spent unloading supplies from the aft hold and loading a hundred bales of noxious weed. McCade's Lakorian troopers swore the stuff was a rare delicacy handpicked in jungle swamps and served in all of the finest restaurants. If so, McCade decided to avoid those restaurants at all costs.

Shortly after the weed was loaded they heard some confused shouts, the splash of a poorly handled bow line, and the loud roar of the hovercraft's twin engines. A few minutes later and they were skimming upriver.

An hour passed and the light started to fade. Then, right at that magic moment when the evening light granted the jungle a soft beauty, the engine noise dropped off and the hovercraft slowed.

"This must be it," McCade announced. "Let's gather up our gear and get ready to bail out of this floating coffin."

There was a loud banging on one of the doors. Rico unlatched it and stepped back with blast rifle leveled.

The captain entered, hands held up in protest. He was short, wrinkled, and solid as the deck he stood on. His standard was something less than perfect.

"Shoot me don't! Friend am I. Arrived have we. Come."

McCade took a look around to make sure they had everything. The soldiers were shouldering backpacks filled with food, medical supplies, and ammo, plus a lethal array of weapons.

Rico wore a backpack com set and Phil carried a flame-thrower with two tanks of fuel.

That left a big black duffel bag that was made out of some sort of water-proof material and equipped with shoulder straps. McCade picked it up. The damned thing weighed a ton. It was tempting to leave it on the hovercraft, de-pend on plan A, and forget the backups. Tempting but stupid.

"Everybody ready?"

There were grunts of assent.

McCade nodded and they followed the captain up on deck. The passage-ways were filthy, the stairs were encrusted with dried mud, and the serfs were as tightly packed as ever. A good many had disembarked at Durn, but even more had trooped aboard, so conditions were little improved.

A child ran out in front of McCade. She wore one of the complicated sarongs that Lakorians loved to lavish on young females. She squealed with joy and headed straight for the gangplank. There was a shout of protest as her mother tried to intervene.

McCade scooped her up and smiled. The little female reminded him of Molly, of all the hugs he'd missed while traveling between the stars, of what he must find.

Frightened by the alien face, the child started to sob. McCade handed her to a grateful mother, shifted the duffel bag to a more comfortable position, and led the way onto the gangplank.

Once they were ashore the captain wasted little time on "good-byes." He gave a curt wave, shouted some orders, and disappeared into the wheelhouse.

The hovercraft made a loud roaring sound as it backed away from the bank and turned upstream. For a moment it looked big, with black skirts, or-ange hull, and a streamlined deckhouse.

Then it grew suddenly smaller as spray flew and the water flattened out around it. Seconds later the hovercraft was gone, disappeared around the next bend, heading upriver.

Something took a bite out of McCade's arm. He slapped it and swore. He wasn't looking forward to the stroll through the jungle, but if they wanted to sneak up on Baron Bulo Lif that's what it would take.

McCade lit a cigar and hoped that the smoke would discourage the rather numerous insect population.

"Sergeant Ven, put your two best troopers on point. Phil, you're next, with scanners running full bore, and the flamethrower on standby. Then comes Ven, myself, and, last but not least, Rico and the rest of the troopers. We shouldn't run into any trouble, but if we do, let's win. Any questions?"

No one had any questions so they set off down the trail. The trail followed the course of the river and had once been heavily traveled. Now, what with hovercraft service and all-terrain vehicles, the path was seldom used. By Lakorians that is.

As they moved down the trail Ven pointed out broken twigs, piles of green dung, and a wide variety of animal tracks.

When asked to comment on these signs, Ven would simply shrug his shoulders and say "very dangerous, very dangerous."

Then Ven would check his auto slug thrower, peer into the jungle, and shake his head sadly as if disaster would almost certainly strike.

McCade took it seriously at first, remembering some of the fauna he'd seen during his first stay, but time passed and he started to relax.

Knowing Ven could be less than truthful he even questioned the Lakorian's veracity. Chances were that the twigs had been broken by passing herbivores, the dung had been deposited by peaceful ruminants, and the tracks had been left by cute little furry things.

Yes, McCade decided, Ven's trying to scare us humans. Chances are he has some sort of elaborate bet going with the troops. Trying to see which one of us will freak out first. Well, to hell with that!

So McCade proceeded to focus all of his attention on the slippery log bridges, the vines that grew across the trail ankle high, and the occasional pockets of deep mud. And that's why he was so surprised when the vebores attacked.

They came without warning, hundreds of leathery little bodies, all teeth and no brains. The vebores were about the size of a Terran gerbil and very fast. So fast that they were in and among the sentients before anyone could shout a warning.

McCade felt a pain in his right calf, looked down, and saw that a small animal had managed to sink its teeth into his leg just above the boot top. He shouted a warning but it was too late. The vebores were swarming out of the jungle and piling onto human and Lakorian alike.

McCade heard the boom of a slug gun and the whine of energy weapons. It was a waste of time. The vebores were too small to make good targets and there were far too many of them.

McCade forced himself to ignore the animal gnawing at his leg. "Cease fire! The river! Run for the river!"

The rest of the party heard and obeyed. At the moment the river was about a hundred feet to the right. A tiny bit of remaining sunlight shimmered across the surface of the water.

Seeing it, human and Lakorian alike crashed through undergrowth, leaped over fallen trees, and tore at the vines that blocked their way.

Twice McCade tripped and fell, and each time he got up there were two or three more vebores locked onto his flesh, their little bodies flapping this way and that as he ran.

Finally there it was, darkly flowing water, and over to the right a small point. McCade shouted to make himself heard over the roar of the river. "Over this way! The point! Get on the point with your backs to the river!"

They heard and, after crashing their way through the thick vegetation that grew along the edge of the river, joined McCade on the point. All except the Lakorian named Kreb.

McCade spun around. "Kreb! Where the hell's Kreb?"

No one answered so McCade started back into the jungle. Strong hands grabbed and threw him down. McCade struggled but Rico and Ven had a good grip on him.

Rico waved at Phil. "Cook 'em, Phil, and make damn sure the little suckers are well done!"

The variant nodded and turned toward the jungle. He got a good grip on the nozzle and aimed it straight ahead. There was a *whoosh*ing sound as he pulled the trigger and the flamethrower sent a long tongue of flame into the jungle.

Though moist, the vegetation was no match for liquid fire, and went up in a roar of displaced air. McCade could feel the warmth on his face as Rico helped him to his feet.

More than a thousand vebores were caught in flames and they made a horrible chittering as they died.

McCade felt a sudden pain and looked down to find Ven was grabbing his vebores one at a time, slicing through their necks, and throwing the bodies into the river.

Then, when all of the animals were dead. Ven used the point of his commando knife to pry their jaws open and free the ugly-looking heads. These too were tossed into the river where they made a small plopping sound and disappeared from sight.

There was a loud pop as Phil killed the flamethrower. Black smoke floated toward them, pulled by the breeze that ran with the river, and heavy with the smell of burnt vegetation.

There was a moment of silence as they thought about what had happened and the fact that they were still alive. Ven touched McCade's arm.

"I am sorry about restraining you, but Kreb went down early on. There was nothing you could do."

McCade shuddered. What a horrible way to go, swarmed under by hundreds of little bodies, literally eaten alive. He forced the thought down and back. The light was almost completely gone. Time to make camp for the night.

First came a big fire, both for the light it would provide and psychological comfort as well. Phil used the flamethrower to get it going, grinning happily as the pile of vegetation *whoosh*ed into flame, extolling the merits of technology over bush craft.

Then came a round of first aid, with everyone taking turns as both doctor and patient, cleaning and dressing their many wounds.

The shelters went up with relative ease, and a good thing too, because it began to rain. Big fat drops that hit the tents hard, exploded into a hundred droplets, and were reunited as they slid toward the ground.

All of them took turns standing guard with the flamethrower, but nothing attacked beyond the scope of their own dreams, and the flickering light of the campfire.

As McCade lay there, he listened to Rico snore and wondered what Molly was doing. Could she be right there on Lakor? Waiting for him to come? Going through God knows what? There was no way to know.

It took him a long time to fall asleep.

EIGHT

The hold was still too small, but half of the gratings had been removed, and those that remained had been covered with thick cargo pads. Most of them smelled and were less than perfectly clean, but they still beat the heck out of bare metal.

Molly sat with her arms wrapped around her knees and rocked back and forth. She still hurt from the beating that Boots had given her. But the bruises had started to disappear, and thanks to the ship's medical officer, her sores were healing as well.

Molly looked around. The crew had rigged more lights, the girls wore clean clothes, cut-down ship suits mostly, and true to Pong's word, they received three servings of slop a day rather than the previous two.

That was the good news. The bad news was that Boots resented these improvements as if they came at her own personal expense and never stopped looking for ways to punish Molly for obtaining them. It was hard to believe that anyone could be so mean.

But Mommy said that some people are sick that way, holding other people down in order to elevate themselves, and it was certainly true that Boots was one of the lowest-ranking people in the crew.

Molly thought about her mother. Was she alive? Oh, please, God, let her be alive, and Daddy too. She bit her lip in order to stop the tears.

There was an intercom in the hold for use when loading and unloading cargo. It bonged twice. Molly looked up in surprise. They'd taken her wrist comp but her internal clock insisted that mealtime was still an hour or more away.

Some of the other girls were surprised as well and gave each other noncommittal shrugs. Whatever would be would be.

The children lined up and climbed the ladder one after another. By allowing the girl in front of her to get a ways ahead, and by climbing quickly past the platform on which Boots stood, Molly managed to escape all but a glancing kick, and a growled, "Hurry up."

Things proceeded normally once they entered the pressurized launch bay, except Molly couldn't escape the feeling that they were eating early, and noticed an unusual amount of activity around one of the larger shuttles.

It wasn't until the meal was over and the girls had lined up for their return that Molly learned the truth.

Boots walked about halfway down the line and stopped. She put her hands on fleshy hips. "All right, you little snots, listen up! At the present moment this ship is in orbit around a planet named Lakor."

Molly remembered the slight nausea all of them had felt about three meals back. Although the pirates hadn't said anything to confirm it, the girls had assumed that the ship was leaving hyperspace, and now they knew where.

Molly's heart leaped with excitement. Lakor! Her father had been there! And Mommy too. They'd helped Baron what's-his-name, Lis or something, and there was a chance that he'd help. Any chance was better than no chance at all! And that's what she had aboard ship.

Molly fought to keep the excitement off her face. She listened carefully.

Boots grinned evilly. "Lakor is well known for its slave markets, and guess what, some of you little creeps are going to see them firsthand. A few, twenty or so, will stay with us."

No one dared say anything but Molly felt the girls on either side of her stiffen. This was it, another step away from home and family, and into the terrible unknown. With the exception of Molly none of the girls wanted to go. They preferred life in the hold to the unknown horrors of Lakor.

"So," Boots continued, "Raz will choose. Those heading dirtside will report to the shuttle on the far side of the bay, and everyone else will stay where you are."

As usual Raz looked like some kind of barbarian warrior, long blond hair hanging down his back, muscles rippling under bronzed skin.

Raz started with the A's and worked his way down the alphabet. He was utterly detached, as if dividing a shipment of robots rather than people, sealing their fates with a laconic "Lakor" or "stays here."

Boots followed along behind Raz with a smile on her beefy face. Whenever Raz said "Lakor," Boots nodded her approval and took pleasure in the girl's dismay.

Finally, after what seemed like an eternity, Raz was one person away. Molly could feel the pulse pounding in her head. She was afraid that he could hear it too.

Raz's voice seemed abnormally loud as he said "Lakor." The girl next to Molly gave a pathetic sob and ran toward the shuttle.

Molly tried to control Raz through sheer force of will. Make it Lakor, please make it Lakor.

Raz stopped in front of Molly, looked thoughtful, and spoke.

NINE

A soft rain fell. It hit the topmost leaves, slid off, and fell to the next layer of vegetation fifty feet below. Raindrops exploded upward as they hit, subsided into pools, and dripped downward to pitter pat around McCade.

A large drop of water found its way down past the neck seal of McCade's Class II Environment suit and trickled between his shoulder blades. It made him shiver.

Like the rest of the team McCade was tired from the hike through the jungle, wet from wading through a seemingly endless swamp, and sore from a long afternoon spent crouched on the hillside.

For the last hour or so they had moved down the slope in tiny increments, on the lookout for old-fashioned trip wires or, Sol forbid, the latest in surveillance technology. So far there was no sign of either one. Not too surprising, since Bulo's bullies spent most of their time in the inn, drinking and chasing barmaids.

Now McCade and his companions were hidden along the edge of the road where the jungle gave way to the village of Durn. Twilight had turned to night, leaving the village little more than a scattering of dark shapes and widely spaced lights.

It was difficult to see, but when McCade brought the night-vision device to his eyes, an astonishing amount of detail appeared. Buildings were transformed into ghostly green rectangles, windows became blotches of red, and power plants showed up as blobs of white. That's why McCade knew that the all-terrain vehicle parked next to the inn had been there for a relatively short period of time. The engine appeared as a ball of white radiance located toward the rear of a reddish haze.

Other than that, and the occasional movement of a blurry-looking guard, there was nothing worth watching. McCade put the device away.

A breeze blew in from the river. It made the vegetation rustle and swish. McCade made a face as the smell of Lakorian body odor hit his nostrils. When exposed to rain Lakorians exuded an oily substance that formed a microscopic layer of insulation between them and the water.

McCade took one last look around. There was no point in waiting any longer. By now Bulo's toughs should be either drunk or asleep. The perfect time to slip into the inn, grab Bulo, and make their escape. Or so McCade hoped.

McCade clicked his mic on and off. There were seven clicks in response. Gently, careful not to fall or make unnecessary noise, Rico made his way down onto the muddy road.

A single streetlight made a pool of sickly yellow light.

Beyond it the town was long and narrow, crushed between hill and river, with its most important buildings toward the center. Of these the inn was the largest, an impressive log structure with a stable on the ground floor and living quarters above that.

McCade watched approvingly as dark shadows flitted across the road to merge with the blackness beyond.

A domesticated animal squealed in protest as its litter mates shoved it up against a wall. McCade's heart pounded in his chest but nothing happened.

Now it was his turn to cross the road. The big black duffel bag seemed to weigh a thousand pounds as he slipped and slid the last few feet down the hill and sprinted across the road. McCade's boots made squishing sounds and his pack swayed back and forth as he ran. Then he was across and slipping between two of the many hovels that fronted the road.

"Over here." The voice belonged to Ven and came from his left. McCade moved with care trying to avoid the considerable garbage strewn between the huts.

Thick fingers reached out to grab his arm and pull him into the shadows. The smell of Lakorian body odor was extremely strong. Ven whispered in his ear.

"There are two guards just ahead, sire. I'll take the left, you take the right."

McCade nodded, realized the Lakorian couldn't see him, and whispered, "Understood. You're left, I'm right."

Ven faded into the darkness as McCade moved forward. There . . . about fifty feet away . . . something moved against the darker background of a building. A sentry.

McCade left his slug gun in its holster and pulled a knife. Silence was critical. One shot, one yell, and they'd lose the advantage of surprise.

Hugging a long, low wall McCade eased his way closer. Bit by bit the smell of Lakorian body odor grew stronger and stronger. There he was, a low blocky shadow with an energy weapon slung over his shoulder. Just a little bit closer . . .

The sentry gave a sudden snort, as if something really putrid had assailed his nostrils, and swung in McCade's direction. As he did so the guard reached for his weapon.

Damn! Either the body odor thing cut both ways . . . or the sentry had unusually good night vision.

Knowing that he'd never be able to close the distance in time, and knowing that if he didn't some sort of sound was inevitable, McCade did the only thing he could.

He brought his arm all the way back, jerked it forward, and let go of the knife. McCade wasn't that good with knives, but he practiced every now and then, and hoped for the best.

There was a gurgle followed by the thump of a body hitting the ground. Not bad! Tiptoeing up to the body McCade was startled to find Ven already there.

Pulling a knife out of the sentry's throat the Lakorian grinned, wiped it on the tough's coat, and slid the weapon into his boot. He gestured to one side. "Your knife is over there, sire . . . sticking in the wall."

McCade looked, and sure enough, his knife had missed the sentry and embedded itself in a log wall. Light gleamed off the blade. Even though McCade couldn't see the Lakorian's face, he knew the alien was smiling. Ven would tell the story for many years to come. Assuming he survived, that is.

McCade returned the knife to its sheath and moved inward toward the inn. There should be at least one more cordon of guards, *would* be if *he* were Bulo.

Pausing to scoop up a rain-slippery rock, McCade rubbed it against his pants leg, and found a comfortable grip.

Determined not to repeat his sorry performance with the knife, McCade tiptoed forward, thankful for his rubber-soled boots. Maybe he'd smell this sentry as well.

But this sentry was sloppy and hit an empty vak bottle with his foot. It made a clinking sound as it rolled away.

Three quick steps and McCade was there, blindsiding the guard with the rock and easing him to the ground. A quick check assured him the sentry was still alive. Good. The less bloodshed the better.

McCade heard a low whistle and knew the rest of the sentries had been accounted for too.

With Ven close behind, McCade slid along the side of the inn's stable searching for the rear entrance. He hadn't gone more than two or three yards when he heard a hissing scream. The entire wall shook as heavy bodies moved back and forth just beyond the log enclosure.

The reptiles! These were hunting mounts, trained for use in the jungle, and attuned to the slightest disturbance. Something, a slight noise, or the scent of alien flesh, had disturbed them. Another animal screamed, and another, until there was a cacophony of sound.

McCade swore and activated his mic. "Okay, team. So much for the subtle approach, go in and get the sucker!"

The words were hardly out of McCade's mouth when Phil kicked the door in, body blocked a surprised guard, and took the stairs two at a time. He had the flamethrower on his back and a machine pistol in his right paw.

Rico grabbed the now-unconscious sentry and dragged him outside, while Ven, two of his troopers, and McCade followed Phil up the stairs.

The inn had its own fusion plant, so lights started to come on, and there was a lot of confused shouting.

A heavily carved wooden door splintered under the force of Phil's boot and banged off an inner wall. He disappeared inside, closely followed by Ven and the troopers.

There were shouts of outrage, followed by the sound of breaking furniture, and the roar of Phil's voice. McCade had just arrived at the top of the stairs when the variant emerged and bowed formally.

"Greetings, sire. Baron Bulo is awake and receiving guests. Please excuse the broken furniture. The palace is undergoing repairs."

McCade grinned. "Thank you, squire. Excuse me while I hasten within. The royal yacht will arrive at any minute . . . and we mustn't be late."

McCade stepped through the door into a small vestibule, from there into a hallway, and from there into a richly appointed bedroom. Ven and his troopers were there pointing their weapons toward the center of the room.

Lakorians of all classes favor canopied beds because they provide excellent protection against leaky roofs and Bulo was no exception. In addition to the canopy his bed was hung with richly embroidered curtains and piled high with pillows.

Bulo occupied the center of the bed, with a presumably comely maiden to either side, and a princely frown on his not-so-noble brow. He looked like a weaker, dissipated version of Lif, especially when dressed in lavender jammies.

"Who are you? And how dare you break into my quarters! Guards! Guards! Kill these intruders and feed them to my mounts!"

McCade shook his head sadly, found a cigar, and stuck it in the corner of his mouth. " 'Feed them to my mounts'? Is that any way to treat guests? Well, I'm sure your brother will teach you better manners. In the meantime, get your royal ass out of bed. You're coming with us."

Bulo crossed his arms. His expression was defiant. "I am not! Run while you can, human. In seconds, minutes at the most, my guards will kill you *and* your traitorous assistants."

There was a loud pop to McCade's left. He turned to see fingers of yellow flame climbing up an embroidered curtain toward the canopy.

Phil waved the nozzle of his flamethrower. Smoke drifted away. "Oops. Sorry about that. My mistake."

Bulo looked at the flames. His eyes grew big. "You wouldn't dare!"

The two females looked at Bulo, looked at the fire, and rolled out of bed. They were gone three seconds later.

McCade walked over, held his cigar in the flames, and puffed. Once the cigar was lit he blew a long streamer of smoke toward the ceiling.

"Oh, yes, he would. There's nothing Phil loves better than fresh meat roasted over an open fire."

Bulo looked at the variant, saw a mouth full of gleaming durasteel teeth, and turned a lighter shade of green. He was careful to stay away from Phil as he rolled out of bed. "Where are you taking me?"

"For a reunion with your brother," McCade replied. "Come on, let's go."

As they left the room the canopy burst into flames.

Phil led the way, with McCade right behind, and Ven, Bulo, and two troopers bringing up the rear.

They were halfway down the stairs when the front door crashed open and Rico dived in. An energy weapon stitched a line of diagonal holes through the door barely missing Phil's sizable feet.

There was a mad scramble to reach the bottom of the stairs and line up along the walls.

Rico stood by sliding himself up a wall. He shoved another power pak into the receiver of his blast rifle. "Time ta haul ya all."

McCade nodded. "Casualties?"

"One trooper dead . . . one missing, presumed dead."

"Damn." McCade had hoped to pull it off without any more casualties. "Any sight of the hovercraft?"

"Nope. Just a lot of bozos with more weapons than brains."

"See?" Bulo demanded shrilly. "My bodyguards are everywhere. Surrender while you still have a chance!"

There was a loud whump as Bulo's entire bedroom was engulfed by flames.

McCade shook his head in disgust. "Sergeant Ven . . . if his supreme effluence says anything more, gag him."

Ven grinned wickedly and slid the muzzle of his blast rifle into Bulo's left ear. The dead troopers had been friends of his.

McCade pulled his handgun and looked around. Everyone was here. No need to use his mic. "All right, everyone . . . head for the pier. Plan one is still operational. Okay, Phil, light 'em up."

Phil sent a long funnel of flame out the door to intimidate attackers and ruin their night sight. Then he released the trigger, shifted the pistol grip to his left paw, and kicked the door open. Phil fired three round bursts from his machine pistol as he headed toward the river.

Ven and the troopers went next, pushing Bulo along in front of them as a shield, firing around him.

Then came McCade and Rico, firing their weapons for effect, zigzagging toward the river.

Energy beams whined overhead, bullets threw up geysers of mud behind their heels, and a heat-seeking missile hit the inn with a loud boom. Rico was right. Bulo's rowdies had more weapons than brains.

McCade heard a roar of sound off to the right. Here came the hovercraft! Right on time and lit up like a Christmas tree! Against all instructions the captain had the vessel's interior and exterior lights turned on.

The hovercraft made a wonderful target. Unable to resist all of Bulo's retainers shifted their fire to the oncoming vessel. A heat-seeking missile hit the rear deck and blew up.

The explosion did very little structural damage, but did sever some control cables and caused both engines to race out of control.

The captain did the only thing he could and shut down both of his engines. Thanks to the swift current he was able to steer toward the middle of the channel. Mercifully the lights went out when the engines stopped.

Although the hovercraft wasn't able to pick them up, it did provide a much-needed diversion, and the entire group made it to the pier unharmed.

By now the hoverboat's captain had mustered a somewhat ineffectual damage-control party. They made dark silhouettes against the flames as they aimed an intermittent stream of water at the base of the fire.

McCade shook his head in disgust, removed the cigar from his mouth, and flicked it into the river.

"All right, everybody . . . so much for plan A. It looks like we're gonna get our feet wet."

"But I can't swim!" Bulo wailed. "I'll drown!"

"That would be nice," McCade said agreeably. "But if you shut up, and do exactly what Sergeant Ven says, maybe you won't."

"Company's coming!" Rico yelled, and sent a stutter of blue energy toward town. Two of the troopers took cover nearby and added their fire to his.

McCade shrugged his way out from under the black duffel. "Give me a hand, Phil . . . this thing's awkward as hell." Together they laid the bag out with the seal upward.

Rico yelled something incoherent and bullets screamed overhead.

Fingers fumbling, heart pounding, McCade broke the seal, found the T-shaped yellow handle, gave it a single turn to the right, and pulled.

The results were quite dramatic. There was a loud *whoosh*ing sound, followed by a series of pops as various air chambers filled, and a final hiss as the now-inflated raft vented a bit of excess air.

"All right," McCade yelled, "massed fire to keep their heads down, then grab the raft and jump together!"

Rico and the two troopers backed toward the river firing as they came.

Phil hit a quick release, dumped the flamethrower, and set it to explode sixty seconds later.

McCade unloaded his slug gun in the general direction of town and got a grip on the boat.

Ven handcuffed himself to Bulo and flinched as a stray bullet whapped through the raft right next to his leg.

"Grab on!" McCade ordered, and the moment they had, he yelled, "Run!"

With bullets zinging around them, and energy beams slicing the night into geometric shapes, they galloped to the end of the pier and jumped.

Then they learned a painful lesson. A well-inflated raft won't sink after a twenty-foot fall, but those hanging on to it will. The force of the fall, plus their own weight, ripped hands loose and pushed them toward the bottom.

The water was cold. McCade kicked toward the surface, unable to see through the blackness, groping for the raft.

Ven got a pleasant surprise meanwhile as Bulo demonstrated a sudden mastery of underwater swimming and towed him toward the surface.

Rico felt a trooper struggling nearby, grabbed his harness, and dragged him upward.

Phil struggled against the weight of his remaining equipment and waterlogged fur, considered going into full augmentation, and decided not to. He would be completely exhausted afterward and that might be just as fatal as drowning. Slowly but surely, forcing himself to stay calm, he kicked his way upward until his head broke the surface.

Most of Phil's attention was centered on the vital process of sucking air into his oxygen-starved lungs, but a distant part of his mind was still able to register a ball of red-orange flame and the thump of a sizable explosion.

The flamethrower had exploded right on schedule taking twelve of Bulo's retainers and most of the pier with it.

McCade was the first one into the raft. As a side current pulled them out and away from shore, he helped others into the raft and urged them to hurry up.

Given the raft's low profile, and its dark color, the boat was almost impossible to see. That didn't bother Bulo's surviving retainers however, they were still firing, hoping for a lucky hit. The fact that they might hit Bulo hadn't occurred to them or just didn't matter.

"Welcome aboard, your wetness," McCade said as he helped Ven, then Bulo, over the side.

The Lakorian noble ignored him as he collapsed in the bottom of the boat.

McCade looked for the hovercraft. It had drifted downriver and out of sight.

Phil was the last one aboard, and as he fell gasping into the bottom of the boat, McCade realized there was a problem. The raft was sinking.

The raft had a number of self-contained air chambers so it wouldn't sink completely, but it looked as if they were in for a long wet ride.

McCade didn't say anything. He didn't have to. The boat told its own story as it sank deeper in the water and began to flood.

One by one they were dumped into the river and forced to find a spot around the raft's sides. Although they couldn't ride in it, the boat did provide flotation and something to cling to.

They talked at first, still high on adrenaline, or the Lakorian equivalent. But as time passed the obvious things were soon said and gave way to periods of silence. These grew longer and longer until conversation stopped entirely and was replaced by swishing, gurgling rhythms of the river. It had a lulling, soothing effect, and McCade drifted in and out of sleep.

Eventually he dreamed that he was far, far away, on a planet where it never snowed and never rained, where Sara and Molly were sunny and full of happiness.

Then a terrible night fell over the land. Molly disappeared into darkness. McCade searched for her, flailing around in the blackness, grabbing squirmy things and throwing them away.

Then a wavelet came and slapped him in the face.

The others were yelling, pointing downriver where the hovercraft was grounded on a sandbar, celebrating their good fortune.

But not McCade. His thoughts were farther downriver, in the slave markets that dotted the coast, with the little girl who might be waiting there.

It took the better part of a day for the hovercraft's crew to complete temporary repairs, and two more to reach the town of Riversplit. It was there that they said good-bye to Ven and his surviving troopers, gave Bulo into the custody of Lif's troops, and met up with Murd.

As before the king's advisor, or gofer, whichever he was, wore a long orange robe and looked somewhat fragile. But appearances can be deceiving as Murd demonstrated over the next few days.

It took a full day to reach the coast and the first slave market. Already tired from his activities in Durn, the trip sapped even more of McCade's energy and left him drained.

Not Murd though, when they arrived at the slave market he was as spry as ever, busy throwing his weight around and generally pissing everyone off.

McCade didn't mind though since Murd's efforts were in his behalf and did a great deal to get things moving.

Though a different slave market from the one McCade had experienced some years earlier, it was still quite similar.

Their all-terrain vehicle had no top. As a result McCade was able to smell the slave market long before they actually arrived.

It was horrible. The unbelievable stench that goes with open sewers and insufficient drainage, but something more as well, something part smell and part emotion.

A feeling of misery, of fear, of hopelessness. It made McCade sick to his stomach.

Then they rounded a bend and saw the stockade made of vertical logs. There were enormous gates that, with the Lakorian tendency to combine old with new, whirred open to let their vehicle pass.

Once inside the vehicle was swamped by a small army of functionaries all vying for the privilege of kissing Murd's ancient rear end.

Ignoring the mob McCade, Rico, and Phil got out of the vehicle and looked around. There was a large expanse of mud at the center of the market, an awning-covered platform where slaves were bought and sold, and rows of enclosed pens where they were housed.

Having spent some time in similar accommodations McCade knew they had dirt floors, a single water tap, and an open sewer that ran along one wall.

The thought that Molly might be locked inside one of those pens made his heart ache.

He turned toward the knot of gesticulating Lakorians. "Murd . . . tell them to bring out the children . . . and to do it now."

Murd, who was enjoying all the attention, considered telling the arrogant human to sit on something pointy but changed his mind. Yes, there was Lif to consider, but more than that the human himself. He had an obvious propensity for violence this human did, and seemed quite agitated.

Murd forced himself to perform a polite bow and issued a long string of orders.

Thirty minutes later the three humans sat and watched one of the most horrible sights they'd ever seen.

The slave market's entire population of human children, some thirty-three in all, were paraded by for their inspection. Little boys and girls, with bony, underfed bodies and hopeless expressions.

Under normal circumstances an auctioneer would be haranguing the audience about the children's virtues, extolling their sexual attractiveness, and reminding them that human fingers are extremely nimble as compared to the appendages found on many other sentient beings.

But this was different. The children trudged across the platform in weary silence, looking neither right nor left, numb to what happened around them.

All three of the men searched for familiar features, hoping, praying to see one or more familiar faces, but none of the children was from Alice.

When the last child had passed the men sat staring at the emptiness in front of them. McCade wanted desperately to buy the children, or simply take them, destroying anyone or anything who got in the way, but knew that was impossible. The three of them had neither the money nor the brute strength to get the job done. No, they must steel themselves against what they saw, and continue the search.

McCade looked at Rico and Phil. Rico had tears glistening on his beard, and Phil's lips were pulled back in a rictus of hate, durasteel teeth almost completely bared.

Murd cleared his throat. "Well, sire? Were any of the cubs yours?"

McCade stood. "No. Take us to the next market."

It was three days and two slave markets later before they found the children. This time there was an actual auction taking place on the main platform, so they were seated inside a striped tent, watching a line of pathetic children straggle past.

Later it was hard to say who saw who first, but McCade heard Phil yell "Mary!" and head a child say "Citizen McCade!" almost simultaneously.

Then there was total pandemonium as twenty-six of the twenty-eight children crowded around the three men, crying and talking all at the same time.

His heart in his throat McCade hugged little girl after little girl, calling those he knew by name, using "sweetheart" on all the rest.

Some of the girls were orphans and didn't know it yet, others would be reunited with anxious parents, but all would end up safe and sound on Alice.

After the first few frantic seconds McCade knew the truth. Molly wasn't there. A wave of grief rolled over him submerging the joy he'd known moments before. Molly was still out there somewhere, waiting for him, or . . .

McCade grabbed the nearest girl, a child named Cindy, and stared into her eyes so intensely that she started to cry. "Molly? Where's Molly McCade? What happened to my daughter?"

The words jerked their way out along with the tears. "Sshee's sstill on the sship."

McCade felt a wave of relief. Alive then. There was hope. McCade pulled Cindy to his chest, and as he apologized for scaring her, he saw something awful over her shoulder.

Two little boys had been brought in along with the girls, the little boys he'd never seen before, but were being led away by a Lakorian guard.

McCade stood up. "Wait! Bring those boys back! Look, Rico! It's John, and his brother Paul!"

Rico looked up from the little girl who was asking about her mother. "Huh? John and Paul?"

Then Rico saw McCade's expression. "Oh, yeah! John and Paul! Hey, boys, don'tcha recognize Uncle Rico? Come over here?"

The younger boy looked momentarily confused, but the older boy put on a happy expression and dragged the little boy with him. "Uncle Rico, sure, I didn't recognize you with the beard!"

McCade smiled in spite of himself. The boy was smart. He'd do well on Alice. They all would.

TEN

Molly waited patiently for the other girls to fall asleep. The dim glow provided by two light switches was enough to see by.

Shortly after the other children had been loaded aboard the shuttle and taken dirtside, the twenty or so remaining girls were removed from the hold and assigned to adjoining compartments. It was a tight fit, but at least they had real bunks and adequate toilet facilities.

Molly still felt certain that she would've been better off on the surface of Lakor, but Raz had kept her aboard, so that was that.

Determined to escape, or at least pave the way, Molly had conceived a plan. A plan that relied on her increased freedom of movement.

Although significant portions of the ship were still off-limits, the girls were now permitted to roam through the rest.

Many of the girls saw their new quarters, and lack of confinement, as a change of heart by the pirates and said so during whispered conversations.

Molly disagreed, pointing out that shortly after they vacated the hold, it had been filled with some sort of cargo brought up from the surface of Lakor. In addition, Molly suggested, the pirates could have hidden motives for allowing them more freedom as well. What if it was part of a plan? A plan in which the girls would wind up colluding in their own slavery? At what point do prisoners cease to be prisoners, and join ranks with those who imprisoned them?

Some of the girls agreed, and were suspicious of pirate motives, but Lia, one of the older girls, was especially critical of Molly's ideas.

"Come on, Molly," she'd whispered, "you griped when we were in the hold . . . and you're griping now. Give us a break. Things are better, that's all. Quit worrying so much."

But Molly *did* worry, and planned to keep right on worrying, no matter what. The pirates had attacked Alice, killed innocent people, and sold children into slavery. Maybe the others could forgive and forget but not Molly. No, she planned to get free, and get even. No matter how long that took.

Because of her attitude Molly had fallen from a position of leadership into that of semi-outcast. She hoped Mommy wouldn't be disappointed, but Lia was wrong, and wasn't there a difference between popularity and leadership? Daddy said so . . . and Molly hoped he was right.

Time passed, and finally, when the last of the whispered conversations had died away, and everyone else was asleep, Molly made her move.

Slipping out from under the covers Molly tiptoed to the doorway and touched the softly glowing circle of red light. The circle turned green and the hatch hissed open.

Molly paused, searched the compartment for signs of movement, and seeing none stepped outside.

Satisfied that she'd managed to slip out of the room undetected, Molly padded down the corridor, ready to claim a stomachache if she encountered a member of the crew.

It felt weird to wear the one-piece black body stocking in the corridor, but that's what the girls used for pajamas, so that's what she'd have on if truly on her way to the sick bay.

This would be her last trip to the S-4 damage-control station. She'd been there three times before, and didn't dare make any more trips after this one. Someone or something was sure to go wrong eventually and trip her up.

Intended for use during a full scale disaster, the station's computer console would provide backup access to the vessel's atmospheric and fire-control systems, allowing the crew to pump oxygen out of various compartments, dump fire retardant in, or selectively cut power to various locations.

As such the computer console located in S-4 had nothing to do with the ship's primary navcomp, or wasn't supposed to, but Molly had written a conversion program that linked both computers together. Or had *almost* linked them together, since she was still in the process of debugging the conversion, and had yet to actually access the navcomp.

By now Martha Chong, Molly's computer instructor back on Alice, would have been mumbling in frustration. The truth was that at least two of the other girls were better with computers than Molly was, but she couldn't trust them. They were friends of Lia's, and the older girl would make fun of the whole thing.

Assuming that she did gain access to the navcomp, Molly planned to obtain a cube dump of the ship's travels for the last month or so. By backtracking along the ship's course she could find Alice. Assuming she had something to backtrack in, which she didn't, but like Mom always said, "Take one thing at a time, Molly. Take one thing at a time."

Like all damage-control stations this one was unlocked. After all, in the case of major damage to the ship's hull, there would be scant time for access codes. Nor was there any way to be sure which crew member would use the station. So, like S-1, S-2, and S-3, S-4 was unsecured.

Molly took one last look around, saw nothing but empty corridor, and palmed the access panel. The hatch slid open, then closed behind her.

It was a tiny compartment with barely enough room for tool storage, a computer console, and an emergency patch kit.

Molly felt her pulse start to pound a little faster. While her stomach ache story might fly out in the corridor, it wouldn't do much good in here. She forced the fear down and back.

A rudimentary seat was held up against the bulkhead by a spring-loaded hinge. Molly pushed the seat down and sat on it. The metal felt cold through the thin body stocking.

Molly slid the keyboard out of its recess and turned it on. Under normal circumstances that would have activated one of the zillion indicator lights located on the bridge, but she had eliminated that function the first time out. Having spent hundreds of hours on her father's ships, Molly had a better-than-average understanding of how they worked.

Molly entered a multidigit code, checked to make sure that no one had tampered with her program, and went to work.

Five minutes later Molly was completely lost in what she was doing. Bit by bit Molly felt her way through the last few interfaces, neutralized two security procedures meant to keep her out, and dipped into the navcomp's huge memory. Not bad for one of Chong's worst students.

Her first question was simple: "Where is the ship now?"

A long string of numbers flooded the screen.

Molly frowned and fingers flew over keys: "Request plain language description of the ship's position using nearest stars or planets as points of reference."

The reply was almost instantaneous: "Ship is en route from Lakor to Drang."

Molly nodded. The ship was headed for Drang, wherever that was. Okay, enough messing around. First she'd get a cube dump on the mathematical stuff . . . then she'd back out of the navcomp, erasing the conversion program as she went. In fifteen or twenty minutes she'd have everything she needed and no one the wiser.

Molly had just started to type when she heard feet scuffle outside. She whirled just in time to see the hatch open.

Lia stood outside, as did a smug-looking Boots and an angry Raz. Lia smiled and pointed a triumphant finger in Molly's direction.

"There she is, sir . . . just like I told you. Thank goodness you caught her in time! There's no telling what harm she might have done!"

ELEVEN

Nexus. That was the name it had given itself, or had been given, depending on which story you chose to believe.

It made little difference to McCade. To him Nexus was a place, a place to look for Molly, or clues that would point in her direction.

At the moment Nexus just hung there, a vast amalgamation of interconnected spaceships, slowly spinning before a distant star.

The ships came in all shapes and sizes. There were tankers, freighters, tugs, yachts, liners, and Sol knows what else, at least a hundred of them, all hooked together in what looked like random order, their various shapes appearing and disappearing as dim sunlight moved across their combined hulls.

Taken as a whole, the ships and the computer that made the gathering possible were known as Nexus.

The purpose of the gathering was simple, to sell things you didn't need, and buy things you did. And to do so without the taxes, duties, laws, and other encumbrances that so often get in the way of free trade.

That's why Nexus was located out along the rim, beyond the jurisdiction of systemic or planetary governments, and a law unto itself.

Nexus was not without structure however, no, it was far too complex to function without rules, and that meant a guiding intelligence.

And that intelligence was supplied by a sentient computer, a machine of rather mysterious origins, which ran Nexus like a personal fiefdom.

There were two theories about the artificial intelligence. One held that the computer had escaped from some sort of governmental research project, while the other suggested that the AI was owned by a huge mega-corp, and provided it with a source of untaxed revenue.

McCade decided it didn't make too much difference which theory was true. Nexus pulled some heavy G's any way you figured it. More than that, Nexus knew the details of every transaction that took place within its sphere of influence, including what was traded by whom.

McCade stuck a cigar in his mouth and puffed it into life. The smoke floated upward and drifted toward a vent.

So, if Pong, or any of Pong's ships, had been here, chances were Nexus would know. In some ways it was a long shot . . . and in some ways it wasn't.

There were a limited number of places where one could sell stolen goods on a large scale, and because Pong had betrayed the pirates during the Vial of Tears episode, he was barred from the brotherhood's markets. The primary one being located on the fortified planet known as The Rock.

That meant he'd have to use one of the others, and there weren't all that many to choose from. There was Tin Town, a free-floating, wide-open, anything-goes habitat, a rather grubby planet called Seed, and a few others, the most famous of which was Nexus.

So, having made sure that all of the children were safely aboard the small freighter that would carry them to Alice, McCade held a council of war.

They listed alternative destinations, discussed the pros and cons of each, and came to a final decision. Nexus. It wasn't controlled by the brotherhood, was relatively close to Lakor, and played a significant role in the slave trade.

Shortly thereafter the group said good-bye to a smug King Lif, climbed aboard their shuttle, and lifted for space.

Once aboard *Void Runner* it was a quick jump into hyperspace and a three-day trip to the point called Nexus.

Most of them enjoyed the trip, or would have had their mission been different, the exception being Rico. He'd fallen into an ever-deepening depression. It was clear that Vanessa's death weighed heavily on his mind.

The activity on Lakor had provided a momentary distraction, something to occupy Rico's mind and body, but now, without anything to do, his emotions were spiraling down.

McCade remembered the glint of gold as Rico had thrown something into Vanessa's grave, and the comment Sara had made just prior to liftoff: "Keep a close eye on Rico, Sam, he's hurting, and God knows what he might do."

At the moment the big man was conning the ship, following orders provided by some tiny portion of the Nexus brain, heading for the point where *Void Runner* would become part of the ever-evolving whole.

For such was the computer's intelligence that it could calculate exactly where to place *Void Runner*'s additional mass, monitor some very complex transactions, and run the habitat all at the same time.

They were still fifty miles away from the mass of interconnected ships when Nexus ordered Rico to surrender control. Conscious of the fact that the computer controlled enough weapons to destroy a small fleet, Rico obeyed.

Numbers and schematics rippled across the command screens as Nexus assumed control, inventoried the ship's offensive and defensive capabilities, and drew the ship steadily in.

Now Nexus could be seen without magnification. The central construct was a globe, and reaching out from it were innumerable black tentacles, each one clutching a ship. The design reminded McCade of the cephalopods of his native Terra.

The comparison seemed even more appropriate when a tube came snaking out to make contact with *Void Runner*'s main lock.

Indicator lights flashed on and off as Nexus ran a final check on the ship's systems, locked out all of her weapons systems, and verified a positive seal with *Void Runner*'s main lock. Like any sentient being Nexus had a well-developed sense of self-preservation.

Somewhere at the hub of the metallic maze an order went out and the heretofore flexible tube turned hard as steel.

Thanks to the tube's rigidity the ship would be held firmly in place preventing the possibility of collision with the vessels that surrounded it.

Lights flashed and numbers vanished from the screens as Nexus withdrew all but a tendril of its intelligence from the ship and turned that part of its attention elsewhere. There were many things to do.

McCade activated the intercom. "Maggie?"

"Yeah?" The chief engineer's voice had an edge to it as usual.

"Meet us in the lounge please."

"Roger."

All four of them were gathered in the lounge five minutes later. It was large enough for twice their number and, thanks to the money McCade had invested in it, quite comfortable.

McCade dropped into a chair and felt it shift slightly to accommodate the shape of his body. Rico and Phil did likewise, while Maggie killed power and lowered herself to the deck.

"Well, here we are," Phil said cheerfully. "Now what?"

McCade checked his cigar, found it was getting a bit short, and stubbed it out.

"Now we take a look around. Find out where the slave market is . . . and look for the children."

Maggie gave a snort of derision.

McCade smiled patiently. "Yes, Maggie? You've got something to add?"

"Only that your plan is stupid," Maggie replied evenly.

"Don't be shy . . . say what ya mean," Rico commented dryly.

"Thanks, I will," Maggie answered, eyes flashing. "If the kids are here, you want to rescue them, right?"

"Obviously," McCade said, somewhat annoyed. "What's your point?"

Maggie met their eyes one at a time. "My point is that we should prepare for success. Think about it. Lets say you find 'em, there's what, twenty or so girls unaccounted for? And the same number of boys? What're you going to do? Take 'em out at gunpoint? If so, you'd better come up with a battalion of marines, cause I've been here before, and if the owners don't stop you, Nexus will.

"Or," Maggie continued, "maybe you plan to buy the children. Tell me, Sam . . . have you got a couple hundred thousand credits stashed under your pillow? Lif paid the freight on Lakor . . . but what happens here?"

There was a long silence while McCade got up and walked over to the autobar. He ordered a Terran whiskey and, when it came, took a thoughtful sip. When McCade turned around there was a grin on his face.

"Thanks, Maggie. I guess I'm so used to rolling over and through problems, I don't always think 'em through. From the sound of things we couldn't take the children by force, and no, I don't have two hundred big ones stashed under my pillow. So, if the children are here, we've got a problem, and if they aren't, we don't. How about you and Rico taking a look around? That way we'll know if we need the two hundred thousand or not."

Maggie found herself nodding in agreement. McCade made the whole thing sound so reasonable there wasn't much choice.

The *Void Runner*'s lock hissed closed behind him. The tube was about seven feet in diameter, slightly ridged along its inner surface, and off-white in color. A yellowish light seemed to ooze around them.

Maggie gestured Rico forward. The tube featured some tight turns and if Maggie made a mistake she'd do so privately.

Rico shrugged and walked away. Within seconds he disappeared around a curve.

Maggie followed, watching the turns, increasingly confident the farther she went. Then the tube straightened out and she saw Rico up ahead. By applying some additional power she was able to reach the main lock only seconds after he did.

The lock opened, they moved inside, and it closed again. A wall screen came to life. On it Maggie saw a softly rounded something with a head and shoulders but no face. It was silver and slightly reflective.

Where a human face would have eyes it had shallow depressions, and where there should be a nose, the thing had a bump. The black background gave it a dramatic look.

This was a new development. Whatever it was hadn't been there during Maggie's previous visit.

Her first impulse was to classify the thing as a robot, an intermediate step between the functional-looking machines used for most tasks and the more humanoid forms favored for domestic applications. But as Maggie was about to learn, this machine was different.

The machine's silvery face was motionless as it spoke, and its voice was neutral, sounding neither male nor female.

"Greetings, and welcome to Nexus. I am a remote, one of four hundred and sixty-three remotes scattered around the habitat, and the direct embodiment of the intelligence known as Nexus.

"I was created to answer your questions, to solve your problems, to make your visit to Nexus as pleasant and productive as possible. Please approach me whenever you need help.

"Before venturing forth, please listen to and memorize my laws: First, no one shall contemplate or take any action that could harm, damage, or incapacitate Nexus, its employees, remotes, or other representatives.

"Secondly," the remote continued, "no one shall possess or use projectile weapons while visiting Nexus."

"Kinda understandable," Rico observed. "Don't mess with the boss . . . and don't punch any unauthorized holes in the habitat."

"Violation of my laws," the remote added, "is punishable by death. Have a nice visit."

"Thanks, ol' sport," Rico said sarcastically, "let the fun begin."

The picture faded to black and the lock cycled open. Clever, Maggie thought to herself. You step into the lock, and presto! A captive audience.

"Come on," Rico said, "let's see the sights."

As Rico stepped out of the lock Maggie heard a tone, and a soft voice that said, "You are leaving lock seventy-seven. Please retain that number for future reference. Should you forget the number, or need other assistance, please approach a remote and ask. I will be happy to help. Have a nice visit."

Maggie floated out of the lock and spun the hover box around. A huge super-graphic of the number seventy-seven covered the entire area around the lock. It should be visible from quite a distance away. Had that been there during her last visit? Maggie couldn't remember.

Rico touched her arm. "Come on, chief . . . the kids, remember? We're supposed ta find out if they're here."

Maggie nodded and whirred along beside him. The hall was huge, and seemed to run straight ahead for a long way, before taking a gentle curve to the right.

The habitat was enormous. And that raised questions larger than the origins of Nexus itself. Who constructed the habitat for Nexus? And why? There was no way to tell.

Except for a path that wound its way down the center of the hall, the corridor was crammed with a bewildering array of cargo modules, vending stands, miscellaneous equipment, and just plain junk.

Moving in and around these objects were humans, robots, aliens, auto loaders, pet animals, silvery remotes, power pallets, cyborgs, androids, and things Maggie wasn't sure of. This at least was as it had been during her previous visit.

Although there were formal venues for selling certain kinds of merchandise, they were in heavy demand and cost a lot to rent.

So the halls functioned as staging areas, and as secondary markets, since many of the merchants had offerings too modest to justify a presentation room.

Maggie looked at Rico striding along at her side. He was uncharacteristically silent. She knew why, or thought she did, and forced herself to make conversation.

"So tell me, Rico . . . why us? Why didn't Sam do this himself?"

Rico came to a sudden stop and turned on her. He looked angry. "Listen here, Maggie . . . I'm gettin' real tired of your crap. I don't know what Sam has up his sleeve. He'll tell us when he's good 'n' ready. Till then I suggest you keep a coupla things in mind.

"First, there ain't ten people on the whole rim that's as savvy as Sam is.

You can take all the cheap shots you want, but if we find those kids, it'll be Sam that gets it done.

"Second, I don't know what your problem is, but you better back off, or by God I'll arrange ta leave your crotchety ass right here on Nexus!"

Maggie felt a variety of emotions. The first was anger. How dare Rico speak to her that way? Leave *her* would he? Not very damn likely! She'd leave him . . . and Sam too . . . there were plenty of berths for a good engineer.

Next came a more rational response. One that recognized Rico's pain, and, more than that, recognized the same old pattern.

In place after place, ship after ship, Maggie had made herself obnoxious and been fired.

That way Maggie never got involved, never came to care, never got hurt. It began with the explosion, with the loss of her legs, and the deaths of her entire crew. But when would it end? A year from now? Two?

Maggie cleared her throat and looked away. "I have a big mouth sometimes. Sorry, Rico."

Rico searched Maggie's face, saw she was sincere, and shrugged. "The truth is that ya have a big mouth *all* the time . . . but what the hell . . . so do I. Shake."

Maggie's hand disappeared into Rico's giant paw and she smiled.

TWELVE

Mustapha Pong was lost somewhere between the past and present.

He sat as he always did under the vast canopy of stars projected on the overhead. The compartment was circular and, except for the pool of light that surrounded Pong, completely dark.

There had been a time many years before when the cabin would've been filled to overflowing with loot, the tangible symbol of his success, the living out of boyhood dreams.

Back then Pong had favored chests brimming over with gold jewelry, ingots of platinum stacked in the corner, slave girls who responded to a snap from his fingers. Raw, open manifestations of power.

But he'd been young and immature then. Raw clay still finding its final shape.

The compartment was different now. Open, nearly empty, boasting little more than a dais at its center, and the custom-designed power lounger that served Pong as both chair and bed.

The cabin was a symbol of what Mustapha Pong wanted to be. Open, centered, at one with the cosmos. A force great enough to move planets, to redefine the course of sentient history, to leave a mark so deep it would still be visible after a million years had come and gone.

The thing on his shoulder stirred and injected a mild stimulant into Pong's bloodstream. As usual the mind slug's thoughts were caustic and mocking.

"Bestir yourself, human, there is work to do, and you are lost in your own ambition."

His reverie broken, and annoyed at the alien's criticism, Pong punched a request for coffee into the arm of his chair. There was a whirring sound and a cup of coffee appeared at Pong's fingertips. The mind slug hated caffeine, and drinking it would serve both as a punishment and a reminder. Pong was in charge . . . and it would stay that way.

Now back to the problem at hand. Pong sipped his coffee. The problem was the one he always faced. How to overcome resistance and work his will on the universe around him.

The larger problem was necessarily subdivided into a series of tasks. Move ships over there, raid that particular planet, invest the profit in certain companies, buy more information, bribe . . .

The Melcetian interrupted. "You are drifting again, O conqueror of the universe. Focus on the problem at hand . . . and drink something else."

Pong frowned and tried to focus. The 56,827 were never satisfied. Now they wanted a full-scale planetary war to observe. A global conflict on a reasonably high-tech world, say level four or five, that would serve to demonstrate the latest in human tactics. Tactics they must overcome in order to enslave the human race.

Pong had laughed the first time they said that, and nearly lost his life.

But that was back before he knew them, when he'd responded to a mysterious but profitable summons, and agreed to function as their sole human ally. Now Pong knew the aliens could do what they claimed.

Not even he knew where the 56,827's homeworld was, but Pong had been to some of the planets they'd enslaved, seen those the aliens had destroyed. Black airless rocks burned clean of the life that had dared to defy them.

But relentless though they were, the 56,827 were cautious as well, carefully studying each race prior to attacking it. That explained their desire for a war, and more than that, their insistence that Pong participate in it. They would see a blade and test it prior to striking a blow.

Pong took another sip of coffee. Drang was the obvious choice since there was a war brewing there anyway . . . but which side should he take? That of the world government? Or that of the corporate combine that hoped to overthrow it? Both had advantages and disadvantages.

"Sir?"

Pong looked up and wondered how long they'd been there, standing on the edge of darkness, waiting for him to respond.

There was Raz, an ugly-looking female guard, and a little girl. The girl was a slave, one of those they'd taken on Alice, a skinny little thing with a mop of curly brown-black hair.

The girl looked familiar, but Pong couldn't place her. A trivial problem most likely . . . but important to the crew. It never seemed to end. If the 56,827 weren't after something, then his crew was.

"Yes, Raz, what is it?"

Raz kept it brief knowing Pong's distaste for unnecessary detail. "Thanks to a tip from another slave, this female was found making unauthorized use of the damage-control computer console located in station S-4."

Pong frowned. "So? Why bring her to me? Can't you people handle anything by yourselves?"

Boots had started to tremble but Raz was unaffected. "There is more, sir. The slave wrote a conversion program that allowed her access to the ship's navcomp via the damage-control console."

Pong sat straight up in his chair. "Really? How interesting. I didn't know such a thing was possible. Let me see her."

Boots gave Molly a shove and she stumbled into the light. The girl looked very familiar, but Pong still couldn't place her.

The mind slug made a tiny secretion and the memory came flooding back. Pong found himself standing in the launch bay, looking down at the girl's ulcerated arms, listening to her arguments. It was all there. The smell of her unwashed body, the echo of a tool hitting the deck, everything.

It took a fraction of a second for the entire conversation to flash through Pong's mind. He smiled.

"So, we meet again. Tell me, child, what's your name?"

Molly felt her lower lip start to quiver and fought for control. "Molly McCade, sir."

Adrenaline surged through Pong's body. It was strong, too strong, and the mind slug worked to buffer it. Pong was jubilant.

McCade! Could it be? Could this be Sam McCade's daughter?"

He worked to hide his excitement.

"Molly McCade . . . a pretty name . . . a familiar name. Is your father named Sam by any chance?"

Something, Molly wasn't sure what, told her there was danger here. But what kind? And was it real? After all, her father knew a lot of strange sentients, and considered many to be friends. Could this man be one? If so, she should tell him the truth; besides Lia would if she didn't. "Yes, sir, my father is named Sam. Do you know him?"

Pong shook his head, and the mind slug shivered a thousand rainbows. "No, child, although I once spoke with him over a com link. Tell me, was your father dirtside when the ships attacked?"

Molly squinted upward into the light. The man looked nice enough, but she was frightened of the thing on his shoulder. Molly wanted to say that had her father had been home, the attack might have gone differently, but she resisted the temptation. It wasn't true for one thing, and might make the man mad for another. "No, he wasn't."

Pong slumped back in his chair. So, it was just as he'd feared. McCade was alive. How unfortunate. Hatred welled up from deep inside. Hatred for Mc-

Cade, for the damage he'd done, for the loss of irreplaceable time. The one thing no one, not even Pong, had enough of.

But hatred would get him nowhere. He must think, he must plan, he must put petty problems aside and focus on Drang.

Raz was waiting, and so was the ugly guard. They didn't care about Drang, they wanted him to pass judgment, to punish the girl in a way that would make their jobs easier.

The problem was that Pong *liked* Molly McCade. It was strange but true. He liked her intelligence, her courage, and her unwillingness to bend.

He'd known a little boy like her once, a boy who grew up hungry in the ghettos of Desus II, a boy named Mustapha Pong.

Besides . . . the girl was Sam McCade's daughter, and there was something delicious about having her under his control.

Pong gestured to Raz. "Who's in charge of the slaves?"

Raz looked at a terrified Boots and back again. "She is, sir. The slaves call her Boots."

Pong nodded. "Give Boots some brig time. Maybe she'll be a little more zealous when she gets out."

Boots flushed red and tried to say something, but a glance from Raz shut her up. He didn't say anything but she got the message just the same. "You may think *this* is bad but it could've been a lot worse."

Pong ignored the byplay. "As for the girl, she'll remain here, where I can keep an eye on her."

He looked down at Molly and smiled. "I could use someone to run errands. Tell the security officer to give her an L-band."

Raz nodded curtly, took Boots by the arm, and marched her to the hatch. It hissed open and closed.

Molly was alone with Mustapha Pong.

An auto loader beeped and Maggie hurried to get out of its way. The markets ran in cycles, and with the fourth cycle about to begin, there was a lot of coming and going.

"You've been here before," Rico said, "where do we go? Where's the slave market?"

Maggie shook her head doubtfully. "Sorry, Rico. Nexus has changed. It's bigger and more complicated than when I was here. Maybe we should ask a remote."

"And maybe we shouldn't," Rico replied with a frown. "Call me paranoid, but the less we tell ol' binary brain the better I'll feel. Come on."

Maggie followed Rico back in the direction they'd come from and over to a vending stand. The electronic reader board said, "Robo guides, by the minute, hour, or day. Fully guided sex tours, market information, ship arrivals . . ."

The vendor was a birdlike Finthian, with saucerlike eyes and a translator hung around its neck. It looked this way and that with a nervous sort of twitch.

"Hello, gentle beings, step right up and get your robo guide. These are the best, the brightest, the —"

"Cut the crap and give me one," Rico interrupted.

The Finthian looked disappointed but did as Rico asked.

Maggie saw credits change hands and watched a tiny robo guide scamper up Rico's arm to perch on his shoulder.

The machine was globular in shape, had three spindly legs, and a single sensor that stuck up periscope fashion above its body. There was a tiny whine like that of a mosquito when the sensor moved.

"Hello," the robot chirped. "I am robo guide thirty-two. My main purpose is to provide you with navigational assistance within the confines of the Nexus habitat. However, my programming includes a wealth of incidental information and commercial messages that I will be happy to share upon request. Where would you like to go?"

"The slave market," Rico replied, "and pronto."

"You are in luck," the robot replied cheerfully. "Cycle four will start soon. Proceed down the hall to lift tube B, go up two decks, and exit to the right."

Rico and Maggie followed the robo guide's direction, and were soon among a crowd of sentients walking, gliding, hopping, and sliding into a circular room.

The programmable seats could accommodate 87.6 percent of known sentient species and were mounted on an incline so that everyone had a good view.

Spotlights washed back and forth across the pit, as if it were a stage and a play were about to begin. But this was no play. This was real. Maggie lowered her hover box next to Rico's seat and waited for the auction to begin.

It didn't take long. For some reason Maggie expected a live auctioneer, a human perhaps, all dressed up like the ringmaster at a circus.

But like most employers, Nexus hired in its own image, and the master of ceremonies was a machine.

A flying machine, that looked like a ball of pulsating energy and arrived with a blare of trumpets. It buzzed as it flew, skimming the crowd, coming within a foot of Maggie's head.

Then with a dramatic display of aerobatics, and the strobe of carefully placed lasers, the machine came to a sudden stop. The robot hung over the pit like a miniature sun and its voice came from everywhere at once.

It came as no surprise to Maggie that this, like most other things on the habitat, was another manifestation of Nexus.

"Greetings, I am Nexus. Welcome to slave cycle four. Being a machine myself, I believe that machines have an important place in the universe . . . but I value natural sentience as well.

"In fact, from a machine's point of view, you sentients are a good buy. You are reasonably intelligent, work hard when properly motivated, and are always eager to replicate yourselves. That's why I own a few sentients myself."

There was laughter from the humans, and a variety of noises from the other sentients, which might have been anything from an amused chuckle to a cry of outrage. Maggie assumed the former.

"Now," the MC said, "let's get down to business. As usual, cycle four will center around oxygen breathers so if you're looking for something more exotic, try cycle five or six.

"So, let's get things started with a nice group of Tillarians."

As the MC spoke six proud-looking Tillarian males were herded into the center of the slave pit. They stood back-to-back, eyes scanning the audience, as if daring the crowd to attack.

They were completely naked, and, with the exception of the bony ridge that bisected their skulls, very humanoid.

Or, Maggie thought to herself, we are quite Tillaroid, depending on your point of view.

In any case the Tillarians would be quite useful on any Earth-normal planet, and were soon sold to a Zord wholesaler, who would parcel them out to a network of retail traders.

During the transaction the robo guide would occasionally chirrup potentially useful information into Rico's ear, like the average price for Tillarian slaves over the last thousand cycles, and the minimum annual cost for maintenance.

And so it went, group after group, race after race until Maggie felt numb inside. Maybe that's how it works, she reflected. If you see something long enough, no matter how horrible it is, the thing becomes commonplace. Bit by bit your emotions grow less intense until eventually you feel nothing at all.

It was Rico who brought her back to the present. "Maggie! Look! Those boys! Aren't they some of ours?"

Maggie looked in the direction of Rico's pointing finger, and sure enough, there was a group of ragged-looking boys standing in the center of the pit. Here and there you could see brothers, or best friends, standing side by side, hoping that some sort of miracle would keep them together.

Outside of Molly McCade, and a few others, Maggie knew hardly any of Alice's children. She spent very little time on the planet's surface. But the expression of joy on Rico's face was all the confirmation she needed.

"I think you're right, Rico . . . what now?"

Rico held a finger to his lips. "Let's listen."

"So," the MC continued, buzzing the perimeter of the slave pit, "here's lot forty-one, a group of twenty-three juvenile humans, recently taken off some slush ball along the rim. They are ice-world acclimated, in good health, and a bargain at ten thousand credits apiece. Do I have a bid?"

Bidding began, and because it was done using the key paid built into each chair, it was impossible to see *who* was taking part.

The Nexus MC provided a running commentary on how much was being bid, but that was beside the point at the moment, and Rico tuned it out.

He turned toward the robo guide on his shoulder. "Can ya tell who's bidding?"

"Of course," the robot replied cheerfully, "it's on freq four. There were five or six bidders a moment ago, but it's down to a couple now, and they're going at it hot and heavy.

"One group is on your right, two rows back, and six seats over. Zords, I think, although it's hard to see with the crummy two-credit vid pickup they gave me.

"The others are over there, on the far side of the pit, the Lakorian in light body armor."

Rico resisted the impulse to look at the Zords but could see the Lakorian without difficulty. He was nothing special, a middle-aged male, dressed in well-worn armor.

Rico spoke from the side of his mouth. "How 'bout the seller? Does Nexus own the boys . . . or is it someone else?"

The robot was silent for a moment as it sorted through a variety of electronic signals. "No, Nexus doesn't own them, and yes, the owners are here. In seats G5, G6, G7, G8, G9 and G10 to be exact."

It took Rico a moment to locate them off to his left, four men and two women, all dressed in ship suits and heavily armed.

Maggie was getting concerned, things were moving quickly, and she didn't understand what Rico was up to. "Rico . . ."

"I have fourteen thousand . . . do I hear fourteen five? Going once, going twice . . ."

Rico ignored Maggie as his stubby fingers danced over the chair's key pad. "Not now, Maggie . . . it's time ta buy the boys."

"But, Rico . . . we don't have any money!"

"Wait a minute, gentle beings," the MC said with calculated enthusiasm, "we have another bid. I have fifteen, do I hear fifteen five? No? Going once, going twice, gone to bid number C-487912!

"Now our next lot consists . . ."

A bored-looking Cellite, with muscles on his muscles, herded the boys out of sight.

"Rico . . ." Maggie started, but stopped when she saw his fingers still moving over the key pad. A minute passed while queries appeared on a tiny screen and Rico tapped in the answers. Then he punched one last button and gave a sigh of relief. "Got 'em."

"But how?" Maggie asked, completely mystified.

"Easy," Rico replied. "I borrowed three hundred and forty-five thousand credits from Nexus, agreed ta pay ten percent interest compounded every thirty-six cycles, and used the boys, plus *Void Runner,* as collateral."

"But that doesn't solve anything. We still have to pay off the loan."

"Right," Rico said patiently. "But it *does* keep the boys here on Nexus. Got it?"

Maggie not only got it, her respect for Rico went up a notch as well. "So what now?"

"So now we follow them," Rico said grimly, nodding toward the group of humans now getting up to leave. "I want a word with that bunch."

A whole cacophony of alarm bells went off in Maggie's mind. "I don't know if that's such a good idea, Rico. Let's find Sam, tell him about the boys, and come back later."

Rico got to his feet. "Sam already knows about the boys, he authorized the lien on *Void Runner.*

"But that's a good idea," Rico said distantly, "you give Sam a hand, and I'll be along after a while."

Something about the way Rico said it, and the look in his eyes, scared Maggie. So she whirred along behind, wishing she could stop him, knowing she couldn't. Deep down Maggie knew this was something personal. Rico would never admit but this had something to do with Vanessa.

The six humans left the venue, laughing and joking, happy with the profit they'd made. Even after the ten percent that went to Nexus, and another ten for Pong, they were still doing very well indeed. Now it was time for a little celebration.

Rico and Maggie followed the pirates down one level and into a recreational zone. There were all sorts of drug dens, sex shops, bars, and restaurants. The pirates turned into the first bar they came to.

Rico followed with Maggie trailing along right behind.

Rico waited until the pirates had seated themselves at a table, selected a booth nearby, and sat down to wait. Maggie did likewise.

The pirates made fun of the blast-burned woman who took their order, used their combat knives to play tic tac toe on the tabletop, and downed their first round of drinks in five seconds flat.

That's when Rico stood up, removed the robo guide from his shoulder, and set it on the tabletop. It scuttled away.

Then Rico walked over to the pirate's table, produced a big smile, and said "Hi."

Most of the pirates snickered, but one replied. He had long lank hair parted in the middle, carefully plucked eyebrows, and a once-broken nose.

"Hi? Don't you mean 'Hi, sir'? That *is* what you meant, right, rimmer?"

Rico nodded. "Yes, sir, that's exactly what I meant, sir."

"Good," the man answered. "Now tell me, rimmer, what the hell do you want?"

"Just a little information, sir. Someone attacked a planet called Alice a while ago, and I wondered if you were there."

Maggie swallowed hard and moved away from the booth. The bar was completely silent. The tension was so thick you could cut it with a laser.

The pirate's eyes narrowed. "Oh, you did, huh? Why's that, rimmer? You from Alice by any chance?"

Rico smiled slowly. "Why yes, sir, I have that honor. Now I'd appreciate an answer."

A woman spoke this time. She had hard eyes, a dope stick hanging from the corner of her mouth, and a whippet-thin body.

"Yeah, rimmer, we were there, the dirties put up quite a fight, but we waxed 'em good. How'd we miss something as big and ugly as you?"

It was the last thing she ever said. Maggie had never seen anything so fast. One moment Rico was standing there, arms hanging loosely by his sides, and the next there was a blaster in his hand.

The first bolt of energy took the woman right between the eyes. She fell over backward.

The next hit the man sitting beside her in the center of his chest, punched a hole through the back of his chair, and turned a neuro-game into a collection of fused circuit boards.

The air felt like quicksand as Maggie slapped the right side of her hover box, heard the panel pop open, and felt the spring-loaded blaster jump into her hand. As the weapon started upward Maggie wondered if it would arrive in time.

Meanwhile, the second woman shouted something incoherent as she put a bolt of blue energy through Rico's shoulder, and died a fraction of a second later.

One of the men stood and brought a blaster into line with Rico's chest.

Maggie fired. Her bolt took the man's hand off at the wrist. It made an audible thump as it hit the deck.

The man screamed and died as Rico put a bolt through his head.

Maggie fired again, saw a man try to cover the hole in his throat, and felt herself fall as raw energy sliced through her hover box.

She didn't see the last man die from her vantage point on the floor, but she heard the scream of energy bolts and saw Rico's boots appear in front of her face.

A second later his face was visible too, full of concern, asking how she was. Maggie saw a wisp of smoke drift away from the hole in Rico's shoulder.

She didn't get to answer, because a bunch of blaster-toting remotes picked that particular moment to show up, but Maggie knew what she wanted to say.

She wanted to say that it felt good to have friends.

FOURTEEN

There was an observatory tucked away far above the ship's bridge, a tiny place where the navigator could get a star fix in an emergency, and the chief engineer could visually inspect thirty percent of the ship's hull. The observatory was hardly ever used and had become Molly's secret hideaway.

At the moment there was nothing to see since the ship was in hyperspace. Still, it was comforting to have a space of her own, where she could think and, if necessary, cry.

She sat on the circular bench, arms around her knees, and stared at the opposite bulkhead.

The headband was tight around her forehead, a constant reminder of Pong and what he could do to her.

The security officer had been a small man, with a shaved head and a walrus-style mustache. As he pulled the loyalty-band around Molly's head and locked it in place, he described how it would work.

"Most o' the time it ain't nuthin', just a headband like ya might wear to keep the hair outta your eyes. But ya try to take it off, or do somethun' the Pong don't like, and blamo! You're history.

"Yasee it's full o' OS-3, carefully shaped ta explode inward, liftin' the top of *your* head off, but keepin' everyone else neat and tidy! It all works off that ring on his right pinky."

The security officer thought he was doing Molly a favor, warning her so she wouldn't mess around with the band and get herself killed, but his lecture had given her regular nightmares.

Every time Molly went to sleep she had the same recurring dream.

It began as she stepped off a shuttle. She could see Mommy and Daddy on the far side of the landing pad. They were alive! Then she ran across the pad, shouting her happiness, waiting to feel their arms around her.

And then, when she was only feet away, something horrible would happen. She would see the bands around their heads, hear Pong laughing, and wake up crying.

It was horrible and caused her to stay awake as long as she could.

But if the headband was terrifying, it conferred benefits too. Molly was allowed to go anywhere she wanted. By order of Pong himself she was accorded the respect shown a junior officer.

She thought it was a joke at first, a strange way to tease her, but now she knew it was real.

On three different occasions she'd given orders and they'd been obeyed. It had been a thrill at first, to suddenly have power, but that feeling quickly disappeared. Now the power troubled her . . . and she didn't know what to do.

Her first impulse was to help the others, but thanks to their already improved circumstances, there wasn't much she could do.

Still, she did what she could, and was able to get them some nicer clothes and holo cubes.

The girls seemed to appreciate Molly's efforts at first, until Lia told them she was a spy, and they turned against her. Now they wouldn't even talk to her.

And that had led to a strange and disturbing encounter. During each twenty-six-hour cycle it was Pong's wish that she spend two hours with him.

Molly didn't see the point of this, because he spent most of the time working and rarely even spoke to her. But her presence seemed to give him pleasure, and Molly had no choice in the matter, so that's how it was.

This particular cycle Pong decided to inspect the ship, an activity he usually left to others, but sometimes did himself.

So with Molly at his side, and the Melcetian mind slug riding his shoulder, Pong started in the bow and worked his way toward the stern.

Most of the inspection was a long succession of worried-looking faces, boring conversation, and trips into odd nooks and crannies.

Molly spent most of the time eyeing the signet ring on Pong's little finger. The ring that gave him the power of life and death over her.

But then something strange happened. They were walking down one of the ship's main corridors when they encountered Lia. She was on hands and knees, polishing the long metal strip that ran along the point where bulkhead met deck. There was no one else in sight.

Later, Molly would wonder *how* Lia came to be in that particular place at that particular time, and *why* Pong would know her name. But it seemed natural at the time and she accepted it.

Pong stopped. Lia looked frightened and polished twice as fast as she had before.

"So," Pong said, "this is Lia."

Molly looked from Lia to Pong. What was he doing? Why the sudden interest in Lia? Did it have anything to do with her?

"Correct me if I'm wrong, child," Pong said thoughtfully, "but Lia's the one who turned you in. Not only that, she did so without any knowledge of what the consequences might be. For all Lia knew, I might torture you or have you killed."

Molly struggled for an answer. Pong *knew* Lia had ratted on her, so why ask the question? And given the fact that Lia *had* acted without any thought for the possible consequences, why protect her? Emotions surged. Come to think of it, Lia was still doing everything she could to isolate Molly and make her life miserable.

Still, to confirm Lia's guilt seemed disloyal somehow so Molly said nothing.

Pong nodded, as if he understood exactly what had passed through Molly's mind.

"Loyalty. A fine quality when deserved. But ask yourself the following question. Does Lia deserve your loyalty? What would *she* say if your positions were reversed?"

Molly had a pretty good idea what the answer to that was. Lia would condemn her without a second's thought.

Lia knew too, and had forgotten to work, staring upward in abject terror. Her eyes pleaded for mercy.

"Right," Pong said as if Molly had spoken. "She would betray you in a second. Not just now, but later too if she gets the chance. She's jealous of you, and wants to dominate the other girls.

"So, here's the problem. Should you forgive her? Knowing that she'll betray you if given the chance? Or kill her, and remove the threat?"

Lia made a mewing noise and started to back away.

Molly felt resentment bubble up from deep inside her, resentment at what Lia had done, *would do* if she got the chance.

Molly's emotions demanded one thing, and her mind another. Her mind won. "No, killing Lia would be wrong."

Pong nodded agreeably. "I understand, and might agree if you were home, dealing with childish squabbles.

"But remember, child, you aren't home anymore. It's unlikely that you'll ever see your mother and father again. I know what that's like . . . I too lost my parents at an early age.

"So the decision is up to you. What do you want of life? What it gives you, or what you can take? Will you be victim or victor? The choice is yours. Just say the word, and Lia will die."

And with that Pong had continued on his way, running a finger along a piece of conduit looking for dust, whistling through his teeth.

Molly had followed, looking backward over her shoulder at a terrified Lia, not knowing what to do or say.

And now Molly felt horrible, because she knew that for one brief moment, Lia had been very close to death.

FIFTEEN

McCade leaned back, left one foot on the deck, and placed the other on the bulkhead behind him. Phil stood a few feet away tapping numbers into his oversize wrist comp.

Four major passageways spilled people and machines into the intersection in front of them. Some paused for a second, looked around, and resumed their journeys. Others knew where they wanted to go, and worked their way through traffic with the determination of fish swimming upstream.

McCade found half a smoked cigar in his breast pocket, stuck it into the corner of his mouth, and puffed it into life.

The bounty hunter had mixed emotions. On the one hand he was glad that Rico had found the boys, but there was no sign of the missing girls, or of Molly. He couldn't help feeling disappointed.

Nexus wouldn't allow them to speak with the boys until they were paid for, but McCade figured they'd been on an entirely different ship, and hadn't seen the girls since the raid.

Well, there was nothing he could do except free the boys as quickly as possible and resume the search for Molly.

McCade removed the cigar, flicked some ash toward the deck, and stuck it back in his mouth. "So what's the tab?"

Phil punched a few more keys, gave a low whistle, and looked up. "Well, what with the three hundred and forty-five that Rico borrowed to pay for the boys, damage to the bar, medical treatment, interest, and a whole bunch of service charges that Nexus tacked on, we're looking at a grand total of five hundred and thirty-six thousand credits. Not counting the money we're spending now."

"A substantial piece of change," McCade said, eyeing the crowd.

Phil nodded. "Yeah, *real* substantial. Do you think we can pull it off?"

"Sure," McCade answered, sounding more confident than he felt.

"There must be a couple hundred sentients wandering around this place with a price on their heads. All we have to do is round 'em up, sell their bounties at a ten-percent discount, and let some enterprising soul haul 'em in. What could be more simple?"

"Training rath snakes to make coffee," Phil growled in reply.

The variant didn't mean it. The idea made sense. Well, not sense exactly, but it might work anyhow.

The alternative wasn't that great either. Sell *Void Runner*, use the proceeds to pay off their debts, and walk home.

"So," McCade said. "Is the holding tank ready?"

"Ready and staffed," Phil replied. "I hired some rather nasty Zords to act as guards."

Smoke dribbled from the corner of McCade's mouth. "Good. How 'bout the scanner?"

"Up and running," Phil assured him. "Both it and the computer are hidden behind the clothes racks across the way."

There was a vendor on the other side of the hall. He sold clothes, accessories, and a scattering of cheap jewelry.

McCade looked, and sure enough, he could just barely see a lens peeking between a couple of leather jackets. The operator was a fourteen-year-old pickpocket. He'd seen Phil, assumed the variant was a rim rube and tried to bump and dip him. A serious mistake for which he was now paying.

"And the escorts?"

"Some mercenaries on leave. They're about fifty yards up corridor. We call, and they come running."

"Okay," McCade said, pushing himself away from the wall. "It's time to open up shop." He dropped the cigar and crushed it under his boot.

Phil pulled the tiny boom mic a little closer to his mouth and whispered something.

On the other side of the hall the pickpocket flipped a series of switches and settled down to wait.

The scanner panned back and forth as it fed images into the computer. The computer took the images, compared them to those McCade had obtained from a public terminal, and notified the boy of a match. At that point the pickpocket would alert his employers and they'd do the rest.

The pickpocket had instructions to lay low after that.

His name was Dawk. He had blond hair, bright blue eyes, and a snub nose.

Dawk was resentful at first, but when Phil explained how the scam would reduce competition and increase profits, the boy became downright enthusiastic. Now he paid close attention as the scanner panned the crowd and waited for a match. It came with surprising speed.

Dawk heard a soft buzz from his earpiece. His heart thumped with excitement. The computer screen split itself into one, two, three equal sections.

Heads filled all three sections, rotated 360 degrees, and squeeze zoomed into the upper right-hand corner. Data flooded the now empty space below. Name, description, crimes, weapons, it was all there.

Dawk fingered a switch. "Dawk here. I've got three positives coming down corridor three. Here's a peek." The pickpocket pushed a button.

McCade looked at his wrist term and swore. Why so many? Why not two, or one? Bad luck, that's why. Well, beggars can't be choosers.

McCade looked up, spotted the three of them right away, and wished he hadn't. They were big, *real* big, and looked very much alike.

McCade glanced down at his wrist term. Looked, hell, they were triplets! And wanted for everything from spitting on the sidewalk to cold-blooded murder!

He looked back up. Each of the triplets was seven feet tall, had a shaved head, and a bushy black beard. All were dressed in matching leather outfits and carried identical weapons. *Lots* of weapons, including blasters, force blades, and Lord knew what else.

Phil nudged McCade's arm. "It's now or never."

McCade wanted to say "never," but the triplets were worth thirty thousand each, plus an extra ten if someone produced the matched set.

"Okay, Phil. Remember to cheat."

Phil grinned wickedly. "You can count on me!"

The two men sidled out into the intersection just as the triplets arrived and began to push their way through the crowd.

McCade went left, and Phil went right.

Then, just as the fugitives passed to the inside, both men turned and sapped the outer triplets from behind. The saps were little more than leather sacks filled with hundreds of tiny ball bearings. They worked extremely well. Both fugitives slumped to the deck.

Stunners had been the other option, but with so many sentients around it would be easy to miss and hit the wrong individual. The same went for blasters only more so.

McCade was still congratulating himself on how well things were going when the third triplet hit him on the side of the head with a ham-sized fist.

This time McCade was the one who hit the deck with a thump, and lay there, wondering what it would feel like when triplet number three jumped on his chest.

Fortunately Phil chose that moment to tap the giant on the shoulder. "Excuse me."

The triplet turned. "Huh?"

That's when Phil delivered a powerful uppercut. It started near the deck, accelerated upward, and hit the man's jaw with a solid thud.

Much to Phil's amazement, the triplet shook his head and moved in for the kill. He was surprisingly fast and had huge hairy hands around Phil's neck in nothing flat.

Phil brought both of his massive forearms up, broke the hold, and kneed the giant in the groin. The man gave a gasp of pain, doubled over, and fell as McCade hit him with a sap.

McCade held his blaster on the triplets while Phil called the mercenaries. They arrived a few seconds later, placed the still groggy giants in triple restraints, and hauled them off to Phil's makeshift holding tank.

With the show over the now-substantial crowd had started to move again. Many were looking at the two bounty hunters and talking among themselves.

McCade knew that word would spread, and knew that fugitives would get harder and harder to find. But that would take time. Five-hundred and thirty-six thousand credits' worth if things went as planned.

Of even more concern however was the fact that three or four remotes had witnessed the incident and relayed what they'd seen to the central processing unit. What did Nexus think of the situation? Did it care?

There was no way to tell, but McCade planned to run the trap as long as he could.

A full hour passed before the computer produced another positive match and notified Dawk. It was a single fugitive this time and not much of a catch.

Her name was Lorina Dep-Smith. She was about two hundred pounds overweight, surrendered with nothing more violent than a loud belch, and swore a blue streak when she understood the situation.

According to the computer Dep-Smith had embezzled some money from a New Britain-based shipping line, and, judging from the paltry five-thousand-credit reward on her head, hadn't escaped with very much.

Still, every credit counts, and Dep-Smith was led away to join the triplets in holding. McCade wondered how the four of them would get along.

The next six hours were quite productive. No one had ever tried bounty hunting on this scale before, and because of the habitat's lawless reputation, there were plenty of fugitives.

They nabbed a twenty-thousand-credit bank robber, a fifty-thousand-credit drug smuggler, a pair of thirty-six-thousand-credit organ runners, and four petty thieves worth seventy thousand total.

Fortunately the triplets were atypical, and with the exception of a minor scuffle or two, all of them surrendered without a fight. The trap was so unexpected that most of the fugitives didn't understand what was going on until it was too late.

Then, just when it seemed as if things couldn't get any better, along came a cyborg with a suitcase full of cash.

The borg was wanted for fraud, and had a paltry thousand-credit price on his head. But the suitcase contained almost a million in cash, and in accordance with Imperial law, the bounty hunters were entitled to a ten-percent recovery fee.

The saps proved completely ineffective on the cyborg's metal brain case but a flying tackle did the trick.

In retrospect the trap had worked better than McCade's wildest dreams, and according to Phil's math, they were only a hundred and eighteen thousand credits short of their goal.

About forty-five minutes passed before the next score came along. It was a big one this time, a psychopath named Hassan, who'd demonstrated his dislike for the elders of his church by blowing them up.

The Empire was offering forty thousand for Hassan dead or alive, and that plus the fifty that had been raised by the membership of the church brought his total value up to a nice round ninety thousand.

There was something about Hassan, something about the twitchy way he moved, that told McCade the man wouldn't surrender easily.

Hassan had a slender build. He was dressed in a high-collared cloak with matching skintight trousers and knee-high boots. While there weren't any weapons in plain sight there could be an entire arsenal concealed under the man's cloak.

McCade nodded to Phil and they moved out into the traffic. Phil circled around behind Hassan while McCade waited in front. A muscle twitched in his left cheek.

When the fugitive was about fifteen feet away, McCade pulled his blaster, gave startled pedestrians a moment to scurry out of the way, and yelled, "Hassan! Hold it right there!"

Hassan didn't even flinch. He pointed a finger at McCade. Something warm brushed past the bounty hunter's left cheek and hit a maintenance bot somewhere behind him. It blew up with a brilliant flash of light.

Hassan had some sort of energy weapon hidden up his sleeve! Whatever the weapon was, it was unusually powerful, and must use a lot of energy. Maybe it would run out soon.

Still, one more shot like the last, and McCade would be little more than a scorch mark on the deck.

Phil tried to club Hassan from behind, but was blocked by a hysterical merchant who threw himself at the variant's feet and screamed, "Save me! Save me!"

The blaster was lighter than the slug gun McCade usually carried and generated no recoil.

Blue light sliced down and across the font of Hassan's cloak. Nothing! The son-of-a-bitch was wearing armor!

Hassan grinned. God protects her own. Now the bounty hunter would pay the price for his impudence. Idolators must die!

Hassan moved his arm a hair to the left and aligned the custom-designed energy tube with McCade's chest. The trigger was a small black ball that Hassan held in the palm of his right hand. His brain told his hand to squeeze the ball but it was too late.

Hassan blew up. Although *he* was armored, his power supply *wasn't,* and McCade hit it. The result was loud and messy.

Disentangling himself from the sobbing merchant, Phil came over to join McCade, still flicking little bits of Hassan off his kilt. "Nice going, Sam. How do we get a reward with nothing to turn in?"

McCade slid the blaster into its holster. He'd been lucky, *damned* lucky, and his hands were shaking. He tried to smile.

"The Empire is quite liberal about such matters, Phil. They'll accept retinas, a full set of teeth, or fingers with prints attached. See what you can find.

"In the meantime I'll help Dawk tear the equipment down. We've pushed our luck far enough."

Phil checked to make sure McCade was serious, saw that he was, and walked away mumbling to himself.

Twenty minutes later a crew of maintenance bots had just finished cleaning up the mess, Phil had one of Hassan's hands in a stasis bag, and McCade was helping Dawk to dismantle the scanner system. He didn't hear the remote approach.

"You will accompany me now."

McCade turned. "Excuse me?"

The remote's face was completely devoid of expression as always. There were six remotes altogether, all armed, all equally featureless.

"You will accompany me now. I wish to speak with you."

McCade knew the "I" was Nexus, and that there was no point in resistance since the AI was all powerful. The computer wanted to talk and, for reasons known only to it, didn't wish to use a remote for that purpose.

There was little doubt as to what Nexus sought to discuss. When Hassan blew up, things had come perilously close to violating law number one, "Don't harm Nexus."

Chances were they'd get a "cease and desist" order. Okay, McCade could live with that, as long as the machine didn't try to block them altogether.

McCade forced a smile and wondered if nonverbal communication counted for anything with Nexus.

"Of course. We'll be right there."

McCade turned. "Dawk, drop Hassan's hand off at our holding tank, and take the computer gear to lock seventy-seven. Ask for Rico or Maggie. Drop by the tank later on. There'll be something extra in your pay."

Dawk looked surprised. "Pay? You mean I get paid?"

McCade looked at Phil but the variant was busy examining his durasteel claws. "Yeah," McCade answered, "no matter what my furry friend may have told you, *all* of our employees get paid. I'll see you later."

Dawk grinned and busied himself with the electronic gear.

McCade turned to the remote. "Okay, we're all yours. Lead the way."

With three of the silvery remotes walking ahead, and three behind, the crowd seemed to melt away. No one wanted to mess with Nexus or get too close to the idiots who already had.

The procession wound its way through a labyrinth of corridors and into a lift tube marked, RESTRICTED—NEXUS ONLY. They stepped out into a large open space a few seconds later.

The first impression was of lights, thousands of them, covering the walls and dome-shaped ceiling, denser than any galaxy, but starlike nonetheless.

They seemed to ripple outward in overlapping circles, like raindrops hitting the surface of a pond.

Suddenly McCade realized that all six of the remotes had retreated to wall niches. They looked like statues.

The deck, which had been a glossy black, was suddenly transformed into a vid screen. Video of the intersection appeared. A variety of shots followed, each covering a different angle, and representing what one remote had seen.

McCade and Phil watched as the triplets, Dep-Smith, and Hassan fell into the trap.

As the video disappeared the asexual voice came from everywhere and nowhere at once. "Explain."

McCade considered a number of lies but couldn't be sure that any of them would hold up. Nexus was no fool and had innumerable sources of information. No, it seemed better to tell the truth, and hope for the best.

McCade cleared his throat. "A few weeks ago the planet Alice was attacked by pirates. A number of children were taken during the raid. My companions and I were sent to find the children and return them to Alice. During slave cycle four, we discovered that twenty-three of our children were for sale, and bought them using funds borrowed from you.

"We are presently engaged in an effort to capture individuals wanted by the Imperial government. We plan to sell their bounties at a discount, use the money to pay off our loans, and take the children home."

McCade turned to Phil. "Did I leave anything out?"

The variant shook his head.

Nexus was silent for a moment, as if thinking, or dealing with something or someone else. Then it spoke. "I disagree with your companion. There is something that you neglected to mention. One of the missing children is your daughter."

McCade looked up at the multitude of twinkling lights and wished the computer had a face. His heart beat like a trip-hammer. How did Nexus know about Molly? Was she here? Was this the end of his search? McCade fought to keep his voice under control.

"That's true. Do you know where she is?"

The answer was emotionless. Machinelike. "No, I do not. However, I do have a personal message for you."

"You have a what?"

Once again the deck transformed itself into a huge video screen. The man who appeared there had blond hair, blue eyes, and was known to billions of sentients across hundreds of systems. Loved by many, hated by some, the face belonged to the Emperor himself.

A man who might still be meditating high in the mountains of the Wind World, learning from the mystics who called themselves Walkers of the Way, if it weren't for Sam McCade.

Yes, Alexander owed McCade a debt of gratitude, but more than that considered the bounty hunter his friend.

And because McCade was untempted by the Emperor's power, uninterested in his wealth, and unimpressed by his rank, he was that rarest of all things, a man Alexander could trust.

The Emperor smiled. "Hello, Sam. I wish this greeting came at a better time. I'm sorry about the raid, worried about Molly, and well aware that it was your service to *me* that put Alice in jeopardy.

"Most people think that I'm all powerful, capable of righting any wrong, but you know better. I'm painfully aware that it is beyond my ability to restore a life, to heal a broken body, or undo the damage done to Alice. Nonetheless I do what I can.

"Descriptions of the children have gone out to every naval base in the Empire, our ships have been alerted to watch out for vessels that belong to Pong, and Swanson-Pierce has his people working on it as well."

A sometimes friend, and sometimes enemy, Swanson-Pierce was none other than *Admiral* Swanson-Pierce, head of Naval Intelligence, and a member of Alexander's personal staff.

"Knowing *you* however," the Emperor continued, "I suspect you are already tackling the problem in your own way, and probably making more progress than we are.

"Still, it never hurts to have a friend in high places, so call on me if there's something I can do. Though not controlled by me, Nexus and I do each other favors from time to time, and it may be willing to help.

"Linnea sends her love. Please let us know when Molly is safe and sound." The picture faded to black.

Silence descended. Seconds became minutes. It seemed Nexus was thinking, or doing other things, or just didn't care.

Of the three McCade thought the last was most likely. There was plenty of Nexus to go around, and had the machine wished to, it could've held a conversation with them *and* covered everything else as well.

Finally, after a good five minutes had passed, Nexus spoke. It was as if no time had passed whatsoever. "So, Citizen McCade, it seems you have an unexpectedly powerful ally, and that will stand you in good stead.

"You will be interested to know that the imperial message torpedo arrived only hours ago. Were it not for the Emperor's intervention this conversation would have turned in a different direction. Your most recent activities threatened not only my personal well-being, but that of my customers as well, leaving me no choice but to discipline you.

"Fortunately you have captured a sufficient number of fugitives to pay off most of your debt. Given the fact that the Emperor is willing to pay off the remaining balance, and given the fact that you are no doubt anxious to leave, I will order my staff to place the children in your custody.

"My staff will also take charge of the unauthorized prison that you and your companions have established on C deck. I will dispose of the fugitives as I see fit."

McCade raised an eyebrow. What did Nexus mean by that? Would the computer turn the fugitives in? Or turn them loose to maintain the habitat's lawless reputation? But as long as Nexus released the children he really didn't care.

The computer hadn't asked for agreement but McCade supplied it anyway. "Thank you. That arrangement will be quite satisfactory."

A section of lights rippled toward the top of the dome. "Have a nice visit."

McCade nodded and started for the lift tube. He was almost there when Nexus spoke again.

"Citizen McCade."

"Yes?"

"Before you turn the prisoners over to my staff you might want to interrogate the woman known as Lorina Dep-Smith."

McCade frowned. "Okay . . . but why?"

The computer paused as if for effect. "Because she commands the ship that brought the children to Nexus."

SIXTEEN

The yacht slowed. The vessel was a wedge of streamlined metal on the outside, and on the inside it was extremely comfortable.

Everywhere Molly looked she saw muted colors, subdued lighting, and carefully chosen fixtures. There was no way she could know, but this was the *Arrow,* the very ship on which Pong had escaped from her father.

Molly sat beside Mustapha Pong on the side opposite the mind slug. She was thankful, because no matter how much time Molly spent with Pong, the Melcetian still made her nervous.

Molly felt both excitement and guilt. Excitement because she liked doing new things, and guilt because she was doing them with Mustapha Pong, and he'd attacked her planet.

And what about the other girls? True, they weren't suffering, but they weren't happy either, and wouldn't be until they returned to Alice. And what had she done to free them?

Nothing, that's what, not since her attempt to access the navcomp, and the placement of the L-band around her head. Not that the other girls *wanted* any help.

Molly felt a sudden surge of anger. Ever since the incident in the corridor things were even worse than before. Lia still hated her, but now the older girl was afraid as well, and cowered when Molly was around. This had the effect of further distancing Molly from the rest of the girls and left her completely isolated.

Yes, Molly thought to herself. Pong's right about one thing. When people betray you it's stupid to give them another chance. Why should I try and help them? Let them stay with Lia! I'll find my own way out of here and leave them behind.

Pong touched Molly's arm. "Look, child, there it is."

Molly looked out of the viewport. The alien ship was huge, large enough to be mistaken for an asteroid, or an errant moon.

Where human and even Il Ronnian spacecraft looked like what they were, this one looked like a big rock. Sunlight moved steadily across its surface as the alien vessel rotated on its axis.

Surely the ship had weapons emplacements, solar collectors, and all the other hardware common to its kind, but Molly couldn't see them.

Molly had never heard of the 56,827 before. She thought that a number made a strange name for an entire race, but Pong had explained that it was the way the aliens saw themselves, as an aggregate comprised of individual numbers.

The total number, and therefore the name of the race, changed with each birth and death. Not only that, but individual names, and their entire social order, stemmed from numbers as well.

If for example someone was born number 32,105, they would forever be junior to individual 32,104, and senior to 32,106.

And, given a long average life span and extremely low birthrate, their relative social position would remain constant for years at a time. This made for a rigid and rather hierarchical social structure.

Because of this internal rigidity Pong explained, the more ambitious members of the race were encouraged to direct their energies outward, and that explained the ship. The aliens were on the lookout for new commercial opportunities.

When Molly asked where the 56,827 came from, Pong replied that they came from somewhere beyond the rim, beyond the limits of human exploration.

As the shuttle approached, the alien spaceship grew even larger. "Are all of their ships that big?" Molly asked.

Pong looked down at her, then out of the viewport. "No, child, as a matter of fact that's the only ship they have."

Molly looked up to see if Pong was teasing her.

The pirate smiled. "I'm serious. They claim one ship is all they need. And what's even more surprising is that in spite of the ship's size, it carries only sixteen individuals, and they think it's crowded."

Molly thought about that for a moment. "They must be huge."

Molly laughed. "A logical conclusion, child, but false nonetheless. They are larger than humans, but not by much.

"No, I'm afraid it's more complicated than that. Due to conditions on their native planet the 56,827 are extremely territorial.

"From what they tell me that stems from the ancient need for individual hunting preserves. Vast lands where they could hunt. With the passage of time and the coming of advanced technology, competition has become more commercial and less carnivorous. The result is the same however. Each adult requires a large amount of personal space."

"And that accounts for the size of their ship," Molly finished for him. "They can't stand to be cooped up together."

Pong clapped his hands in approval. "Exactly, child! Correct as usual. Now excuse me while I deal with an incoming message."

Molly couldn't hear the message because it came in via the small plug in Pong's left ear. And due to the fact that the pirate subvocalized his reply, she couldn't hear that either.

Returning her attention to the alien ship, Molly saw she was right. It *was* more mechanical than it appeared. A section of the planetoid's surface had opened to reveal a spacious landing bay. A complicated latticework of laser beams reached out to touch receptors on the shuttle's hull and guide it in.

Fifteen minutes passed while the shuttle touched down inside the otherwise empty hangar, the outer door slid closed, and a breathable atmosphere was pumped into the bay.

Freed from her seat, Molly passed the time in the shuttle's control compartment, asking the pilot questions and playing with the vessel's external cameras.

The pilot, a humanoid-shaped cyborg, didn't like Molly messing around with the controls but was afraid to object. Like the rest of Pong's crew, the cyborg didn't understand her leader's relationship with Molly, and had no desire to test it.

Oblivious to these concerns, Molly activated a vid cam located halfway down the shuttle's port side, and moved it around using a small joystick. It was fun to track the robots as they scurried hither and yon, fueling the shuttle and getting in each other's way.

Molly turned a knob that caused the vid cam to zoom in and out. As the robots became larger and smaller Molly noticed something strange. Many of the robots were extremely dissimilar. Startlingly so.

Take the matter of locomotion for example. Some of the robot's walked, while others hopped, rolled, and crawled. Why so many variations? It was as though the robots had been created by different designers with wildly different ideas of how they should look and function.

As Molly watched the robots she remembered Daddy saying that mechanical artifacts vary tremendously from race to race due to environmental, physical, and cultural differences.

For example, human house bots tend to look humanoid, while their Finthian equivalents have a distinctly birdlike quality. Given that, which one of these machines looked like the 56,827?

Molly looked from robot to robot but still couldn't find many similarities. Of course form follows function where utility bots are concerned . . . so that might explain it.

Mustapha Pong interrupted her thoughts. "What are you thinking?"

Molly pointed at the screen. "The robots look different from each other. Were all of them designed by 56,827?"

Pong was startled. This girl never ceased to amaze him. Without realizing what she'd done, Molly had put her finger on the aliens' greatest secret, and their one weakness.

The truth was that the 56,827 hadn't built *any* of the robots, or the ship either for that matter, and were frightened of more technologically advanced races.

The ship was a good example. Pong knew that the 56,827 had forced another more sophisticated race to build and arm it.

Ah, but there was one thing the aliens did very well indeed, and that was fight. Pound for pound, tooth for tooth, they were among the most vicious carnivores in the known universe.

And even more importantly the 56,827 had the will to win, the absolute ruthlessness it takes to eradicate an entire race, and do so without compunction. That was the quality Pong found absent in so many humans and admired in his secret allies.

But none of this could be shared with Molly so Pong ignored her question and glanced at his wrist term instead.

"Come on, Molly, our host awaits."

Molly slid off the copilot's chair. The Melcetian mind slug quivered and color rippled across its surface.

Molly positioned herself on the opposite side of Pong's body.

"Our host? One of the 56,827?"

The pirate nodded. "Number 47,721 to be exact. You will be one of the few humans privileged to meet a member of the 56,827."

Pong almost added ". . . and survive," but decided not to.

They went alone, just Pong and Molly, down a ramp and into the bay. There was a lock set into the left side of the bay, and from the height of the controls, Molly judged the aliens were at least a foot taller than Phil.

The door whirred open, then closed. Pong whistled tunelessly while they waited. The pirate seemed preoccupied so Molly passed the time counting the number of rivets in a section of bulkhead.

Then the inner hatch slid open and Molly gave a gasp of surprise. Where she should be looking at a utilitarian corridor, or at most a reception area, there were rolling grasslands giving way to a distant forest. And where there should be gray metal, nearly invisible behind duct work, conduit, and pipe, there was a dim lavender sky. Everything looked dark and murky.

Pong smiled at her consternation. "Amazing, isn't it? A clever combination of carefully regulated biosphere and electronic trickery. As you can see the 56,827 are rather fond of their home planet and take a likeness of it wherever they go."

Molly nodded wordlessly and followed as Pong stepped out onto a dirt path and followed it up a slight rise toward a stand of strange-looking trees. Or was it "tree" singular?

Whichever it was had grown in a circle, with hard vertical trunks forming an outer stockade, and rich purple foliage hanging down into the center. They looked dark and foreboding.

They were about ten feet away from the grove when something stepped out from between the tree trunks and turned their way. Molly grabbed Pong's arm. She'd met three or four different types of aliens nose to snout, beak, or whatever, and seen holos of many more.

Over and over Molly's parents had told her that regardless of how strange another race might look to human eyes, regardless of how they sounded or smelled, what mattered was the way they behaved. Were they truthful? Ethical, by their own standards at least? Compassionate? These were the measuring sticks Molly had been taught to use.

But try as she might Molly couldn't suppress the overwhelming fear that burbled up from some primeval well deep inside her. This thing reeked of such raw unrepentant evil that it made her blood run cold.

Number 47,721 stood about seven and a half feet tall. Its head consisted of two distinct parts. A cigar-shaped section with eyes mounted at either end and, set at right angles to that, a pair of lethal-looking jaws. They parted slightly to show rows of teeth. A long rope of salivalike mucus dribbled out.

The alien had narrow shoulders, heavily muscled arms, and ivory, almost-translucent skin. 47,721's torso curved backward slightly, reminding Molly of the Terran insects she'd seen on study tapes, and was balanced on a pair of powerful legs. Each of its feet had three toes, each toe ending in a two-inch claw, each claw razor-sharp.

Pong gave Molly's hand a reassuring squeeze. "Greetings, 47,721. This numberless one comes seeking an audience."

Molly gulped as the alien looked her way. Now she saw that its eyes were huge, multifaceted, and probably much better at collecting light than hers. Molly noticed the translator hung around its neck. It spoke standard like a machine, free of accent, and without intonation. "I hereby grant the audience you seek. Is this one of the juveniles?"

Pong frowned as if hearing an undertone he didn't like. "Yes, this is a juvenile, but not one of those we discussed. This one belongs to me."

Molly looked upward at Pong. Juvenile? Discussed? Belongs to me? What were they talking about anyway?

Mucus drooped down from the alien's jaws. Its voice dropped an octave. "Careful, numberless one. *Nothing* belongs to you save that which the 56,827 grant you. But enough of this. We have much to discuss. Leave the juvenile here. It will be safe enough as long as it stays near the trees."

Pong turned to Molly. "Stay here, child. 47,721 and I have business to discuss. Do as he says and stay near the trees. I'll be gone for an hour or so."

Molly nodded silently. Much better to stay here alone than go with the alien. It was even worse than Pong's mind slug.

Pong gave her a nervous smile and turned to 47,721. "The numberless one is ready."

The alien made an inarticulate grunting sound and turned toward the path. Moments later alien and human alike had disappeared around the side of a small hill.

Molly just stood there for a moment, staring after them, half hoping that Pong would reappear. When he didn't she walked a few yards away from the trees and sat down in the grass. It smelled good.

It was silent at first. But bit by bit sound returned as tiny insects buzzed around Molly's head and a breeze rustled its way through the grass.

Had the sun been brighter, it would have been enjoyable, sitting there on what seemed like solid ground after countless days aboard ship, feeling the sunlight on her face.

But the strange twilight that surrounded Molly made her shiver instead and wish that she'd brought a cloak.

Still, Molly started to feel bored after a while, and stood up in order to look around.

Surely she could explore the immediate area without running into anything dangerous. Though somewhat dark the countryside was peaceful and quiet.

Molly saw a pile of boulders downhill and to the left. There were holes in them, big round openings that looked perfectly symmetrical and might be fun to crawl through.

Molly made her way down the slight incline and was about fifty feet away from the jumble of boulders when a voice said, "Are you old enough to speak?"

Molly looked around. She saw nothing but gently waving grass, the boulders, and forest beyond. "Yes, I'm old enough. Who are you? Where are you?"

"Right here," the voice said, and a triangular-shaped head appeared followed by a skeletal-looking body. It stood erect, but looked more sauroid than human. It wore a complicated-looking vest with a multitude of pockets. Busy hands fluttered this way and that as if searching for something to do. The creature's leathery skin was the same color as the grass and made it hard to see. "My name is Jareth."

Now Molly remembered 47,721's warning and took a step backward. "I thought I was alone."

The creature snorted softly. "Not very damned likely. This ship is too small. You were headed for the rocks. That's a bad place to go."

"Why?"

"You see the holes?"

"Sure, they look innocent enough."

"Throw something toward one."

Molly bent over, picked up a loose stone, and threw it toward the boulders. Something black flashed out, snatched the rock from midair, and disappeared back into its hole.

Molly swallowed hard and took a couple more steps backward. "What was that?"

"Something bad," the creature said noncommittally.

"You speak standard."

The creature took a few steps forward. It made a sign with its left hand. In the same way that 47,721 seemed evil, this alien felt nice. Molly stood her ground.

"Yes, we runners are good at languages, and I met one of your kind before . . . bigger though and even more frightened. I learned your type of sound talk from him."

Molly thought about that. A grown-up even more scared than she was. It seemed hard to believe. "Where is he now?"

The creature swayed back and forth. "Death came. The you-thing ran. Death found it."

"Death?" Molly looked around. If black things were hiding in the rocks, then what else was lurking around?

"Yes, that is what we call them."

"We?"

"Runners. Those that look as I do."

"So you don't like them?"

Jareth blinked. "Who?"

Molly forced herself to be patient. "Them. Death."

"Not very damned likely," the runner replied. "Would you?"

"Would I what?" Molly asked, grinning when she realized she was doing it too.

"Like death, if it ate you," the alien said.

Something cold and hard tumbled into Molly's stomach. "They eat you?"

Jareth swayed back and forth for a moment before cocking its head to one side. "Yes, that is what we are here for. That, and repairing the ship. We built it, you know."

Suddenly Molly understood or thought she did. The spacecraft was a true biosphere and contained its own ecosystem. An ecosystem in which the 56,827 fed on the runners and used them to maintain the ship as well. "That's horrible!"

"Yes," the alien said calmly, "it is."

There was silence for a moment. Molly broke it. "So death ate the one like me?"

"Yes," Jareth replied. "Only the hard-supporting things were left. Do you want them?"

Molly shuddered. "No, it wouldn't do any good."

"No," the runner echoed, "it wouldn't do any good."

"Molly!"

Molly turned and looked toward the trees. Pong was there, looking in her direction, hands cupped around his mouth. The thing called "death" stood beside him.

Molly turned back but the runner was gone.

SEVENTEEN

McCade lit the latest in a long series of cigars and let his eyes drift along the line.

Phil stood three people back, talking with a down-at-the-heels roid rat, but McCade passed over him. It might or might not pay to have an open friendship. Time would tell.

The line stretched the length of the hall, wound its way down three flights of rickety wooden stairs, and out into the poorly lit street. The vid ads said, "All you can eat and a hundred credits a day." There were plenty of takers.

McCade shifted his weight from one foot to the other and stared at a graffiti-covered wall. Like most of the real estate bordering HiHo's spaceport, this building was waiting for a really heavy-duty lift-off to shake it down.

He was tired. Very tired. Things had moved along rather quickly after the interview with Nexus. The boys were freed and just as McCade feared, they knew nothing about the girls.

But the stories the boys told about life on a pirate ship made McCade's blood run cold. Had Molly been through the same sort of thing? Was she going through it now? Or was she dead? Some of the boys hadn't made it. Pitiful little bundles ejected out of a utility lock as if they were so much garbage.

Looking at the boys' emaciated and sometimes scarred bodies, McCade saw Molly in his mind's eye.

So as he hugged the boys, and did his best to answer their questions, McCade was close to tears. Pong had caused all this pain, all this misery, and Pong would pay.

But in order to punish the pirate he'd have to find him and that's where Captain Lorina Dep-Smith came in.

She was reluctant to talk at first, but after five minutes of private conversation with Phil, she became suddenly voluble.

In talking to Dep-Smith it became quickly apparent that she was little more than a hired hand, useful for running errands to places like Nexus, but not privy to Pong's long-range plans.

She did possess one piece of useful information however, something Pong could hardly deny her, and that was her next destination.

After leaving Nexus, Dep-Smith was headed for a planet called HiHo, where she'd load elements of a mercenary army and receive further instructions. She didn't know where the army was headed, or why, but she knew Pong would be in command.

So after giving the matter some thought and discussing it with his crew, McCade came up with what he hoped was a workable plan. Since they didn't have enough money left to send the boys home on a chartered ship, they'd cram them aboard the *Void Runner.* Rico was still recovering from his wound, but was healthy enough to act as pilot, and Maggie would handle everything else.

Meanwhile, McCade and Phil would sign aboard Dep-Smith's ship as replacements for the crew that Rico and Maggie had killed, and work their way to HiHo. Once dirtside the pair would join Pong's newly formed army and look for an opportunity to snatch him. Their plan had a lot of potential flaws, but it was better than nothing.

One of the potential flaws surfaced right away. Though appropriately threatened, and simultaneously bribed, they couldn't trust Dep-Smith further than they could throw an Envo Beast.

Once aboard her ship, and en route to HiHo, they were almost entirely at her mercy. The ship carried a crew of twelve, which meant they were outnumbered six to one if it came to blows, and given Dep-Smith's smoldering resentment, the battle could come at any time.

So, between Dep-Smith's efforts to make sure that they got all the ship's most unpleasant jobs, and the fact that they were cooped up with ten sociopaths, the two of them got very little sleep. Regardless of the shifts they were assigned, one was awake at all times, blaster in hand, waiting for the attack that never came.

McCade yawned. A wooden door slammed open and a burly man with the look of a professional noncom stepped outside. There were no badges of rank on his brand-new camos and he didn't need any. The man had "sergeant" written all over him. In spite of the fact that they were only five feet away from each other, the noncom yelled "Next!" as if McCade were at the other end of the hall.

Having spent hours waiting to hear that word, McCade wasted little time stepping inside. The door slammed closed behind him. McCade found himself standing in front of a large med scanner. It came close to filling the room.

The sergeant appeared at McCade's elbow. He wore his hair high and tight, had bushy eyebrows, and the beadiest eyes McCade had ever seen.

"Lose the stogie, and listen up. You will take five steps forward, enter the med scanner, and follow its directions. Having done so, you will take six additional steps forward and assume a brace. Major Mike Davison will ask you some questions. You will answer them honestly, completely, and with the respect due an officer. Do you understand?"

McCade dropped the cigar into a spittoon and heard a hiss as it hit the water. "Yeah, Sarge, I understand. Five plus six, and a brace. Major Davison. Straight scoop and no bull."

The sergeant gave a slight nod, as if acknowledging someone he knew, and jerked a thumb toward the scanner. "Good. Hit it."

McCade took five steps forward. The med scanner came to life and closed in around him. It was like standing in a small closet. It was completely dark outside of the single red light located directly over his head.

"Stand completely still."

McCade obeyed the machine's orders and felt a number of artificially warmed pads make contact with his body. The bounty hunter was completely immobilized once they were in place.

A minute passed. Waves of white light rippled up and down as the machine scanned his body in layers, starting with McCade's skin and working its way through all of his internal organs.

There was a whirring sound as the pads were withdrawn.

"Place your hands in the lighted receptacles."

McCade saw a pair of lighted slots appear in front of him. He did as he was told. His hands slid into a warm jellylike substance that held them firmly in place.

McCade flinched as needles drew blood from both of his index fingers.

"You will feel a pinprick in each index finger," the machine said belatedly, "stand by."

McCade swore softly and withdrew his hands.

The red light went out and the machine parted in front of him. There was a doorway ahead and a rickety old desk just beyond that. A porta comp sat on top of the desk and a man in crisp camos lounged behind it. He looked up at McCade's approach.

Major Davison had black hair, even features, and a neatly trimmed beard. The latter marked him as a merc since anything more than a neatly trimmed stash was forbidden to Imperial officers. Like his noncom, Davison wore brand-new camos.

Remembering the sergeant's instructions McCade took six steps forward, popped to attention, and rapped out his name. Or in this case the name he chose to be known by. "Sir, Blake, Roland, reporting as ordered, sir."

Davison was silent for a moment, looking McCade over, tapping his lips with a silver stylus.

The whole thing took McCade back to his days at the Terran Naval Academy, and his frequent visits to the cadet captain's office. Like then he was careful to keep his eyes focused on a spot one foot over Davison's head.

"So," Major Davison said softly, "a vet. Good. We need experienced people. We've got enough plow boys out there to start an award-winning farm. But experienced at what? Give me your last outfit, slot in the TO, and rank at separation."

"Yes, sir. Imperial navy, sir, special ops, lieutenant commander."

That was false of course, but McCade had known a Roland Blake in his navy days, and he might be a lieutenant commander by now.

Davison's eyebrows shot upward. "Special ops? Lieutenant commander? Explain."

McCade kept his eyes on the dirty green wall. He had a story prepared for this situation, a story that was partly his, and partly that of an officer he'd heard about. "I refused a direct order and was court-martialed, sir."

The officer leaned backward in his chair. "And the order was?"

"We were retrieving a recon team, sir. I was in command. If the indigs spotted the team and engaged, I had orders to lift without them."

"And you ignored those orders."

"Yes, sir."

"And the recon team?"

"Killed in action, sir."

"And the consequences of your decision?"

"Substantial damage to my ship, sir."

"So you were wrong?"

"No, sir."

Davison smiled. "You'd do the same stupid thing all over again?"

"Yes, sir."

Davison nodded thoughtfully. "You interest me, Blake. I like officers who are loyal to their people, but I won't stand for disobedience."

Davison's hand jerked forward and the silver stylus flashed by McCade's head to stick quivering in the wall beyond. The bounty hunter remained motionless.

The merc smiled. "Sorry about that . . . but you'd be surprised how many of the vets who come through that door have lost their nerve." Davison leaned forward slightly.

"I'm going to ask you three questions. If you are what you claim to be, you'll know the answers."

McCade felt his heart beat a little faster. Davison was no dummy. It was clear that he'd been an Imperial officer himself. Would McCade know the answers?

Davison looked thoughtful. "Who commands Naval Intelligence?"

McCade came close to laughing. Finally, his old enemy and sometimes friend would do him some good! "Admiral Walter Swanson-Pierce."

The merc smiled. "Good. The second question. What is the motto inscribed on the plaque in front of headquarters on Terra?"

McCade's throat felt dry. "Headquarters," meant headquarters for Naval Intelligence, and the fact that he knew the answer was pure luck.

> *"The first to see,*
> *The first to hear,*
> *The first to know,*
> *The first to die."*

Davison nodded. "Excellent. Here's the last one. Everyone who works special ops is given a life-long code name . . . what is yours?"

McCade swallowed hard. A life-long code name? He'd never heard of that, but NI had lots of secrets, and code names were the sort of nonsense they loved. Still . . . McCade took a chance.

"Sir, I have no life-long code name."

"I'm glad to hear it," Davison said cheerfully, "because as far as I know, no one else in NI does either. At ease, Blake, and welcome to the brigade." Davison got up from behind the desk.

"Sorry I can't give you something equivalent to your last rank, but I do have a slot for a captain, and who knows? If a sufficient number of people die you might move up!"

McCade shook Davison's hand, replied that captain was just fine, and started toward the back door. He stopped and turned around. "One question, sir . . . is there a chance that you'll assign me to something like special ops?"

Davison pulled the stylus from the wall and wiped plaster off the needle-sharp tip. "It's too early to say for sure, but the idea had crossed my mind."

McCade gave mental thanks. The plan was working. An assignment to special ops would keep him out of the trenches, give him more freedom of movement, and a better chance to get at Pong.

"Yes, sir, I'd like that, sir. There was a variant in line behind me. He's big and looks like a Terran bear. Ex-recon if I'm not mistaken, sir. If you decide to create a special ops team, he'd make a good officer or senior noncom."

Davison pushed the button at one end of the stylus and watched the lethal-looking tip vanish inside the barrel.

"Thanks, Captain, I'll keep him in mind. Don't get wasted tonight. We'll be up at 0500 trying to turn this herd of dirt technicians into an army."

McCade grinned. "Yes, sir. Thank you, sir." McCade let himself out as another potential recruit stepped in.

The back door gave access to a hall, where a bored-looking trooper ascertained that McCade had been accepted, and directed him to an office down the hall.

Once in the office a civilian clerk asked McCade dozens of questions and dutifully typed the bounty hunter's lies into his computer.

And then, because McCade was an officer, a lance corporal took him down two floors into a warehouse area. It was filled with row after row of tables, each heaped high with different kinds of gear, each manned by a uniformed trooper. A long line of recruits was shuffling its way through the tables stuffing gear into camo-covered duffel bags.

With the lance corporal leading the way McCade was allowed to practically zip through the line cutting an hour-long process down to fifteen minutes.

The newbies looked resentful and the pros looked bored. Officers took care of each other. Always had and always would.

After that it was a few steps outside to a waiting command car, a bumpy ride to a well-lit camp, and total collapse on a folding camp bed. It felt heavenly. He was asleep in seconds.

The next few days were extremely busy. Everyone worked long hours. The goal of putting the entire brigade together within a month had seemed impossible at first but was actually starting to happen. In spite of Davison's comments to the contrary, most of their recruits were *not* fresh off the farm and had some sort of previous military experience. As a matter of fact most were fairly well trained.

That, plus a masterful job of organization by their XO, a legendary merc named Colonel Mary Surillo, had made the impossible seem increasingly likely.

The brigade was coming together in a huge field outside HiHo's main city of Ness. Thanks to the season, and a stretch of especially good weather, conditions were as good as they could be.

Just as he'd hoped, McCade was given command of a special ops team with Phil as his senior noncom. The team consisted of twenty-six men and women, all with recon or equivalent experience, which was good because McCade had none at all.

Interceptor pilots don't spend much time snooping and pooping dirtside, but like Phil, McCade did belong to Alice's militia and had picked up the basic infantry tactics in the process. So the trick was to hide his lack of knowledge behind a seemingly taciturn exterior and rely on his junior noncoms to structure most of the team's training.

Unfortunately *their* idea of a good time was to run the perimeter of the base yelling "One, two, three, four, I love the Marine Corps," while carrying an unarmed surface-to-air missile on their shoulders. Or like today, running over every hill in sight, dressed in class II combat gear.

Although McCade had considered himself to be in fairly good shape at the onset of training, he now knew differently. His lungs were on fire, his heart was trying to beat its way out of his chest, and it felt as if someone had filled his legs with solid lead. This in spite of the fact that the troops around him looked fresh as a daisy. Still under the pretext of giving *them* a break. McCade ordered a halt.

They stopped just below the summit of a sizable hill. Even McCade knew better than to do that at the top of the hill where they'd be outlined against the sky. The team scattered before Phil could yell, "One grenade would get you all!" and settled in smaller groups.

Trying to hide his desperate need for more oxygen, McCade turned his back on them and used a pair of mini-glasses to scan the valley below.

Seen from a distance the camp consisted of orderly looking streets, each crossing the others at right angles, and lined with identical pop-up shelters. The shelters were inflatable and capable of housing a full platoon of troops.

Spotted here and there were vehicle parks, supply dumps, landing pads, training areas, com trailers, and other less identifiable installations.

And surrounding the whole thing was a computer-designed perimeter. It took into account the lay of the land, the distance between it and the hills, the areas of deepest shadow, indigenous life forms, the consistency of the soil, and much, much more.

As a result the perimeter seemed to jig and jag in what looked like random patterns but weren't. Every foot of the perimeter was not just guarded, but guarded with the weapons and personnel perfect for that particular spot, making it damned hard to penetrate.

Very professional, very high tech, and very strange. A computer-designed perimeter was something McCade would expect from the Imperial Marines, but not from a mercenary outfit thrown together by a pirate.

McCade moved his glasses across the camp. He saw rows of brand-new armored personnel carriers, hover tanks, missile launchers, supply trucks, and a lot of snappy-looking troopers.

Now that he thought about it, McCade realized that it wasn't just the computer-designed perimeter, *everything* was top-of-the-line brand-new. The camp and everything in it looked like something a child would set up on the floor of their bedroom. It was too damned perfect.

Not only that but most merc outfits were specialists, ground pounders say, or tankers. Hardly any of them had the resources to assemble a miniature army with everything from infantry all the way up to heavy armor.

McCade lowered his glasses. Why? Why had Pong spent so much money on a picture-perfect army? And speaking of Pong, where was the bastard anyway, and when would he take command? Soon. It had to be soon.

McCade found a half-smoked cigar in an outside pocket of his body armor. He sucked it into life and blew smoke out toward the valley below. He thought about Molly and whispered to himself, "Hang in there, honey. I'm getting closer."

Mustapha Pong was frustrated. The planet Salazar was the last place in the universe that he wanted to be. Especially given his many business deals, his army forming up on HiHo, and the war brewing on Drang.

Of course that was the problem, the war on Drang, and the question of who would win it. Because the 56,827 wanted a full-scale, human-fought war, and because they wanted Pong to accept a personal role, it was important to stack the deck as much as he could.

Pong looked out the window. It was winter. Snow fell steadily from a lead-gray sky, swirling through the aircar's headlights, to cover the city of Segundo with a cloak of white. It was beautiful.

Pong longed for the cold kiss of a snowflake on his cheek, the bite of frigid air, and the wonderful silence that snow brings with it.

Then, after a brisk walk in the snow, a glorious retreat into the yellow warmth of a good cafe. The kind he stood outside of as a child, peering in through steam-fogged windows, marveling at the wonderful things that people ate.

"And unless you pay attention that's exactly where you will be," the Melcetian reminded him tartly, "on the outside looking in."

"And so what?" Pong asked resentfully. "As long as there's blood in my body, what do you care?"

"My, my," the mind slug replied sarcastically, "touchy aren't we? But let's discuss that. You made a lot of promises to the 56,827. In essence you promised them the entire human race. How will they react should you deliver something less? How much blood will you give me then?"

The Melcetian was right. There was a lot at stake and this was no time to make mistakes. Pong forced himself to concentrate.

Thing were heating up on Drang. For years now a combine of large corporations had been gathering power, buying off as many elected representatives as they could, and working to counter the rest with an army of paid lobbyists. Now, things were coming to a head and everyone knew it.

The combine officials were determined to fight rather than surrender what was left of the government. So, with hostilities about to begin, and both sides looking for an advantage, Pong found himself in the perfect situation.

In order to satisfy the 56,827's desire to witness a war, he was offering a brand-new, first-rate army at a bargain basement price. Both the world government and the combine wanted his help in the worst way.

And after careful consideration of both alternatives, Pong had decided in favor of the world government. The combine was strong, but according to Pong's intelligence the government was just a little bit stronger, and more likely to win.

In a few short minutes the aircar would land, Pong would meet with representatives from Drang's government, and the deal would be done.

Shortly thereafter he would make the short hop from Salazar to Drang, take command of his brand-new army, and win the ensuring war. Then, with backing from the 56,827, the boy from the slums of Desus II would turn the Empire on its head.

"Ah, such dreams," the mind slug said acidly. "And should they come true, what then? The new Emperor will be a slave to the 56,827, that's what."

"Perhaps," Mustapha Pong thought back, "or perhaps it will be the other way around."

"Ah," the Melcetian said amusedly. "Even more delusions of grandeur."

But even as the alien formulated the thought it also injected a chemical reward into Pong's bloodstream. The mind slug knew that the resulting physical pleasure would reinforce the human's ambition and encourage him to act on it.

Suddenly Pong felt warm and happy. He turned to look at Molly. He'd given her a red ball. She was playing with it and staring out the window.

Molly had been quiet, almost taciturn since their visit to the alien ship, and Pong was sorry that he'd taken her along. 47,721 scared her, that was clear, but there was something more as well. Something she refused to talk about. The ball, made from emergency hull sealer, had been by way of an apology.

Pong turned back to the window. This time there would be nothing more frightening than some government bureaucrats to deal with, and if the meeting went quickly, maybe they could sneak away for a walk through the snow. Maybe they'd stumble across a toy store and Pong could buy Molly something nicer than a ball made of sealant.

Up ahead a fancifully sculpted high-rise towered over all the rest. It was covered with black glass and surrounded by an invisible force field. Just part of the elaborate security measures required by both sides.

The pilot murmured something into her mic and the force field went down long enough for the aircar to slip inside and settle toward the carefully cleared roof.

The aircar touched with a gentle thump and a hatch slid open. A blast of cold air entered and brought a few snowflakes with it. Molly moved her finger under one and urged it to land. The snowflake shied away and fell toward a leather-covered seat. The snow reminded her of Alice.

Pong had to bend over to make his way out of the car. It was a single step to the ground. The fur-lined coat was custom-tailored to accommodate both Pong and the mind slug. The coat felt good as Pong pulled it close around him.

Raz and three of Pong's best security people took up positions around him. Raz wore the top half of some black body armor as a concession to both the situation and the weather. Like the others he was heavily armed.

Pong turned to help Molly out of the aircar. She looked cute in the brown hat and matching fur coat. She smiled briefly and it warmed Pong's heart. He subvocalized.

"Is everything clear?"

"We swept it twice, boss," Raz replied. "It's clean as a whistle."

Pong nodded. "Good. Let's get this over with."

With Molly at his side and guards all around him, Pong marched through a dusting of snow to the roof-top lobby. Doors swished aside and a uniformed security guard snapped to attention. Pong waved a hand in acknowledgment before coming to a halt in front of an open lift tube.

Raz and a tough-looking woman stepped aboard, waved detectors through the air like wizards casting a spell, and nodded their permission.

Pong stepped aboard and turned around. The doors closed and the platform started to descend. The inside walls were alive with vid-art. Color swirled. Abstract shapes appeared, melted, and merged to become something else.

Pong didn't like it. He preferred art that had substance and definition. Something you could count on.

The platform came to a smooth stop and the doors hissed open. The security guards got off, detectors scanning, weapons ready to fire.

A tall man with a long solemn face waited patiently for the security team to complete its inspection. He wore a formal-looking robe with gold trim and a high collar. The man bowed as Pong stepped out of the lift tube.

"Citizen Pong. We are honored. My name is Ethan Mordu, Drang's envoy to Salazar, and host of today's meeting. I apologize for our rather wintry weather."

Pong delivered a small bow. "The honor is mine. As for your weather, I find it quite refreshing."

Mordu smiled and looked down at Molly. "What a pretty little girl. Your daughter perhaps?"

Pong placed a possessive hand on Molly's shoulder. "No, though I'd be proud if she were. Molly, this is Envoy Mordu."

Thanks to her mother's position on the planetary council Molly had been to any number of formal occasions and knew the drill. She gave a slight curtsey, the kind reserved for minor diplomats, and considered throwing herself on Mordu's mercy.

Molly wondered what he'd do. Nothing probably, and that plus the L-band cinched tight around her head cautioned silence.

The two men made small talk as they walked down the wide shiny hall. The walls were paneled with a light-colored native wood. They glistened with wax.

Molly liked the way her heels made a clicking sound on the hardwood floors and tried a couple of surreptitious variations. Nobody seemed to notice.

Then the clicking sounds disappeared as they passed through large double doors and entered a large, well-carpeted room. Two well-dressed women and a man stood to greet them. Except for a circular table, and some comfortable-looking chairs, the room was otherwise empty.

Molly waited for Pong to introduce her, curtseyed in turn, and drifted away as the adults began to talk.

Each wall was completely different. One was hidden by a curtain of rich-looking fabric, another consisted of floor-to-ceiling glass, and the third boasted an enormous holo tank. But it was the last wall that caught and held Molly's attention. It featured a heroic mural.

The painting showed a man, woman, and child in the foreground, and behind them a colony ship that was already being stripped of useful metal. The mural incorporated lots of detail, including some of Salazar's most famous wildlife, and Molly studied it while the security team inspected the room.

Pong shrugged apologetically as Raz looked behind the curtain. "I'm sorry about that, but you know how security people are, once they get going there's no stopping them."

The others nodded sympathetically, well aware that the security people were following Pong's orders, and not in the least insulted. They would've taken similar precautions had positions been reversed.

Once Raz had signaled his satisfaction with security, Pong chose a seat with his back toward the holo wall, and wasted little time getting down to business. Molly took a seat right next to him with the security team fanning out behind.

Under normal circumstances the conversation would have centered around price, but given the fact that Pong was offering his army at cost, the discussion went off in another direction.

Not knowing of Pong's relationship with the 56,827, or their existence for that matter, Drang's officials assumed that his low asking price equated to ulterior motives. Pong was after something, but what was it? The mineral rights presently held by the combine? A role in Drang's government? What?

The officials needed answers to these questions and more before they signed a formal agreement.

Pong understood these concerns and knew how to handle them. The key was to show a little greed, but stop short of scaring them and breaking the deal. In other words it should be a rather enjoyable process that ended up the way Pong wanted it to.

So as the adults plunged into their negotiations Molly eased her way out of the chair next to Pong and drifted away. The guards ignored her.

First Molly looked out the window, wrote her name on the slightly fogged glass, and watched the snow fall. But the snow reminded Molly of home, of Mommy, and made her hurt inside.

She walked across the room, running a finger along the smooth surface of the holo tank, and over to the mural. It was a truly wonderful painting, full of interesting detail, and bright clean color. It absorbed Molly's interest for a full five minutes.

Then, without conscious thought, the ball left Molly's hand and bounced off the floor. The carpet absorbed the sound. She caught it and looked toward the adults. No reaction.

Molly smiled and bounced the ball again, and again, and again, until it hit the toe of her boot and hopped away. Molly followed as the ball headed straight for the drape-covered wall and rolled underneath.

Molly looked at Raz but the bodyguard was looking in another direction. She checked the other security people. Ditto.

As Molly turned back something strange happened. The ball rolled out from under the curtain, and just as it did, Molly saw the tip of a highly polished boot. There was someone behind the curtain!

Curious, Molly waited for the ball to reach her, and bent to pick it up. Now she saw more boots, at least six in all, suggesting three people. Molly straightened up and pretended interest in the ball.

Why would people hide behind the drape? And where had they come from? Molly remembered how Raz had pulled the curtain aside and looked behind it. She'd seen no sign of a door. A secret passage then! Like in the books she'd read.

Something cold fell into Molly's stomach. Suddenly she knew that the people shouldn't be there.

Forcing herself to walk very slowly, Molly ambled toward the table and took her seat next to Pong. Except for a glance in her direction the adults took little notice.

Trying to hide her action Molly tugged on the side of Pong's tunic.

Pong felt Molly pull at his tunic and felt annoyed. Couldn't she see that this was the critical moment? In a minute, maybe two, he'd call for closure. And given the way things were going there was little doubt that he'd get it.

Molly tugged again. Pong forced a smile. "Excuse me. You know how children are. This will only take a moment."

Pong turned toward Molly. His voice was an urgent whisper. "Damn it, child, can't you see this is the wrong time to bother me?"

Molly bit her lip. Was she wrong? Was there some simple explanation for the people behind the curtain? Would Pong know that and be angry with her?

"I dropped my ball," she whispered, "it went behind the curtain. Someone kicked it out to me. When I bent over I saw three pairs of feet."

Pong started to say something irritable, stopped when he realized what Molly had said, and turned slightly pale. He subvocalized and smiled as he turned toward the officials.

"Wouldn't you know it? She needs a bathroom."

Then all sorts of things happened at once. Molly found herself on the floor, Raz and the others sprayed the curtain with stun beams, and a man fell forward bringing the entire drapery down with it. Then two more men toppled over, weapons falling, bodies hitting the floor with a soft thump.

At that point Pong's security team shouted orders, one of the officials pulled a blaster, and fell facedown when Raz stunned her. The woman's head hit the conference table with a loud thud.

A few seconds later and Raz had guards on the secret passage and the room's man entrance. Reinforcements would get a big surprise.

Silence descended on the room. Pong was on his feet. During the confusion a small slug gun had materialized in his hand. The barrel was touching the inside of Ethan Mordu's right ear.

Mordu looked distinctly uncomfortable.

Pong caught Raz's eye, nodded toward Mordu, and removed his gun from the diplomat's ear. Turning toward Molly he bent to help her.

"Are you alright, child? Sorry about throwing you down but there wasn't much time. What you did was very brave."

Molly didn't *feel* brave. She felt cold and shaky inside.

Pong turned his attention to Mordu and the two other officials who sat frozen in their seats, hands on top of the table, faces etched with fear. "So, were the assassins just an option, or were they the entire plan?"

The officials looked at one another but remained silent.

Pong shook his head sadly. "Come, come. No need to be modest. It was a good plan and would've worked except for my little friend here."

Mordu cleared his throat. "The assassins were an option. In case negotiations broke down."

Pong nodded understandingly. "I understand. Quite sensible. Always have a backup."

Pong smiled. "Of course it helps if the backup works."

Raz put a hand to his ear as if hearing something. "The aircar is almost here."

Pong pulled on his coat and looked around the room. "Excellent. You may prepare our exit."

Raz swiveled toward the window and squeezed the trigger on his automatic weapon. The slug thrower made a roar of sound.

Molly held her hands over her ears as the window shattered and fell in a shimmery cascade of glass. She staggered as air rushed out through the opening, taking loose pieces of paper with it. An alarm sounded out in the hall.

Then the aircar appeared and hovered just outside the window. It looked huge and somewhat ominous with its flashing beacons and ugly-looking guns.

"So," Pong yelled over the whine of the aircar's drives, "that brings this meeting to a close. In just a moment Raz will say good-bye as only he can."

Something about the way Pong said it, and the look on his bodyguard's face, told Molly what would happen. The moment Pong climbed aboard the aircar Raz would kill them. She pulled at Pong's coat.

"Don't kill them! What good will it do? We survived. That's the important thing."

Pong frowned, started to say something, and changed his mind. He looked at each official in turn. "This is your lucky day! The child is right. Killing you will accomplish nothing. But when my army comes, and pulls your government down, remember this moment. You brought this end upon yourselves."

A cold wind entered the room, picked up some papers, and threw them down. Snowflakes settled toward the top of the conference-room table.

Pong took Molly's hand and led her toward the aircar. "Come on, child, let's go for a walk in the snow."

NINETEEN

"Hammerfall leader, this is hammerdrop one."

McCade chinned his mic. The drop module was only slightly larger than his combat-equipped body. He could smell his own sweat. "Hammerdrop leader. Go."

"We are five to the zone. Repeat, five to the zone. Stand by."

McCade swallowed hard. In less than five minutes he and his special ops team would fall through Drang's atmosphere, pray that their drop mods would hang together long enough to get them below the government's radar, and hope that their electronic countermeasure gear was as good as the sales literature claimed it was. If not, they'd be easy targets for the government's air defense battalion.

McCade chinned the team freq. "Hammerfall leader to hammerfall team. We are minus five and counting. Auto sequence and sound off."

McCade flipped a switch and pushed a button. There was an armored box under his seat. Inside the box was a mini-comp. It ran an auto check on the module's systems, found everything to its liking, and lit a green light on the instrument panel.

Meanwhile the special ops team checked in.

"Mod one . . . green board."

"Mod two . . . green board."

"Mod three . . . green board," and so on, until all twenty-four men and women had checked in. Two members of McCade's team had turned up at sick call. Some kind of virus. Lucky bastards.

"Roger," McCade replied. He eyed the digital readout in front of him. "Prepare for drop. One-thirty-six and counting."

Time became plastic and seemed to stretch. The readout worked its way down with frustrating slowness until there were fifteen seconds left. At that point Major Davison's voice came over both command and team freqs.

"Hammerdrop one here. We're in the zone. Ten, nine, eight, seven, six, five, four, three, see you dirtside, hammerfall team! Good luck!"

McCade was thrown violently sideways as the egg-shaped module shot out of the port launch tube and began its journey toward the planet below.

McCade couldn't see them, but knew that eleven modules had followed his, with twelve more to starboard. Phil's would be last. The variant would assume command if McCade were killed.

The team was heading dirtside two rotations prior to Pong's main force so it was important to avoid detection. There was no point in providing the government with an early warning. That's why the techs had gone to the trouble of installing an expensive launch system in a tramp freighter. After it had dropped McCade's team into the upper atmosphere the ship would land and unload a legitimate cargo.

The module jerked as it hit a slightly thicker layer of air and McCade felt the temperature start to climb.

Outside the tiny passenger compartment layer after layer of ceramic skin was burned away as the egg fell. And as the layers of protective material became increasingly thin, more and more heat was conducted inside.

Eventually, after the module had fallen through all of Drang's interlocking radar nets, the hull would disintegrate and a parachute would open. At that point McCade would float gently to the ground.

Or so the techies claimed. Needless to say none of them had tried it.

McCade's vision blurred as the module began to vibrate. He strained to see the instrument panel and couldn't. The egg tumbled end over end, stabilized when the mini-comp fired the module's steering rockets, and fell like a rock toward the reddish orange planet below.

Strange things went through McCade's mind. Unconnected memories of places that he'd been and things he'd experienced. He remembered Sara, Molly, and his long-dead parents. He thought about Molly's birthdays, and how many he'd missed over the years, always assuming that there'd be more.

McCade blinked sweat out of his eyes and whispered a prayer he hadn't used since childhood.

The module began to shake and shudder again. Pieces flew off. Air pushed its way in through the holes, roared around McCade's head, and spun the module like a top. Blackness appeared where the instrument panel had been just moments before. The rest of the hull leaped away in chunks, broke into smaller pieces, and spread itself out over twenty square miles of desert.

The chair, with McCade still in it, continued to fall. And fall, and fall, and fall.

The chute? Shouldn't it be open by now? Scooping air and slowing his fall? Something must be wrong. It was time to pop the reserve chute. McCade had flipped the protective cover up and was closing his fingers around the lever when the main chute opened. It made a loud cracking sound.

Air filled the chute and McCade felt as if it was pulling him upward. The force of it pushed him down into the chair's padding. Things slowed. The chair twirled under a canopy of fabric.

Still on duty, the mini-comp used radar to make a tightly focused sweep of the terrain below. It located the best place to land and activated a pair of servos.

Lines grew taut, air spilled from one side of the chute, and McCade felt himself slide toward the ground. He braced himself. The chair fell away a few seconds later. With less weight pulling down on it the chute slowed even more.

There was a distant thump as the mini-comp blew up and took the chair with it.

Air rushed around McCade's face. He was worried. Sure, the mini-comp had aimed him in what it thought was the right direction, but mini-comps could be wrong. What if he landed on some rocks? In a river? Right on top of a missile battery?

McCade strained to see the ground but couldn't. There was a scattering of lights to the right, many miles away, but only blackness below. Should he switch to night vision?

The ground came up with unexpected suddenness. McCade's legs absorbed most of the impact and he managed an awkward roll. He scrambled to his feet. How the hell were you supposed to roll wearing body armor and a day pack? Who thought of this stuff anyway?

McCade hit the chute release before a sudden gust of wind could pull him off his feet. He touched a pressure plate on the side of his helmet and watched a ghostscape appear around him.

Most of the things around him were a sickly green, except for the rocks, which retained enough of the daytime heat to show up as fuzzy red blotches.

McCade spilled the last bit of air from his chute, gathered it into his arms, and looked for a place to hide it. A black patch between a pair of red blotches suggested a crevice. McCade walked over and found that the chute fit with room to spare. A loose rock went on top.

Good. Now for the team. Where were they? And was everyone okay?

McCade removed the small tac comp from his combat harness and flipped it open. He touched some buttons and a map appeared. It looked weird via night vision but was still readable. A glance told McCade that he was located just fifteen miles west of their target. Not bad.

His position was marked by a red star with a scattering of blue dots all around. Twenty-three in all according to the data summary at the bottom of the tiny screen.

McCade frowned and pushed another button. The map vanished and was replaced by words:

> Subject: Zemin Mary Ann
> Serial number: NB965471
> Status: KIA, Drang
> Cause: Module Failure
> Disposition: Explosive Disintegration
> Threat Factor: 001

McCade swore softly. He had liked Zemin, in fact, with a couple of exceptions, he liked the whole team. Zemin had been cheerful, competent, and their best electronics tech. There were others, each member of the team was qualified in at least three specialties, but none of them was Zemin. There had been only one Zemin and she was dead. Dead in a stupid war, on a stupid planet, in a stupid universe.

McCade cleared the screen, touched a key, and looked around for a place to wait. Somewhere out in the darkness twenty-three men and women would hear a solid tone in their headsets and follow it to this position. If they had trouble tracking the tone, a quick check of their own tac comps would solve the problem.

McCade pulled a weapons check, found that his slug gun, blast rifle, and force blade were all where they should be, and retreated between a couple of boulders. With any luck at all his body heat would blend in with the warmth stored in the rocks and shield him from infrared detection.

McCade readied his blast rifle just in case. After all, there was always the chance that government troops had located him somehow, and were on the way.

Ten minutes of almost total silence passed before McCade heard gravel crunch under someone's boot. He grinned as a ghostly red blob appeared ten feet away and looked around. It was Martino, easily identifiable due to the launch tube strapped to his back, hoping to catch McCade by surprise.

Moving carefully McCade picked up a small rock and tossed it in Martino's direction. It made a soft thocking sound as it bounced off the mercenary's helmet. Martin spun around, auto thrower ready to spit lead, and swore when he saw McCade. "That wasn't very nice, Skipper . . . I damn near messed my pants."

McCade chuckled. "Sorry . . . I couldn't resist. Besides, it isn't nice to sneak up on your CO."

Martino grinned unashamedly. His teeth looked green.

The two men repositioned themselves in the rocks and waited for the rest of the team to show up. They came in ones, twos, and threes, whispering the password prior to closing on the rocks. It was like a ghostly echo out of the night, "Hammerfall, hammerfall, hammerfall," until all were present. Everyone was okay outside of some bumps and bruises.

Phil came in third from last. He checked to make sure the team had established a defensive perimeter and huddled with McCade. "Too bad about Zemin."

"Yeah," McCade replied. "I hope it was fast."

"Yeah," Phil agreed somberly. "I hope so too."

McCade flipped his tac comp open and pushed a series of buttons. Because the entire area was flat the tac comp dispensed with contour lines and gave him what amounted to a simplified road map.

The target showed up as a pulsating orange square. According to the tac comp it was some fifteen miles to the east. That would be the lights McCade had seen from the air.

The mission itself was relatively simple. The team would cross fifteen miles of desert, infiltrate the town of Zephyr, and find one particular home. And according to McCade's information, that should be relatively easy.

The home belonged to one Nigel Harrington and by all accounts it was huge. A mansion really, spread all over two acres of land, and as eccentric as its owner.

It seemed that Harrington was the patriarch of the entire Harrington clan, and taken together they owned Harrington Industries, the very heart of the combine.

The combine feared, and Pong agreed, that the moment his fleet showed up government forces would try to take Nigel Harrington hostage. The old man would provide considerable leverage. And because he lived in a small town, far from the combine-dominated cities, it would be easy to do.

Over and over Nigel Harrington's sons and daughters had pleaded with the old man to stay with them, and over and over he'd refused. Zephyr was where his wife was buried and Zephyr was where he'd stay.

The family had reinforced the mansion's small security force but couldn't do much more than that without alerting the army unit stationed in town.

So it was McCade's job to reach the mansion, defend it for the better part of two days, and keep Nigel Harrington alive. Of more immediate concern however was the fifteen miles of desert between him and the Harrington mansion.

The first ten miles looked relatively easy. Open desert mostly, crisscrossed with dry riverbeds and dotted with unmanned oil pumps. The original source of the Harrington family fortune.

Closer in things got more complicated. There was a five-mile-deep defense zone around the town, ostensibly created to defend against raids by the nomadic indigents, but actually placed there because the Harrington family wanted it to be. Like all wealthy families the Harringtons lived in fear of thieves, kidnappers, and assassins. Between the efforts of their well-bribed government representatives and their army of lobbyists, the proposal for the Zephyr defense zone had sailed through the parliament.

Now, however, their government-funded defenses might work against them. In addition to fortified positions and motorized patrols, McCade and his team would have to deal with an unknown number of robo sentries. These were of some concern not only because of their heavy armament but due to their sensors as well. The team would have to be very, very careful during that last five miles.

"Well," McCade said, "time to move out. We've got fifteen miles of desert to cross and about six hours left to do it in. When morning rolls around, and the sun comes up, the desert will turn into a frying pan. Not only that, we'll be visible for miles around."

Phil nodded soberly. The very thought of all that heat made the ice-world variant start to sweat. "Right, Sam. What do you want?"

McCade flipped the tac comp closed and attached it to his harness. "Put Evans and Kirchoff on point, with Abu Rami running the left flank, and Stobbe guarding the right. I'll go first and you ride drag."

Phil nodded and whispered into his mic.

Three minutes later the special ops team was up and running. They were spread out to lessen casualties in case of an ambush, or land mine, but thanks to the enhanced optics built into their visors still in sight of each other most of the time. Radio traffic was kept to minimum and all-out speed was sacrificed to a ground-eating jog. Every now and then the team would top a slight rise and see lights in the distance. They got brighter all the time.

Time passed and McCade fell into a comfortable rhythm. Thanks to the conditioning on HiHo he felt pretty good. His boots made a steady crunch, crunch in the loose gravel. His breathing was deep and steady. His pulse pounded evenly through every vein and artery. In spite of Molly, in spite of what lay ahead, it felt good to be alive.

TWENTY

Mustapha Pong was awake although his eyes were closed. He heard the swish of the hatch sliding open followed by the click of boots on the metal deck. He recognized the step as belonging to Raz. "Yes?"

"The Harrington party has come aboard, sir."

Pong opened his eyes and blinked in the light of the overhead spot. It felt good to be back aboard his ship safely ensconced in the privacy of his own cabin. He hated the prospect of making small talk with the Harringtons but it had to be done. They'd hired his army, and as representatives of the combine had a right to see what they'd paid for.

Pong nodded. "Thank you, Raz. Show them into the wardroom. I'll make my entrance after they've had some time to stew."

Long accustomed to Pong's ways, Raz nodded and withdrew.

Pong closed his eyes. He directed a thought toward the mind slug. "Show it to me again."

The alien gave the Melcetian equivalent of a sigh. Pong never seemed to tire of the fantasy and demanded to see it at least once or twice a day. The mind slug secreted some chemicals, waited for them to take effect, and projected the appropriate thoughts.

Color swirled in front of Pong's eyes, paused, and gradually took shape. A vision emerged, an omnipotent vision such as God might have, in which entire solar systems and galaxies were little more than pieces laid out on a table of black marble.

Here and there Pong saw bursts of light as stars were born, black holes as others collapsed, and collisions so monumental that entire planets were turned into clouds of cosmic debris.

But these were trivial events, no more important than a spring rainstorm on Desus II. Of more importance was the vast sweep of sentient activity. He could see it drifting across the blackness like star dust, succeeding here, failing there, all according to chance and the work of a few unusual minds. Minds like his.

Well, not exactly like his, because Pong could see the possibility of order within the chaos. He could conceive of something greater than the stars themselves. A single civilization, with him at its center, reaching across known space and beyond, to wrap all races and cultures in a single embrace, an organism so big, so powerful, that it would live for a million years.

Yes, that was a vision worth working toward, worth sacrificing to. Humans, Il Ronnians, and, yes, the 56,827, all of them would kneel to Pong.

The chemicals ebbed from Pong's system and his eyes snapped open. The vision had the effect of reenergizing him. Now he was ready to deal with trivial annoyances like the combine and its somewhat arrogant leadership.

Pong got down off of his thronelike chair and headed for the hatch. It swished open at his approach. Raz and Molly waited outside.

Ever since the assassination attempt Pong had insisted that Molly be with him at all times. Pong had always liked and respected the little girl, but this was something more than that, an almost superstitious belief that she brought him good luck.

After all, since Molly's abduction from Alice Pong had yet to suffer a single defeat, and she had literally saved his life. Surely it would be wrong to ignore such an obvious talisman.

Pong smiled at Molly, and she smiled back, but it was polite and somewhat distant. Oh, how he hungered for a real smile! The kind he saw on those rare occasions when she was swept away by the joy of the moment. Like the precious hours they'd spent walking the streets of Segundo, the aircar hovering above them like a guardian angel, Raz practically dancing in his eagerness to get Pong off the planet.

Those had been magic moments during which Molly had forgotten herself, and her parents. Yes, her parents were the problem, and one with which he would eventually deal. Perhaps Molly's mother had been killed in the attack on Alice. If not, a hired assassin could finish the job.

As for the almost-legendary Sam McCade, well that might be a little more difficult, but where there's a will there's a way. The trick would be to kill Molly's parents in such a way that their deaths could never be traced to him. And then, with that accomplished, arrange for Molly to find out. She'd be sad for a while, but children are resilient creatures and recover quickly. With all hope of being reunified with her parents gone, Molly would gravitate to him, and Pong would see those smiles a good deal more often.

Yes, just two more of the many small details that must eventually be dealt with. Pong took Molly's hand and together they walked down the corridor toward the ship's wardroom.

Pong cut it extremely close. By the time he entered the wardroom Marsha Harrington, the most senior of the Harringtons present, was just short of a boil. No one kept her waiting on Drang, and by God no one should keep her waiting here either, especially some jumped-up mercenary general. Her escort, a rather junior officer named Naguro, had done his best to stall but had run out of small talk five minutes before.

So as Pong entered the room, Marsha Harrington turned her somewhat beefy body his way and was just starting to speak when he preempted her.

"Citizen Harrington, this is an enormous honor. I knew the president and chief executive officer of Harrington Industries was brilliant . . . but I had no idea that she was beautiful as well."

Being far from beautiful, Marsha Harrington flushed at this unexpected compliment and found herself completely disarmed. Pong was entirely different from what she'd been led to expect. Quite pleasant in fact, and, aside from the grotesque alien draped across his shoulder, dangerously handsome. She found herself babbling like a schoolgirl.

"The honor is mine, General Pong. May I introduce my brother Howard, and my cousin Nadine?"

Howard, a rather sallow man in his mid-thirties, gave a stiff bow, and Nadine, a dissipated-looking creature in a custom-tailored Harrington Industries business suit, nodded. She looked at Pong like a rancher judging a prize bull. "Charmed."

Pong smiled. "Likewise I'm sure. Hello, Lieutenant Naguro, it's good to have you with us."

Naguro, a nervous little man, nodded jerkily and did his best to fade into the background. Pong, and the rainbow-colored thing on his shoulder, made Naguro sweat.

"Now," Pong continued, "if you'll take a seat around the table, we'll review the additional forces now at your disposal. With the landing only two rotations away I'm sure you'll agree that time is of the essence."

The next two hours were so boring that Molly had a difficult time staying awake. Aided by a long series of holos, Pong droned on and on about ships, troops, equipment, logistics, and drop zones. And if he wasn't talking, then it seemed as if Marsha Harrington was.

Making the situation even worse was the fact that the wardroom was extremely spartan. Outside of the occasional holos there was nothing to look at.

The only interesting moment came about halfway through the presentation, when Boots, Lia, and two of the girls entered the room with trays of refreshments. Boots had been out of the brig for some time now . . . and made no secret of her hatred for Molly.

Molly could understand that, but still hoped to make friends with Lia and fix things with the others.

Molly smiled, hoped for some sort of friendly response, and was quickly disappointed. The girls ignored her, while Lia put on a show of exaggerated deference, and hated Molly with her eyes.

So Molly just sat there, staring miserably at the floor, wishing she were dead. Didn't they realize how she felt? Couldn't they see that she was a slave too? Subject to Pong's slightest whim?

No, Molly realized, they couldn't. The fact that they served while she did nothing had blinded them to the way things really were. Finally, after what seemed like an eternity, the girls left the room.

"And so," Pong said, plucking a grape and popping it into his mouth, "that completes our review. The government's forces are strong, but so are yours, and with the addition of my troops the advantage is ours."

Marsha Harrington nodded agreeably. Pong's presentation had compared favorably with the reports of her own intelligence apparatus. Not only that, but the mercenary had kept self-serving exaggeration to a minimum. She liked that. There was only one question left.

"An excellent presentation. Thank you, General. One more question before we leave. Can you tell us anything about my father? With hostilities only hours away, and his home almost completely unprotected, we can't help but worry."

Pong did his best to look appropriately concerned. He searched his memory and came up empty. Damn. There were so many things to track. The mind slug filled the gap. Pong seized the information and put it to use.

"Of course. I'm pleased to report that a special operations team under the command of Captain Roland Blake has landed on Drang and is en route to your father's home. They should reach the mansion within the next few hours."

Marsha Harrington beamed, while her brother nodded dutifully, and her cousin examined perfect nails. "Thank you, General Pong. I can tell we are in good hands. To a successful campaign." She raised her wine glass.

Pong smiled and raised his wine glass in return. "Yes. To a successful campaign."

TWENTY-ONE

McCade and the rest of his team were spread out along the edge of a dry riverbank. Five miles of reddish desert stretched away in front of them, the last five miles before their objective, and the most dangerous of all.

The problem was that they were quickly running out of time. They'd been forced to hide twice, once when the soft rumble of engines filled the air, and again when spotlights made tunnels through the night. They'd escaped on both occasions but paid a price in time.

Now a jagged line of light had crept its way across the horizon and separated earth from sky. The bushlike plants that dotted the desert had begun to stir, waking from night-long hibernation, to creep up and out of the river bottoms.

Within an hour or so they would line the top of the riverbanks like a silver hedge, soaking up energy with their shiny leaves and storing it against the cold of night.

Later, when temperatures started to soar, they would retreat to the river bottoms and the shade cast by high-cut banks. From there the plants would sink tap roots down toward the water hidden deep below.

Which is fine for the plants, McCade reflected, but doesn't help us at all. When the sun comes up we're dead.

McCade flipped up his visor and took a look through the binoculars. He panned from left to right. Nothing. It made him nervous. Where were the robo sentries they'd briefed him on? There weren't many, that was true. Maybe four or five in the entire Zephyr defense zone. But given the fact that they stood nearly three stories tall, and carried enough armament to destroy a light tank, how many did the government need? One would be enough.

Well, robo sentries or no, they couldn't wait any longer. McCade stashed the binoculars and activated the team freq.

"Okay, listen up. We've been lucky so far, but don't get overconfident. There could be all sorts of stuff up ahead. Keep your eyes open and pay attention. And if you notice something that stands about thirty feet tall, and has lots of weapons sticking out of it, don't hesitate to let me know."

There were chuckles followed by some rude comments.

McCade grinned. "Okay, let's hit it. Maintain your spacing, and watch where you put your feet."

"Yeah," Martino added wryly, "you could step in some deep doo-doo."

Nobody laughed.

McCade waved Evans and Kirchoff forward, gave them a few seconds to take the lead, and followed. After hours of running it was easy to slip into a ground-eating jog.

The desert was deceptively beautiful in the early morning light. A soft inviting palette of earth tones that gave no hint of the searing heat yet to come.

The ground was treacherous however, full of holes that could turn an ankle, and loose gravel that skittered underfoot.

But time passed and McCade began to relax. The town of Zephyr was clearly visible from every rise, a cluster of twinkling lights, shimmering in the distance. A peaceful sight reminiscent of small towns everywhere.

Then came a cracking sound. The force of the explosion threw Evans ten feet into the air. Her body cartwheeled and landed with a heavy thump.

Phil yelled, "Land mine!" over the team freq and everyone came to a sudden halt. A quick check confirmed that Evans was dead.

McCade swore under his breath. Another casualty. Another life gone in defense of what? Of the combine's right to line its pockets? What a waste.

The team hurried to pile loose rocks on top of Evans' body. She'd get a formal burial after the main force landed if things went well.

A trooper named Slotman carried their only mine detector. He took the point and waved the wandlike device in front of him like a shaman seeking water. The rest followed, careful to stay in line behind him, slowed to little more than a fast walk.

McCade wanted Slotman to move faster but resisted the urge to tell him so. He scanned the horizon instead. Surely someone had seen or heard the explosion. What would they do? Send a patrol to investigate? Assume that a wild animal had set it off? All he could do was wait and see.

The first sign of trouble was a shard of reflected light. It came in low and from the left. McCade stopped and brought his binoculars to his eyes. What he saw scared hell out of him.

It looked like an insect at first, a metallic beetle, on long skinny legs. Slowly but surely it got to its feet, rising up from the hollow where it had been hidden, to turn in their direction. Light glinted off its shiny skin.

A robo sentry! Lying in ambush! McCade spoke into his mic. "We've got a robo sentry two thousand yards to the left! Stay behind Slotman and we'll run for the next riverbed!"

Blue light slashed past them and hit a large boulder. It exploded throwing superheated chunks of rock in every direction. Something stung McCade's cheek.

Slotman stashed the detector wand. He was running too fast for it to function effectively. He glanced back over his shoulder. The next member of the team was a full hundred feet behind him. It confirmed what Slotman already knew. *He* was the mine detector now. If he lived, the way was clear, and if he died, it wasn't. Simple but effective.

It got so that Slotman dreaded the impact of his boot hitting the ground, the necessity of lifting it up and putting the other one down. Would this be the one? The final footfall? A sudden flash of light followed by eternal darkness?

Blue fire ripped the ground ahead and something exploded. A mine! The robo sentry had triggered a mine! A mine he might have stepped on.

Slotman ran straight toward the patch of smoldering ground and pounded his way through it. The riverbed was just ahead. Slotman knew because the silvery bushes had aligned themselves along its edges and spread their leaves to catch the morning sun. Just a few more yards, a few more feet, and he'd be there.

Slotman dived through the plants and tumbled into the riverbed below. The rest of the team were right behind him. They half jumped, half fell into the bottom of the cut, and scrambled to find defensive positions.

What was the robo sentry up to? A bend in the riverbed blocked the view. McCade was in the process of scrambling back up the bank when a shaft of blue light hit the bushes. They absorbed part of the blast and reflected the rest, sending shafts of coherent energy in every direction. One skimmed the length of McCade's left arm and left a black scorch mark on his body armor.

Straining to keep his balance on the steep bank, McCade fumbled the binoculars to his eyes. The robo sentry was closer now, using the riverbed as a highway, its four podlike feet kicking up clouds of dust each time they hit. No wonder the machine hid. Otherwise people would see it coming from miles away.

All sorts of energy projectors, gun barrels, and launch tubes stuck out of the robot's shiny torso. One moved slightly and burped light. The section of riverbank in front of McCade became a thick liquid and dribbled downward.

McCade took the slope in a series of small jumps. "Martino! As soon as that monster comes around the bend nail it with your launch tube! And don't forget to move afterward!"

"That's a rog, Cap," Martino said, already hidden behind a large rock.

"Spread out," Phil ordered, "and fire thermal grenades when it comes into view."

The ground shook as metal pods hit one after the other and the robo sentry came into full view. A lot of things happened all at once.

Martino fired all five of his launcher's mini-missiles and sprinted for another boulder knowing that the robo sentry's tac comp would compute a reciprocal course and fire on his last position. He'd barely dived behind another rock when an auto cannon turned the first one into gravel.

Those armed with grenade launchers fired thermal rounds, not at the robo sentry itself, but out and away from the team. They made a gentle pop and burned white-hot as they fell toward the ground. The thermals pulled two of the robo sentry's heat-seeking missiles away from the ops team and disappeared inside fiery explosions.

Meanwhile, boulders popped like party balloons as the robot's energy weapons probed among the rocks searching for life. Rock shrapnel screeched through the air and McCade heard someone scream.

Ignoring the danger, Abu Rami rested his long-barreled rifle on its custom-designed tripod, removed a magazine of hollow points, and inserted one filled with armor-piercing rounds. Rami looked through the electronic sight. The robot was huge and menacing. The sniper felt a sudden need to relieve himself. He struggled to remember the machine's weak points.

The robo sentry's ECM gear fooled three of Martino's five mini-missiles but couldn't confuse the other two. They were dummies, with no more intelligence than bullets have, flying where the launch tube had directed them to go. They exploded against the robot's belly.

The robo sentry's designers had anticipated such a possibility and armored the underside of the robot's torso. But while the missiles were unable to penetrate the robot's armor, they did spray chunks of hot metal in every direction.

One piece penetrated a joint, sliced through a cable, and cut power to both rear legs. Undeterred, the machine used its front legs to pull itself forward. There was a horrible screeching noise as metal was dragged over rock. Meanwhile the robot sentry continued to fire in every direction.

McCade was scared. It seemed as if nothing could stop the metal monster. Explosions rippled across its top surface as Martino fired another salvo of missiles. They didn't even slow the robot down. It just kept coming, dragging its useless legs behind it, a mindless killer.

Knowing it was a waste of time McCade fired his blast rifle and waited to die.

Abu Rami made a fine adjustment to his scope. Then, wrapping a finger around the trigger, he took a deep breath. Somewhere in the back of his mind

Rami heard the hunting prayer his father had taught him. He let out half the breath, squeezed the trigger, and absorbed the recoil with his shoulder.

The armor-piercing bullet ran straight and true. It sped across the intervening distance, smashed through a thin-skinned sensor housing, and tunneled its way through the robot's tac comp. Denied all control the robot's weapons fell suddenly silent.

This didn't stop the machine from dragging itself forward however, metal screeching against rock, like a wounded beast returning to its lair.

One by one the team came out from their hiding places, some with bloodstained battle dressings, all with shell-shocked expressions. For a moment everyone just stood there, staring at the wounded machine, amazed at how harmless it had suddenly become.

McCade felt something warm touch his cheek and realized that the sun had topped the edge of the riverbank. All around them the silvery bushes were root-walking to the edge of the bank and sliding downward. It was time to go and then some.

A quick check turned up the fact that while no one had been killed, a trooper named Banks was badly wounded.

Because the energy beam had cauterized the wound on its way through Banks' thigh there was very little bleeding, but it hurt like hell just the same. Phil gave him an injection. Banks was smiling sixty seconds later.

McCade found Abu Rami and thanked him for making the critical shot.

Rami listened politely, acknowledged the compliment with a nod, and turned his attention to the rifle. A thin layer of dust covered its outer surface. That would never do.

A stretcher was assembled from the pieces some of them carried and Banks was strapped onto it. It was difficult getting the stretcher up and over the lip of the bank but they made it.

They formed a column of twos and ran toward Zephyr. It was only two miles away. McCade could see the whitewashed buildings shimmering in the sun. With the enemy warned, and the sun up, there was no time for mine detectors or other niceties. McCade was gambling that the robo sentry worked along the inside edge of the mine field. If so, this area should be clear. If not, it was just too bad.

And now there was another danger as well, a danger they couldn't do a damned thing about. It lurked above them in the clear blue sky, or could, and might descend at any moment. A fighter, a chopper, an armed aircar, any and all of them could, and would, turn the team into chopped liver.

But when danger came it was on the ground. The first sign of it was a dust cloud coming straight toward them from Zephyr. Someone *had* noticed their run-in with the robo sentry and was coming to investigate. That pretty much ripped it, but if they were forced to surrender, McCade wanted to do it from a position of relative strength. Assuming that the government was willing to take prisoners, a proposition that was far from certain.

"There's company coming," Phil said laconically, the words jerking out with each breath.

"Yeah," McCade replied, "I see 'em."

Still running, the world rose and fell around him as McCade looked around. Outside of the oil pump off to the left there was no place to hide. "Okay, everyone, head for the oil pump, it's the only cover around."

They swerved and jogged toward the oil rig. A glance toward the growing dust cloud assured McCade that they'd make it in time. There was only one vehicle as far as McCade could tell, a troop carrier perhaps, or a military truck. Something big anyway, big enough to carry plenty of troops and a lot of weapons.

There wasn't much to the oil pump. Just a vertical mount, a steel cross-piece, and some shiny pipe that disappeared into the reddish soil. It went up and down, up and down, like a bird pecking at the ground. Standing next to it was an equipment shed and some empty oil drums.

The team spread out, found what cover they could, and got ready for their final battle.

The dust cloud was bigger now, much bigger, and McCade could see the vehicle that caused it. First he frowned. Then he brought the binoculars to his eyes, looked, and looked again. Then McCade recognized the conveyance for what it was and laughed.

A bus! A school bus, or crew bus, with a white flag flying from its antenna! It was big, lime green in color, and equipped with huge desert tires.

McCade triggered the team freq. "Hold your fire and stand by. This could be a friendly."

It could also be a trick, McCade thought to himself, and watched as the bus approached, then skidded to a stop. The enormous tires sprayed gravel in every direction. Now McCade could see the words "Harrington Industries" printed along the vehicle's dented flank.

A door hissed open and a man stepped out. He had white hair, a deeply tanned face, and an athletic body. The man was dressed in short-sleeved white shirt, khaki shorts, and a pair of beat-up desert boots. He summoned them with a wave.

"My name's Harrington. You folks look like you could use a lift. Climb aboard, and let's get the hell out of here. We can expect a flight of T-40 fighters in about twelve minutes. Their base is a couple hundred miles away so it's taking them a while to get here."

McCade knew that it could still be some sort of an elaborate trick, but didn't think it was, and decided to take the chance. "All right, everybody . . . you heard the man . . . let's get aboard!"

Phil entered first, his ugly-looking submachine gun at the ready, making sure the bus was empty. It was, and he waved the rest of them forward.

Once the team was aboard, Harrington wasted little time in closing the door and accelerating away. McCade noticed the older man was wearing a headset, and from the speed with which they were traveling, McCade suspected that he had a means of tracking the T-40s. If so, they were coming on strong.

The bus swerved to avoid a rock and threw McCade against hard metal. He smiled. This was silly. Not only was Nigel Harrington a good deal different from the helpless old man that he'd imagined, the industrialist also showed every sign of rescuing his rescuers, and doing so with a good deal of panache.

Zephyr was clean and crisp up ahead, safe behind a carefully maintained wall, all curves and rounded corners. Then McCade saw the iron gate, the pillbox located next to it, and the troops spilling out of a government truck.

Harrington's voice boomed over the PA system. "They're on to me, so hang on, folks, we're gonna dent some government property!"

An automatic weapon opened up from the pillbox, but the gunner hadn't fired at a real target before, and put all of his slugs where the bus had been instead of where it was headed.

An officer waved her arms, mouthed some sort of order, and dived out of the way as Harrington accelerated toward the gate. There was a crash as the bus hit, a snow storm of shattered safety glass, and the stutter of hand-held weapons. McCade sensed rather than saw government troopers falling away as members of his team fired out through the windows.

Up front Harrington yelled, "Yahooo!" and put his foot down. The bus fishtailed around a corner, sideswiped a lamppost, and screeched its way up a well-kept boulevard.

Just then three barely glimpsed somethings roared overhead, shaking the bus with their combined slipstreams.

"That's the T-40s," Harrington yelled happily, "they can't fire on us without hosing the entire neighborhood! Most of my neighbors are government officials. Silly bastards!"

McCade made eye contact with Phil a few rows back and on the other side of the aisle. The variant shook his head in amazement and smiled. It was easy to see why Harrington Industries had been so successful.

The aircraft made one more pass during the time it took for the bus to wind its way down some residential streets and roar toward a pair of massive gates. They opened like magic and closed behind the bus as it bounced inside and slid to a screeching halt.

McCade was impressed with what he could see through the broken windshield. In the foreground were carefully planned rock gardens, thoughtfully interspersed with desert plants, and crisscrossed by well-swept walkways.

Farther back was the mansion itself, a huge rambling structure, all of which was blindingly white.

Harrington tried to open the vehicle's door and found it wouldn't budge. Not too surprising, since it had sustained a good deal of damage during the crash and was badly twisted.

A heavily armed security guard, dressed in a paramilitary uniform with a Harrington Industries logo stitched to his breast pocket, managed to pry the door open with a crowbar.

They unloaded Banks first, with the rest of the team tumbling out after that, and McCade last. Nigel Harrington was there to greet him. There was a smile on the older man's face. His grip was dry and firm.

"Captain Blake, I presume. Welcome to my home. I received word of your arrival a few hours ago."

Harrington gestured toward a tall spindly tower that soared up from the corner of the mansion. "Margaret had that built, God bless her soul. Used to sit on the observation deck and paint. I saw the whole battle from up there. Nasty business that. Could've been worse though. The night patrols were in and the day patrols were getting ready to go out. Idiots don't have enough brains to overlap their patrols. Be surprised if we don't whip the whole government in a week."

McCade thought Harrington's projection was more than a little optimistic but didn't say so. "We sure appreciate your help, sir, we owe you one."

Harrington waved the comment away with a smile. "Not for very long. I'll be owing you pretty soon."

Harrington looked around at his mansion, the gardens, and the pristine grounds. "I wonder how much of this will still be standing two days from now."

Three fighters flashed by overhead, their wings almost touching, the roar of their engines nearly drowning Harrington's last words.

McCade watched the fighters go. Afterburners glowed red as they stood on the tails and screamed toward the sky. He met Harrington's eyes. "That's hard to say, sir, but one thing's for sure, now's the time to dig in."

At exactly 0300 Mustapha Pong gave an order and death fell toward the planet Drang. It came in the form of drop modules, assault boats, bombs, missiles, and beams of pure energy.

And as Pong struck, so did the combine, quickly securing generous landing zones for the invading forces.

But the government forces were tough and, thanks to good intelligence, well prepared for the attack. They'd known since Salazar that war was inevitable, and that Pong would side with the combine. So they gave ground, but did so grudgingly. Every LZ was contested, every target defended, and every victory paid for in blood.

The night was full of fire. Assault boats blossomed into flowers of flame, aerospace fighters exploded, and cities glowed reddish orange. Death was everywhere.

As in most wars Drang's civilians came in for a large share of the suffering. There was no way to protect them against a damaged assault boat cartwheeling out of the sky, a pod of misdirected bombs, or a heat-seeking missile that couldn't tell the difference between a residential power grid and a military one.

But thanks to a common need to win popular support, both the government and the combine avoided civilian target as much as possible.

And because both sides wanted to live on the planet when the war was over, they refused to use nuclear weapons. Of course the fact that nuclear war was grounds for intervention by the Emperor might have had an impact on their thinking as well. Neither group wanted to live on a planet governed by Imperial Marines.

So, some five hours after the attack had begun, Pong was quite satisfied with the way things had gone. His forces had suffered casualties, but nothing unexpected, and thanks to the excellent leadership provided by Colonel Surillo, 81.7 percent of the primary objectives had been taken. A high score indeed.

Pong had watched the first hours of the battle from orbit with 47,721 at his side. A special booth made of one-way glass had been set up inside the flagship's situation room to protect the alien's identity.

Just one leak, one whisper of a previously uncontacted race, and Imperial intelligence would be all over the place. That would be inconvenient, and potentially disastrous as well, since Pong's plan depended on surprise.

Forewarned is forearmed, and if the Empire knew about the 56,827, there was a fairly good chance that they could win the ensuing war. Regardless of what the aliens believed, Pong knew his fellow humans were a tough lot and capable of amazing stubbornness. Not only that, they were also a good deal more technologically sophisticated then the 56,827, and mean as hell when threatened.

No, Pong thought to himself, I mustn't let that happen. Victory depends on a surprise attack by an absolutely ruthless race using weapons the Empire hasn't seen before. It would start when the moon-sized alien ship dropped out of hyperspace into near Earth orbit and cut loose with everything it had. A few hours later man's ancestral home would become little more than charred rock.

The Emperor would be killed along with his entire family, the seat of Imperial government entirely eradicated, and the home fleet destroyed. The rest of the Empire would burst like an overripe fava fruit, split into warring factions, and finish the process Pong had started.

And then, with some key victories over the Il Ronn, and a few other space-faring races, a new order would be born. A new order conceived by *him*.

"By *us*," the Melcetian put in waspishly.

"Of course," Pong responded impatiently. "That goes without saying."

"It better," the mind slug replied, but thought better of it, and slipped Pong some soothing chemicals.

Completely unaware of Pong's thoughts, or his interchange with the Melcetian, 47,721 shifted in his seat. It was of 56,827 manufacture and served to cradle the alien's backward curving midsection. Both of its outward bulging eyes were swiveled forward in order to follow the action.

The privacy booth included three sophisticated holo tanks, twelve different video monitors, and a sophisticated com set.

Using video supplied by hundreds of spaceships, assault boats, drop modules, combat vehicles, and individual troops, a rather sophisticated computer had woven it all together to provide them with a live blow-by-blow account of the battle.

So skillful was the computer's manipulation of incoming information that it took on the quality of a holo drama, complete with ongoing characters and running subplots.

More than once Pong and 47,721 were watching when a particular video source disappeared from the screen and never returned. Often there was natural sound, explosions, or screams followed by silence.

Each time Pong was conscious of the fact that real men and women had just died, yet because it was little different from watching a well-executed holo drama, it didn't seem to mean much.

Not to Pong anyway, although 47,721 grew somewhat agitated during the scenes of personal combat, and his toe claws had left scratches in the surface of the durasteel deck.

All around the booth there was the quiet murmur of com traffic, an occasional burst of static, and the gentle hiss of air-conditioning. All of it comfortably distant from the battle that raged below.

But not for long. In a few minutes Pong would depart for the surface where he would take personal command of his troops and prove his worthiness to the 56,827. Silly but necessary. He turned to 47,721.

"So, we are well on the way to victory. In a few weeks, a month at the most, our work will be done. In the meantime I must join my troops."

A long rope of saliva drooped out of the alien's mouth parts and plopped to the deck. "Yes, numberless one. You have done well. I shall remain here for a while and monitor the battle before returning to my ship."

Pong delivered a small bow of acknowledgment. He eyed the hood and cape arrangement thrown over the back of 47,721's chair. It would protect the alien's identity between the situation room and the shuttle. The crew was curious, but so what. With the exception of Molly, none of them had seen anything more than the outside of the alien's spaceship. And for all they knew, it was an asteroid transformed into an elaborate habitat and crewed by Lakorian swamp dancers.

Pong cleared his throat. "Do you need anything before I leave?"

The alien was quiet for a moment, as if giving the question his full and undivided attention. "Yes, as you know, our success stems in part from the care with which we prepare for battle."

Sure, Pong thought to himself. If you never take chances you never lose.

Out loud Pong said, "And quite right too."

"So," the alien continued, "I will take the juveniles along with me as I return."

The 56,827 had made their desire for some human children known early on, and Pong had saved some from the slave markets of Lakor specifically for that purpose. And up till now he'd never dared to ask why.

But flushed with the successful attack on Drang, and more confident of his position, Pong decided to indulge his curiosity.

"Of course. I will have the children prepared. May I ask what you'll do with them?"

The alien's reply was matter-of-fact. "Of course. Some of our more sophisticated weapons kill by disrupting the enemy's nervous system. However, due to the fact that neural systems vary from species to species, it is necessary to fine-tune our weapons prior to battle. Some of the juveniles will be used for that purpose. Others will provide an interesting variation to our rather monotonous shipboard diet."

Pong shuddered. Although well aware of the 56,827's preference for dinner on the hoof, it was something he'd tried to ignore. On one occasion they'd invited him for dinner and it had taken weeks to get over it.

Pong thought of the slave girls who'd been captured with Molly. What a horrible way to die. Still, a deal's a deal. He would give the necessary orders.

As for Molly, well, she was safe. Remembering her fear of 47,721, Pong had ordered Molly to remain in his cabin while the alien was aboard, and during his trip dirtside as well. Much as he enjoyed Molly's company, Pong knew it would be dangerous on Drang, and wanted to protect her. He stood to go.

"The juveniles will be ready, 47,721. May your hunts go well."

"And yours," the alien replied politely, before returning his attention to the video screens. A small city was on fire and he didn't want to miss it.

TWENTY-THREE

"Incoming!" The voice was an unidentifiable croak in McCade's ear.

He dived behind the wreckage of a once-graceful water fountain. Like everything else in and around Nigel Harrington's home, it had been reduced to little more than twisted metal and shattered masonry. The mortar shells made a loud cracking sound as they marched across the driveway and rock garden leaving large craters behind. The barrage ended as suddenly as it began.

"Here they come!" This time McCade recognized the voice as belonging to Phil. He rolled over and poked the brand-new assault rifle up and over a chunk of broken duracrete. There was no shortage of weapons and ammunition thanks to Nigel Harrington's underground arsenal.

But what good are weapons if you don't have troops to fire them? Only twelve members of McCade's team were still alive. They, plus the five surviving members of Harrington's security force, were all that stood between the industrialist and the government troops that were trying to capture or kill him.

The air was full of dust and smoke. A couple of dozen dimly seen figures sprinted through the wreckage of the main gate. Their armor was covered with powdery white dust. It puffed away as they ran.

Auto throwers stuttered, energy weapons burped, and a grenade went off as the government troops came straight at him.

McCade fired in ammo-conserving three-round bursts, methodically working his way from left to right, watching the soldiers jerk and fall. He cursed them for coming, for running at him through the smoke, willing them to turn and flee.

But they kept on coming, their bullets dancing through the rubble around him, screaming incoherent war cries.

The deliberate *thump, thump, thump* of a heavy machine gun came from McCade's right, and he watched as geysers of dirt exploded upward next to the troops and then among them.

Bodies were thrown backward, loose weapons flew through the air, and the *thump, thump, thump* continued. Continued, and stopped, when there was nothing left to kill.

McCade dropped down and rolled over onto his back. The sky was partially obscured by drifting smoke. Then a momentary breeze blew it away and he saw contrails crisscrossing the sky. The battle for Drang was well under way.

McCade wondered how the battle was going, who was winning, and who was dying.

He thumbed the magazine release and fumbled for another. The bounty hunter didn't even look as he shoved it home. The magazine made a loud click followed by a clack as the bolt slid forward.

"Fighters! South side, six o'clock low!"

McCade looked to his left and swore. What was this? Their seventh sortie that day? Their eighth? He supposed it didn't matter much. About five or six hours after the team arrived the government had evacuated the rest of the neighborhood and called for an air strike. The planes had been strafing and bombing the hell out of the place ever since. The entire neighborhood had been leveled.

McCade rolled to his knees, scrambled to his feet, and sprinted for a bolt hole. It had been a basement window once, but it was no more than a hole now, one of the many passageways they maintained in and out of Harrington's underground shelter. All around the mansion others were doing the same thing. They didn't need orders. The planes came and you hid. It was as simple as that.

McCade heard the roar of the approaching planes and the growl of their mini-guns. The black hole was just ahead. He dived through it and landed on the mattress placed there for that purpose.

The world outside was suddenly transformed into a hell of exploding rockets, bursting bomblets, and flying lead. Wave after wave of death flowed across the land churning the rubble and sending up great clouds of smoke and dust. The noise was almost deafening.

McCade put his hands over his ears just as the voice came through his tiny receiver. "Blake . . . Harrington here. They won't attack as long as the planes are here. Come on down for a minute."

McCade got to his feet and staggered out of the small storage room and into a richly paneled hallway. He followed that for thirty feet or so and came to a heavily armored door.

McCade turned his face so the security camera could get a good look at him and was rewarded with a loud click. He pulled on the door and it came open.

A wide set of stairs led downward. McCade pulled the door closed and made his way down the stairs. Cool air rose to meet him, along with the smell of fresh coffee and the odor of cooking.

Built to protect the Harrington family from everything up to and including nuclear war, the shelter was much more than the name would imply.

Powered with its own fusion plant, and stocked with five years' worth of supplies, it included all the basic necessities and then some.

Harrington's sentient servants and house bots had retreated underground along with him. So, as McCade entered the large sitting room, everything was sparkling clean and a maid was in the process of serving coffee. The thick rugs, modernistic furniture, and expensive art all gave the impression of relaxed luxury.

One entire wall, the one that almost screamed for a window, was given over to a huge vid screen. It was filled with a shot of dramatic-looking boulders, some stunted greenery, and a crystal-clear pool of water.

Like the view from a picture window it was absolutely static, except for small details like an eight-legged reptile scampering over the surface of a sun-warmed rock, and a bird skimming the surface of the water in search of insects.

McCade assumed the shot was live, piped in from somewhere out in the desert.

Harrington wore light body armor, still dusty from a stint on the surface a half hour before, and marked here and there with impacts from flying debris. The industrialist was a damned good shot and had done his share of the fighting and then some. How old was he anyway? Sixty? Seventy? Whatever the industrialist's age he was tough as hell. Harrington gestured toward a comfortable chair.

"Excellent work up there, Captain Blake. Have a seat. Nancy, coffee and cigars for my guest."

A middle-aged woman who looked more like an executive secretary than a maid nodded pleasantly and went to work. Within moments McCade had a humidor full of expensive cigars at his elbow and a coffee cup in his hand. It made an unbelievable contrast with the surface. McCade took a sip of coffee, it burned his tongue.

"You wanted to see me, sir?" It felt good to sit down and rest, but McCade couldn't leave his team for very long.

Harrington touched a remote. The desert scene disappeared from the huge vid screen and was replaced by a wide shot of the Harrington compound. A line of explosions marched through the debris as a plane roared by overhead. Harrington turned the sound down.

"No need to worry, Captain. Most of my vid pickups have been destroyed, but as you can see, I still have one or two left. They're still at it, and as long as they are, your team is safe."

McCade nodded and lit a cigar.

The older man waited until the cigar was drawing satisfactorily and smiled. "I used to enjoy them but was forced to quit. Even with anticancer shots and all that other medical hocus-pocus old age eventually has its way."

Harrington waved a hand. "But enough of that. I have good news. The initial battle is winding down. Your forces have landed and in most cases linked up with the combine. Within an hour, two at most, Zephyr will be in friendly hands."

It *was* good news. McCade knew he should be happy but wasn't. Half his team were dead, and the outcome of the war didn't matter to him. What mattered was a little girl, and a woman on another planet. He forced a smile.

"I'm glad to hear it, sir. The truth is I'm not sure we could've held for another day."

Harrington nodded. "No, I think not."

McCade grabbed a handful of cigars, stuck them in a breast pocket, and got to his feet. "Thanks for the news, sir. I'll go topside and tell the team."

Harrington nodded and watched him leave. A tough-looking man, a soldier from all appearances, but something more as well. Something more complicated than a hired killer. But what? Just one of the many questions he'd never get an answer to.

It was actually more like five hours before a flight of the combine's fighters swept in to control the sky and soften up the government's ground forces, and two hours after that when a flight of choppers landed and disgorged two companies of Pong's best infantry.

First they surrounded what was left of the Harrington mansion, then they swept through the town of Zephyr and secured that as well.

McCade was sitting on a chunk of garden wall smoking one of Harrington's cigars when Major Davison found him. Although it was clear from the condition of his armor the other officer had been in or near the fighting, he looked disgustingly fresh.

"There you are! I've been looking all over for you! Nice job, Blake, damned nice. So nice that the old man wants to shake your hand. Fred's too."

Frederick Lambert was the name Phil had taken.

McCade raised an eyebrow. "The who?"

"The old man, the general, Mustapha Pong himself."

McCade's heart beat a little bit faster. Finally! A chance to meet Mustapha Pong! Maybe he'd know Molly's whereabouts, and even if he didn't, there was a score to settle. A *big* score.

McCade stood up and flicked the cigar butt away. "The old man. Yes, sir. Ready when you are, sir."

The wounded had been flown out minutes after the combine swept in, but McCade found the others and thanked them one by one. Martino, Abu Rami, Kirchoff, and a few others were completely untouched. Then, with Phil at his side, McCade climbed aboard the waiting chopper and watched Zephyr shrink below him.

Then, stretching out on a pile of cargo nets, McCade went to sleep. Davison shook him awake two hours later.

"Rise 'n' shine, Blake. This is brigade headquarters. Before we came it was a nice little hell hole called Foley's Folly, and don't ask, because I don't know why they called it that."

McCade yawned, stretched, and sat up. Over on the other side of the chopper Phil did the same.

Without the breeze blowing back through the open hatch it was hot, damned hot, and McCade's mouth was dry. Not only that, his neck hurt from sleeping on the cargo nets, and he smelled like rancid vat slime.

Davison grinned. "Well, Blake, I hope you feel better than you look, cause you look like hell."

McCade got to his feet. He squinted toward the hatch. The sun was high in the sky and the glare off the desert was incredible. "Thanks for the pep talk, sir, I feel better now."

Davison laughed and waved them toward the hatch. "Come on, Captain, Sergeant, let's get you cleaned up. We can't parade you in front of the general looking like that."

The sun fell on them like a hammer as they stepped down onto the fused sand. Engines roared all around them, as insect-like choppers took off and landed, their rotors blowing sand sideways forcing McCade to turn his head.

Once off the landing pad Davison ushered them into an open combat car. The vinyl seats were hot as hell. Phil looked terribly uncomfortable, panting heavily, his fur matted with sweat.

A private sat behind pintle-mounted twin-fifties, looking bored and doing her nails. She didn't even glance their way. The driver was a cheerful-looking corporal. He had bright brown eyes, black skin, and a gold earring in his right ear.

"Welcome aboard, sirs. Where to?"

"The O club and step on it," Davison replied.

McCade was thrown backward as the car spun away, spraying a nearby work party with sand and reinforcing all the negative images they already had regarding officers.

The corporal liked to drive combat cars, and saw each errand as an opportunity to hone his skills. As a result the trip from the helicopter pad to the O club was transformed into a high-speed sprint through an imaginary combat situation, with piles of camo-netted cargo modules standing in for tanks, and rows of inflatable tents representing troop carriers. This made the trip fast but somewhat terrifying as well. McCade was thankful when the car skidded to a stop in front of a large tent. A steady stream of officers was coming and going through the front entrance.

Davison thanked the corporal, turned his face away to avoid the inevitable spray of sand, and waited for the combat car to clear the area. He turned to Phil.

"Here . . . pin these tabs to your armor. I put you in for lieutenant and we'll assume it's been approved. Can't have sergeants in the O club . . . might contaminate the beer or something."

Phil laughed, did as Davison requested, and followed the major inside. It was soothingly dark, redolent of smoke and beer, and filled with the low mumble of conversation. There were thirty or forty folding tables, about half of them filled.

Davison led them to the bar, bought a round of beers, and watched as they chugged them down. Phil chased his with a full pitcher. When it was gone the variant wiped his muzzle with the back of a furry hand, belched, and said, "Thank you, sir, that hit the spot."

With their thirst quenched, Davison sent them to the rear of the building where they stripped down and entered the male showers. There was no such thing as cold water, but it felt wonderful to stand in a steady stream of tepid water, and let it wash away days' worth of desert grime.

McCade soaped and rinsed three times before he felt really clean.

Phil, always given to singing in the shower, did so, his prodigious baritone filling the area with sound. At least one officer thought about asking Phil to stop, but caught a glimpse of the variant's bulk, and decided to let it go. A few minutes later they had the showers to themselves.

Finally, two bars of soap and many gallons later, they emerged much refreshed and ready for the new uniforms that Davison had waiting. Phil's was an extra large, triple X, and barely fit.

Davison nodded approvingly when they joined him at the bar. "Better . . . much better . . . and just in time too." The major glanced at his wrist term.

"We're due to appear in front of the general at 1730. The general's not much for handing out medals and that sort of thing, but he's got the combine to consider, and Marsha Harrington is real pleased about the way you took care of her father. So the heroes are about to receive their just due, along with some other fortunates who had the good sense to save a combine factory. We're off."

It was a shock stepping out of the air-conditioned O club into the late afternoon heat. Fortunately for them the HQ bunker was a short distance away. It was more than a bunker actually, being a fairly good-sized freighter, which had been landed in a specially prepared ravine and buried under tons of rock and sand. The result was a hardened command post that was nearly invulnerable to attack.

The entrance was inside a small tent some fifty yards from the command post itself. It was heavily guarded. All three were subjected to an identity check and asked to surrender their weapons prior to admission.

Up to this point McCade had been looking forward to a confrontation with Pong, unsure of exactly how things would go, but determined to make something happen. Now, stripped of his weapons and surrounded by Pong's personal troops, that seemed suicidal. But thanks to the fact that Pong had never seen him before, he could accept the medal and leave. After that he'd get together with Phil and make a new plan.

Somewhat comforted by this analysis McCade turned his attention to following Major Davison through the underground tunnel. The walls were made of fused sand and chem strips lighted the way. The exaggerated zigzag of the tunnel was no accident. Each corner represented a place where defenders could take cover while their attackers were forced into the open. It was very professional.

There was another identity check once they reached the ships's lock, followed by a pat down, and a trip through a standard metal detector.

Phil's durasteel teeth and claws set the detector off right away and caused quite a stir. Finally, after much arguing and explaining by Major Davison, they were allowed to pass.

A junior rating led them through the freighter's interior to a specially modified cargo hold. Half the space was filled with banks of com gear and people, most of whom were milling around a centrally located tac tank. It shimmered and swirled with distant battle.

Folding chairs had been set up in the other half of the hold and most of them were already filled. The occupants looked tired and extremely bored.

"A bunch of ground pounders," Davison whispered, "you know, the ones who saved the factory."

McCade nodded and took one of the few empty seats. Phil sat beside him.

Five or ten minutes passed during which nothing seemed to happen. Then a hatch hissed open and a man stepped through. A rather pleasant-looking man with a Melcetian mind slug riding on his shoulder. The alien rippled with reflected light.

McCade felt adrenaline pour into his system. His heart beat like a trip-hammer.

Mustapha Pong! The man who had stolen his daughter, wounded his wife, and murdered his friends. Where's Molly? What have you done with her? McCade wanted to scream it, and was half an inch out of his chair when Phil touched his arm.

"Not now, Sam, Not here. We'll get our chance, but not now."

The voice was calm, logical, correct. McCade fell back into his chair and looked around. Had anyone noticed? No, not as far as he could tell anyway.

The room had grown quieter, whether from Pong's presence or actual orders, McCade couldn't tell. A stern-looking woman in perfect body armor nodded to Pong and turned toward the small audience. She had heavy black eyebrows, a predatory nose, and a stern mouth. The woman cleared her throat.

"Hello, I'm Colonel Mary Surillo. It's my pleasure to welcome you to brigade HQ. Being mercs, we don't give out a lot of medals, but when we do they really mean something. Each one of the medals given out today comes with a cash award."

The ground pounders gave a cheer and Surillo nodded approvingly. "That's right . . . the stuff we fight for. Here to present your awards, and to congratulate you on behalf of the combine, is General Mustapha Pong."

Surillo nodded toward Pong and took a step backward.

Pong produced a smile, stepped forward, and let the mind slug feed him what he needed to know. "Thank you, Colonel, it's a pleasure to be here. As I give your names please stand up. First I'd like to recognize Major Elroy, Lieutenant Deng, Private Hoskins . . ."

Pong's voice became a dull drone as he listed the ground pounders, their sterling service on behalf of the combine, and their various rewards.

McCade watched the pirate's face, wondering how such evil could lurk behind those banal features, and wishing he could do something about it right then.

McCade felt a nudge from Phil and realized that their turn had come. The ground ponders had taken their seats, and Pong was about to speak.

"And that brings us to our next set of winners. Captain Roland Blake and Second Lieutenant Frederick Lambert, please stand."

McCade stood, as did Phil, and Pong had just launched into a description of what they'd done when a loud squawk came from the other side of the room.

McCade looked just in time to see Captain Lorina DepSmith step out of the crowd, belly jiggling, and point a pudgy finger in his direction. Her voice cut through the noise like a knife through soft butter. "Roland Blake my foot! That's Sam McCade!"

TWENTY-FOUR

Molly huddled in one corner of Mustapha Pong's vast cabin, half asleep, half awake. She was fantasizing about home, reliving a wonderful afternoon when she, Mommy, and Daddy had gone up to Uncle Rico's summer place for a picnic. Everything was cozy and warm inside the cabin, while outside the snow fell thick and heavy, covering the world with a layer of white frosting.

There had been a big blazing fire, lots of good food, and the pleasant drone of her parents' voices. There was nothing exciting about the trip, nothing special, just the warm fullness of being cared for and loved.

Molly remembered how it felt to have Daddy throw her into the air, while Mommy cautioned him to be careful and smiled from the other side of the room. Oh, what she wouldn't give to be back there, reliving that moment, feeling strong arms around her.

A tear trickled down Molly's cheek and she wiped it away as the hatch hissed open. There were loud footsteps as someone walked into the center of the room and stood in the cone of light that bathed Pong's chair. A knot formed in Molly's stomach when she saw who it was. Boots! What was she doing here? Molly cowered in the corner and hoped the woman would go away.

Boots laughed, a horrible cackling sound, full of hate and satisfaction. "So! Hiding in the corner, eh? Get out here!"

Molly did as she was told, wondering what was going on and wishing Pong would appear. He didn't.

Two quick steps and Boots had her by an ear, pulling Molly along, towing her through the hatch and down the corridor. It hurt, and just to emphasize that fact, Boots gave her ear an extra jerk every once in a while.

Molly bit her lip, determined not to cry, and looked around for help. Crew members passed them in both directions. Where was Pong? Raz? Surely they'd help her. But no one came to her rescue or even looked especially interested. Slaves, even ones favored by Mustapha Pong, were still slaves.

Bit by bit it became clear that they were headed for the launch bay, and sure enough, when Boots came to a halt it was outside robo lock four.

The hangar had been depressurized so that shuttles could come and go freely, but a limited number of accordianlike robo locks allowed direct access to high-priority vessels, and it seemed Molly was destined for one of those.

Aha! Molly felt suddenly better. Pong had sent for her. Boots would put her aboard his shuttle, and that would be that.

But that hope was snatched away when the rest of the girls were herded into the area, all nineteen of them, with Lia leading the way. The older girl had a sneer on her face.

"Well, look who's here! Little Miss Privileged. What's the matter, Molly, did Pong get tired of wiping your nose?"

Molly ignored her and did her best to figure out what was going on. It wasn't just her. They were taking *all* of the girls off ship. Why?

Boots counted noses. "Well, that should be the lot of them."

"Yup," the other crew member agreed, checking his porta comp, "let's get 'em on board. Chow's in twenty minutes. We wouldn't want to be late."

Boots shoved Molly toward the lock. "Get moving, brat . . . it seems Pong came to his senses. We're well rid of you."

Molly stumbled, caught herself, and stepped into the lock. She felt an emptiness inside. Pong had sent her away. It shouldn't matter, but it did.

Molly knew Pong was a horrible man, knew he was capable of destroying entire planets to get what he wanted, and liked him anyway. She shouldn't but she did. He'd been kind to her, or as kind as he knew how to be, and seemed to like her. That's why Molly felt betrayed. What had she done to displease him? Why was Pong sending her away?

A tremendous wave of self-pity rolled over Molly as she groped her way through the dimly lit tube. It wasn't fair! Why her? Why?

The question found no answer as Molly knew it wouldn't. She saw a dimly lit lock up ahead. The light had a lavender hue. It reminded Molly of something she couldn't quite put her finger on.

She entered the lock along with Boots and five other girls. There wasn't room for more. Much to Molly's relief Lia was back toward the end of the line.

Boots hummed as the lock cycled through, and was so pleased with the occasion that she allowed Molly to slip by untouched.

It was dim inside the shuttle and it took Molly's eyes a moment to adjust.

Then Molly's heart jumped into her throat. She saw dirt where the deck should be, vegetation to either side, and a lavender sky overhead. The shuttle was a smaller version of the moon-sized ship! The ship that belonged to the horrible aliens!

Molly whirled and headed for the lock. She shouted, "Run! Run!" but it did no good. The other girls stayed right where they were; Boots cuffed her on the side of the head and kicked her as she went down.

Molly struggled as Boots dragged her toward the shuttle's stern, doing her best to tell others what was waiting for them, screaming with frustration when they ignored her.

An openhanded slap sent Molly reeling as the rest of the girls poured into the small compartment and a metal gate slammed into place. Boots stood on the other side of the gate and grinned. Molly grabbed the bars and shook them.

"Let us out . . . please let us out . . . they plan to kill us!"

But Boots laughed and disappeared into the near darkness of the corridor. Hands pulled Molly away from the bars and held her while Lia moved in front of her.

"Now listen, and listen good. You're going to shut up and do as you're told! We're tired of being abused while you sit around playing princess. From now on you'll do what *we* say when *we* say to do it. Understand?"

Molly jerked her arms free and looked Lia in the eye. "I understand all right . . . I understand that you're an idiot! Do you know where we're headed? And what will happen once we get there?"

Some of the other girls looked interested, but Lia crossed her arms and spat the words out one at a time. "No, and you don't either! Now shut up and sit down!"

Molly shrugged and looked for a place to sit down. Information is power, and by bottling it up, Lia hoped to control the situation. It was stupid and immature but effective nonetheless.

A quick look around confirmed Molly's earlier impression. The shuttle contained a miniature biosphere, but unlike the mother ship's, this one seemed limited to plants and insects. Not enough room for higher life forms, she supposed.

A half hour passed during which the other girls wondered at their alien surroundings and ignored Molly.

Then came a rustling sound, followed by the whir of a hatch closing, and the slow swish of something moving their way. Molly had a pretty good idea of what it was and moved toward the rear of the compartment, while the other girls jostled one another trying to see.

Then 47,721 stepped out into the half-light. He was hidden by a black cloak, but looked ominous enough to elicit a collective gasp and start a general movement away from the gate.

Molly shuddered. She saw some drool hit the dirt by the creature's feet and knew it was one of them. The alien moved its head as if looking at each one of them individually.

Then, with a grunt that might have meant anything, it turned and left.

Eva, one of the younger girls, was first to speak. She was short, chubby, and plainly terrified. "Wha-what was that?"

Molly started to answer but Lia held up a restraining hand.

"Don't be so xenophobic. It doesn't matter what's under the cloak. We all know that biological form flows from environmental conditions. There's nothing to worry about."

Eva and the rest of the girls didn't look so sure, but Lia's domineering approach left no room for dissent, so they remained silent.

Molly smiled. You had to give Lia credit. Her answer sounded good, and would've pulled an "A" back in school, but didn't answer Eva's question. Worse than that, it left all the girls ignorant of what was coming.

Anyone who was standing, and that included Lia, fell as the shuttle moved up and away.

There was a long slow period of acceleration, followed by what felt like nothing at all, as the ship reached cruising speed. Molly waited for the momentary nausea that often signals a hyperspace jump but it didn't come. It seemed the alien mother ship was relatively close by.

Molly wrapped her arms around her knees and rocked back and forth. There was nothing to do but wait. She couldn't help but dwell on her first exposure to 47,721, and his inquiry about "the juveniles." The alien wanted human children. Why? And what for?

Time passed, exactly how much was hard to say, since none of the children had a watch. But judging from how hungry Molly was when the shuttle started to slow, she figured it had been six or seven hours, maybe more.

The knot in her stomach grew larger and larger.

Finally, after what seemed like an eternity, the ship settled into place with a discernible thump.

All of the girls watched the gate and, in spite of Lia's insistence that everything was okay, looked very apprehensive. All of them wondered the same thing: What now?

Time passed and Molly heard movement, a shuffling sound from the corridor. Then 47,721 appeared. The cloak was gone now and even Lia whimpered with terror. All the girls took a step backward. The gate slid open as if by magic. Molly tried to disappear.

The alien entered the cell, drool plopping into the dry dirt, and looked at each of them in turn. The process seemed to last forever. Then, with his decision made, 47,721 raised a bony finger and pointed at three of the girls in quick succession.

"Come." The word grated its way out of the translator that hung around its neck.

All three of the girls whimpered and looked at Lia. She forced a smile. "Go ahead . . . I'm sure it'll be okay."

Molly wanted to scream, "Don't do it! Don't go!" but knew it wouldn't do any good. 47,721 would take them away regardless of what she or Lia said or did.

Karen, Suki, and Niki looked back over their shoulders as they stepped into the corridor, and 47,721 shuffled along behind. All four were quickly lost to sight. The gate slid closed.

Molly heard the hiss of equalizing pressure as the lock cycled open. The gate slid open five minutes later. The message was obvious. They were free to go.

The girls looked at Lia. She smiled. "See? I told you not to worry. We can leave anytime we want."

Molly opened her mouth to speak but closed it when Lia looked her way.

Satisfied that she had the situation under control, Lia did her best to look confident, and stepped into the corridor. The other girls followed. Molly waited for someone to give her orders, and, when they didn't, stayed right where she was.

Once they were gone, Molly tiptoed through the leafy corridor and found that a durasteel hatch barred the way to the control compartment. She palmed the lock. Nothing. 47,721 was a lot of things but stupid wasn't one of them.

Unable to see any advantage to staying on the shuttle alone, and afraid that one or more of the aliens might show up, Molly left the ship. Making her way through the lock and down a ramp, she found herself in the same landing bay as before. There was no sign of the others.

Stepping up to the same lock that she and Pong had used, Molly touched a heat-sensitive panel and waited for the hatch to cycle open.

Once inside she saw that one of the girls had lost her comb. It lay on the deck in a pool of alien goo. Molly didn't blame her for leaving it there.

When the opposite hatch whirred open Molly stepped out to find that everything was as before, with the possible exception of the sky, which seemed a little bit brighter. A little earlier in the simulated day perhaps.

Everything was the same. The path, the hill, the strange-looking trees at the top.

Lia and the others had followed the path partway to the top where they stood huddled together looking around. Molly knew how they felt. She also knew that they should scatter, hide wherever they could, and hope for some sort of miracle. Perhaps the runners would help them.

Lia grew visibly tense as Molly approached and did her best to look commanding. Molly expected some sort of comment on her late arrival but was ignored instead.

"All right," Lia said importantly, "let's spread out and see what's going on. Marsha, check out the tree things toward the top of the hill; Eva, take a look at those boulders. I see some holes down there and we might need some shelter."

Eva started downhill but Molly grabbed her arm. "Don't do it, Eva . . . there's some sort of creature living in those rocks."

Lia gave an exasperated sigh. "Here we go again. I thought I told you to shut up? Ignore her, Eva. There's nothing to worry about."

"Oh, yeah?" Molly asked. "Well watch this."

So saying she picked up a rock and threw it toward the boulder. Nothing happened.

Molly stared downhill in openmouthed amazement. Where was the black thing?

"See what I mean?" Lia sneered. "Molly lies like a rug."

With a show of nonchalance, the older girl stuck her hands in her pockets and strolled downhill. Molly ran after her and grabbed Lia's arm.

"Don't do it, Lia! I've been here before. Something lives in the boulders, honest!"

Lia jerked her arm away and walked even faster than before.

Molly threw another rock hoping that the monster would reveal itself. Still nothing.

Unable to do anything else Molly stood and watched. Maybe Lia was right after all. Maybe the creature had gone somewhere else.

Then, without any warning whatsoever, the black thing lashed out and dragged Lia into its hole. There was a scream, a horrible crunching sound, and total silence.

Molly just stood there for a while, staring at the spot where Lia had disappeared, unable to accept what she'd seen. Poor Lia. She'd been mean and nasty but didn't deserve to die for it.

Molly turned and made her way back up the hill. The girls gathered around. Molly had been elected to lead them without a word being said. Some were crying and all of them looked scared. Molly forced a smile.

"Come on, kids. We've got a friend around here somewhere. Let's find him."

TWENTY-FIVE

They tried to run but it was hopeless. Within seconds McCade and Phil were surrounded by gun-toting military police. There were at least fifteen weapons aimed at them. Not even Phil could beat odds like that.

As he turned toward the front of the room and Mustapha Pong, McCade felt a tremendous sense of disappointment. To come so far, to be so close, and lose. It didn't seem fair.

Mustapha Pong smiled. He felt good. Very good. He'd waited a long time for this moment.

The Melcetian, who saw the human tendency to gloat as a complete waste of time, stirred slightly. "We have a lot to do . . . so keep it short."

Pong ignored the alien and moved forward.

The ground pounders got up and left. They didn't know what was going on and couldn't care less. They had their bits of brass, some money to spend, and were well satisfied. How stupid when the universe was full of larger and more important goals.

The MPs shifted slightly in order to make room. Pong was careful to stay well out of reach. "Sam McCade. So, we finally meet. I should've killed you when I had the chance."

McCade remembered the moment well. He'd been searching for the Il Ronnian Vial of Tears, and along with some others had been standing on the surface of an asteroid. Pong's cruiser had hung over them like some omnipotent God while the pirate's voice boomed into their helmets. "Which one of you is Sam McCade? Raise your right arm."

McCade had raised his arm and a spear of white light had flashed down to pin him against the ground. But instead of an energy weapon, it was a spotlight, and McCade had lived. Up till now anyway.

McCade forced a crooked smile. "You'll have a hard time getting any sympathy from me."

Pong smiled indulgently. "A sense of humor . . . I like that in a dead man. Tell me something. If we hadn't invited you here ourselves, what then?"

McCade shrugged. "I would've found some other way to get here."

Pong nodded agreeably. "Of course. You're resourceful if nothing else. Well, I'm glad things turned out as they did. I'll feel better knowing that you're adding some much-needed nutrients to Drang's soil. It'll be my little contribution to the planet's ecology."

McCade knew that Pong was hoping for a reaction and refused to provide it.

Pong laughed and walked away. He hadn't gone more than five feet before he stopped and turned. "Oh, and one more thing. My compliments on your daughter. Molly's a wonderful little girl. I plan to raise her myself. Just thought you'd want to know."

Rage boiled up from deep inside and McCade threw himself in Pong's direction. If only he could wrap his hands around the pirate's throat and kill that evil brain, his own death would be worthwhile.

But the MPs grabbed McCade and beat him with their rifle butts until blessed darkness pulled him down.

There were moments, brief episodes, when McCade floated to the surface. He felt rough hands pick him up, heard coarse voices give unintelligible commands, and saw shapes move around him. Then came movement and a constant bumping up and down as he hovered somewhere between light and darkness.

And there was pain, a dull throbbing in the back of his head, and something more as well. Another pain that was sharp, like an animal's bite, and came at regular intervals. What could it be? This intermittent pain that came between him and peaceful darkness?

It was curiosity as much as anything that caused McCade to open his eyes and look around.

He was in the back seat of an enclosed military vehicle, either a command car, or something very similar. There was desert outside. The same desert Pong planned to bury him in.

McCade turned his attention to the vehicle's interior. A driver and a guard sat up front, and directly behind them were two MPs on fold-down seats. They faced backward and looked mean as hell.

The woman seated directly in front of him wore a ruby stud in the side of her nose and the skin along the left side of her face had the patchy look that comes with a recent skin graft. Like the pro she was, the woman had her side arm out and pointed to one side. If the weapon fired accidentally, the slug would hit the door instead of her partner.

The second guard was handsome in a sort of sallow way, his dark brown eyes darting here and there like little animals, searching for something to eat. Every once in a while he would reach up to tug on his left earlobe. Like the first guard his weapon was drawn and aimed to the side.

This amused McCade because both guards could have aimed their guns at him. If the car hit an unexpected bump and the guns went off, so what? They planned to kill him anyway so why worry?

They were pros, that's why. Regardless of uniforms the guards were hired killers. It would be a mistake to kill him accidentally and they didn't make mistakes.

McCade felt a sharp pain in his right arm. What the heck was that anyway? Carefully, letting his head drift with the motion of the car, he looked to the right.

And there, in all of his furry majesty, sat Phil. His wrists were chained together in front of him, but there was just enough slack for the variant to cheat them left, and prick McCade's arm with the top of a durasteel claw. Phil saw the subtle movement of McCade's head and his eyelids drooped downward in silent acknowledgment.

Now McCade understood. The pain was Phil's way of bringing him around. The variant was ready to make his move but wanted McCade conscious when he did it. Overpowering the guards would be extremely difficult, doing it alone would be close to impossible.

McCade moved slightly, almost imperceptibly, checking to see what kind of restraints they'd placed on him. Handcuffs and leg irons. Good. No nerve shackles, thank Sol.

The vehicle shook violently as the driver pushed it through a series of chuck holes. McCade swayed, apparently in response to the motion, and fell forward in the woman's lap. By doing so he blocked both her handgun and legs. That's when Phil went into action.

With twenty-five percent of the opposition momentarily immobilized, the variant brought his feet up and kicked as hard as he could. Because guard number two had turned to look at McCade, Phil's boots hit him in the side of the head and snapped his neck like a dry twig. The ice-worlder caught the man's body as it slumped forward, felt for the gun, and couldn't find it.

McCade was having trouble too. Still woozy from the earlier beating, and something less than a hundred percent, it was hard to keep his opponent under control.

First she tried to throw him off and, having failed at that, brought her forehead down on the top of his head. Darkness swirled and threatened to roll him under.

The weapon! She'd try to use it. McCade's hands found hers and fought for the gun.

The driver heard the commotion in the back, saw it from the corner of his eye, and stood on the brakes.

As the command car started to slow, the third guard yelled something incomprehensible and looked for an opportunity to fire. With the vehicle skidding, and the bodies swaying to and fro, it would be easy to hit the wrong person.

The driver, a rather ruthless individual known to his friends as Snake, saw the flaw in this approach and said so. "Shoot, you idiot! Shoot *all* of them!"

Unfortunately for Snake, the third guard wasted precious seconds analyzing the order and understanding the logic behind it.

So, by the time the guard had made the decision to obey and had started to squeeze the trigger. Phil had located the second guard's gun and freed it. There was no time to bring the weapon up, align it with the third guard's face, and fire, so the variant did the only thing he could. He pointed the gun toward the front of the vehicle and squeezed the trigger.

The weapon made a dull thumping sound as the slugs ripped through the second guard's already dead body, the thin partition behind it, and hit guard number three in the abdomen.

Guard number three looked surprised. Something hurt. What the hell was going on? Then he toppled over and crashed into Snake just as he brought the command car to a complete stop.

Meanwhile, with the gun trapped between them, McCade and guard number one were still struggling for control. She had wiry little fingers and they moved in and around McCade's to pull the trigger.

McCade felt the weapon jerk under his hand and felt the impact of a slug punching its way through his left arm. Damn! McCade twisted the gun barrel in what he hoped was the right direction and felt the weapon go off again.

The woman stiffened, tried to say something, and slumped sideways.

Phil swore as Snake bailed out of the driver's side door, slipped, fell, and got up running.

The variant flexed massive muscles, snapped the durasteel chains on cuffs and leg irons, and tried the door. It was locked and the handle came off in his paw.

It took a moment to find the key card in guard number two's pocket, slide it into the proper recess, and push the door open. Once outside Phil saw that the driver had a huge head start. A really well-aimed shot might bring him down, but why bother? They were free, and that was the important thing.

Now, with the adrenaline draining away, McCade's arm was starting to hurt and he felt dizzy. He tried the door and found it was locked. He was just getting ready to search for a key card when Phil pulled it open from the outside.

McCade swayed and Phil grabbed him. There was blood all over the place. "Whoa, Sam, you took one through the arm. Sit down and keep some pressure on it while I look for a first-aid kit."

McCade did as he was told and felt a little better. His arm still hurt but the dizziness began to fade. He heard a flight of aerospace fighters scream by overhead.

The restraints fell away at the touch of the electronic key that Phil had retrieved from guard number one's pocket. McCade rubbed his left wrist where the handcuffs had chaffed his skin.

Phil found a well-stocked first-aid kit under the driver's seat, cut McCade's sleeve off, and examined the wound. The bullet had passed through the fleshy part of the bicep and missed the bone. Both the entry and exit wounds were reasonably small.

The variant cleaned both holes, ignored the things McCade said when he poured half a bottle of antiseptic over them, and used butterfly strips for closure. The strips weren't as good as sutures but were better than nothing.

After that it was a simple matter to apply self-sealing dressings, bind them in place with gauze, and slap an injector against McCade's good arm. The bounty hunter couldn't feel the antibiotics going to work, but the pain killers made a big difference, giving McCade a warm fuzzy glow. He stood up and rotated his left arm.

"Good work, Phil, I feel good as new."

"Well, you aren't," the variant replied sternly, "so don't get carried away. You could do a lot of damage to that arm."

McCade nodded absently as he fumbled around for a cigar and eyed the horizon. They were exposed as hell, sitting right in the middle of the open desert, only miles from Pong's HQ. The camp was a clearly visible smudge from which a variety of aircraft came and went on their various errands. A makeshift spaceport sat slightly to the south, clearly marked by fingers of flame as ships landed and took off.

McCade found a cigar butt and lit it. The words came out with puffs of smoke. "Phil, we need to tidy up. Take what we need, lose the bodies, get our act together. We'd look real suspicious to a patrol or a recon drone."

The variant nodded, as if expecting something of the sort. "And then?"

McCade's eyes narrowed. "You heard him, Phil. The bastard has Molly. You can do whatever you want . . . but I'm going after her."

Phil snarled. "You mean *we're* going after her. I'm her godfather remember?"

McCade nodded soberly. "I remember. But the odds aren't very good. You've done more than your share already."

Phil gave a disapproving snort. "What a lot of bull. Let's clean up. We've got work to do."

Two hours later the command car rumbled up to the outermost checkpoint and came to a stop. The spaceport was a temporary affair, little more than fused sand and a collection of prefab buildings.

It boasted some impressive defenses though, at least three rings of them, and the checkpoint was the first. It was little more than a break in the huge antitank ditch that surrounded the complex. A ditch that had been sown with mines, was preregistered with Pong's computer-controlled artillery, and could be flooded with burning fuel.

The corporal was reluctant to step out from under the square of plastic that protected her from Drang's sun. She bent over to look in the driver's side window and eyed the tabs pinned to McCade's collar. The bounty hunter had ripped his right sleeve off to match his left, a practice that was nonreg, but winked at in Drang's heat. He figured the battle dressing was safe enough this close to the front. A transport rumbled into the sky behind her. She waited for the noise to drop off. "Good afternoon, sir. Can I have your pass please?"

McCade smiled reassuringly. "Of course. Here it is."

So saying McCade gave her the plastic card that they'd recovered from guard number three's body. Phil had seen him use it as the command car made its way out of the main compound two miles to the north. With any luck at all the card, and the password that went with it, would work here as well. Their plan depended on it.

But what if the spaceport used different codes? Or the driver had warned Pong's MPs? Or a million other possibilities?

The sentry smiled politely. "Thank you, sir. I'll be back in a moment."

As the woman walked toward her rectangle of shade, and the computer terminal that rested there, McCade eyed the boxy-looking vehicle that sat a few yards away. He could hear the hum of its auxiliary generator and found himself staring into all four of its automatic cannons. Just one word from the sentry and those black holes would burp sudden death. Within seconds he and Phil would become little more than meat frying on what had been a command car.

"Sir?"

McCade jumped. The sentry had approached from his side this time. She handed his card through the open window. "You're cleared all the way through. Today's password?"

"Trident."

"Thank you, sir. Have a nice day."

McCade croaked something appropriate, and for the first time noticed how pretty she was.

The vehicle jerked as Phil stepped on the gas, then rolled through the checkpoint, and roared toward the next checkpoint.

Though even more formidable than the antitank ditch, the second and third lines of defense were even easier to pass through, since they'd already cleared the computer checkpoint.

In each case Phil simply slowed down, growled the password, and was waved through. In fact, the worst danger came from the hover truck convoys that were headed in the opposite direction. The trucks were heavily loaded with supplies and highballing for the front more than ninety miles away.

They took up two thirds of the gravel road and their fans stirred up miniature dust storms that peppered the command car's windshield with flying debris. The dust made it hard to see, and by way of adding insult to injury, the drivers took great pleasure in hitting their air horns.

McCade breathed a sigh of relief as the command car rolled off the access road and into a large parking area. Another convoy was forming up and a small army of specialized robots was whirring back and forth as they loaded the last few trucks. They looked strange in their desert camouflage, like huge insects, gathering food for their nest.

The combined noise of hover truck engines, auto loaders, and spaceships was almost deafening.

In the middle of all this, striding about on a stiltlike walker, was a stocky-looking officer. His face was concealed by a bulbous command helmet. From the way the officer moved, and the robots scurried around him, he was obviously in command.

McCade was still debating the merits of asking the man for information when the decision was made for him. The officer took two giant steps and blocked their way. His voice boomed out of twin loudspeakers mounted on the exoskeleton's ten-foot-long metal thigh bones. Noisy though the area was he had no difficulty in making himself heard.

"Hey, you in the command car! What the hell are you doing in the middle of my loading zone?"

Based on the officer's belligerent tone, McCade assumed he carried lots of rank, or was some kind of a mean S.O.B. It seemed like a good idea to humor him either way.

McCade triggered the command car's PA system. "Sorry, sir . . . we've got an important package for General Pong. Could you direct us to his ship?"

A beam of red light shot out from the walker to touch a distant ship. McCade did a quick count and found it was sixth in a row of eight. The light vanished.

"You see that?"

"Yes, sir."

"That's the general's ship. Now get the hell out of my way before I load your car on a truck and send it to the front."

"Yes, sir."

Phil tromped on the gas, swerved around a train of power pallets, and scooted onto the burn-blackened surface of the spaceport itself. Here there was even more activity as maintenance crews swarmed over ships, robotic fuel hoses snaked their way between pieces of equipment, and ground vehicles dashed in every direction.

McCade hoped the hustle and bustle would help cover their activities.

They passed ship after ship, boxy-looking freighters for the most part, until Pong's lay just ahead. It looked like a greyhound sitting among mongrels. Slim and obviously fast it crouched low on its landing jacks as if ready to leap off the ground at any moment. The main lock was open and a short set of metal stairs reached down to touch the ground.

Seeing the command car, and assuming it contained at least one officer, the single sentry popped to attention and delivered a rifle salute. He wore light armor, a combat helmet with the visor pushed back, and looked very warm. The sun was blistering hot, and the heat radiated off the surrounding ships, plus that reflected off the surface of the landing pad itself, made things even worse. Sweat rolled off the sentry's farm-boy face.

The command car screeched to a halt and McCade jumped out as if in a big hurry. The sentry knew his lines. "Sir, this is a class-three restricted vessel. Please present your class-three authorization code."

McCade summoned an officer-type frown. "At ease, Private. Tell me, is the general aboard?"

"No, sir," the sentry answered uneasily, "but he's due soon."

Good! McCade felt downright jubilant. Things were definitely looking up. The sentry was their only remaining obstacle.

McCade smiled disarmingly. "Excellent. I made it just in time. I have an important message for the general's pilot. Is the pilot aboard?"

The sentry remembered the somewhat arrogant cyborg who'd gone aboard earlier and shuddered. He didn't like cyborgs. "Yes, sir, the pilot's aboard, sir, but no one goes aboard without the correct code."

McCade nodded understandingly. "Of course, but this is an emergency. Why don't *you* go aboard, tell the pilot I need to see him, and enjoy some of that nice cool air-conditioning? That way you obey orders, I get the message through, and there's no harm done. I'll stand guard in the meantime."

The sentry's face worked along with his thoughts. This was a difficult situation. This was a captain and therefore a deity. The private didn't wish to offend such a lofty being. But lofty or not, the captain was minus the necessary code, and other even higher gods must be taken into consideration. Their commands left no room for doubt. What about the captain's proposal? Surely that was permissible.

The sentry would enter the ship, careful to enjoy the air-conditioning for as long as possible, and find the pilot. The pilot would emerge, get the emergency message, and everything would be fine.

The sentry grinned. "That should be fine, sir. Shall I leave my blast rifle with you?"

McCade peered at the name embroidered just above the sentry's left-hand breast pocket. "Good idea, Platz. That way I'll have something a little more potent than my side arm in case there's trouble."

Platz looked worried and McCade realized his mistake. "Not that there will be any trouble, mind you." McCade waved toward their surroundings just as a Destroyer Escort roared into the sky. "I mean what could go wrong in the middle of all this?"

Platz looked relieved as he removed his helmet, placed it on the stairs, and handed McCade his blast rifle. "There you go, sir . . . I'll be right back."

The sentry's boots made a clanging sound as he climbed the metal stairs.

McCade looked at the command car and nodded toward the hatch.

Phil slipped out of the vehicle, winked at McCade as he started up the stairs, and disappeared into the lock.

McCade did his best to look sentrylike as he surveyed his surroundings. So far so good. The nearest ship was a reentry-scarred freighter. A group of techs were busily relining a tube with help from a sturdy-looking robot. They were completely uninterested in McCade's activities.

But then, just as McCade turned back toward the ship, he saw movement on the northern perimeter of the spaceport. It was a command car, newer then his, and flying some sort of pennant from a long whip-style antenna. The car was moving like a bat out of hell and heading straight at him. It didn't take a genius to figure out who was in it. Mustapha Pong himself!

In spite of Drang's oppressive heat McCade felt suddenly cold. What to do? He couldn't run, not with Phil trapped inside, and he couldn't just stand there either.

McCade heard a burst of static followed by some unintelligible gabble. The sentry's helmet! They were calling Platz and warning him of Pong's arrival. And unless they got some sort of answer, and got it real soon, all hell would break loose!

McCade picked up the helmet, slipped it over his head, and pulled the visor down. The mirrorlike surface would cut the glare and would make him faceless besides. A female voice blasted both ears. "Platz! Wake up, you idiot! The general's on the way."

McCade chinned the radio on. "I read you. The general's on the way. Sorry . . . I had my helmet off for a moment."

"Yeah?" The voice came back, "Well, keep the damned thing on. You okay, Platz? You sound different."

"Just the heat I guess," McCade mumbled. "I'll be fine."

"If you say so," the woman replied doubtfully. "I'll bring you something to drink when I make my rounds. Take a salt tablet."

The radio clicked off and McCade snapped to attention. All he could do was pray that Pong didn't notice his officer's tabs, or try to speak with him.

The command car came to a dignified halt. Pong got out, said something inaudible to the driver, and hurried toward the lock. The Melcetian didn't like direct sunlight and urged him on. Pong didn't even give McCade a second glance as he made his way up the stairs and disappeared into the lock. The moment Pong was gone the command car pulled away and headed toward one of the spaceport's prefab buildings.

McCade took one last look around to make sure no one was watching, slipped up the stairs, and entered the lock. It was well lit and, outside of some racked space suits, completely empty. Good. McCade palmed the control panel and heard the outer door close behind him.

As he waited for the inner hatch to open, McCade removed the helmet, put it on a bench, and drew his slug gun. It had been the property of guard number one and it felt good in his hand.

The inner hatch whirred open allowing a blast of cool air to fill the lock. Trying not to expose any more of his body than was absolutely necessary, McCade peeked into a long, narrow corridor and found himself looking straight down the barrel of a gun. A big gun in a furry paw. McCade gave a sigh of relief and stepped out of the lock.

"What are you trying to do? Give me a heart attack?"

Phil held a massive finger up to his muzzle and jerked his head toward the ship's bow. McCade nodded and followed along behind as the variant moved up the corridor.

Suddenly Phil paused, held up an enormous paw, and opened a door. McCade looked inside. Instead of the emergency equipment the locker was supposed to contain there was Platz, bound, gagged, and trying to signal McCade with his eyes.

McCade smiled, winked, and closed the door. Thanks to Phil, the sentry was safely out of the way.

From there the two of them eased their way up the corridor and paused outside the hatch marked Control Compartment. Pong was clearly visible. He and a humanoid-shaped cyborg were busy reviewing some date on the ship's navcomp.

McCade took one last look around, verified that no one was in sight, and got a nod from Phil. The variant had checked, and outside of the cyborg and Pong, they had the ship to themselves.

McCade stepped into the control compartment and cleared his throat.
Pong turned, clearly startled.

McCade pointed his gun at the pirate's chest and smiled. "Remember me? Surprise!"

TWENTY-SIX

Molly squirmed her way to the top of a low rise and peered through low-lying vegetation. A small valley was spread out in front of her, the same one she'd seen before, but from the opposite side. Although the light was dim Molly could see the gathering of boulders where the black thing lived, the hill where the strange-looking trees grew, and a small discontinuity that could be the lock. Molly was too far away to be absolutely sure.

"I'm hungry," Eva whined from beside her. "When do we eat?"

The question was unfair and made Molly angry. She forced the anger down. Leaders who squelch stupid questions suppress intelligent ones as well. At least that's what Mommy said. Molly tried to keep her voice even and calm. "We'll eat when we find food."

Eva didn't say anything but her discontent was obvious. Remembering field trips in school, Molly had asked the girls to pick buddies and spread out. If a member of the 56,827 showed up, they had orders to run in different directions and meet back at the lock. At least some of them would survive and the buddy system would help them deal with whatever dangers they encountered.

The plan had a flaw however. After everyone had chosen their buddies, and registered their choices with Molly, Eva was left over. Which meant that Molly was stuck with her. Still another benefit of leadership.

Molly scanned the valley again. She'd chosen this position because it was away from the lock but not too far away. Until such time as she could make contact with the runner named Jareth, or another of his race, Molly had no way to navigate. The lock represented a reference point and their only chance of escape.

Eva began to say something just as Molly saw movement. She held a finger to her lips and shook her head. What was it? Jareth? One of the 56,827?

The answer came with blinding speed. Jareth, or another just like him, emerged from some tall grass and ran. He, she, or it was extremely fast. No wonder they referred to themselves as "runners."

But if the runner was fast, so was the horrible-looking thing that followed, and it was closing the gap with a series of tremendous leaps.

The runner changed direction, angled off to one side, and headed for the protection of a thicket. But there were low-lying rocks barring the way and tall grass slowed it down, so the pursuing alien drew even closer. There was no doubt about the outcome anymore. 47,721, or one of its brethren, was going to win.

That's when the runner did something strange. It stopped, turned, and waited for death to come. And come it did, with such unrelenting violence that Molly couldn't watch. Her eyes met Eva's.

"Did you see that?"

Eva's eyes were big as saucers. She nodded slowly.

"Good. That's what I've been warning you about. That's what they look like without a cloak. Get the others. Bring them up here in pairs. I want them to see what we're up against."

Eva did as she was told, running down the slope and notifying the nearest pair of girls. They laughed, giggled, and gave Molly curious looks as they followed Eva up the slope, crawling the last few yards. Then they looked, gasped with horror, and ran down the hill. Some were crying and others looked like they wanted to throw up.

Molly didn't blame them. By now the creature the runners referred to as "death" was consuming its prey.

Molly remembered the way the runner had stopped and turned toward certain death. She knew hardly anything about the runners, but that single action spoke volumes. It communicated intelligence, bravery, and a tremendous dignity. She would remember it for the rest of her life, short though that might be.

When the last pair of girls had returned from the top of the slope Molly convened a council of war. The dim sunlight had almost disappeared, suggesting that a period of complete darkness was about to begin. The girls were tired, hungry, and scared. But their attitude toward Molly had undergone a radical change. When Molly spoke they listened.

"All right. You've seen what we're up against. The 56,827 use the runners for both crew and food. There's little doubt what they have in mind for us. Our only chance is to get help from the runners. If you see a runner, an alien that looks different from the one you saw aboard ship, let me know right away."

Molly looked around. She could practically hear what they were thinking. Since the aliens eat sentients, and number 47,721 took Niki, Karen, and Suki away, did that mean what they thought it meant?

Molly swallowed hard. "I know you're hungry, but the artificial sun's going down, and there isn't much we can do until it comes back up. Blundering around in the dark could be extremely dangerous. Stay with your buddy and get some sleep. Four of us will be awake at all times. Does anyone have a watch?"

There was silence for a moment, then a girl named Linda spoke up. "Sasha does . . . she stole it aboard ship."

Sasha had dark hair and flashing black eyes. She started to deny it but Molly held up a hand. "Good going, Sasha. You and Carla take the first watch along with Eva and myself. We'll wake the next group in three hours. Any questions? No? Okay, let's get some sleep."

The night passed slowly. It was quiet for the most part, with only occasional stirrings by unseen animals, and the usual absence of wind. Once, about halfway through Molly's watch, it rained. It was warm and felt good.

The rain stopped fifteen minutes later just as suddenly as it had begun. Molly wondered if it rained at the same time every night. She suspected that it did.

Finally it was Molly's turn to sleep but she found that difficult to do. There were so many things to worry about, so many people depending on her, and so many things to go wrong.

Molly remembered her mother's parting words. "Never give up hope. No matter where they take you, no matter how long it takes, Daddy will come.

He'll hunt them clear across the universe if that's what it takes. Be ready There'll be trouble when Daddy comes, and he'll need your help."

But Molly had survived so much, and waited for so long, that rescue didn't seem possible anymore. If Daddy were coming, surely he'd be here by now. Maybe he was dead and Mommy too. There was no way to know.

Eva was sound asleep, sucking her thumb. Molly raised her head and took a quick look around. There was no one close enough to hear so she allowed herself to cry.

Deep sobs racked her body, until the need for them had passed, and then, as Molly wiped her face with a shirtsleeve, she found that one of Eva's chubby little arms had found its way around her middle. The other girl didn't say anything, but she'd heard, and was offering what little comfort she could.

It felt warmer with Eva snuggled up beside her and Molly fell asleep.

Molly awoke to a feather-light touch. With it came awareness of where she was and her eyes flew open. Alien eyes stared at her from only inches away. Molly started to push herself away but stopped when she realized who and what it was. The alien was seated next to her and wore a complicated vest.

"Jareth? Is that you?"

The triangular head moved slightly. "Yes, it is I."

"Do you remember me?"

"Of course. That is why I approached you rather than one of the others."

The others. Molly got up on her knees to look around. It was lighter now, and although some of the girls were up and around, none seemed aware of Jareth.

He seemed to read her thoughts. "Do not be angry with them. They kept watch as well as they know how. This is, how do you say it, my 'home,' and I am good at hiding."

Jareth dangled something from bony fingers. It took Molly a moment to recognize what it was. The L-band! Her fingers flew to her head, and sure enough, the explosive device was gone.

"I hope you do not mind," Jareth said apologetically. "But this is a dangerous device, and should not be worn around your head."

"No," Molly replied gratefully, "I'm happy to get it off. How did you know it was dangerous?"

Jareth blinked. "I knew."

Molly tried another approach. "How did you disarm it. Wasn't that dangerous?"

The alien made a sign. "Not very damned likely."

He reached into one of his multitudinous pockets and pulled out a tiny box. "This produced an electronic signal that entered the trigger mechanism, neutralized it, and withdrew."

"Thank you," Molly said solemnly. "It might've killed me."

"Death is bad," Jareth agreed evenly.

Molly thought of the other runner, the one who'd been eaten. "I . . . we . . . saw a member of the 56,827 chase one of your people."

Jareth made some sort of a sign with his left hand. "Yes. That was Mizlam. It was her turn to die."

Molly frowned. "Her turn to die? What does that mean?"

Jareth cocked his head to one side. "Did I say it improperly? I meant that others have died in the past and this was Mizlam's turn."

Molly had forgotten how frustrating Jareth could be. "So you take turns dying?"

"Yes," the alien replied. "Oldest first, youngest last. Izliak is next, followed by Threma, followed by Dorlia."

Molly searched the alien's face. It bore the same expression. "Why? Why do you take turns?"

Jareth made a complicated gesture with his left hand. "Because it is fair."

Molly remembered how Mizlam had died, turning to face death, meeting it with dignity. She shook her head in amazement. "I admire you and your people, Jareth. You are strong and brave."

When Jareth blinked, Molly saw that his eyelids were almost transparent. "Thank you."

Molly gestured to the surrounding area. "Can you help us?"

"I will try," Jareth replied. "What do you need?"

Molly sat up and wrapped her arms around her knees. "We need water, something to eat, and a way to defend ourselves from the 56,827."

Jareth seemed to consider her request. "Water is easy, and the food also, if you can eat what we do. I cannot satisfy your last request however. There is no defense against death."

Molly searched the runner's face and found no information in the alien features. "Jareth, I don't understand. Your people built this ship, you run it, surely you have a knowledge of weapons."

Jareth made a hand sign. "The knowledge yes. This entire ship is a weapon. A weapon so powerful it can destroy entire planets. But we cannot operate such weapons."

"Can't? Or won't?"

Jareth blinked. "There is no difference. We cannot, and we will not use such weapons. Our ancestors rose to sentience by running faster, thinking better, and organizing more effectively than their enemies. We are and always have been vegetarians. We have no experience at killing things. More than that we have a—how do you say?—a revulsion? A dislike for violence which prevents us from using it on others. Killing isn't fair."

Although Molly had read about pacifists in school, she'd been exposed to violence all her life and couldn't imagine doing what she'd seen Mizlam do. All of her training, all of her experience, suggested that the runner should've fought to the death no matter how hopeless that might be. Molly respected the runners, and their beliefs, but was personally unwilling to give up her life without a struggle. She frowned.

"I understand, Jareth, but our races are different, and humans *are* willing to use violence. Most of them anyway. Is there anything that prevents you from giving us weapons?"

Jareth cocked his head to the other side. "Weapons? Are you and your companions old enough to use them?"

Molly grinned. "On the planet I come from everybody's old enough to use them. We have no choice."

Jareth wiggled his fingers. "What kind of weapons?"

Molly shrugged. "Small stuff, you know, slug guns and blasters."

"Slug guns? Blasters? What are those?"

"Small hand-held projectile and energy weapons."

Jareth blinked. "I have no personal knowledge of such weapons but will ask the others. There is water nearby, I will show you where and bring you food."

Molly nodded solemnly. "Thank you, Jareth. And there is something else as well."

"Yes?"

"The 56,827 took three of our kind. They are somewhere aboard ship. Could you help us find them?"

Jareth stood, causing some of the girls to scatter. "We will try. But remember, little one, if they are alive, it is for a short time only."

Molly nodded. She understood all too well.

TWENTY-SEVEN

McCade felt better and worse than he had in a long time. Better, because he was closing in on Molly, and worse, because the medication had begun to wear off, he was tired, and his arm had started to throb.

McCade forced the fatigue aside and squinted through a haze of his own cigar smoke. Drang was a brownish ball that filled half of the main screen, and there, miles ahead, light winked off Pong's flagship.

In fifteen minutes, twenty at most, they'd be aboard. McCade imagined Molly rushing into his arms and tightened his grip on the blaster he'd taken from Pong's arms locker. Sol help anyone who got in his way.

The control room was comfortable to the point of being luxurious. There was the soft glow of instrument lights, the steady hiss of air through carefully located vents, and the comfort of the leather acceleration couches. A rather pleasant compartment except for the tension that filled the air.

The cyborg occupied the pilot's position, her plastiflesh face completely impassive as she conned the ship, her metal-ceramic composite fingers dancing over the keys.

And beside her, with weapon drawn and fangs showing, sat Phil. The variant watched the pilot the way a cat watches a mouse, conscious of her slightest move, ready to pounce if she tried to escape.

The com set buzzed softly. The cyborg looked at Phil. The variant nodded. She pushed a button. A male voice flooded the compartment.

"CF warship LC4621 to approaching vessel. Provide today's recognition code or be fired on."

The cyborg glanced over her shoulder at Pong. The pirate looked at McCade, the bounty hunter nodded his permission, and the pilot pressed a key. Then she read off a series of numbers and touched another key.

There was silence for a moment followed by the male voice. "Acknowledged. Out."

McCade made a note of the abrupt tone. The shuttle had lifted in something of a hurry, and a whole barrage of inquiries had followed them into space, making it clear that Pong's staff knew something was amiss. The dead guards, the missing sentry, and the massive violation of lift protocols had made sure of that.

Yes, a reception committee would be waiting aboard Pong's ship, but with the pirate as a hostage, McCade thought he could handle it. Would *have* to handle it.

Pong sat on McCade's right just behind Phil. The pirate was uncharacteristically silent. The reason was simple. Pong was scared for the first time in years.

It was McCade's eyes that frightened him the most. They were like cold, hard stones. He saw no weakness there, no sign of the greed, fear, and lust for power that Pong usually saw in others, or in himself for that matter. No, this man could not be bought, intimidated, or tempted.

Pong wondered if he was going to die. He directed a thought toward the Melcetian.

"Well? I notice you missed this development. What do you suggest we do now?"

The mind slug had oozed its way toward Pong's right shoulder, gradually putting more and more of the pirate's body between itself and danger, already plotting what to do if its present host was to die. The alien's reply was caustic.

"First of all, I believe it was *you* who insisted on raiding this man's pathetic planet for reasons of revenge, and *you* who insisted on turning his offspring into some sort of personal mascot. So, if you wish to place responsibility, look no further than yourself.

"As for what to do now, well that seems quite simple. I suggest that you give this man what he wants as quickly as you can. Why sacrifice all of your hopes, all of your ambitions, to the rather understandable desire of a father to rescue his child?"

Pong thought it over. In the strictly logical sense the Melcetian was correct. He should use the girl to buy his way out, allow them to escape, and forget the whole thing. There were worlds, nay, an entire universe to conquer. Why let this get in the way?

The answer was pride, and more than that emotion, things the Melcetian knew very little about. Yes, he'd look like a fool if he allowed McCade to take Molly away, but worse than that, he'd lose something he treasured. Molly herself. She was more than a good-luck charm.

Molly was the one person Pong could rely on to say what she thought, to be herself, to accept him as he was. And because Molly was a child there was no need to worry about her true motives, her allies, or her ambitions.

Pong knew she didn't like him all that much but so what? Affection would come with time. No, logic or no logic, Pong wasn't ready to surrender Molly to her father. Not yet anyway.

McCade watched Pong's flagship grow steadily larger until it ran off the edges of the screen. What had been little more than a white dot, had slowly transformed itself into a rectangle, and then into a large hatch. He could see the gleaming deck within, a variety of smaller spacecraft, and the stutter of alignment beams.

The cyborg fired the ship's retros, and McCade felt the shuttle slow as three delta-shaped fighters arrowed out of the larger vessel's bay and accelerated away. Then, with a tiny increment of thrust from the main drive, the pilot moved them forward.

McCade admired her touch. The *Arrow* seemed to float inside the launching bay, where the retros slowed her again, and the ship settled gently toward the durasteel deck. It touched with an almost-imperceptible bump.

Outside the shuttle a huge pair of external doors slid steadily closed. McCade watched them on two of the control compartment's smaller vid screens. When the bay was sealed Pong's crew would pump an atmosphere into the bay allowing the shuttle's passengers to disembark without space armor. A routine courtesy extended to Pong? Or part of a trap? McCade grinned. The second possibility seemed the most likely. Once the doors were closed the shuttle would be immobilized. The time had come to make some preparations.

Thirty minutes passed before McCade was ready to leave the *Arrow*. During that time the bay was pressurized and fifty or so heavily armed crew members had taken up positions around the shuttle. They wore reflective armor and looked like toy soldiers.

Raz stood in front of them, chest almost bare to the frigid air, his face expressionless as the lock whined open. He had snipers stationed at various points around the hangar. They'd kill the bounty hunter and his furry friend the moment they emerged.

There was a gasp of surprise as Mustapha Pong stepped out. He had gray repair tape wound around his head, and more than that, something taped to his left temple. A blaster! A blaster bound to the bounty hunter's right hand by a ball of tape! Even if the sharpshooters managed to kill McCade before his brain sent a message to his right index finger, the weight of his falling body would apply pressure to the firing stud and send a bolt of energy straight through Pong's head.

Raz brought a small radio up to his lips. "Don't fire! I repeat, don't fire!"

All over the bay fingers came off firing studs and weapons were lowered.

Seeing this McCade gave an internal sigh of relief. He felt the tension ease a little. So far so good. Now for the next step. His voice carried well within the open bay.

"Hi there, everybody . . . let's keep this nice and simple. You've got some children aboard, slaves taken from a planet called Alice. I want them, and I want them now."

McCade pushed the blaster against Pong's head. "How 'bout it, Mustapha? Got anything to add?"

The pirate glared at McCade and turned his attention to Raz. The bounty hunter's blaster left Pong with very little choice. "Do as he says. Bring the girls here. Be sure to include the one called Molly."

Raz nodded stiffly, started to turn, and stopped when a petty officer touched his arm. There was conversation. Raz turned back. "I'm told the girls were taken off-ship, sir, on *your* orders."

"He's right," the Melcetian reminded Pong, "you gave them to 47,721."

Now Pong remembered. He'd given the alien some of the snotty-nosed kids . . . but not Molly. He'd never agree to that. Someone had gone into his quarters and taken her! Anger sent blood pounding through Pong's veins.

"Find the person or persons who put the children aboard the shuttle! Bring them here!"

McCade felt something heavy fall into his stomach. Taken away? Shuttle? He'd missed her again? When would it end?

Raz nodded. "Yes sir." He said something into his radio and four guards jogged toward the nearest lock.

There was movement to McCade's right and a flash of light. Someone screamed and a body fell. Phil's voice boomed through one of the shuttle's external speakers.

"Stay where you are. As you can see, the secondary lock is well protected, and there's no point in getting killed."

And they *had* seen. Smoke drifted up and away from the crumpled body. Nobody moved.

Eight extremely long minutes passed before the guards returned. They dragged a man and woman between them. The woman was crying, begging for mercy, and doing her best to blame everything on her companion. The man was silent, looking around, trying to understand.

Then the woman saw Pong, the blaster, and the man with the cold gray eyes. The whimpering stopped as Boots searched for a way out. Pong was in trouble. Could that work in her favor?

Pong ignored the man and focused his attention on Boots. She'd been in charge of the slaves and she'd been punished for allowing Molly access to the Navcomp. A motive perhaps?

Pong's voice was soft and reasonable. "Boots, isn't it?"

Boots nodded, pleased that Pong remembered. Things were looking up.

Pong smiled. "The man with the blaster pointed at my head is looking for the children that were aboard this ship. Did you put them on a shuttle?"

Boots did her best to look innocent. "Yes, sir, I was ordered to, sir."

Pong nodded understandingly. "Of course. Now tell me, Boots, did you have orders to load *all* of the slave girls? Or was there an exception?"

Boots frowned as if trying to remember. This is where it got tricky, but Pong's phraseology, plus his tone, suggested a way out. "I don't remember any exceptions, sir."

"I see," Pong said sympathetically. "And did you happen to remove the slave girl known as Molly from my quarters? And having done so, load her aboard the shuttle along with the others? This man would like to know."

Boots did her best to look rueful. "Yes, sir, now that you mention it, I did, sir, it was my understanding we were to load *all* of the girls."

Pong looked thoughtful and McCade felt silly holding the blaster to his head. Pong had taken control of the situation and it seemed as if their positions ought to be reversed.

"I see," Pong said calmly. "Well, Boots, that's too bad. I left Raz in charge, and if your information is correct, then the whole thing's *his* fault. Tell me, Raz, was it your fault? No? I didn't think so. So here's what I want you to do, Boots. Go get your space armor, suit up, and get the hell off my ship."

"But I'll die!" Boots wailed. "I'll run out of air!"

"Probably," Pong agreed, "but not before you get a good look at Drang. A nice long look. Consider it my little gift."

Boots tried to run but the guards caught and dragged her away.

Unable to turn his head because of the blaster, Pong swiveled his eyes toward McCade. "I know where Molly is. She's in great danger. We could be there in a few hours."

McCade was surprised. Why so cooperative? A trap? Then it hit him. What Pong had said about raising Molly was true! The pirate liked her! More than that, wanted her for himself!

McCade felt a lot of things, jealousy and fear foremost among them. Pong liked Molly. Did she like him? Had she changed? And what about the danger Pong referred to?

Pong cleared his throat. "Time is of the essence, McCade. We need to leave *now*. I suggest that we bring some of my troops."

McCade shook his head. He believed Molly was in trouble, but wasn't about to bring any of Pong's troops. There was no way that he and Phil could control additional people. "No troops. Tell them to clear the bay and open the outer doors."

Pong did as he was told, and the double doors slid open fifteen minutes later. The doors were still in motion when the cyborg took *Arrow* out. Phil ran the sensors at maximum sensitivity but no one followed.

With the tape undone, and everyone back in their former positions, McCade was about to ask Pong some questions when an unexpected hand touched his shoulder. "Coffee, sir?"

McCade spun his chair around to find Platz standing there with a tray of coffee containers. He looked rumpled but otherwise no worse for wear.

Phil grinned. "Platz is out on good behavior. It was a bit cramped in that storage compartment."

McCade nodded and accepted a container of coffee. "Thank you, Platz. Sorry about this, but you were in the wrong place at the wrong time."

Platz shrugged and offered Pong some coffee. It was sealed in a zero-G bulb making it useless as a weapon. "That's okay, sir. Phil explained what's going on, and I hope you find your daughter."

McCade smiled and turned toward Pong. "Which brings us to you. Where's Molly? And what sort of danger is she in?"

Pong didn't hesitate. He told McCade about the 56,827, their ship, and their so-called death experiments. It was true that 56,827 were his secret weapon, but he couldn't save Molly without admitting their existence. If things went the way he hoped, McCade would die aboard the alien ship, and if they didn't, well, those were the breaks.

The Melcetian listened but made no attempt to interfere. The alien had computed all of the most likely outcomes, and while it still had hopes for Pong, was ready to find itself a new host if necessary. Number 47,721 might make a good candidate. Disgusting, but completely ruthless, and sufficiently ambitious. Yes, the best plan was to lie low, and see where the advantage lay.

As the bounty hunter listened to Pong's description of the 56,827, their planetoid-sized warship, and his plans to take over all of known space, McCade was more and more amazed. Not only did the pirate propose murder on a scale hitherto unknown, he did it with the calm, measured prose of a businessman describing plans to enter a new market, or an architect discussing his latest design.

If not actually insane Pong was the next closest thing to it. It showed in Pong's total selfishness, his complete lack of empathy for others, his inability to see them as anything more than pieces in some elaborate game.

Although the pirate liked Molly, and was clearly determined to save her, the other girls meant nothing at all. Only Molly had something to offer Pong personally, so only she was real.

Although McCade had encountered a large number of sociopaths during his days as a bounty hunter, Pong was the worst by far. Still, if he wanted to save Molly, he'd need more information and that meant playing along.

"It's an amazing plan, Mustapha, and if anyone could pull it off, you could. There's something I don't understand though. If you want to help Molly, and these aliens are friends of yours, why is she in danger?"

For the first time during their conversation Pong looked slightly embarrassed. He cleared his throat. "Well, I don't approve mind you, but the 56,827 have some rather unpleasant ways. For one thing they insist on performing what they call 'death experiments' on a representative sample of the sentients they plan to fight, and for another, they are rather actively carnivorous."

It took McCade a moment to decode the last part of Pong's statement, and when he did, the bounty hunter was incredulous. "'Death experiments'? 'Actively carnivorous'? Does that mean what I think it does?"

Pong refused to meet McCade's eyes. "Yes, I'm afraid it does."

McCade's eyes narrowed as he leaned forward, his hands working in and out of fists, only inches away from killing Pong then and there. "You mean you took little girls, Molly included, and handed them over to be tortured? Or eaten? Or both?"

Phil growled, a long, low rumble that made Pong's blood run cold, and Platz gave an involuntary gasp of surprise.

Pong knew death was extremely close. He also knew that McCade wanted some sign of sorrow, of contrition, so he provided it. "I'm sorry, I really am, and I tried to protect Molly. Things went wrong, that's all. It wasn't my fault."

Only the need to get aboard the alien ship and find the children kept McCade from wrapping his fingers around Pong's throat and choking the life out of him. McCade forced himself to lean back in his seat. His eyes were little more than slits and his hands shook with suppressed rage. Once they reached the alien ship, once the children were safe, Pong would pay for the things he'd done. And if they arrived too late, if . . . McCade forced the thought away. Silence fell on the control compartment and time slowed to a virtual crawl.

TWENTY-EIGHT

McCade and Phil stood watches, two hours on, and two hours off. When he wasn't on duty McCade slept and, in spite of his bone-deep fatigue, dreamt of monsters that ate little girls.

But the rest did him good, and that, along with another round of medication from Pong's well-stocked first-aid kit, put him in reasonable shape by the time the alien ship filled the screens. He was surprised by the ease with which the *Arrow* was permitted to approach and enter the larger vessel's bay.

Pong shrugged. "The 56,827 have a simple policy. Admit the *Arrow* and destroy anything else."

McCade thought about what life would be like under such rulers and shuddered. It reminded him of the larger problem. Even if they found the children, and managed to neutralize these aliens, there was the rest of them to worry about. But first things first.

McCade spent the next twenty minutes quizzing Pong about the 56,827, the interior of their ship, and anything else he could think of. Good intelligence is absolutely critical when you're forced to fight on enemy ground.

By the time the shuttle landed inside the bay McCade and Phil had added blast rifles to their already extensive armament, agreed to let Platz come along on the condition that he was unarmed, and rigged up some leg shackles that would slow Pong down should he attempt to run.

When the ship was secure, they wasted little time locking the cyborg in the head and cycling out into the bay.

There was no sign of the 56,827, or the children either, so they headed for the ship's lock. It was already open. McCade stepped inside, found it empty, and motioned for the rest to follow. They did and the hatch closed behind them.

McCade lit a cigar and blew smoke toward the inner hatch. Pong stared straight ahead, face impassive, mind churning through his options.

Phil smelled something foul, something he'd never encountered before, and allowed his lip to curl away from durasteel fangs. A growl came from deep inside his massive body.

The Melcetian shimmered, throwing light in every direction as it repositioned itself on Pong's shoulder, and monitored the human's thoughts.

Platz looked around as if seeing a lock for the first time, saw a comb lying on the deck, and bent to pick it up. But there was some kind of goo on it so he let it lay.

The hatch whirred open and McCade stepped through. He held his blast rifle up and ready to fire, but saw nothing more threatening than a dim lavender sky and an alien landscape. There were rocks, strange foliage, and some distant trees. Or things that *looked* like trees anyway. The others followed.

McCade was just about to ask Pong where the dirt path led when there was a stirring in some nearby bushes and the sound of a hesitant voice.

"Citizen McCade? Is that you?"

McCade's heart leaped into his throat. "Yes! Who's there?"

"We are," the voice answered, and one by one a group of bedraggled little girls emerged from the bushes. McCade inventoried each dirt-smudged face until a small group stood in front of him and Molly was nowhere to be seen. McCade bit his lip. He recognized some of the children but not all.

The girls looked from McCade to Phil and back again. The same one, a girl named Linda if he remembered correctly, spoke again. "Is it really you? You came for us?" Her upper lip trembled.

McCade managed a smile. He wasn't sure, but he thought that Linda's father was dead, buried below the permafrost on Alice. A tear ran down his cheek. McCade got down on one knee. He bit back the desire to ask about Molly and forced himself to wait. "Yes, it's really us, and we came for you."

The girls cried, threw themselves at McCade and Phil, and bombarded them with questions. "Is my mommy all right? Did you find my brother? Can we go home now?"

Platz beamed and Pong whistled through his teeth. Finally, when the pirate couldn't take it anymore, he said, "Save it for later, McCade . . . where's Molly?"

McCade peeled two little girls away from his chest and held a finger to his lips. "He's right. There'll be lots of time to celebrate. Where *is* Molly? Are there any others?"

The story spilled out in fits and starts, first from one girl, then from another, until McCade had the whole picture. It seemed three of the girls had been taken away by one of the 56,827, presumably for the "death experiments" Pong had mentioned, and Molly, with help from a friendly alien called Jareth, had gone after them.

And then, about three hours after Molly's departure, another member of the 56,827 had swung through the area. Hunting, exercising, the girls weren't sure what. But they had orders to scatter and proceeded to do so. The alien lingered for a while, then left. After that it was a relatively simple matter to regroup around the lock as Molly had instructed them to do, and that's where they were when McCade arrived.

As McCade listened he was conscious of Molly's leadership role, and found himself alternating between pride and fear.

McCade held Linda by both shoulders. "Do you know where Molly went? Can you show us which direction?"

Linda nodded. "Jareth showed her the way. He said he wouldn't fight but he gave Molly some sort of gun."

"A gun? Molly has a weapon?"

Linda nodded again. "Yes, she said you'd taught her how to use it."

McCade remembered putting an empty meal pak on a snow-covered rock, helping Molly to wrap cold little fingers around the grip of a blaster, and watching as blue light burped past the rock to hit the scrub beyond. He tightened his grip on Linda's shoulders. She winced and he let go.

"Show us, Linda, show us where Jareth and Molly went."

Linda turned and started down into the valley. The others followed as Linda made a wide detour around the boulders where Lia had disappeared, took them past the pile of still bloody bones where the runner called Mizlam had faced death, and climbed the slope beyond. When Linda reached the top of the hill, she looked back to make sure the others were with her, and disappeared from view.

By the time McCade topped the hill, and had started down the other side, Linda was already at the bottom of the slope pointing at a rock.

"That's where they went, Citizen McCade . . . and they never came back!"

McCade came to a stop in front of the rock and looked quizzically at Linda. "They went where?"

"Under the rock," Linda answered impatiently. "It lifts up."

McCade bent over, got a grip on the rock, and pulled. It came up with surprising ease. And no wonder, since one glance at the rock's underpinnings showed that it was hydraulically assisted. The rock concealed a rather standard maintenance tube.

It made sense when McCade thought about it; biosphere or not, the ship would require maintenance, and as a member of the crew this Jareth character would know his way around.

Metal rungs extended straight down, rungs spaced farther apart than would be comfortable for humans, and disappeared into darkness. Molly had climbed down those rungs and ended up where?

McCade wasted little time. "Okay, Phil. Take Pong's restraints off. We've got some climbing to do. Platz, come here."

The trooper obeyed. His open-featured face radiated trust. "Yes, sir?"

McCade held up his blast rifle. "What would you do if I gave you this? Would you shoot me and ask Pong for a bonus?"

Platz didn't even blink. "No, sir. I'm not stupid, sir. If something happens to you, the general will kill me and try to keep all of this secret."

Pong raised his eyes heavenward but didn't attempt to deny it.

McCade nodded and handed Platz the rifle. "You've got that right. I'm leaving you in charge of the girls. Take them back to the lock. If you see any of the 56,827, shoot to kill. Wait for three hours, if we aren't back by then, put the girls on the ship and get the hell out of here..

"Take them to the nearest Imperial Navy base and ask for Admiral Swanson-Pierce. They'll give you lots of guff but hang in there. Use my name a lot. Walt will show up eventually, and when he does, tell him I promised you ten thousand credits. The same for the pilot. He'll make it good, and get the girls home to boot."

Platz listened with a look of complete amazement, as did Pong, who raised one eyebrow. "You've got some interesting friends, McCade. I suspect I underestimated your influence."

McCade turned toward the pirate. "Shut up and listen. I'm going into the maintenance tube first. You're second, and Phil's third. Just one wrong move and we'll kill you. Got it?"

Pong shrugged. "Got it." For the moment he had no choice but to do what McCade said, but figured the 56,827 must be well aware of their uninvited guests, and would make an appearance sometime soon. That would be his chance.

"Good," McCade replied. "Okay, girls, do what Citizen Platz says, and I'll see you in a little while."

The girls looked doubtful, many wishing that he would stay, but waved gamely as Platz led them away. McCade was pleased to see that the soldier held the blast rifle at port arms and was watching both his flanks.

McCade checked to make sure that his remaining weapons, a hand blaster and a slug gun, were secure, and lowered himself into the tube. Pong followed, as did Phil.

Sensing a certain amount of mass and movement within the tube, a distant computer turned on the lights. The lights were circular like the passageway itself, and came at roughly ten-foot intervals, as did the tiny rivet-sized surveillance cameras that fed video to alien eyes.

Looking down between his feet, McCade could see lights stretching away for what seemed like forever. He continued downward.

Their boots rang on the metal rungs, and the farther down they went, the warmer it became. Four or five times they went by intersections where horizontal tubes connected with their own, and on two occasions they heard the sound of rushing water, as if some sort of large conduit paralleled their tube.

The intersections were troublesome, since Molly and Jareth could have used any one of them, but each of the horizontal tunnels had a fine layer of dust at the bottom, and as far as McCade could tell none of them had been used for a long time.

Then, just when McCade was sure they were descending into hell itself, the tube grew suddenly cooler and continued that way until it bottomed out.

Here too the dust came in handy, clearly showing the scuff marks where Molly and her alien companion had headed toward the right, showing McCade where to go.

McCade was cautious now, sensing they were close to something important, glaring at Pong to make sure that the pirate understood.

This was more a corridor than a tube, and dark at the other end. McCade slid forward, his left hand maintaining contact with the bulkhead, his right wrapped around the comforting weight of the slug gun.

From Pong's description of the 56,827 a weapon with some stopping power would be best. The problem with energy beams is that they tend to go right through the target without producing any hydrostatic shock. Not very good if your opponent is large and has lots of inertia.

Lavender light flooded the corridor. By the time McCade's eyes had adjusted, and his brain had processed the new information, the alien was in motion. It came straight at him and the bounty hunter responded automatically.

The slug gun made an enormous booming sound within the close confines of the corridor. McCade could see where the hollow points hit, punching their way through the alien's thin exoskeleton and blowing huge chunks of flesh and bone out of its back. Although it didn't seem possible the alien kept on coming.

McCade fired again, and again, expecting each slug to put the creature down, but it just kept coming, staggering with each impact, but refusing to die.

Finally, when a slug cut through the second of its redundant spinal cords, the alien tripped, fell forward, and slid almost to McCade's feet. He jumped backward as the alien's still dying nervous system caused it to jerk and snap.

Turning, McCade found Pong plastered against the bulkhead, and beyond him, Phil looking down at a second crumpled body. It had a hole the size of a dinner plate burned through its bony chest. Goo drooled from its mouth.

The variant caught McCade's look and gestured upward. The aliens had known where they were and attempted to box them in.

McCade started to sidestep the body, felt his foot his something, and heard it skitter away. Light bounced off a shiny object. McCade bent to pick it up. An energy weapon of some sort, the butt felt awkward in his human hand, but there was still no doubt as to its function.

McCade held it up for Pong to see. The pirate nodded. "It's like I told you before. The 56,827 like to hunt, and while willing to use weapons when they have to, consider them demeaning. Especially where personal combat is concerned."

McCade smiled grimly. "Yeah? Well guess what . . . from now on they're gonna be known as the 56,825."

McCade thumbed the magazine release on his slug gun, slammed a fresh one into place, and pulled the hand blaster too. The aliens were damned hard to kill. He'd need every weapon he had.

They eased their way around the dead alien and headed for the hatch at the end of the corridor. Just before they reached it McCade grabbed Pong and pushed him forward. "Time to earn your keep, old sport . . . open that hatch."

Fear ran through Pong's body like an icy stream. Anything could be, and probably was, waiting beyond that door. Pong considered begging but knew it wouldn't work.

As Pong crouched low and reached up toward the control plate, he felt the Melcetian ooze down as far as it could. The miserable piece of worthless fecal matter was using him as a shield!

Pong's hand touched the heat-sensitive plate and the hatch slid open. They waited for a barrage of slugs and energy beams but it never came.

McCade felt his heart beat just a little bit faster as he eased his way forward and peeked through the door. He found himself looking into some sort of equipment room, where metal catwalks turned and twisted through a maze of metal pipes, and the air seemed to shimmer with radiated heat.

McCade looked at Phil, got a nod in return, and stepped out onto a catwalk. The response was almost instantaneous. Two aliens stepped out from behind a cluster of pipes and opened up with energy weapons. One of the beams cut through a piece of conduit at McCade's elbow and showered him with sparks.

McCade fired the slug gun five times in quick succession, saw each of them jerk, and burned them down with the blaster before they could charge.

McCade heard Phil roar something incoherent, and turned to find the variant firing down the tube way, his blast rifle stuttering blue death.

As the bounty hunter added his fire to Phil's, three more of the aliens struggled forward and died in the combined fire of three weapons.

"Behind you!"

McCade spun around on Pong's warning just in time to find one more creature charging him. The bounty hunter emptied the slug gun into the alien's head, just barely destroying the thing's brain before the insectoid body hit and bowled him over. It took the alien a moment to flop around and die.

McCade crab-walked backward to get away, scrambled to his feet, and checked his weapons. Then, with a new magazine in the slug gun, and a fresh power pak in the blaster, he was ready once again.

With Pong following close behind and Phil bringing up the rear, McCade made his way through the maze of pipes to another opening.

Once again Pong was forced to open the hatch, and once again there was a lack of reaction.

They waited for a full minute. Still nothing. McCade motioned for the pirate to step through the door. Pong started to balk, but the bounty hunter waved his slug gun, and the pirate changed his mind. He stepped through the door and looked around.

"McCade! There they are! There's Molly!"

McCade came through the door in a low crouch, weapons in his hands, eyes searching for trouble. He found himself in a large circular area. It had a crude dirt floor, a source of lavender light high above, and at least twenty tunnels spaced equidistantly around its walls. Each was identified with some sort of pictograph. Maintenance tunnels? Private entrances for the super-territorial aliens? It made little difference.

And there, right at the room's exact center, was some sort of cage. It contained three or four children and a type of alien McCade had never seen before. The one called Jareth?

The thought was pushed aside as his eyes met Molly's and he heard her voice. "Daddy! Watch out . . ."

But the warning came too late.

Strong arms wrapped themselves around him, immobilizing both of his weapons. McCade heard Pong laugh, and knew the pirate had seen the ambush, but failed to give warning.

The bounty hunter felt both handguns ripped away and heard a growl from behind as Phil struggled with assailants of his own.

Within seconds both of them were completely immobilized. There were two of the aliens controlling McCade, and no less than four struggling to hold Phil.

There was a scraping sound and McCade turned to see an alien walk out of a tunnel. There was a translator hung around his neck, and when the creature stopped, the device swung back and forth. The alien addressed itself to Pong.

"So, numberless one, you come bringing death with you."

Pong shook his head and forced a smile, forgetting that it had no meaning for 47,721. "I was forced to come and bring them with me. That one, the creature that looks like me, was searching for his daughter."

"Daughter?"

"One of the juveniles. One of those," Pong said, pointing at the girls. "She is his—how do you say it?—progeny."

47,721 swiveled toward the cage. "Which?"

Pong frowned. He didn't like the way this was going. "The one with the black curly hair. But what difference does that make?"

47,721 didn't answer. It walked over to the cage, undid the latch, and opened the door. Jareth placed himself in front of the children, but 47,721 brushed the runner aside. Long heavily clawed fingers locked themselves around one of Molly's arms and pulled her from the cage. She struggled but it made no difference.

"Pong!" McCade shouted. "Don't let him touch her! You said you cared about her, you said you liked her, how can you stand there and let this happen?"

Pong took a hesitant step forward. "Leave her alone, 47,721. You can have the rest, but leave that one alone."

The alien paused deliberately, Molly still clutched with one hand. "You forget yourself, numberless one. I do as I wish, and since I'm hungry, I shall eat. A meal that will not only satiate my hunger, but teach this human a lesson."

Pong saw Molly, the obvious terror in her eyes, and tried to take another step forward. But the Melcetian wouldn't let him. The mind slug projected emotions into his head and poured chemicals into his bloodstream.

Pong found that each motion took tremendous effort. It was like walking underwater or in heavy gravity. The mind slug's nervous system had been integrated with his for years now, and the alien had developed a tremendous amount of control, more than Pong had ever imagined.

"Let her die!" the Melcetian screamed in Pong's mind. "You're throwing away everything I worked for, everything I wanted, all for a stupid child!"

The words echoed through Pong's brain as he willed himself forward. What was it the mind slug had said? "I?" As in "everything *I* worked for, everything *I* wanted."

And suddenly Pong knew something he should've known long before, that his "I" and the Melcetian's "I" were entirely different. This was no partnership, no sharing of similar ambitions, this was slavery. The alien was, and always had been, his master.

Reaching deep into some hidden reservoir of energy Pong found strength and used it to hurl himself forward. He felt his hands close around 47,721's neck, and saw Molly spin away as the alien turned its attention to him.

Pong felt something tear deep inside his body as the Melcetian pulled itself loose. The mind slug had waited until the last moment before separating itself, hoping that Pong would come to his senses, and now it was too late.

A terrible agony lanced through Pong's nervous system. He screamed, and as he did, the mind slug screamed too.

47,721 gloried in the feel of his razor-sharp hand claws slicing through alien flesh. His first few strokes cut the soft shiny thing to ribbons and the next cut deep four-inch channels through the human's upper torso. Then with a single darting motion of his oblong head, 47,721 administered the *Natawkwa*, or killing bite. A sticky red fluid sprayed across 47,721's face and he gave thanks for the hunt. There would be much meat when this was over.

Then, as the killing rage began to fade, 47,721 saw that things had changed. The hairy thing, the one the humans called a variant, had broken loose. 47,721 dropped Pong's remains in order to watch. His venturing companions would make short work of the human.

Phil had waited, hoping to avoid going into full augmentation, knowing he'd be worthless for days afterward. But when the alien grabbed Molly, and Pong threw himself forward, Phil knew there was no choice.

The variant activated certain triggers planted deep within his subconscious, felt chemicals pour into his bloodstream, and saw the world around him slow. His reactions were speeded up, his muscles chemically augmented, his entire body a murderous machine.

Now a single jerk from Phil's arms was enough to free him from his alien guards. A spinning kick and one went down, its leg broken at the joint, screeching loudly. Another kick broke its neck.

The others rushed him, confident of their superior strength, eager to give the *Natawkwa.*

Phil roared his approval, rammed a fist through the first one's chest, and pulled something out.

A whitish fluid sprayed everywhere as Phil grabbed another alien by the skull and turned it around. The creature dropped like a rock.

The variant felt something slice through fur and flesh and turned to grab it. As he hugged the alien to his chest, Phil felt bones crunch and heard organs pop.

"You want a fight?" the variant roared. "You want combat? Well how's this!"

So saying Phil lifted the already dead alien up over his head and bounced it off a bulkhead.

In the meantime Molly had been sent tumbling head over heels. As she hit the cage it knocked the wind out of her. Molly struggled to breathe as the alien did something horrible to Pong. Blood spattered on her boots.

Then Molly saw Phil break loose from his guards and spin-kick one of them. Meanwhile Daddy was struggling to break free.

Molly saw a gun, one of Phil's knocked loose in the struggle, slide across the packed earth. She dived forward and felt it heavy in her hands.

Daddy shoved and kicked but to no avail. One of the 56,815 still had hold of his arm. Molly tried to aim but was afraid that she'd hit Daddy instead of the alien. She ran forward and pressed the muzzle against the alien's torso. The slug gun practically jumped out of her hand when she squeezed the trigger. It made a muffled bang.

Mortally wounded, the alien let go and McCade yelled, "Molly! Give me the gun!"

Molly tossed the gun to her father and backed away as the remaining alien moved toward her. It staggered as McCade pumped four slugs into its back, took two more steps, and toppled onto its face.

Both of them stared at it for a second until Molly saw something over her father's shoulder and pointed. "Daddy! Behind you!"

McCade whirled to find 47,721 coming straight at him, a horrible-looking sight with saliva dripping from its jaws, and Pong's blood smeared all over its torso.

The bounty hunter brought the gun up in a two-handed grip, fired shot after shot into the alien's chest, and kept on firing as it slumped to the deck. He stopped when the gun clicked empty.

There was silence for a moment as all of them looked around, surprised to be alive and extremely grateful.

Then McCade was on his knees, with Molly in his arms, both crying and trying to talk at the same time.

Molly heard herself talking, heard herself say, "Oh, Daddy, Mommy said you'd come, but it took so long! And I was scared, and every time I did something it went wrong, and everything was awful. Is Mommy okay?"

And she heard her father reply, saying, "You did a great job, honey, and I'm sorry it took so long to find you. Yes, Mommy's fine, and waiting for you to come home. I love you, Molly. Thank God you're safe."

But years later, long after Phil had recovered, the remaining alien had been hunted down, and the effort to find their homeworld had begun, Molly would remember other things.

She'd remember the strength of her father's arms, the familiar smell of his clothes, and the fact that he'd crossed a thousand stars to find her. Molly was home.